"The goal is not
to be an adult, but to
mature down to be a
child."

To Barbara, a dear
friend and colleague,
with gratitude for having
gotten to know you,
and appreciate so much
who you are and
what you do.
With love,

7/19/13

Blackfire

Blackfire

The Books of Bairnmoor, Volume I

By James Daniel Eckblad

RESOURCE *Publications* · Eugene, Oregon

BLACKFIRE
The Books of Bairnmoor, Volume I

Resource Publications
An Imprint of Wipf and Stock Publishers
199 W. 8th Ave., Suite 3
Eugene, OR 97401
www.wipfandstock.com

ISBN 13: 978-1-61097-936-8
Manufactured in the U.S.A.

For
My sons and daughter:
Marshall
Michael
Jack
Peter
Carolina

Critical reading friends, Ronald Damholt and Rebecca Swan, and son
Michael

Alex Emma, whose life has inspired the character bearing his name

Herbert Ellis, Literary Editor

and, most of all, for Barbara, without whose encouragement and love
this story could never have been written.

Thanks to Aristotle for his remark concerning literary theory, "Probable impossibilities are to be preferred to improbable possibilities." ("Poetics," Part XXIV, Public domain), and to Jorge Borges, who said, "Any life, however long and complicated it may be, actually consists of a single moment—the moment when a man knows forever more who he is." ("A Biography of Tadeo Isidoro Cruz," in The Aleph (1949); tr. Andrew Hurley, Collected Fictions (1998))

~ONE~

ELLI ADAMS LIVED AS if she were always leaving, and people who are leaving are always different from those who aren't, and so different from virtually everyone else. It wasn't that Elli Adams *wanted* to leave, or *had* to leave, or even that she *knew* she was leaving. No, it was simply that she *felt* she was going to be leaving—whether she wanted to or not, and she didn't know why. Maybe *that* was why she was so different from the other children—and why they knew she was different. Or maybe it was simply the "separation" issues that attend many children who, like Elli, are adopted.

But, actually, Elli did have to leave—she needed to be at the library—there was a book she wanted to read, and she was hoping they might have it. It was a book of poetry. Elli loved poetry. None of the other kids in school did. And those few who knew she liked poetry would tease her about it. But, then, most kids teased her anyway—if you could call it teasing. It wasn't funny—at least, not to her. And it wasn't actually funny to them either, even though they laughed. It simply gave them pleasure to say unkind things to her. But to her, it was like having hyenas gnawing at her back. Wherever she went it seemed there were boys and girls waiting to say unkind words to her as she walked by.

It was certain to happen again as she made her way to the library today. It was Saturday, and there would be lots of kids from school hanging out on the sidewalks. But she was willing to pay the price for another book of poetry. She loved poetry—and she loved poetry because of what it did to her small and confining world in Millerton; poetry took the small, ordinary parts of her every day life and transformed them into something extraordinary—not just seemingly extraordinary, but truly extraordinary. Because poetry took the individual, specific aspects of her ordinary, mundane world and made them into something that was true for the whole world: poetry about a brook, for example, that transformed it—and so the tiny river in town—into the journey that is all of life—transforming the

1

particularly small into the universally large. Perhaps it was, as her adoptive mother alleged, with a tone of disapproval, a form of escape. But if it was a kind of escape, it was only because it allowed her to leave a small world for a much larger one.

Elli walked around the corner toward the library that was three blocks away. She was relieved to see there were no kids on the street. But she had walked only half a block when five or six kids appeared quite suddenly from a doorway across the street—and crossed the street behind her and began to taunt her. "Hey moon-face! Any astronauts land by mistake? Or just asteroids?" And then they laughed. The kids called her moon-face because of the pockmarks or "craters" that a serious bout of the chicken pox had left behind. She didn't say anything. It only made them tease her more. So, with tears welling, but Elli not daring to let them fall, she continued her journey to the library. It was about the time when she could no longer hear what the kids were saying that she at last reached the large, double bronze doors of the old stone building.

Under vaulted ceilings with low-hanging fluorescent lights, Elli ran a fast check with the computer catalogue and then walked with confidence toward the circulation desk, as if she and the floor beneath her were bosom buddies. She was only 14 years old, but she had had her own library card for nearly 8 years, and she and the librarian, Ms. Simonson, had become good friends. Indeed, there was no place she liked to be more than at the library, and especially when Ms. Simonson and she would sit at the reference desk during slow periods on Saturday afternoons and talk about poetry and literature. She thought it odd that Ms. Simonson was not at the reference desk—and surprised to see a new face at the circulation desk.

"Yes, dear?" the desk clerk inquired.

"I'm looking for a certain book of poetry," she replied.

"Have you checked the computer catalogue to see if we have it?"

"Umm . . . Yes, I did. But that's the thing. It said you have the book, and that it's not checked out, but I couldn't find it on the shelves. In fact, I didn't see any poetry on the shelves at all."

"Oh, that's right. The new Library Board instructed us to put all of the poetry downstairs to make more room for the expanding technology section. It seems no one checks out the poetry any more."

"But *I* do, and I would very much like to check out this particular book. Could someone please find it for me?" Elli asked, as she laid a tiny scrap of paper with scribbling on it in front of the woman.

"I'm afraid I'm the only one at the circulation desk today—perhaps if you came back on Monday someone could help you then."

"Oh, but I so very much would like to have it today. Will Ms. Simonson be here in a bit? I think she would be willing to help me."

"I'm afraid Ms. Simonson is no longer with us; the board ordered staffing cuts this past week—and I was hired just two days ago to manage the library on Saturdays. I've never worked in a library before young lady, and I'm still trying to learn the procedures. Again, I'm sure someone will be able to help you on Monday."

Elli heard nothing of what the woman said beyond her saying that Ms. Simonson was gone. Forgetting about the book momentarily, she asked, "How soon will there be a replacement for her?"

"My understanding is there will be no replacement, and that they plan to hire out the management of the library to an operations management company." She added, as if she were signaling sudden expertise in the area of concern, "There is really very little need for librarians any longer, now that we have the Internet."

Elli had no idea what the woman could possibly have meant by the remark, and considered it useless to carry the conversation any further. "Would it be possible for me to go downstairs and find it myself? I could spot it easily, I know, and it would only . . ."

"Young lady," the woman interrupted, seeing that a small line had now formed behind Elli, "I can't be of any help to you today. You will simply have to return on Monday when someone else besides me will be here. Now," she added quickly, looking at the man who was behind Elli, "may I help you?"

The man actually reached over Elli's head and put his books on the desk in front or her. Elli slipped aside to let the man get to the counter. She simply stood there and wondered: why couldn't she herself go to the basement? That was what she was trying to ask the woman at the desk, but she was never given the chance. She thought to herself, "No one told me I *couldn't* go to the basement!"

Elli glanced about the large reading room and noticed to her delight that what appeared to be the door to the basement was not only not behind the circulation desk, but was also open—as if it had been opened just for her, she pretended. Actually, the dark, oak paneled door, just around the corner behind the drop-off counter, wasn't open very far—just an inch or so, as if someone had intended to close it, but had forgotten to make sure it was closed tightly—or had shut it, but, like many older doors, it just opened by itself. The bright light from the reading room poked through the partially opened door, allowing Elli to see that just to the other side was a flight of stairs—going down.

That *had* to be it, she thought. But maybe she'd better try to ask permission again before going any further. Elli moved a little closer to the front of the line where she had just surrendered her position to the man whom the woman was now helping. The woman's eyes caught Elli's and, sensing that Elli was not going to give up her quest just yet, she glared at Elli with a look that said, "I am not going to talk about this anymore." And with that, as if sensing Elli's thoughts, the woman, while walking past the basement door with a stack of return books, pushed hard on the door to make it shut, as if by the slam she was announcing both her authority and a final decision. She followed this with a dismissive look that was enough to persuade Elli to try to find the book on her own. When the woman returned to the circulation desk, Elli caught her eyes, stepped out of line and then headed straight for the bronze doors through which she had entered the building only minutes earlier, hoping the woman would think she was leaving.

When Elli was about four feet from the exit, however, she began to turn ever so slightly to her left—while looking back and giving a furtive glance toward the woman at the desk. When Elli saw that the woman was fully occupied with another young girl, she turned and headed back into the library around the many tall shelves of books, as if she had been the hand of a clock that had moved suddenly counterclockwise from twelve o'clock to nine o'clock, and then to five o'clock, where she located the basement door just twenty feet ahead of her. She could see, peeping above a row of books from the end of a shelf, that the woman at the desk was still occupied. But it was also apparent that Elli would be in her peripheral line of vision were she to make a dash for the door. Elli waited for just the right moment. The woman turned, as if suddenly ordered to do so by a commanding officer in an army, and began walking quickly in the direction of Elli, causing Elli to wonder if she had been discovered. But then, as if suddenly remembering she had forgotten something, the woman turned abruptly on one heel back toward the desk. Elli realized instantly that this was her best and perhaps only opportunity, and made a quiet dash for the door.

Elli tried the knob and found the door locked. She looked for a key and found a rather large and old one on a nail next to the door. She grabbed the chain holding the black skeleton key, unlocked the door and then slipped inside, shutting the door ever so gently behind her.

The head of the stairs she had noticed earlier through the slightly opened door was no longer in sight, and she was standing in pitch-black darkness.

Elli stood still in the small space, not wanting to fall down the stairs, and groped the three close walls enveloping her for a light switch. Like a blind woman trying to "see" another's face with her hands, Elli let her probing fingers dance lightly over the surfaces of the cracked plaster walls, not wanting to miss the one spot where the switch was located. She found nothing. Perhaps it was a bulb with a switch or pull chain hanging from the ceiling. Elli stood on her toes and waved an arm throughout the impenetrable darkness while she leaned against one wall and then another to keep from falling. Still nothing.

All of a sudden, Elli heard the sound of the heels worn by the *acting* librarian. They were getting louder—and closer. Elli had to decide either to open the door and disclose her presence or, still in the dark, to lock the door and go quickly down the stairs. With little time for consideration, Elli locked the dead bolt and then groped for the handrail she had discovered in her search for a light. She found it and began an initially swift, but careful, descent. Elli descended no more than a few steps when she heard the knob jiggle, indicating, apparently to the woman's satisfaction, that the door was locked as she had intended it to be. Elli then heard the heels walk away, as if in victory.

Elli assumed that the bottom of the stairs must be near, and that surely there she would discover a light switch. However, the handrail suddenly disappeared and the steps turned abruptly into stairs of stone that spread themselves like an unfolding fan into an ever-widening spiral. It was, she felt, as if she were a young woman in a wide skirted gown slowly descending the staircase of an elegant mansion to join her waiting escort.

Elli continued her descent on the stairs that, to her astonishment, seemed to have no end, and on a spiral that seemed ever to widen, as if the spiral staircase never intended to reach any sort of ground or pavement whatsoever, but simply existed for its own sake. She balanced herself against the stone wall as she stepped, careful with each footfall to make certain there was always another step or, better, a landing. To be sure to not lose the key, Elli placed the chain about her neck, tucking the key inside her shirt.

"Surely," thought Elli, "I must have made a mistake—this couldn't possibly be the stairs to the basement!" Elli stopped and turned, paused for an indecisive moment, and then began walking back up the stairs. But as soon as she began her ascent, Elli heard a door open just several feet below, and the bluish light from the doorway cast a large shadow of her small body on the stairs above her. Elli stopped, startled, and was about to run the rest of the way up the stairs when the voice of what had to be that of a very old man said to her kindly,

"Now, young lady, why would you be leaving when you are almost to the book?"

Elli, more puzzled than frightened, but duly fearful, too, turned toward the door that had opened from the wall only five steps below her, but with the stairway itself still continuing to descend into the darkness beyond the light. She could not see the man, but she could see through the doorway rows of dark wooden bookcases containing what she thought must be hundreds, if not thousands, of old books. The musty odors drifting onto the staircase made her think of what she guessed to be the scent of old monasteries, their libraries filled with devoted scribes and scholars laboring with ideas and words that mattered.

"Hello?" said Elli, as if not quite certain she was saying it to anyone there at all.

"Come in, come in," the man said with quiet enthusiasm, as if he had been expecting her for hours, or days, or even a much longer time, ago.

With tentative steps and ready to turn and run if required, Elli descended the stairs to the doorway and stood there, looking in. She still saw no one—just a narrow, but deep, room with a number of bookcases that seemed endless in their length.

"Hello?" she asked again.

"Come in, come in!"

Elli took one step into the room and noticed immediately a small man sitting at a very small wooden desk, his face bent over a large old book, the pages of which appeared to have been turned many times over the course of many years.

The man turned a page and then spun around in his chair to look at Elli over a pair of tiny horn-rimmed spectacles. The man, who she judged could not have been more than three feet in height, nor less than a hundred years of age, was dressed in a brown, threadbare robe that was tied at the waist, not unlike those worn by monks she had seen in pictures. And he had a very large head on top of which rested a rather precariously tilted tall, pointed hat. His face reminded Elli of the faces often depicted as those of the man in the moon. He had a wide mouth, a small pug nose, bulging cheeks, and long, half-closed eyes, except that his cheeks and mouth were scrunched toward the center of his face, as if the hands of an unseen mother were pushing them together out of anger at her child. He wore brown leather boots with a metal hook on the top of each upper sole.

The man jumped from his chair, held out a hand for Elli to shake, and said, "I'm Peterwinkle, and I understand that you are looking for a certain book of poetry."

"Ye . . . yes," Elli replied, with surprise in her voice. "But how did you know, Mr. . . . Mr. Peterwinkle?"

"No, no . . . it's not Mr. or Winkle or Peter, just Peterwinkle—all one word! Please, just call me Peterwinkle," he said politely, so as not to seem scolding toward Elli.

"So, Peterwinkle, how did you know I was looking for a book of poetry? Did the woman at the circulation desk tell you I might be coming, and is she angry with me? And are *you* angry with me?" Elli asked.

"Oh, heavens no, dear girl! No one is angry with you—at least," he added soberly, with a faraway look in his eyes, "not at this moment." And he smiled.

Eager to obtain the book and be on her way, Elli said, "I'm looking for a book by an Adams, entitled . . ."

"Yes," interrupted Peterwinkle, "I know the book. By 'Adams,' with no first name, and the title being simply *Poetry*."

"Why yes! But, how did you know?" Elli asked, incredulously.

"It's the only book of poetry that in all these years has never been checked out. And the only person wanting this book would be the only person to have found me. And so, here you are. And so you must be . . . ?" he asked.

"Elli Adams," she replied.

"Precisely! Finally!" Peterwinkle said, with a controlled and uncertain gleefulness. "And," he added, in a voice suggesting that he had almost forgotten the most important part, "it is dedicated to you, by one who will have written the book a very long time ago!"

"To me? . . . and 'will have been written?'" Elli asked, with complete puzzlement.

"Yes, most definitely! It says: 'To Elli Adams, without whose life this book could not have been written.' Now, the only problem, dear girl, is that I don't have the book at this time."

"You mean someone else has checked it out? Or . . . it's lost?!" Elli asked.

"No, no, Elli. None of that," Peterwinkle assured her. "No one else has it, and it most definitely is not lost." He paused to sigh deeply, and then he continued, "It's just that the book has not been written yet, I'm afraid to tell you." He paused again, and then said, "And, the only question is whether it *will* be written. I have, you see, the book, with its covers and pages, but there is nothing written on them except, as I said, the title, the author, and the dedication to you."

"Well," Elli said, "this is all so very confusing, Peterwinkle, and I'm disappointed that you don't have the book and that, obviously, I'm simply wasting both your time and mine. So, thank you, and I'll be on my way," she said while turning to go.

"But, Elli," Peterwinkle replied, almost matter-of-factly, "the book will only have been written if you provide the story for the poet."

Elli turned abruptly back to face the little man. "You're frightening me now, Peterwinkle, and I shall be going at once," Elli said as she turned to leave once more.

"Of course I'm frightening you, dear girl! The world is a frightening place, as you well know, and it's understandable that you should be frightened by me and all that I've said, but that doesn't mean you have to run from that which frightens you." Peterwinkle smiled kindly at Elli, and made no gesture to suggest he would physically discourage her from leaving.

"Please, come in, Elli, and at least have a cup of tea or lemonade with me, and let me try both to un-confuse you and to un-frighten you."

Elli turned again, and Peterwinkle motioned toward a small chair next to his desk. Elli sat down, but with the open door in her peripheral vision, just in case.

"Now, Elli, let me tell you a brief story, the rather lengthy ending of which I will have to leave for another time together. Oh, would you like some tea or lemonade?" Elli shook her head slightly, as if not even hearing the question.

"A long time ago, there was a very grand and beautiful queen named Taralina who ruled the world of Bairnmoor, imbuing it with her love and kindness that became the source of all well-being and happiness throughout the land. She thought little of herself, except as an instrument of all that was good for her people. She desired nothing in return but the love and affection of her people, asking only that they also love each other in the same fashion that she loved them. Prosperity prevailed for all her people for thousands of years, and there was not one who did not enjoy the favor of her rule.

"But, there were a few of her subjects who wanted more, who became envious of her position and power, and who decided to rise up against her. Those who rose against her, whom we will call the 'insurrectionists,' knew she had no army—no real defense—except perhaps her stone castle that was built and used for benevolent, not defensive, purposes.

"Of course, the insurrectionists knew there would likely be many who would rally to her defense, but they were clever, and played upon the minds and emotions of the queen's subjects, telling them that the queen was withholding from them much that they could yet enjoy. There would be larger plots of land, bigger homes, more impressive machines to assist them in their work, and greater freedom to do as they pleased, especially the freedom to rule themselves.

"There ensued a great battle, and many lives were lost on both sides, but in the end the insurrectionists prevailed and then enslaved virtually the entirety of the people, rewarding with wealth and privilege those who advanced the insurrectionists' rule and punishing those who resisted with terrific poverty, imprisonment, torture, and death.

"The Queen, who was thought to possess enormous power from an unknown source, was easily locked away in the deepest regions beneath the castle, where to this day she remains. No one knows for certain what has happened to her, and the depths beneath the castle remain closed, with the Queen in a locked chamber and the most horrible of creatures guarding both castle and chamber beneath. It is said that another must release her for her power to return and defeat her enemies, taking control once again of the land—and this time ruling forever.

"It is further said, as has been said for centuries, that there is one who is to come who is alone able to release the Queen and who must do so before the insurrectionists have destroyed both the land of Bairnmoor and your world, Elli, sending both into the nothingness from which they can never return. So you see, the world in which you now live is entirely dependent on the world of Bairnmoor for its own continued existence, so that it is not only the future of Bairnmoor that hangs in the balance.

"It has been assumed that this one who is to come to release the Queen will have special powers that will enable that one to accomplish the mission that can be accomplished by no other—if, indeed, it can be accomplished at all. How, even with the greatest of powers, the Queen can be released, is unknown and incomprehensible for me to imagine. Yet there is one—and one *alone*—who is able to attempt the mission."

It was not clear whether Peterwinkle had concluded his story. He glanced up at Elli and said nothing further. "Peterwinkle," Elli said, after a lengthy pause, "I don't know why you are telling me this story. I don't even know, with all due respect, sir, whether I believe it or not. All I want is the book of poetry by Adams, and if it does not exist, then I should be on my way, although I am very pleased to have met you," said Elli, as she straightened her shirt for departure.

"Oh, Elli," replied Peterwinkle softly, "all of this has very much to do with you."

"I should be going now," Elli said curtly as she rose from the chair.

"Elli," Peterwinkle said, with a deep longing in his eyes, "the Queen is depending on you." He paused, and then added, looking imploringly into her eyes, "Everyone is."

Elli sat back down, ever so reluctantly, overwhelmed in both her mind and her heart, her thoughts and her emotions, and with an emerging credulity for the story from which she wanted to flee with her entire being.

"Elli," said Peterwinkle, as if the statement to be made was simply indisputable, "you are the one chosen to attempt this—yes, this *incomprehensible*—endeavor, and I am the one chosen to tell you so."

"But, Peterwinkle, even if any of this—even if all of this—is true, the part that is otherwise false is that this Elli Adams is but a girl of fourteen, and I have no special or great powers whatsoever. So, there is a mistake— and probably someone else who is to come after me—and I am deeply sorry to tell you that, for I see that you have already concluded that I am this one you've been waiting for."

"No, there is no mistake, Elli. You alone are the one to whom this book is dedicated; and the mere fact that you profess to no powers only confirms the veracity of your place in this business. Elli, it is not that you *have* great powers, but that you *will have* great powers in the undertaking of this mission. And you are not to do this alone. Indeed, you cannot do this alone. You will have companions to assist you, both from your world and from Bairnmoor, and without whom you would not be able to accomplish what is set before you—if it can be accomplished at all," Peterwinkle added quickly, as if forgetting an obligatory phrase.

"But, who are these companions you speak about, Mr. Peterwinkle, and why do you continue to say that the mission may not succeed?" Elli asked, a bit perturbed.

Blackfire

"How can anyone assure the accomplishment of anything in the future, Elli? All that one can control is what one does, not the results. But, without your efforts, there is no hope—for any of us."

"But, I must know, Mr. Peterwinkle: who are these companions of which you speak? Are they great adults, and is it they who will provide the great powers?" Elli asked, insistently, as if to create the answer to her question.

"Oh, Bumblesticks, no, Elli! You will have no adults with you. Only children. For only children will be able to enter the kingdom now, and only children will be able to save it."

"Then, who are these children you speak of?" Elli asked, now pressingly. "I have very few friends, Peterwinkle, and I can think of none who would want—or be *able*—to accompany me, even if they believed the story was true."

"Elli," Peterwinkle giggled kindly, and then said, as if ignoring her doubts, "it will be three other children whom you most would trust to be without guile, to be loyal to your mission, and to protect your heart. It would be those who would say nothing false, and who would say nothing true they thought would injure you, and who would do all they could against others, regardless of the circumstances, who would seek to hurt you in any way. And," Peterwinkle added, with a sense of prescient knowing, "I suspect that you know already about whom I am speaking. Am I correct?"

Reticent to speak, for any of a number of reasons pressing upon her mind and emotions, Elli simply nodded and said quietly, "Yes, I believe I do." Peterwinkle sat silently, fingers folded together on his lap, waiting to hear more.

"There is Beatríz, also my age, who was born in Chile and," she added, looking firmly into Peterwinkle's eyes, "who has been blind since birth. And there is Jamie, who is a year younger than I and who comes from a really bad home and spends most of his time alone, with no self-confidence whatsoever—and other kids know it, so they tease him mercilessly, calling him weak and scared and good for nothing." Elli paused, manifesting an appearance of general incredulity. "And, and . . . then there is Alex. Alex has Down syndrome, and is three years older than I. He's in the same grade, but he has the mental capacity of someone younger than I. I eat and spend recess at school with these three, but, other than a couple of us occasionally meeting at the library, none of us spends time with any of the others outside of school; it's safer that way. Guys who pick on us would be more inclined to get rough with several of us than with just one, if you know what I mean." Peterwinkle nodded affirmatively.

"All of us like each other, and I can't imagine that any one of us would say anything unkind about the others. I'm certain of that, since each of us has been hurt lots of times by others, and we all know how awful it feels." Elli paused, and then said, conclusively, "I know of no others, among children or adults, to whom I'd trust my heart."

Peterwinkle nodded his head approvingly. "I think you should be going—and then returning as quickly as you are able with your friends, for time is of the essence. You may, of course, decline to return, Elli, and you will not see or hear from me again. And no one but you and I and your friends will know of this conversation, and no one in either world will think more or less of you. Life will return for you as it has been, but with one exception. In this moment you have the opportunity that few in any world have, which is to find out who you really are. And the same may be said, I suspect, concerning your friends."

Elli shivered at Peterwinkle's final words and said nothing further. Exhausted in mind and heart, she mulled over all that Peterwinkle had said. She left the room, glanced furtively toward the wide staircase descending into the darkness below, and then carefully made her way back up the stairs and out the door, keeping the key with her.

~TWO~

WHEN ELLI ARRIVED HOME, she was surprised that so little time had passed since she had left for the library. She told her mother that the book was not available and that she was hoping to have several friends over for the evening, and would it be okay with her. She explained they would spend the night in her room and then go together to the library late on Sunday morning. Although surprised by the uncharacteristic request, Elli's mother said it was okay as long as it was okay with her friends' parents.

Elli called each of the three friends about whom she had conversed with Peterwinkle, saying it was imperative they get together, and that she would tell them about an adventure unlike any other, guaranteed.

When all four had gathered on Elli's big bed, and the door had been shut, Elli proceeded to tell them everything that had happened to her that day at the library. There was Beatríz, a tall and lithe girl with black hair that hung in joyful waves all the way to her waist. Alex was short, especially for his age, but he was built like a middle linebacker, naturally and uncommonly strong, and sported the same buzz cut he had had since he was a small child. Jamie, as uncommonly short for his age as Alex was strong for his age, had a slight, but wiry, build, harvest blonde hair that flopped over his ears and forehead, and sad eyes—as if they were drawn that way on his face.

With their eyes and ears glued to Elli, not one of the three friends doubted in the least that something very strange had happened to her at the library, and none doubted that Elli was telling the absolute truth—or at least what she thought was the truth, which itself frightened Jamie. But no one said anything, except a few scattered and whispered "wows." After about a minute of complete silence, Beatríz finally said, "Well, I think the least we can do is go back to the library and see what happened to you, Elli. And, then . . . if it's all as you have described things, Elli, we can—all of us—decide, okay?" All nodded in agreement.

After a restless night of intermittent conversation and a bit of sleep, the four left the house at ten thirty, to be certain to be at the library when the doors opened at eleven.

Armed with the key and her pattern of stealth past the circulation desk and through and around the aisles of bookcases, Elli and her friends stood in complete darkness just inside the door to the basement. Without hesitation, Elli led them in single file with feeling hands and feet down the stairs on which Elli had descended the day before. Without talking, and with only the sound of whispering shoes on the smooth stone stairs, the four companions proceeded, as if out of reverence for the space or the moment. Elli, who was leading the group, watched in the blackness for any hint of light from the open doorway casting itself on the steps below. Elli worried that perhaps they had already traveled too far down the stairs; she also sensed that someone—or something—else was close by when she felt a slight and chilly breeze pass in front of her.

But then Elli saw the familiar light of the opened door below her on the steps. Elli led her friends into the room and looked for Peterwinkle at his desk. When she saw that the chair was vacant, she called for him. "Mr. Peterwinkle?"

In a moment, Peterwinkle appeared from behind a bookcase, carrying a stack of volumes. "Come in, come in," he said warmly, as he laid the books on his desk, dusted them and himself off, and then sat in the chair, his pointed hat cocked to one side. He pushed the hat back to its proper place, chuckling, "I try to not hit my head on the hard ceiling when climbing the ladder, but the hat is not always so successful; but, better the hat than my head." He giggled and paused awkwardly. "And," he added, "I have the hooks on the tops of my boots to keep me from falling off the ladder. I still fall rather a lot, but at least I don't fall very far, and I get an entirely different perspective on the books while hanging upside down!

"Well, young lady," he said, looking at Elli, "I see you've returned, and with your friends. Please, sit down." He invited them with a gesture to sit on the floor. Then, Peterwinkle himself sat on the floor and began to tell the story to all four of them, just as he had told it to Elli—and just as Elli had told it to her friends. He concluded by saying to them that it was up to Elli to decide first if she was going to accept the mission, and then up to the rest of them to decide, one by one, whether they would be joining her on this difficult and uncertain journey. The decision had to be made then and there, and the moment of decision would be irreversible when they passed through the doorway: either remaining in their world by going back up the stairs, or journeying to the land of Bairnmoor, by continuing down the dark staircase.

When Peterwinkle had finished speaking, the group remained silent for a long time, each one considering whether to turn left and go back up the stairs or to depart to the right and go down the stairs, descending further into the darkness—and the unknown.

Beatríz spoke first. "Mr. Peterwinkle, what about our parents and school?"

"From the moment you turn to the right, your absence will be time-less. You will be traveling perpendicular to time, returning, if you survive this mission, at the same moment of your departure—unless," he interjected as an appending thought, "you decide otherwise at the moment of your return. You will simply have been to the library today, regardless of how many days or weeks and months, or even years, you will have spent in the land of Bairnmoor."

"And if we are not successful, Mr. Peterwinkle, and . . . " Beatríz said and paused. Then she continued, somewhat haltingly, "If we do not return, Mr. Peterwinkle, then what will happen to us here?"

"I'm afraid I am not able to answer that question, Beatríz, with any certainty, that is. I would suppose your existence here would be . . . non-existent. But, I simply don't know."

"Peterwinkle," Elli said, somewhat pensively, already missing those wonderful parts of her world in which she at that moment yet lived, "I knew somehow when I left you yesterday that, regardless of how I felt or what I thought, I would be going to Bairnmoor."

"I'm not letting Elli go alone; if she's going, then I'm going, too," Beatríz said.

"Me, too," said Alex.

The three of them lowered their heads while waiting for Jamie's answer.

"I don't see how I can be of any value to Elli, or to the rest of you, and I have some very bad feelings about all of this, but if you are going, and you want me with you, then I guess I'm in," said Jamie, finally.

Then, as if part of a liturgical mantra, each of the others repeated, in succession, "I want you along."

"Well, then," said Peterwinkle, placing his palms together, "it's been decided. Besides each other, you will have to assist you a leather backpack from me containing some essentials. You will find in your packs a canteen of water, a week's supply of special wheat crackers, some chocolate, and room for whatever else you may be provided by others throughout your journey."

"Peterwinkle," said Elli, "can you tell us anything else about the land of Bairnmoor, or how we will go about carrying out our mission?"

"Once more, I am sorry to say, I do not have answers for you. It was a long time ago when last I was there. I was but a small boy, then. I am now a very old child, and I remember very little; my memory betrays me, and so much has changed. I do know there will be those of one sort or another who will assist you, and that you will come to know who they are, including some who will likely surprise you. I have been set apart only to discover you, to tell you the story, and to send you on your way in the direction you are to go. And, oh, yes, it is imperative that you not tell anyone else about your mission, even if someone already seems to know about it. Finally, I have been set apart to thank you on behalf of the Queen and her people who do not know you, and to say, 'Fare thee well.'" He then added, rather sadly, "It may be that I shall not be seeing you again."

The four rose when Peterwinkle got to his feet. He went behind the bookcases from which he had appeared earlier and returned with the four promised backpacks. When Elli and her friends had put on their packs, Peterwinkle ushered them gently through the door, careful that he himself did not cross the threshold with them. He said, "Oh, I almost forgot! You must not remove the key, Elli, for you will require it to return to your world. Fare thee well." And then he closed the door.

Once again the friends were enveloped in darkness. "Well," said Elli quietly, "thank you, each of you, and all of you, for coming with me. I guess we should be going." And with those words, Elli took one step down the stairs, and then suddenly stopped. She reached far back to touch the door, and, just as she suspected, it was no longer there.

And so they continued their descent, the four children in the dark, toward what they could not fathom. Each of them began the journey harboring private thoughts and emotions, feeling mutually only fear and the greatest wonder imaginable, and perhaps also a shared disbelief that this was all really happening to them, except in a dream.

They followed the hard stone steps downward in a still ever-widening spiral. After an hour or so, the balls of their feet becoming sore, they decided to stop and rest. They had rested for perhaps five minutes when all of them began to shiver. A damp and chilly wind was descending upon them from above. "We'd best be going," said Beatríz.

"Yes, I think so, too," replied Elli.

In the grip of heavy weariness more than just physical, they continued their descent, each one panting in rhythm to his or her own rapidly
beating heart. Jamie, who was following Alex and sensed Alex's fatigue,
gasped, "Elli, I need to stop for awhile. I never thought going *down* a set
of stairs could be so tiring." Elli was about to agree when she noticed that
the key was glowing, ever so slightly, through her shirt. "Wait. Something
is changing."

"What?" asked Jamie.

"The key . . . it's glowing, but the light's not coming from the key.
Look. When I point it down the stairs, it glows, just a little; but it definitely
glows. But when I turn it in any other direction it stops glowing. Come
on—just a little further." With each successive step, Elli could see the key
glowing more brightly, although she could see no light ahead. Then, all
of a sudden, Elli noticed a faint glow in the distance, almost like the pale
light of the moon when it settles softly on thin wisps of clouds that hover
over a marsh. "Guys, there's light up ahead; it can't be far. C'mon!" Elli said,
feeling for the first time since meeting Peterwinkle the excitement she felt
when she was first going down the stairs in search of the book of poetry.

With the light ahead of them getting brighter as they continued their
descent, they were finally able to see ever-so-faintly the stairs on which
they were stepping, giving them greater confidence and more energy. As
they got closer to the light, Elli could see it was in fact passing through a
fog that was gradually surrounding them. As the fog deepened, the light
became more luminescent. Then the stairs abruptly ended, and as they
stepped onto a soft surface, the fog began to lift and the light began to dim.

There, in front of them, in the middle of a forest clearing, was a fire
whose flames were nearly spent, leaving behind a large mound of glowing
embers. The fire was enclosed in a sort of hemispherical hut cut vertically in half and made of thin bamboo stalks. The opening was facing the
staircase.

Sitting on one of several woven rugs that lay all around the fire was
an elderly looking woman in layers of worn, but elegant robes. She had
long and beautiful gray hair that trailed behind her to the ground and
framed her face in front—a face that was undoubtedly old, but that re-
tained distinct soft features and large open eyes reflecting the glowing embers like tiny spherical mirrors. Her small, thin-lipped mouth was smiling
and relaxed.

The woman seemed not to notice Elli and her friends, or at least she
provided no such indication. She sat on her knees facing the fire, the glow

from which danced delicately on her face and hands. Elli was about to politely announce their presence when the woman, as if she had expected them, politely invited them to sit around the fire and warm themselves. As the children ever so quietly walked toward the fire, Elli glanced back toward the stairs and noticed that, like Peterwinkle's door earlier, they had disappeared.

The children sat close together around the fire across from the woman. Awkward silence ensued, and then Alex, without prompting, said, "Ma'am, we ah . . ."

"Shhh, Alex!" whispered Elli, firmly. Alex left his statement hanging, half-finished. "Don't say anything," Elli said to the others so only they could hear her. The three friends stared at Elli, waiting for her to do or say something. She did do something—saying nothing, making her companions anxious. Finally, the woman broke the silence.

"Please tell me who you are, from where you have come, and where you are intending to go," she said, as if beginning a polite interrogation.

"We can't do that, Ma'am, if you please," Elli replied, just as directly, but with a note of respect for someone older, as her mother had taught her.

"I don't know whether it will please me or not, but just the same I want to know who you are, from where you have come, and where you are going," the woman said, in the same tone. Elli, as if fencing with the woman, repeated her own reply, and with the same tone.

"Suppose I told you I could help you—help you go where you want to go and do whatever you are intent on doing, perhaps even ensuring both your safety and the accomplishment of your mission? And," she added following a long pause, "what if I told you that you will surely perish if you do not answer my questions?" said the woman, her tone now unfriendly.

"What does . . . does 'paiwish' mean?" Alex asked Elli, keeping his voice low.

"It means to die, Alex," Elli, said, now staring straight into the eyes of the woman who, across the fire, was staring straight at Elli. The woman slowly lifted her left hand and, immediately, out from the shadows at the edge of the clearing appeared an animal, which was growling menacingly. It was an awful looking creature, not unlike a cross between a large snake and a badger. It had a long tail that was bare of fur and coiled tightly against its body. The creature was itself perhaps eight feet in length and covered in coarse hair, and had four pairs of legs—two pairs at the front and two at the rear, with each paw having numerous thin, curled and barbed claws. The head was nearly that of the badger, except that along with its badger-like ears and deep-set beady eyes, it had a very long and pointed nose and a pair of upper tusks that folded neatly over its lower lip. Blood from a recent kill dripped from its mouth and moistened its feet. The loud growl was more than merely threatening, but the creature did not appear to be about to attack—at least, not without a further order from the woman.

Elli never expected so great a challenge, or so great a decision, at the very beginning of the long journey. She had wondered to herself all along how she would respond when faced with such a crisis. Now, she was going to find out—and find out how the others would respond, too.

Beatríz, of course, could not see the beast, but she could hear and smell it, and her imagination was more than capable of filling in the missing pieces fairly accurately. Yes, she was terrified, but she knew she couldn't survive the journey very long without finding sustained periods of relief from the fear and the crippling effects that almost invariably accompany it. She needed to assume the worst right now, and meet it head on, defeating her fear with courage, believing either she was going to die sooner rather than certainly later—or face the real possibility of death all over again, perhaps on numerous occasions, and go through the same terror.

Beatríz could, of course, decide to plead with Elli to be compliant with the woman, out of fear and against the express instructions from Peterwinkle, and so give into fear and thereby perhaps defeat the mission at the outset—and still be killed by the beast. If she could not control the consequences of her actions, she could at least control the actions themselves, and control was what she at this moment needed most. If she could defeat her fears now, then perhaps she could defeat them from that moment forth.

A new and wonderful sense of certitude and peace came over Beatríz. "Don't tell her, Elli."

Jamie, in the process of scheming a way of escape, also said, "Don't tell her, Elli."

All Alex could think about was protecting Elli. "If you twy to make Ewi die, I wiw stop you!" Alex blurted out.

Elli gripped Alex's knee with one hand while she fingered the key through her shirt with the other. She knew the woman had complete control of the beast. "We will not answer those questions, Ma'am," Elli said firmly, "and thank you for the hospitality, but it is now time for us to leave."

Elli rose to her feet slowly, but without hesitation, and the others began then to get up as well. The growling of the animal increased immediately and markedly, as if before an attack.

"Wait. Please. Sit down again, dear children," the woman said, more warmly than even her initial invitation, as if she were suddenly someone who knew them as family for a very long time. Ever so slowly, and with the deliberateness of having chosen to do so, rather than having been coerced, Elli and her friends sat down.

"I know who you are, Elli, and where you come from, and where you are intending to go, and what you are trying to do," the woman said, with an attempt at reassurance in her voice.

But Elli broke in, demandingly, "Then why did you deceive us?"

"I cannot apologize, for that would mean being sorry for doing what I did; yet, I do feel terribly bad for having scared you so. But," she added quickly and with emphasis, "I needed to be absolutely certain of who you are and that you would be able to withstand the awful—and what will most certainly be the continual—pressure to answer those questions or otherwise to tell the story about which you've been sworn to secrecy. Had you answered me, the mission would have been lost before it had barely begun." She then added, but only after pausing to give weight to what followed, "Did I deceive you? Under ordinary circumstances, the answer would be an unqualified yes. But since I did so not for my sake, but for yours, the answer is no."

As soon as the woman had begun to speak, the animal became silent. While speaking, the woman raised her right hand, and the beast retreated, hind legs first, back into the concealing shadows at the edge of the clearing. "Elli," the woman said, "my name is Hannah, and you are now in the land of Bairnmoor, once ruled by Queen Taralina. It is ruled now by the one who deposed the Queen—Sutante Bliss, under the control of the Evil One." Hannah then went on to tell her own version of the secret story, all of which was consistent with everything Peterwinkle had told the children.

"The source of all things, the Good, has chosen you for this incomprehensibly difficult and uncertain mission through the mouth of a messenger situated between the world you left and the world in which you now find yourselves. As with Peterwinkle, I do not know how you are to release the Queen. You will need the greatest of powers to undertake such a mission, and from where those powers will come, the Good only knows.

"But, among other valuable items, I have something to give you that could assist you on your journey. It is an amulet, Elli, to protect your hand in battle; but it is also something that will help you know the truth. If, for example, you want to know whether something being said is true, whether by you or another, the amulet will begin to glow. If the bracelet does not glow, then what has been said is either false or ambiguous. Ambiguity would exist whenever there is a combination of truth and falsehood presenting itself to you. But a word of caution: The amulet will only respond if you *want* it to, and the answer it provides may be other than what you had thought or hoped; in addition, the answer provided by the bracelet will not direct any decisions you make regarding the answer. There may be times, then, when you will not *want* to know the truth, if for no other reason than because the answer will make no difference regarding either what you should do or what you otherwise may already have decided to do."

Hannah reached out a hand containing a wide silver bracelet. Elli went to Hannah and took the bracelet and then sat down again, placing the plain but elegant item on her wrist.

"Look now at the amulet, Elli. Ask it in your heart, whether aloud or in silence, whether the words that I have spoken are true."

Elli looked at the bracelet and asked out loud: "Are the words spoken by Hannah all true?" Immediately, the amulet began to glow softly.

"The amulet is glowing, is it not?" asked Hannah.

"Yes, it is," replied Elli.

"You can trust the bracelet, Elli. But remember: it will respond only when you want it to." She paused, then said, "Remember also on your journey that all things ugly are not bad and all things beautiful are not good. And, finally, do not under any circumstances tell your story to anyone." Hannah paused again. "I will give each of you a knife. It will assist you in many ways yet unforeseen, and it can be used also as a powerful weapon—and with extraordinary power on any one occasion you desire. However, you may use your knife as a weapon with extraordinary powers on one occasion only, so you must take great care to not squander its efficacy prematurely on lesser moments when greater moments of need may be yet to come. In that moment of extraordinary need, you will simply use it with the words, 'in the will of the Good.' Otherwise, it will still assist you immensely in battle and in other ways. Remember, however," Hannah said with particular emphasis, "success in battle, large or small, may not necessarily be of benefit to you. The knife will not give you the wisdom of when to use it or not in its extraordinary capacity."

Speaking as if she had just remembered a crucial piece of information, she said, "You must do all you can to avoid being seen by those who are the enemy, because your mere presence will alert them to a great anomaly they believe will threaten their power and so raise alarm throughout the kingdom. They may not know, at least at the outset, what your mission happens to be, but they will know you are not from this land simply because you are children; there have been no children in Bairnmoor since the ascent of Sutante Bliss. Indeed, since all children and any evidence of childnessness have been destroyed at the instance of Sutante's rule, he will want to destroy you as soon as possible, and especially so since what he considers to be only legend nevertheless refers to the prophetic coming of a child to restore the kingdom to Taralina. Regardless of whether he believes the prophecy or not, he will take no chances, and will do anything and everything in his power to bring about your destruction as quickly as possible.

"All of us must now go our separate ways, for there are forces of evil approaching nearby from the west, and they may already be aware of your presence, so prevalent are there spies serving Sutante in all parts of the country. There are a few, like me, who will assist you on your journey. Nevertheless, regardless of their friendly questioning, you must not answer the questions I have posed to you or otherwise tell your story. If they are friends who have been set apart to assist you, they will know that part of the story they require to assist you, and they will insist on no more. But, be prepared for them to test you.

"Before you depart, I want you to put on clothes I have for you, and to hide your knives behind your backs; it will be best if all whom you encounter along the way see, first, that you anticipate peace." While saying these words, Hannah brought out from the dark interior of the hut an outfit for each child, including a knife and sheath. There were short, dark brown leather skirts for the girls and loose leather trousers for the boys, all of which to the children seemed surprisingly lightweight. She gave to each a thick, long-sleeve linen shirt the color of toasted bread and a pair of knee-high boots made from water snake skin. In addition, Hannah provided each of the girls with leggings that were both lightweight and durable, designed to keep their legs warm, even in extreme cold, and cool in the heat.

The children put on their new clothes that would blend more easily into their surroundings, sequestered their knives, and at Hannah's request hesitantly cast their old clothes into the fire. The fire flamed brightly for a few minutes before becoming only glowing embers once more.

All that remained of their former world, apart from themselves, was the library key.

"Now, it is time for you to go, and without any further hesitation," Hannah said.

"But, Hannah, which way do we go?" Elli asked.

"I'm afraid I do not know, dear children," she said, rather sadly Elli thought, with her voice trailing off as if she had herself already left their presence for the depths of the darkness encircling them. And, then, as Hannah retreated into the seemingly impregnable forest, the children could just barely hear her final words. "The castle is far to the north, beyond The Mountains. Fare thee well."

~THREE~

THE CHILDREN STOOD LOOKING at Elli, waiting for her to provide direction. As Elli considered their next move, the others noticed at once the slow appearance of the beast, Beatríz alerted to its presence from the slight, tight gasp that came from Alex. The creature was advancing to within several feet of the children, all frozen in place, when Alex stepped quickly in front of Elli in a posture of defense while reaching back to pull out his knife. And then, just as Alex had the knife in front of him, the beast lay down on all eight legs and gave out a tiny pleading sort of whimper, as if asking to not be left behind.

"Wait, Alex. I think he wants to follow us," Elli said.

"I hear a rumbling not all that far away, and I don't think it's thunder," said Beatríz.

"Then let's go," said Elli.

"Wait," Beatríz said. "Can anyone see anything beyond the fire?"

"No," said Jamie, "no, not at all, Beatríz."

"So choose a direction and let me lead. I can move best in the dark, I think. I can 'see' with my hands and feet and ears probably better than the rest of you," Beatríz concluded.

"Good," replied Elli. "Feel which way I'm facing, Beatríz, and lead on."

Beatríz stood in front of Elli and then stepped forward into the forest with Elli, Jamie, and Alex trailing close behind by the aid of sound and touch. The beast followed Alex, but at a distance. The forest was dense, with thick vines draping from trees, requiring the children to lift and duck beneath them. They struggled to avoid entanglement, and the going was slow and tiring. The rumbling was not far away, and getting closer. No one said a word. There was nothing to say. The only sounds were those of the forest being disturbed by the four visitors—or, perhaps, trespassers—and the beast. Beatríz stopped to rest, and then all of them stopped and stood quietly, hearing only the slight whispers of their breathing and nothing from the creature following supposedly on their heels. All of them felt a heavy cold wind passing by. Perhaps, thought Elli, it was the same wind that had marked its presence on the staircase, shortly after they had left Peterwinkle. In any event, she had the same feeling that something other than the beast was close and noticing them.

They resumed their slow march. Within a minute or so, however, Beatríz, still in the lead, stopped again. "What is it?" Elli asked.

"The wood has just ended here, and the ground is beginning to slant sharply downward. I'm going to get down on my stomach and feel where it leads, and whether we can go any further in this direction," said Beatríz.

Beatríz lay down and stretched out her arms in front of her head. She crawled forward just a bit. "Elli—Jamie, Alex. Hold onto my legs and don't let go. There seems to be some sort of drop-off here, but I don't know how steep it is or how far down it goes." Beatríz, now secured by the others, crawled downward until soon she announced, "I've hit what seems to be flat ground covered with flattened long grass. Let go of my legs and I'll crawl a little further."

Beatríz crawled through the grass for a couple of minutes before she came to the same kind of ridge from which she had just descended. "It seems like a circular depression, maybe thirty feet across. I think I'm at the other side. Why don't two of you follow along the ridge in opposite directions and see if I'm right."

The children discovered that they were in some sort of clearing just a few feet below the forest floor, and that the tall grass was pressed to the earth and warm, as if a collection of creatures had lain there recently.

"Well, we haven't heard the rumbling in a while, and I can't stay awake any longer," said Elli. "Let's get some sleep, guys." All four of them lay themselves down, one next to the other, as if trying to fit into one bed, each one's head on his or her backpack and an arm around another.

"Has anyone seen The Beast?" Elli asked, in a tone suggesting that the creature now had a name. All said no. "Goodnight," Elli said.

"Goodnight," each of them responded. And all four, with thoughts of home, a deep abiding fear of every next moment, and an inescapable weight of drowsiness, as if caused by the fear itself, went to sleep.

Beatríz was the first to awaken, feeling uncomfortably warm. "Guys! Guys! Is that the sun I feel?"

Alex awoke next, sat up quickly to the sound of Beatríz's voice, and said, "Yes! The sun! And . . . hewz The Beast!" The Beast was lying, in a coil, next to Alex's feet, its tiny beady eyes wide open. The creature licked his upper lip between his fangs and waited, as if obediently, for an order from someone. All four sat up, rubbing thick sleep from their eyes. If this were their home world, it would have been noon in the summertime. The sun was high overhead, and the sky around it was light blue and cloudless.

"What do you see?" Beatríz asked the others. The others were looking almost straight up, with amazement showing on all their faces.

"We are in a clearing, as you thought last night, Beatríz," said Elli, "and the depression pretty well takes up all of it. But the trees—the trees around it are so high that we can barely see the leaves at the top. And the sky is like a small blue hole cut out of the trees, with the sun taking up almost all of the space. No wonder it's so dark around here, even during the day.

"And the trees are so tall and dense, Beatríz, that it could be noon in the middle of the forest, and still we'd think it was night," added Jamie. "Heck, it could have been daytime while we were traveling yesterday in the dark. I'm not sure in this forest it makes any difference whether it's day or night. It's just always . . . dark."

In their hunger, they noticed, while the sun was still shining overhead, some yellow berries in the bushes growing tightly next to the forest's edge. Elli took a closer look, wondering like all of them if they were okay to eat. They looked like yellow cherries, with thin blue lines encircling them, like the rings of Saturn. She picked one apart, and a single seed fell to the ground. Jamie noticed there were lots of seeds scattered about the bushes, including within the depression itself, and that all but a few were clean of any berry flesh.

"Guys," Jamie said, "other things have been eating these. They must be okay."

While the quickly waning light remained, the children decided to gather some of the fruit for their late breakfast and then gather some more to wrap in leaves and save in their backpacks for later. The berries were refreshing and renewing, as well as surprisingly filling. There were lots of long thorns growing around each berry, like sentinels standing guard in a tight circle, so Beatríz's job was to take the berries picked by others and do the wrapping and packing.

They had nearly completed their work, all the while gathering and packing while eating, when the rumbling they had heard the day before at Hannah's, and again while traveling in the dark, sounded shockingly loud and close. They also heard a brutal hacking noise near the rumbling, not unlike what one might imagine the sound of a hundred axes hitting simultaneously a stand of trees to be like. The combination of ominous sounds was so near now that the children had no time to lose in fleeing back into the forest. The chilling problem, however, was that they could not ascertain from which direction the threatening sounds were approaching, or whether those making the sounds had actually surrounded them and were rapidly tightening the circle.

"Ewi," Alex asked, with urgency in his voice, "hwew do we go?"

"Which way, Elli?" asked Beatríz, with a tone of desperation.

"Look!" Jamie yelled and pointed. "The Beast is heading into the woods over there!" The Beast had trotted quickly to the forest's edge and then stopped and looked back at the children. "I think he knows the way and wants us to follow him!"

"Let's go!" ordered Elli. As the children headed for The Beast, he padded on beneath the leafy shroud of darkness.

They hadn't gotten very far into the forest before the darkness was complete, despite the sun being still high in the sky, making listening attentively for the sound of his swift movement in the ancient undergrowth the children's only way to follow The Beast. Not more than five minutes and about a hundred yards had passed when the children no longer heard the sound of hacking. In its place, however, they heard even louder rumbling accompanied by grunting—as if words were being growled.

The creatures making the sounds were now very close, evidently gathered in and around the clearing, voicing both their discovery of the children's recent presence and their vile excitement at the thought of an imminent killing or capture. All of the children and The Beast stood still, waiting to learn what the creatures' next move would be. The children then heard some low and barely audible conversation and bickering before all became once again deathly still.

Then, the rumbling began once again, together with strident screeching and triumphant yelling, as the creatures swarmed toward the children. The Beast continued his leading with greater speed, and the children struggled to keep up. But as fast as they went further into the dense, vine-entwined forest, it was all too evident that the gap between them and the creatures was fast closing, and that it would be only minutes before the enemy was upon them.

Beatríz, still leading the others, stopped suddenly for what was to be only the briefest of moments to listen for The Beast's movements, but heard nothing, except the approaching creatures and their own panting of panicked alarm.

"Get down on your stomachs everyone, and stay quiet; maybe (just miraculously, she was thinking) they will pass by us," Beatríz said, with a note of feigned hopefulness in her voice. They all immediately lay themselves down—and waited, in silence. Then, quite suddenly, the sounds coming from the creatures changed, no longer seeming to be approaching them. The children heard the collective hateful roaring of the enemy and, along with it, the shrill screech of a lone challenger summoning them to battle. The children lay frozen in fear as they listened to the roaring and screeching and wailing of pain in the tumult of battle. All four of them wondered, without saying a word to one another, and with tears welling in their eyes, whether The Beast was sacrificing himself to buy them time to escape. Elli wanted to give the order to move on, but she was uncertain about the direction to take now that they no longer had The Beast to lead them. Perhaps, she thought, they should simply remain where they were until they learned what the creatures would do next, but she just as quickly realized the inadvisability of that decision.

All at once, Alex, who just as inadvisably had raised himself in an effort to see what was pursuing them and how close they were to the ongoing battle nearby, said, in a loud whisper, "Ewi!"

"Shhh, Alex!" Elli said, and just as quickly added, sensing he was no longer on his stomach, "And get back down—we don't know what they can see and how far in the dark!"

"Ewi!" Alex replied, in a louder whisper and more insistently.

"Alex, you *have* to get back down and be quiet until we all move together!" Elli insisted.

"But, Ewi, thew ah wites ovew thew!" Without hesitation, Elli got up on her knees and looked quickly all about. She saw the lights—perhaps two dozen—in a single grouping, and not far away.

"C'mon, guys!" Elli ordered. "Follow me—fast—toward the lights—over there to the left!" They scrambled to their feet and pushed against the forest toward the group of tiny lights, stumbling and scraping and bruising themselves in their struggle through the woods that seemed resolved to resist any further penetration into their ancient community by the four young strangers. All of the children found themselves becoming increasingly tangled in coiled vines and twisted branches that impeded their progress, and it was impossible in the dark to ascertain what, or how far away, the lights were. The din of rumbling and hacking had not only resumed, but was once again closing in on them.

"Use your knives!" Jamie yelled, no longer concerned about whether the enemy could hear them or not. All of them—except Jamie, ironically—pulled out their knives and began to hack and cut with surprising ease the vines and branches that were entangling them. All except Jamie were now moving, and moving faster than they had ever moved in the forest to this point. They pushed toward the lights that, nevertheless, seemed to be constantly moving away from them while keeping the same distance, as if intending to lead the children. But Jamie, who alone had remembered the knives, was so entangled that he was not able to reach his knife with either hand. "I'm caught! I can't reach my knife!" Jamie yelled against the noises of the advancing enemy.

The others were by this time far ahead of Jamie, and only Beatríz was able to hear him. "Jamie's stuck—way back there!" she yelled.

"I'll double back," Elli said, "but you two keep going toward the lights."

"Elli!" Beatríz yelled back. "We don't even know what the lights are, or even if they're friendly!"

"They can't be any worse than what we're running from!" shouted Elli, as she attempted to backtrack in the direction of Jamie.

Jamie continued to try unsuccessfully to reach his knife. Then, suddenly, before Elli could reach him, the branches and vines were pulling themselves—or being pulled—away from Jamie. When Jamie was finally able to get to his knife, he was already free to move again. "I'm out—I'm coming!" he yelled to the others. In a minute or so he caught up with his three companions who had stopped and were waiting for him.

Elli barked another order. "Okay, let's keep going—faster, if you can! The creatures will be on us any minute now!" They resumed their push through the heavy growth and seemed, finally, to be getting closer to the lights. The rumbling and hacking behind them, however, was also growing louder and closer. Elli, in the lead once again, noticed the lights had stopped, not more than forty yards ahead. She noticed also, much to her dismay, that they were disappearing, one by one, until there was only a single small light remaining—hovering, barely visible, just ahead of them.

The children could now feel the vibrations from the movement and destructive work of their pursuers. The ground beneath them began to shake from the enemy's heavy feet, and the children were hearing trees falling and feeling bursts of wind from their crashing to the forest floor.

Finally, when they had nearly reached the light, it moved suddenly away once more, leaving them with hopes quickly dashed. As the enemy forces were gaining on them, Elli noticed the single light move to the right where she spotted, with newfound hope, the other lights. Far from having gone out, they had been hovering in the darkness beside a tall thin beam of light created by some sort of opening that was more than ten feet high and about a foot and a half wide.

The enemy, with lights of their own, at last saw the children, not more than twenty yards ahead of them, and roared with the certainty of impending triumph. Then, to their astonished surprise, the children vanished. When the creatures reached the spot where they had just seen the children, there was only a single large tree standing nearby. The tree, being one of the biggest in the forest, was too big to hack down, even if the children were somehow within it, which seemed all but impossible. The leader of the enemy forces ordered his warriors to halt and be quiet, hoping to hear the children who had somehow been able to elude them. They looked and listened with keen eyes and even better ears, but saw and heard nothing. At that point the leader motioned for a number of his forces to encircle in opposite directions the trunk that was the width of a house, assuming, with an ugly smug smile of accomplishment, that he would shortly discover the children hiding on the other side of the tree. But, again, there was nothing.

In anger, they attacked the trunk with all of their resources, including the "hacking machines," but the tree was impenetrable and incapable of being taken down, and the thought, finally, that the children would some-how be *in* the tree struck them as ludicrous. They then began working away at the forest in the direction they had been heading in their pursuit of the children only minutes earlier. They were determined to follow the children as long as it took to capture or kill them, even if it meant clearing the entire forest to do so. Besides, should the small ones reach the other side of the forest, which was highly unlikely, they would be met with nothing more welcoming than those now pursuing them.

Just as the creatures were about to see and pounce on them, all four children had frantically squeezed themselves through the narrow opening in the trunk from which the light was emanating, stumbled to the uneven floor inside the tree, and then heard the sound of a massive wood door slamming shut behind them. They looked back, but saw no one. The door seemed to have closed of its own accord before disappearing entirely by blending perfectly into the rest of the tree.

They looked around, frozen in silent wonder—each where he or she had tumbled to rest on the floor. The light had seemed bright at first against the pitch blackness to which their eyes had been accustomed outside, but as their eyes adjusted, they realized that the light was soft, streaming in all directions from healthy flames in a stone fireplace on the other side of the large circular room in which they were sitting. The mammoth door that had closed behind them, likely not heard by the enemy above their own loud noises, sealed out the darkness and greatly muffled the sounds of the enemy raging and assaulting the tree.

The children remained quiet, examining their surroundings and unconsciously enjoying their first sense of well-being since they had first arrived in Bairnmoor. It became evident that they had landed on the solid wooden floor of a circular room inside a tree, the diameter of which was about forty feet. There were no windows, and the smooth walls of the room curved gently upward into a circle of shadow that obscured the height of the ceiling—if, in fact, there was any ceiling at all. In the room was a large round wooden table with thick and gnarled branches surrounding it, as if they were a circular barrier to anyone or anything actually being able to use the table. There were also similar tree limbs and branches protruding in a number of different places from the continuous wall of the room, as if they were growing inside the tree and weaving themselves together into complex knots. And although the children could not imagine how anyone could sit in them, there were several articles of twisted limbs scattered about the room that vaguely resembled high backed chairs.

There were also two tall wooden cabinets spread apart along the wall, and perhaps five or six stacks of sticks leaning against them, or against each other, as well as some cups and plates on the table containing remnants of recently eaten food.

Now that she could no longer hear any sounds from the enemy outside, Elli ventured a modestly loud "Hello?" She paused just a bit, out of politeness. "Hello? Can anyone hear me?" she now yelled.

"You don't have to yell so, especially given the acoustics. I can hear you very well, indeed," a voice somewhere inside the room or beyond the shadow of the ceiling replied.

Elli, Alex, and Jamie looked wide-eyed around the room, straining to see where the voice was coming from, but saw no one or anything else that appeared able to speak. Beatríz said, "I'm sure the voice came from right behind us, near the door that slammed shut."

"But of course!" the voice said.

Jamie looked back after having looked there already. "All that's there, Beatríz, is just an old stack of tall sticks."

"Well, this 'old stack of tall sticks,' as you call me, had just pulled *you, sir*, out of an entanglement a few minutes ago," the voice said, directing his remarks at Jamie.

"What?" Jamie exclaimed, utterly confused.

"Wait!" said Elli. "I saw what looks to us like a stick move in that stack, and I don't think it's a stack of sticks anymore than we are piles of bones! It's a . . . a . . . ."

"A person, I think you mean!" the voice said, whereupon the apparent stack of sticks unfolded and spread itself into a creature that looked like a huge walking stick with two bulbous, knot-like protrusions at the top of the tallest "stick" that opened next to each other as large round eyeballs. The creature blinked a few times at the children, seeming to be not nearly as surprised to see *them* as they were to see *him*.

The three children who could see were staring into the creature's eyes when it spoke to them again. "If the four of you are persons, then I am surely a person, and I suspect that you are persons, so that, therefore, I also am a person, although," he said a bit wryly, "I have to say that you don't *look* very person-like, at least from *my* perspective. But, if you'll concede the argument, then I'm satisfied." He then walked rather giraffe-like over to one of the chair-like articles of tangled branches and, one might say, made a sitting-down movement, finishing it off by crossing one leg over the other.

The person had two legs, and two arms nearly as long as the legs, with four thin fingers and two just-as-thin thumbs at the end of each limb. He had two distinct, porpoise-like holes the size of dimes well below his eyes that constituted his nose, and, just beneath those, a most diminutive horizontal slit of a mouth that seemed almost to move about his face when he talked.

"So," the stick man said, once he had settled the ontology of their mutual existence—and himself into the tangled wood that resembled a chair, "I suspect that you are persons in the form of children, and that, since there are no known children remaining in the land of Bairnmoor, although at one time they constituted the primary form of personhood here, you are strangers in this land." He paused and rubbed his chin, ruminating on what self-ascribed profundity he had just uttered, and then added, "Am I correct?"

"Yes," said Elli, before anyone else could speak, and especially before Alex spoke, "but that's all we can tell you."

"By the way, Mr. . . . um . . . person," said Jamie, to break the ice, "I want to thank you very much for saving me earlier."

"Not a thing. Not a thing," replied the stick man. He pulled out a beautifully grained wooden pipe from a hidden pocket on one of his legs that looked like a typical bulge on a branch, and lit it.

"But," Jamie continued, "why did you save me? And why did you save all of us? And who and what are you—I mean," catching himself quickly, "besides a person, I mean? And, um . . . what were those lights that led us to your place?"

"So, you have a lot of questions for me, do you? But," said the stick man who then paused to puff a couple of puffs. "But, you apparently won't answer *my* questions; is that correct?"

"We can't!" Alex interjected himself into the conversation. "Mistuw Petuwinckuw said w'w' we caan't tawk . . ."

"Alex, stop talking! Please!" Elli insisted, interrupting him. "Let me do the talking for us."

"And what, young lady, can you talk to me about?" the stick man asked, with little sense of urgency about the conversation, but with his eyes protruding toward her as if they were going to pop completely out of their sockets in the expectation of a forthcoming—and acceptable—answer.

"Sir, I can tell you who each of us is, and that we are not from this land, and that we mean you no harm, but I cannot tell you more."

"So, you . . . *are*?" the stick man inquired, his voice rising in pitch at the end of his short question.

"My name is Elli," she said compliantly, "and these are," she pointed in succession, "Beatríz, Alex, and Jamie. And, of course," she added, "we are children."

"Hmm . . ." the stick man said, continuing to look at Elli and puff his pipe. "Well . . . my name is Thorn, and I am what is called a Dactyl. My family and I lived along with other Dactyl families in this forest, and this is my home—at least . . . my home as long as the forest lasts," he added, his voice trailing off and his eyes staring through Elli, as if he saw something behind her that had grabbed his attention.

"What do you mean by 'as long as the forest lasts?'" asked Elli.

"But," the stick man said, as if not even hearing Elli's question, "I must hear more. Whatever are you doing in this forest—and where are you going?"

"I cannot tell you why we are in this forest, sir, except to say that we found ourselves suddenly surrounded by this forest and, to flee from some creatures that were pursuing us, we simply ran further into the forest in whatever direction The Beast was taking us," Elli replied.

His eyes suddenly retreating back into their sockets, Thorn asked, "And who or what is this thing called 'The Beast?'"

"Oh, of course. Well, we don't really know what he is—or was—exactly, but it appeared that he wanted to eat us, and then he became our friend and wanted to lead us away from those who were chasing us. We just called him 'The Beast.' The sad thing, Mr. Thorn, is that we believe he is already dead—that maybe he sacrificed himself to give us time to find safety from the creatures when they were just about to reach us."

"Ah, yes, so he did," said Thorn, sadly. "I mean died in this battle you've described." Thorn chewed on the stem of his pipe and added, glancing at each of the children briefly, "I saw the entire skirmish from above in the trees; it was this Beast you speak of that actually initiated the contact, rushing headlong into the clearing where your enemies had gathered. I don't of course know whether he intended to sacrifice himself. What I can say with certainty is that without that distracting conflict we would not be having this conversation." Thorn blinked. "But, none of this tells me why you are here in this land in the first place."

"I'm sorry, sir, but none of us can tell you that. We are sworn to secrecy—and nothing will make us tell you, with all due respect," Elli said, resolutely, but politely.

Thorn smiled a most tiny, barely visible, smile with his lipless mouth. "Well," Thorn then said, "I simply needed to make sure."

"To make sure of what?" asked Jamie.

"To make sure you wouldn't tell me anything," Thorn said.

"But," Jamie added, "that's what the woman . . ."

"Jamie!" Elli whispered loudly.

"I know what Hannah must have said to you," Thorn said.

"So," Elli replied, in a question veiled as a statement, "in other words, we don't need to tell you anything because you already know—like Hannah!"

"Well," said Thorn, rather matter-of-factly, "I'm not at all certain that I know all that Hannah knows. I only know that Hannah has told me—and others through the 'maven-line' as we call it—that if I ever encountered those who resembled you, I was to provide you safe passage through the forest—that is, as long as the forest lasts—and that I would know you because you would be children who would not tell me anything of your mission here."

"Mr. Thorn," Elli began.

"Just Thorn—no Mr. Thorn. Please." He smiled, signaling with twirling fingers for her to continue.

"What do you mean by 'while the forest lasts?' I believe you've mentioned that twice now."

"The forest, as large as it still is, was yet much larger when the Queen ruled this land. But Sutante Bliss, who now rules, has been depleting the forest of trees to build huge fortresses and palaces and many things associated with roads and bridges, as well as wood to sell to others for heat and light against the darkness and cold that have overshadowed so much of the land since the Queen's death."

"The Queen's death?" asked Elli, with a stunned and troubled look of surprise.

"Why, yes. Did you think she was still living?" asked Thorn, with a puzzled look of surprise that included one eye rolled higher than the other.

The other children looked at Elli, wondering what those words meant, and what she'd say, and what they'd now do.

"Are you quite certain, Thorn? I mean, about the Queen being dead?" Elli asked, meekly.

"Oh," he replied sadly, "I'm afraid that I am all too certain. I saw her killed, Elli, by the sword of Sutante Bliss. And I saw them bury her deep below the castle. No, I am quite certain, Elli, that the Queen is dead." He paused and looked kindly upon Elli. "Does it matter to your mission, Elli?"

Elli glanced at the silver amulet on her wrist and asked it in her mind, with great reluctance, not being at all certain she wanted to know the answer, whether what Thorn had said about the Queen's death was true. As she feared, and with a visible shudder, Elli saw the amulet begin to glow. "But, if true, then what does that now mean for our mission?" she asked herself. And she then wondered whether Hannah and Peterwinkle knew.

"But," Thorn added, following another couple of puffs, awaiting patiently a response from Elli, but not expecting to get one, "why does it matter to you, Elli?"

"I cannot tell you anything about the mission, as you've already acknowledged, Thorn. Nor can I tell you whether it matters or not that the Queen is dead," Elli said, forlornly, while looking away with tears in her eyes.

"But, Elli," said Jamie, "doesn't it matter that . . ."

"Jamie!" Elli said sharply.

"Dear young lady, Elli," Thorn said, with a soft and sympathetic voice, placing a hand gently on her shoulder, "I feel bad that none of you knew about the Queen's death, and that it troubles you. But whatever this means to you I have pledged to Hannah to do everything I can to see you safely through the forest, and that I will do regardless." Thorn then added, "I would ask you which way out of the forest you wanted to go, but since there is only one way, it will have to be that way."

Thorn puffed a couple of times on his pipe, which was no longer lit. "We will talk about all of this tomorrow. Now we shall go to bed. I am sorry to say I have no beds that will suit you. However, I will lay some vine rugs on the floor next to the fire and give you some soft coverlets made from skins. I will tend the fire, as needed, throughout the night. You must get some sleep, for your day tomorrow will be a long one."

"Excuse me, Thorn," Elli said, changing the subject deliberately, "but what are these creatures pursuing us? We have only heard them; we have never seen them."

"And a good thing, too," Thorn replied. While he made ready their meager sleeping arrangements, he continued. "They are called Rumblards and Thrashers, and are fashioned from the wicked art of joining together animals and former persons, or, Unpersons. The Rumblards are fashioned from Unpersons and elephants—hence, the rumbling of their movements. The others, the Thrashers, are made from Unpersons and Sawfish. Both are tools of Sutante Bliss and are tended by others called Wolfmen—who are half wolf and half Unperson—and by Unperson warriors from the north. All of these have been pursuing you, no doubt."

"But," Elli asked, with a voice of incomprehension, "how does Sutante Bliss create these creatures—these Rumblards and Thrashers and Wolfmen?"

"He doesn't. In fact, Sutante Bliss can create nothing; he can only destroy. But, he provides the *illusion of creation* with evil, and the creatures I have named are the products of *destruction* only." The children looked puzzled, but Thorn did not elucidate—and they were too weary to pursue any more questions, including Jamie, who wondered about the lights.

When Thorn had prepared the children's beds, he pulled himself up and onto one of the protruding sets of tangled branches located along the wall, covered himself with an animal skin, said "Goodnight," and went immediately to sleep, evidenced by a slight, rather bottled snoring sound drifting from his bed.

Except for the presence of the skin, there was nothing else to distinguish the place where Thorn was sleeping from any of the other protruding sets of branches, or even from Thorn himself, so well did Thorn "become one" with his bed, as he must have "been one" with the forest itself.

Perhaps surprisingly, the children slept soundly through the night, falling asleep nearly as soon as they had lain themselves down.

~FOUR~

WHEN MORNING BROKE, IT made very little difference either inside or outside Thorn's home. The sun had been rising for several hours, but since it was not yet nearly overhead, the large clearing around the immense tree in which the five had been sleeping had the appearance of dusk. Though it was becoming slowly and steadily lighter, it was nevertheless impossible for anyone to see more than three or four feet into the surrounding forest.

Inside the tree, it was the darkest it had yet been because Thorn had let the fire die down to dusty flickering embers. Thorn awoke well before the children had even begun to stir into consciousness, lit various lamps hanging on the wall, and pulled out a preparation table from one of the tall cabinets. He then put coffee on to simmer over the fireplace coals and cut up some bread and fruit.

It was actually the smell of the coffee simmering that awakened the children, one by one. And while none of them actually liked coffee, the smell comforted them with the familiarity of home.

The children rose and took nourishment with Thorn by the low fire, even to the point of drinking the sweetened coffee and actually enjoying its taste and warmth. No one had yet said anything, as if the meal was meant to be eaten that way—in meditative silence.

When all had finished, Thorn addressed them. "In a few minutes we shall set out. As I said last night, regardless of where you expect your journey to take you, you will, in any event, have to leave the forest first, and there is only one—that is to say, one *safe*—way. And that is *underneath* the forest, following the main root from this tree to where it emerges from the ground many miles from here. There is a narrow tunnel which the Dactyls excavated a long time ago that follows alongside the main root. However, I will need to lead you, since there are numerous other tunnels made for various purposes by a variety of creatures, including some into which the main tunnel divides or that break off from it. There are also tunnels that ground waters have created that would confound you, sending you easily and truly—and literally—to a dead end, with no hope of ever being found.

"We will each of us carry in our rucksacks water, fruit, and dried sweet bread, as well as a skin for warmth when we need to rest or sleep."

"How long will it take us, Thorn?" asked Jamie.

"If we make good time and not encounter any, shall we say, 'interferences,' we can make it in three to four days. We will carry no torches for light, since the air is scant as it is simply for breathing. You will feel as if you are climbing up high into some mountains instead of descending deep into the earth as the air becomes increasingly thin and you tire more easily.

"We will, however," Thorn said, with a note of the fortuitous, "have the light of my eyes to guide us. Indeed, just as you will be able to see my eyes when they are open, so I will be able to see what lies some several feet ahead of me, my eyes casting a dim light upon our path whenever I open them. However, just as *you* will be able to see my eyes when they are open, so, too, will other creatures that may be hidden in the dark beyond the reach of my glow.

"I will have Beatríz follow immediately behind me. Her keen sense of hearing that I noticed when you first arrived may assist us most valuably during our journey. I will have a rope tied about my waist, and each of you will take hold of it, one after the other. And, by all means," Thorn said, as if this was the most critical instruction of them all, "do not under any circumstances let go of the rope. You may never find it again—or the rest of us you."

Having finished his instructions, Thorn doused the coals with water, blew out the wall lamps and led them in the dark across the floor with his glowing eyes to the other of the two cabinets. He then moved the cabinet aside and, with his thin fingers pressed into several small holes in the wall, pulled out and slid to the side on a hidden track a small door, not unlike the door of an airliner. Thorn reached into the pitch black opening and took out a rather long thick rope with a loop to go around the leader's waist and a number of knots along the length of the rope against which those following could rest their grips.

With each one in place along the length of the rope, beginning with Thorn and ending with Elli, Thorn slid the door shut, enveloping the children once again in that darkness that had become all too familiar a traveling companion since they had first descended the library's basement stairs a few days earlier.

The tunnel that, at the beginning, was little higher than eight feet, would never reach that height again during the course of their journey underground. At times, they would find it considerably smaller. Thorn, who was himself nearly eight feet tall, would have to travel most of the way bent forward at the waist as much as ninety degrees, looking as if he were the feeblest of old men. Beatríz thought the tunnel, in general, had the odor of dry black dirt. There were times, however, as they passed by unseen passageways off of the main tunnel, when the odor reminded Alex of those times when he would dig in the moist nocturnal grass for large worms that would surface only when the sun had set. The ground descended gradually with firm, packed earth, as if it had—as, indeed it had—been traveled for hundreds of years by thousands and thousands of creature feet.

Like a slow-rolling and soundless train, the four "cars" that were the children and the "engine" that was Thorn with two eyes for "headlamps" that appeared to be low on their batteries, moved steadily through the tunnel. Every once in a while Thorn would slow to a stop, examining with a wagging glow a fork in the tunnel or something amounting to a T intersection to determine down which tunnel the main track was running. It was not at all clear to the children how deep underground they had traveled, or were going to travel, but they had been descending silently for hours, and each was becoming short of breath. Thorn heard their rapid and shallow breathing and halted the train.

"Let's rest for a few minutes and then continue; there will be a multiple passageway intersection not far up ahead that will give us a sufficient area on which to stretch out and sleep for a few hours. It's another hour ahead, and it will be time to stop for the night anyway. By then we should have logged a good eight hours—plenty for our first day, I'd say. You'll need to sleep double that time in this thin air to recoup your stamina, but I will keep watch. Unlike you *human* persons, I need very little sleep."

They sat and ate some fruit. While eating and drinking, Alex's breathing was getting faster and louder. He was beginning to wheeze and then starting to cry. Elli told him to relax and keep quiet—that his fast breathing and crying would only make it harder to breath. But Alex only breathed faster and cried louder.

"I can't bweeth! I can't bweeth!" Alex tried to shout in a panicked voice.

"Try your best to relax, Alex," Thorn said while laying a reassuring hand on Alex's knee. "You're panicking and hyperventilating and, as Elli said, only making it more difficult for yourself. And," he added, "if there is anything else in this tunnel within half a mile, it will now know that we are here."

Alex suddenly stood up, hitting his head against the roof of the tunnel, and began to jump in place, yelling as loudly as he was able under the circumstances, "I can't bweeth! I can't bweeth! I have to go back! I have to get out of hew! I do! I do!"

"Alex!" Jamie yelled. "You have to stop! Sit down! You're making things worse for everyone!"

But Alex only continued to yell the more, in a harsh, tight and aspirating voice, "I have to get out of hew!" Then, all of a sudden, he started to run back into the tunnel from which they'd come.

"Alex, stop!" yelled Thorn.

Elli wasted no time to think. She jumped to her feet and ran as fast as her (rather fast) legs would carry her while bent at the waist. "I'll get him!" yelled Elli.

"Don't go, Elli!" Thorn shouted. "You'll both get lost!"

But Elli caught up to Alex quickly and tackled him at the legs, bringing him down with a thud and holding tightly onto his ankles. "Stop, Alex!" Elli screamed at him.

"Ewi," Alex cried weakly, with no air behind the voice, "pweez wet me go!"

"Thorn!" Elli yelled, in a composed voice, "I have him, but I need help to bring him back!"

Alex had no energy remaining either to run or to resist. Thorn and Jamie helped carry Alex back to where Beatríz had remained alone. They laid him on a skin, gave him some tea that Thorn had packed in a bottle, and let him in his utter exhaustion drift from semi-consciousness into a deep sleep.

"We'll simply try to rest here," said Thorn, quietly, "until Alex awakens on his own. If he is still intent on going back, we will acquiesce. At least, that's what we will tell him. If I must, I will tell him we are returning, but we will nevertheless continue our journey out of the forest. If lying is the most loving thing I can do, then lie I will. I don't know if anyone or anything has heard us, but the sooner we can continue the better."

All but Thorn fell asleep. Unbeknownst to them, they slept more than a dozen hours, each of them awakening at roughly the same time, feeling rested and eager to be on their way, including Alex. No one said anything to Alex about what had happened a half day earlier, and Alex himself said nothing, behaving as if he didn't recall the incident at all. They resumed their journey in the darkness, only Thorn able to see just an arm's length or so in front of them. Within what seemed only minutes, the five had arrived at the open space created by the intersection of several passageways. Thorn stopped to ascertain which way was for certain the correct one. He bore into the sides of the various tunnels with a single finger, feeling for what he believed to be the side of the main root. He was able to feel a root alongside two of the tunnels, but his sense was that neither was the main one. "We'll go off to the far right; it's the passage that has the hardest-packed earth. Ready?" All answered in the affirmative.

They continued their shallow descent, and within a short time found the tunnel widening and increasing in height. Thorn stopped abruptly, closed his eyes, and said to the others in the lightest of whispers, "No noise from anyone."

Elli reached around and gently touched Alex's lips. "Shhh." They stood still for several minutes, Thorn listening intently and the children awaiting further instructions. Thorn could feel a slight vibration in the earth beneath his feet.

Beatríz tapped Thorn on the shoulder and whispered, her lips touching the side of his head, "I hear a light clicking noise in the distance, Thorn, and it's getting closer."

As if he immediately understood the implications of what Beatríz had told him, Thorn whispered to the others, "Go back, Elli, and take the first passage to the left that you come to. It's probably going to be pretty small, so you'll likely have to crawl to get into it. Go in as far as you can until I tell you to stop—but back in! Remember to back in! I'll be right behind you! Let's go, quickly!"

Suddenly, all of them could hear the rapid clicking, as of a hundred drumsticks drumming lightly on a board, and getting rapidly louder. "Quickly, everyone! Quickly!" yelled Thorn, realizing they had already been discovered by what was fast approaching from up ahead. Elli, holding firmly to the rope, challenged the others with her speed and agility. She found the low passageway within a matter of seconds and crawled in backwards on all fours, all the while pulling on the rope to assist the others until she heard Thorn yell, "I'm in! You can stop! We're okay for the time being."

After they had all caught their breath, Jamie asked Thorn, "What is it?"

"From that awful drumming sound, I can tell that it's a Mortejos. We call it simply, a 'Death Eyes.' It is a giant millipede that has hundreds of bony legs and crawls low to the ground, almost on its stomach," explained Thorn. "When standing, it is more than four feet high, as well as being about ten feet long, but even on its stomach it's nearly three feet high, so it won't be able to follow us into this passageway—which is important, because it's almost here!" Thorn paused, and caught his breath. "On the other hand . . . "

Thorn was interrupted, first by the rushing sound of the millipede's legs clicking in their joints in their inexorable march toward them and, then, by the appearance in the glow from Thorn's eyes of the creature's hissing mouth and bared teeth at the passage opening. Thorn instructed everyone to remain still and not talk. Then, after about ten minutes, the creature left the opening and retreated back up the tunnel a short distance before stopping.

"As I was attempting to say earlier," Thorn said, sounding relieved, "the Death Eyes will simply wait us out, even if it takes weeks, which, of course, we do not have. We can perhaps get by with the provisions we have for two or three more days, not including the remaining time it will take to emerge from the tunnel, but that's as long as we have, especially with the water which remains. What I'm saying, unfortunately, dear friends, is that we either remain here and die or we somehow face the creature by executing the best plan we can to improve our odds against it."

A long silence ensued.

"Thorn," asked Elli, "why do you call the Mortejos 'Death Eyes?'"

"Because," answered Thorn, "it captures its prey by first hypnotizing it into paralysis. Once another creature of any sort looks into the Mortejos's eyes that creature becomes instantly immobilized. Then, the Death Eyes merely has to walk up to its prey and bite off its head."

"But, what if a creature doesn't look at the eyes, Thorn?" asked Jamie.

"It never happens. You simply cannot face the creature without looking into its eyes—they are the only thing you can see of the creature in the dark—and it takes only a fraction of a moment to be frozen in place."

All became still again, each one pondering the nearly impossible jam they were in, while the creature patiently awaited its opportunity for a substantial meal. Finally, Thorn said, "I have a plan, and I think it will work. Elli, you will tie the rope around your waist and the rest of you will take hold behind her, beginning with Beatríz and ending with Jamie. At the moment I determine best, I will slip out of the tunnel and run *back* toward my home. The Mortejos will immediately come running after me. I can run fast, so I may be able, with my speed and eyesight, to elude the creature for sometime before I have to dive into a side tunnel to hide, expecting then that the creature will continue to run past me.

"As soon as the Death Eyes pursues me, you, Elli, will lead the others out of the tunnel and turn to the right, continuing the journey as quickly as you can. If you hurry, you can make it almost immediately to the multiple-tunnel intersection where you will take the second tunnel to your right, which will be too small for the creature to follow you into. Once in that tunnel, you can continue until you rejoin the main root tunnel in some three hundred yards. By that time, the creature will have learned of your escape, but frustrated because it cannot pursue you any longer, it will go back to its customary place of rest. Once back in the main tunnel you will be starting to ascend. Just continue to stay on the packed earth tunnel that ascends, and you will find yourselves emerging from underground within another day or so. The air will continue to thicken and enrich itself, so you will have more energy and be able to make better time. I can't guarantee that you won't encounter any other obstacles along the way, but this is your best chance. I will try to join you before you've gotten far, but that depends on how long it takes for the Mortejos to get beyond me."

Thorn paused to catch his breath and steel his mind, while focusing on the softening of his heart that he hadn't experienced in many years. He knew that his death at the jaws of the Mortejos was virtually inescapable, and perhaps even imminent, but he also knew that these four children whom he had already come to love had only this opportunity to live and, perhaps, complete their mission that quite likely was the last hope of his beloved Bairnmoor. "So," Thorn said, with an almost cold resolve, "time taken is time wasted. Elli, ready your companions. As soon as I leave and you hear the Mortejos running by the tunnel after me, leave the tunnel immediately and run as fast as you can in the other direction, saying nothing to each other and, of course, not letting go of the rope." Thorn rummaged quickly in his rucksack. "Here, Elli, take this torch and some matches; but do not make any light until you have reached the next tunnel to your right."

Thorn, crouched on all fours, moved next to the passage opening. He turned to look one last time into the children's eyes and then braced himself for a dash.

"Wait! Wait!" yelled Beatríz. Thorn had started out the tunnel, and then stopped, pulling his head back in.

"Beatríz," said Thorn, firmly, "there is no other way."

"But, there is—I'm quite sure of it, Thorn. And if I'm right, then you won't have to die to save us—and we all know that that's what's going to happen if you leave us. And we need you! And I really believe there is another way. Please, just hear me out!" Beatríz pleaded. Without waiting for Thorn's answer, she continued. "You said the Death Eyes paralyzes its prey so that it's in no hurry to kill it, correct?"

"Yes," said Thorn.

"Well, what if *I* confronted the creature just outside the tunnel and *pretended* immediately upon looking toward him that I was paralyzed in place? I would already have my knife held above my head when I turned to face the creature. You would tell me when I'm directly facing the creature. Once frozen there, I will simply wait for the Mortejos to come to me. As soon as his head in within reach, you will yell, 'Now!' And I will then plunge the knife into its head—that would kill the creature, wouldn't it—or at least severely injure it?" Beatríz could hardly believe it was she who had just spoken.

The other children looked into Thorn's slowly blinking eyes, waiting for his response, not knowing either what he would think or what they were to think about the alternate plan.

"Yes, it would." Thorn said. "But, Beatríz, if you would move yourself the least little bit once you pretended to be paralyzed, the Death Eyes would rapidly fall upon you and kill you. There would not likely be time for us to help you. Do you understand this?"

"Yes," said Beatríz, "I do, and I still think it's the best plan if there is any hope at all for all of us to survive."

"But, Butweece," said Alex, almost weeping, "ahnt you afwade?"

"Yes, Alex, I am afraid—more afraid than I had ever imagined being afraid. But we are here on this journey for a reason, and this Good that Hannah and Peterwinkle talk about must want us to succeed, so we have to trust in that—*I* have to trust in that."

Reluctantly, filled with fear and sadness and unspoken incredulity, they adopted Beatríz's plan to fool the Mortejos into believing it had paralyzed Beatríz and so meet its death at her hands.

"But," asked Alex, "what if it doesn't wook? What if it doesn't wook?"

"It will, Alex. It has to," answered Beatríz.

"Are you sure you want to do this, Beatríz?" asked Thorn, offering a final chance for her to withdraw. "You don't *have* to do this, Beatríz."

"Mr. Thorn, I really *don't want* to do this." She gulped softly. "But, I believe I am *supposed* to do this—that someone or something has called me to do this, Mr. Thorn, and so I know that I have to."

Each of the others, with unseen tears in their eyes, laid a gentle hand on Beatríz's shoulders.

"Are you ready?" asked Thorn.

"I don't know how to be ready, Thorn, and, even if I did, I don't think I ever would be, so let's just get on with it," Beatríz replied, feeling strangely detached, as if she were more a spectator to what she was about to do.

"Do you have your knife out, Beatríz?" Thorn asked. She fumbled behind her back.

"I do now," she said.

"Beatríz! Remember what Hannah said—about the knife and its extraordinary powers!" whispered Jamie, sharply.

"Yes," Beatríz remembered. "In the will of the Good," she said to the knife.

"As soon as you exit the tunnel, Beatríz, stand up with your knife held fully aloft and ready to strike. Then, start turning to your right. I will yell 'stop!' when you are facing the Mortejos. At that moment, with your eyes open, freeze, and do not move—or even flinch. You should, within a few moments, hear the creature creeping slowly toward you. It will sound like it's moving faster than it is because of its many legs, but it will advance casually, unless it receives signals that you are not paralyzed. As soon as it is within striking distance, Beatríz, I will yell, 'now!' Then, strike down in front of you with all your might. Do you think you have it?" asked Thorn.

"Yes," said Beatríz, under her breath, as if she were in the middle of praying—which she was, but to whom or what she could not have said.

"Okay, on three," ordered Thorn. "One, two, three!"

So much was her adrenaline rushing that Beatríz shot out of the tunnel like out of a gun. She immediately stood up, her knife held aloft, and began turning to face the Death Eyes. Already everyone could hear the creature stirring, with grunting and a random clicking of legs, as if it were awakening suddenly from sleep, followed by a shrill hissing of both surprise and anger.

"Stop!" shouted Thorn. Beatríz froze herself in place, facing the enemy with her eyes wide open—and struggling to not tremble. There was an interminable moment of silence when the Mortejos must have been staring straight into Beatríz's eyes. Then, she heard the din of the millipede's woody legs clicking and clacking with a regularity that told her it was advancing toward her.

Suddenly, when the Mortejos was a mere ten feet away, Beatríz started to tremble, and the creature, its mouth wide open and baring dozens of thin sharp teeth, rushed at Beatríz! Immediately, a horrified Thorn screamed, "Now!"—hoping against hope that Beatríz would hit the Mortejos before the creature hit her.

At the same time that Beatríz's arm struck downward, the creature planted its teeth into her abdomen while Thorn dove at the creature with his knife. Beatríz fell fast and hard on her back, the creature's mouth clamped to Beatríz's body and its own body lying lifeless, the knife belonging to Beatríz plunged deep into one of the creature's awful eyes. Finding the Mortejos dead, Thorn pried its jaws away from Beatríz's belly. She also seemed to be lifeless, and Thorn began to sob. The others had by this time scrambled out from the tunnel and, in the eerie light of Thorn's eyes, knelt around Beatríz, touching her head and hands, whimpering, and saying, "No, Beatríz! No! No!"

Thorn gained his composure quickly and began to examine the wounds to Beatríz's abdomen, finding to his surprise that her stomach was only badly scratched, the jaws of the Death Eyes having progressed no further than the depth of Beatríz's leather skirt. "She may be alive! She may still be alive!" yelled Thorn, with unrestrained hope. "The jaws never entered her stomach—just her clothing! She killed it at the last possible moment, and she's unconscious, but the Mortejos could not have killed her, at least not by biting her," Thorn continued, while he checked her pulse and breathing.

Thorn could find no pulse, so he put his face under Beatríz's nose to learn if she was breathing. All waited quietly for the verdict, staring at Beatríz's inert body in the soft glow enveloping her. "She's breathing!" yelled Thorn. "Not much, but she's definitely breathing. Jamie," ordered Thorn, "cradle her head in your lap and pat her cheeks lightly. Elli, Alex, gently pat her hands; I'll get some water."

Thorn returned quickly from the side tunnel with a leather pouch and began sprinkling drops about Beatríz's face. The four of them continued their various tasks for more than an hour. Beatríz was still breathing, ever so barely, but there was no discernible movement in any part of her body.

"C'mon, Beatríz!" Jamie said, encouragingly.

"Please, Beatríz!" pleaded Elli.

"Pweez don't be dead, Butweece!" said Alex, with a softly sobbing voice. "Pweez!"

A short while later Thorn checked Beatríz's breathing again, but this time discerned nothing. He was about to say to the others that it was time to stop, when, like an eruption, Beatríz sat up, just missing hitting Jamie's head that was bent over hers. She coughed deeply and then screamed, "Elli! Elli!" and reached into the bluish darkness for Elli's face.

"Beatríz, I'm right here! Here!" exclaimed Elli, as she placed Beatríz's hand on her face for Beatríz to see that it was true. Beatríz embraced Elli and began to cry—Elli held her for several minutes, saying nothing.

Her head once again cradled in Jamie's lap, Beatríz asked quietly, "What happened? Where is the Mortejos?"

Thorn smiled. "You killed it, Beatríz! You killed it, just as you had planned. Its body is right here—and quite dead, I can assure you."

"*I* killed it?" Beatríz asked again, with more of a statement than a question.

"Yes," said Thorn, his voice soft and reassuring—and punctuated with celebratory chuckles.

"But . . . but how did that happen?" Beatríz asked, in disbelief. "The only thing I remember is all of us in the tunnel and my suggesting I confront the Mortejos."

Elli laughed and said to Beatríz, "You did just that, Beatríz, just as you and Thorn planned it—and so bravely, too! And you saved all of our lives!" Elli squeezed one of Beatríz's hands with both of her own and gave her a kiss on the cheek. All four of Beatríz's companions beamed smiles of gratitude and pride.

Then, after what seemed like a grand ceremonial pause, Thorn spoke. "We must begin moving again as soon as we can. Who knows what else has heard the commotion that will not be kindly disposed toward us. Beatríz, how are you feeling? Can you move, even if only slowly and with assistance?"

"Actually, other than a bit of a headache and a sore stomach, I think I'm fine. If we need to move, then I'm all for it."

"Okay. Get your things and follow me—just as we were before this business with the Mortejos began."

Thorn was in the lead, his eyes now popped entirely out of their sockets for maximum light. They had walked for perhaps ten minutes when they heard in the distance behind them a distinctive sound, as of many pieces of wood breaking apart. Thorn stopped. "This is good," he said. "It means that other creatures who might otherwise be chasing after us are, instead, eating the Mortejos. By the time they're finished with it, we will be much too far from them to worry about."

The five continued at a relaxed, but productive, pace. They soon arrived at the T intersection and turned to the right. And, as Thorn had informed them earlier, the tunnel began gradually to ascend and the air began to thicken, making it easier for them to breathe and move with less effort.

After traveling for nearly eight hours following Beatríz's victory over the Death Eyes, and with only a few brief stops to rest, they found another significant widening of the tunnel where they could sleep for the night. Thorn, however, who needed very little sleep and who could remain alert at will for days on end, once again said that he'd keep watch. But before allowing the children to crawl into their skins, Thorn made sure there was a small tunnel opening nearby into which all of them could crawl in the event of their need for a fast escape.

The four children slept soundly for nearly sixteen hours while Thorn remained alert, but with his eyes closed—opening only occasionally to check on things. Thorn then awakened them and, once all had eaten some breakfast, they continued on what was supposed to be the final leg of their journey through the forest underground. Indeed, it was about eight hours following breakfast that they ascended more sharply toward the world above and began to hear muffled noises and feel vibrations beneath their feet. Within two to three hours of reaching close to the surface, all heard the slight, but distinct and chilling, sound of the Thrashers clearing trees just above them. They paused and then moved on. Once they had left the sound of the Thrashers behind them, there was only the sound of their boots treading softly on the compacted earth and their breathing to disturb the otherwise complete silence.

Then, abruptly, Thorn stopped and sat down, bidding the others to do so as well. "This is where I leave you, my dear friends."

"But," interjected Alex, "we ah stiw in the tunnow."

"The tunnel ends after another fifty yards, and you will find yourselves outside the forest. I'll see to it that you get to the opening. From there I do not know which way you are to go, because I do not know your destinations, either intermediate or ultimate. What I can tell you is that you will be on the eastern side of the forest."

As she began to feel the reality of their impending separation, Elli asked, sadly, "What will we find outside the tunnel, Thorn?"

"I don't really know, Elli. I haven't been outside the tunnel at the eastern edge, or otherwise within sight of that part of the forest, for many decades," Thorn said pensively. "And the last time I was outside the tunnel, it was still the forest. But apparently it hasn't been forest for more than a century now at tunnel's end, or so I've learned from others."

All five of them simply sat, their shoulders slung forward and their eyes staring wide open into the darkness ahead, tears in every one of the children's eyes sparkling from the two lightly glowing lanterns which were now fully retracted into Thorn's head.

"Thorn," Elli asked, forlornly, "can't you please come with us?"

"I can, but I may not."

"Why may you not, Thorn?" asked Elli.

"Because I have fulfilled my mission given to me by Hannah, and I am not charged or called to do anything further on your behalf," Thorn replied.

"But can't you come anyway? You don't have to be part of our mission, or even know any more about it than you know now. Just help us for a little while longer, simply as a friend," Elli pleaded. "We need you. And, and . . . we all love you, Thorn." The others nodded fiercely in assent.

"Only one person could enable me to continue with you," said Thorn, in a tone that indicated resignation to the impossible.

"And who's that?" asked Jamie.

"Only the one with the key, Jamie—the one for whom we have been waiting for centuries to free us. But, it's just a story now—a sacred one perhaps, but, still, just a story. It leaves us with something to hope for—and maybe in." He paused and then concluded, "Perhaps something to *hope* we can hope in one day."

All became quiet, and the other three children were staring at Elli. Elli fingered the key through her shirt. Finally, she broke the heavy silence.

"Thorn?"

"Yes, Elli," he replied, happy to delay, if only for a moment, their parting that would perhaps be forever.

Elli unbuttoned the top two buttons of her shirt and lifted the key to her neck for Thorn to view. "Thorn, it's certainly not the one you are looking for, but I have a key. It's just an old library door key from the world my friends and I come from." She then added, "Still, it is a key."

Thorn glanced at Elli with moist eyes. And then, like a couple of jack-in-the-boxes, Thorn's eyes popped out of his head with a kind of cork-popping sound. His tiny mouth dropped open as far as it could drop. "Oh, my!" Thorn said, as if he'd won a lottery. "Oh, my! Oh my! Oh my!"

"I don't think this is the key that you are referring to, Thorn, but if you believe it is, will you now join us beyond the forest?" asked Elli, noticing a tone of authority in her voice.

Thorn continued to stare at the key. It was the exact likeness of the drawing of the legendary key that had been secretly passed among the Queen's loyalists since her demise; the only exception was that . . . the key in the drawing was made of solid diamonds, and not of something entirely black, like the aged alloy of some sort of metal that this one seemed to be. But there was no mistaking the shape of the key. And those who were "people of the key," who were loyalists to the Queen and to her reign of love, had a sign that they would give to each other to show their membership in this secret society of brothers and sisters of the Good. Two fingers would be held aloft, and then the arms would cross on the chest, with each palm resting on the opposite shoulder.

Thorn made the sign of the key. "Oh, Elli. You are, I believe, the one who is to release our land from the imprisonment of Evil, and at your command I will do as you bid."

"Thorn," replied Elli, humbly, "I, as you know, can tell you nothing about our mission. What I can tell you is that it is likely impossible to accomplish, even with your help. But," she added, after a long pause, "if you will come with us, we would be very grateful for you to do so, even if it's only for a little while longer."

"Then, Elli," pronounced Thorn, "it will be as you request. And I will continue to accompany you for as long as you want my services, even to the conclusion of your mission, regardless of what that might be."

An abundance of smiles and tears of joy were shared all around.

"Elli," said Thorn, with confidence and joy he could not recall having in a long while, "lead us out of the tunnel and into whatever we find ourselves."

~FIVE~

WHEN THEY HAD REACHED the end of the tunnel, what had been an opening decades earlier was no longer there, having been closed by the accumulation of organic matter, dirt and growth, as well as the absence of use. Thorn took his stick and poked it into where he thought the opening was located. After a couple of thrusts he hit what sounded and felt like solid wood, likely part of a root system. After a number of other thrusts in other locations, Thorn was able to say, "I found it! It used to be near an exposed root of a large tree, and the tree and root have now grown over most of the hole. I think I can widen the hole with my stick, but it's going to take a while—maybe a couple of hours, I'm afraid. The earth above is pretty thick and compacted."

"Thorn," said Jamie, "here, use my knife; it's supposed to be a special tool." Thorn took the knife to claw away at the ground above him. The work was virtually effortless, and, within only a few minutes, Thorn was able to push his wide head and narrow torso through the hole and into the light of day.

"Well," Thorn yelled down to the others, "not exactly what I was expecting, but it's safe. C'mon out!"

The Thrashers had been employed decades earlier to remove the trees where the tunnel emerged, but they had been away from their vile work for so long now that new growth had established itself, so that Thorn and his companions were actually standing in a young forest all around them, with the older trees growing in the west and the younger ones surfacing in the east. And so the five of them stood—horrifically thirsty for light and soaking up the sun—in the midst of much shorter and far fewer trees, separated by spaces allowing for tall grass, hearty bushes, and an abundance of sunlight. What had once been the towering tree that had grown mightily over the old tunnel exit was now merely a broad stump with a few stems, one of which hopefully someday would have the opportunity to become a tree of majesty.

It was late in the afternoon when they emerged into the upper world, and soon the plummeting sun was casting beams through the branches, mottling the forest floor with the flickering shadows of leaves that were enjoying a final dance in the sunny, gentle breezes.

It would be dark before long, so Thorn suggested that they remain where they were for the night. The large stump next to the tunnel opening, together with its extensive and expansive root system, had defeated all attempts by other trees and bushes to take root in the soil they occupied. Thus, there was a sizable, even if uneven, clearing around the stump. As the late afternoon light dissipated rapidly into dusk, the four children gathered wood for a fire while Thorn used the stealth of his natural camouflage to catch a rather large rabbit for a rather small supper. Even the largest of wild rabbits was not much supper for five hungry souls, four of whom yearned for anything besides the berries and dried bread that were their lot since entering Bairnmoor.

But with the fire blazing and the supper roasting, and all sitting side by side in the friendly light and welcoming warmth and smells, everyone felt safe and at peace for the first time in several days. Elli and her friends joked about roasting marshmallows, with each of them using a different part of Thorn's body, and they laughed. They laughed louder when one of them suggested that, in this case, they could eat both the marshmallows *and* the sticks! And they laughed louder still when Thorn said that, from what he could gather from the conversation, the marshmallow idea sounded tasty and they could count him in!

The children stopped laughing when Thorn announced that supper was ready. They ate with a slow savoring of the meal, not certain when they'd eat like that again, and all surprisingly were satisfied. Following supper, as was the case during their meal together, they remained pleasantly silent, listening to the strong happy sounds of the still-blazing wood crackling and spitting as if in an unconstrained private celebration on which the children were eavesdropping. Each was lost in private thoughts and emotions, some experienced for the first time.

Elli puzzled over Thorn's statement about her being the one to release the land from evil apart from any apparent knowledge of either their mission to liberate the Queen or the role of the key in it.

She was also surprised that she was not homesick and that she didn't miss her parents. She had known she was adopted since she was very young—really, for as long as she could remember. But that never bothered her. Her parents talked about *choosing her*, which was special, they said, by comparison with other children who, without election, had simply been born to parents who, therefore, were virtually obligated to love them. But Elli's parents had indeed *elected* her, and so that, they said, made her more special. But she didn't *feel* more special than other kids—quite to the contrary, at least as far as other kids were concerned. And even with respect to her parents, she had to admit to herself that she never really felt as if they *knew* her and loved her for who she was. And while she always felt cared for and safe, she never quite felt that she was *at home* with her parents in the way that other kids seemed to feel at home in their families, including others she knew who also had been adopted. And now this—this thing she was living right now that at times seemed more like a dream than reality and that at other times seemed far—no, truly—more real than reality itself.

Now Alex? Well, he was mostly just tired. He missed his family for sure, however: his mom and dad—and sister and brother, both of whom were older than he. And he missed his music that he listened to on his ear buds, seemingly all the time and with the same songs holding their excitement for him. And he missed the special attention he got from his mom and dad, and even from his sister and brother; but he also felt better about himself somehow since being with Elli. Truth be told, he felt less special with Elli, but he also felt more confident in himself, and more like everyone else around him. Here in Bairnmoor he was *expected* to be like everyone else around him; and that was new, and kind of scary, but also kind of good. He liked how he felt when he was protecting Elli, and he wasn't sure if he had ever felt better than that. He didn't really know why, but, then, he didn't really ask that question. For now, he was homesick, for sure. But he was also okay—for sure, for now.

Beatríz was thinking about how absurd and amazing it was that she was on a journey like this with her disability; it wasn't really reasonable, or even remotely rational, that she was doing this. The picking of someone else among millions and millions of others would have made so much more sense; even *she* knew that. The liabilities of having her along would far exceed anything she could contribute. It wasn't that she didn't have a genuinely large and valuable role to play in the world, but this wasn't the sort of role that would ever come to anyone's mind—except Elli's! And Mr. P's! She smiled and laughed under her breath at the absurdity of it all. And yet . . . and yet, she couldn't imagine any experience in life in her normal world that could match in importance and drama and meaning the experiences she had already accumulated in her brief time in Bairnmoor. Indeed, she thought, if it all came to an end tomorrow, happily or not, she felt she had lived a far more purposeful and courageous existence than anyone she knew, and a more purposeful and courageous an existence than any she would have been permitted—much less have attempted— back home.

Ever since she volunteered to face the Death Eyes, it was as if she had come into her own, timid no longer. She was proud of that—not in the way that says, "look what I did," but in the way that says, "even *I* am able to do something significant, and I'm not worried about whether I'm able to do it or not, or whether I get credit for it or not—or even whether anybody else knows about it or not." Thinking about the future was hard, though. She had become accustomed to having to focus on the immediate. But, here, she was being asked to think first about the future, and only secondarily about the present. And that wasn't easy—or comfortable. Yet it seemed necessary. And she wondered whether, or how, she would be up to all that might be asked of her in the coming days. She was beginning to think there existed far more wonderful things than anything she had ever wanted or wished for, or could even understand.

Jamie was wondering what his role in all of this was supposed to be. It didn't seem that the group *needed* him; if it had been just Elli, Beatríz, Alex, and Thorn, the mission would be just fine without him, he thought. So . . . why him? He certainly had no special abilities—or even notable qualities. Even Beatríz had the unusual qualities of a heightened sense of smell and hearing. And Alex? Well . . . he had that passion for loyalty that existed beyond questioning and understanding. He was going to hold fast, no matter what. But he—Jamie? Would he hold fast no matter what? Would he remain loyal and brave? Could he handle any greater pressure than what he had already experienced? And did he want to? Probably not. After all, he was not even a true believer in the mission. And if he could go back now, would he? Probably, he thought. Probably.

Thorn was convinced that Elli was "the one," given the key and her mere presence as a child in Bairnmoor. But Elli, it seemed to him, wasn't convinced of her importance. In fact, she didn't place much value on the key and suggested that her purpose for being in Bairnmoor was far less crucial than the one he was suggesting for "the one with the diamond key." And, of course, there was nothing diamond-ish about the old black key that Elli was wearing. But something big and wonderful was afoot and, in his view, worthy of his attention, and even worthy of his life—and worthy of his life whether this "something" amounted, in the end, to anything at all. Of that much, he was certain.

As the fire quieted down, the soft flicker of light on their faces suggested to each of the children that all the others looked somehow older, perhaps even a bit different. And the odd thing was, it was as if each one looked to all the others as if he or she was *more* of a child, but yet a more mature one, whatever that meant. Thorn, who was staring the entire time into the fire, appeared the same to the children, reflecting what might best be described as a soothing quality of changelessness and permanency that provided the children an abiding source of comfort.

Thorn added more wood to the fire, stirred the coals and took his place of watch, sitting against the large stump. He sat facing the slightly older part of the forest and away from the light of the fire, hidden in the shadows and so able to see without being seen. The others rolled their skins tightly around them and drifted off to sleep.

The next morning, following a pleasantly chilly night, the sun rose and awakened the children early with light through the trees, prompting them to rise. They ate what remained of their bread and berries, and packed up for the next leg of their journey that would lead them east to the edge of the forest and to—they knew not what.

They walked with increasing ease as the woods became thinner, the vines less frequent, and the ground less cluttered by dead limbs and branches. None of them felt any need to stop, except for water, and by the time the woods was coming to a scraggily end toward the middle of the afternoon, the five missioners found themselves facing a long, steep hill that was treeless and covered with a carpet of knee-high grass. The final three hundred yards of their climb to the ridge would be the first time since their journey began below the stone stairs that they would be easily visible, at least to anyone or anything that would happen to be looking across the grassy knoll. Little did they know that there would, indeed, be eyes ready to notice them once they stepped from the veil of the forest's edge into the open.

Before leaving the cover of the trees, Thorn instructed them to move swiftly and say nothing until they had crouched just below the ridge.

"If there are Fire-eyes watching from the grass, we will not be able to see them in the daylight. I would suggest that we wait until dark, but that would only give any enemies behind us more time to catch up. Besides, as soon as we see them, they will already have seen us. Off we go."

Side by side they left the forest and ran onto the grassy slope, Beatríz at one end holding onto Elli's shirttail. The ground beneath the grass was hard and even, so all of them, including Beatríz, were able to move with remarkable speed. At the slope's steepest point, not far from the ridge, Beatríz tripped over her own feet, losing her grip on Elli's shirt. Neither she nor Elli said a word, each knowing that Elli would reach back quickly for her, which she did. Soon, all were lined up, crouching in the grass within arm's length of the top of the ridge.

In the darkening twilight, which had already settled on the other side of the knoll, they could hear indistinct voices and an occasional cracking sound, not unlike the sound of two boards being clapped together. Far below and behind them several Fire-eyes, having sold their souls to the Evil One, through Sutante Bliss, in exchange for the promise of bodies, watched from the cover of tall grasses near the edge of the forest. Then, concealed by the grasses, the Fire-eyes flew wide of the travelers to the top of the ridge and over. Little did *these* Fire-eyes know, however, that the Fire-eyes who had led the children to Thorn were, from just inside the forest's edge, watching *them*. As soon as the stealthy Fire-eyes that were watching Thorn and the children were out of sight, off flew the other set of eyes northward.

Thorn crawled several feet further to the top of the ridge to get a peek at what was waiting for them on the other side. Thorn raised his head just enough to see through the tops of the grasses, looked without moving for several minutes, and then uttered a quiet "Hmmmm . . ."

"What is it, Thorn?" whispered Elli.

Thorn slipped back to where the children were bunched together. "Well," said Thorn, his eyes appearing thoughtful and looking at no one. "What we have is this. Below us on the other side is a cluster of maybe ten large mud huts and a larger building made of logs with a tower on top. They are located on this side of the river that runs right to left. To the right of the huts, and stretching for dozens of acres on both sides of the river, are fruit trees. There are a number of Unpersons who, even at dusk, are tending to the trees, and a number of people from this part of the kingdom are clearing the land to plant new trees, or so it would seem. They are turning the soil and carrying away rocks. Unpersons are supervising them, and overseeing the entire operation are an uncertain number of Sutante Bliss's warriors, including a few Wolfmen. I could see three of the troops in the tower, but there have to be more inside the log building. What we are hearing are the voices of the overseers giving commands and cracking whips."

"Thorn," asked Beatríz, "who are these *people* you speak of—and are they slaves? And, are they also Unpersons—or becoming so?"

"The people in this part of the kingdom had been some of the most loyal subjects of the Queen. Those who did not resist the forces of Sutante Bliss were promised leniency: they, like others elsewhere, became Unpersons, turning against their own people, betraying the Queen and losing all childnessness as they embraced evil in a host of ways, either intentionally or simply by refusing to resist.

"Most of those who resisted were forced into servitude, though some were simply killed. You will see they will look old and very worn, but they will have, to a partial extent, the distinct facial features that you yourselves possess because they refuse to accept the rule of Sutante Bliss, and have refused to renounce the core of who they are—their childnessness—which is said to be at the heart of the Good. However, they no longer possess the power of the Queen and her community, and are barely able to remember what it means to follow the Good and manifest childness. Mostly, they do not believe any longer, even though they will not defer to evil."

"Do not believe any longer in what?" asked Elli.

"The source of all things, the Good, and in its power to overcome Sutante Bliss and his vile deeds, much less the Evil One, who is the ultimate source of all evil."

Thorn paused for a moment, turned to Jamie—who had first asked about the Fire-eyes—and then continued. "Some, however, have had their eyes removed and their bodies killed and burned. What remains of them are what we call the Fire-eyes, left to wander the world bodiless. A few of the Fire-eyes remain loyal to the Queen and the Good, even in their unending state of disembodiment, like the ones that led you to me. However, most of the Fire-eyes were promised new bodies if they served Sutante as his spies, and in this way came under his authority."

"Do they actually *get* bodies?" asked Jamie, skeptically.

"Yes. Some have already been given bodies. Sutante Bliss will simply replace the eyes of the body of a resister with Fire-eyes from among those most loyal to him. You see, the soul is in the eyes—not in the body—and it is the eyes that give the body life." Thorn replied.

"Can you kiw the Fiuwise?" asked Alex.

"Actually, no." said Thorn. "Once the eyes are removed they no longer have flesh and so cannot themselves be held captive or killed. It is not any longer fear of Sutante Bliss, but the incentive to once again have a body, that captures the loyalty of the Fire-eyes. And," he added, as if to punctuate the point, "that is a powerful incentive."

The thoughts of each of the children were now spinning, like the swirling of dry autumn leaves, endeavoring to comprehend all that Thorn had just told them. Thorn suggested that they wait until dark to crawl over the ridge and then continue crawling in the long grass toward the river where they could hide in the tall reeds and cattails that lined the riverbank. Once under cover again, they could make their way in the water quietly downstream—to the left and away from the watchtower. All agreed that this was a good plan, each one wondering in the deepening twilight on this side of the hill what lay in store for them in the dark on the other side.

At last, the large red sun settled softly below the tops of the forest trees behind them, and darkness began to creep up and over them from the other side of the ridge. Soon, night had unrolled its shroud, revealing from east to west an amazing display of stars, like so many thousands of crystals and sequins sewn onto the black velvet fabric of the sky.

When it was well past nightfall, Thorn gave the final instructions. A slight iridescence covered the earth, as if the stars themselves had ever so lightly dusted the grasses and trees. The plan was to crawl on their stomachs over and down the hill through the grass toward the river, aiming for a spot in the cattails some one hundred yards downstream from the tower.

"Everyone ready?" Thorn asked. They were. "Remember—slowly, and as quietly as possible; follow me." And so, like five black salamanders hugging the dewy ground, they slithered and slid over the crest of the hill and down, one after the other. At a laboriously slow pace they moved silently down the hill, their bodies barely visible above the tall grass. Any slight scraping and rustling noises they made against the ground and through the grass were sufficiently covered by the croaking and chirping of toads and frogs drifting up from the water's edge—as if, on behalf of the children and Thorn, the little creatures intended by their noise to prevent discovery by the enemy.

The descent seemed never-ending, but finally they were within fifteen yards of the cattails. At this point the five were beginning to feel some small degree of success and relief. It was also at this point that those in the tower were feeling an even greater sense of impending victory. Having been warned earlier in the day by the spying Fire-eyes of the intruders' presence, the warriors were waiting until the five had crawled nearly to the water's edge. Then, the captain in the tower would give the signal, and a dozen warriors armed with swords and axes and knives would storm from the log building and capture the enemies for deliverance to Sutante Bliss.

At last, Thorn could see through the grass that the cover of the shoreline was now not much more than ten yards away. Hope was rising in Thorn.

"Attack! Attack! Attack!" shouted a voice from the tower. At that same moment, two doors of the log building were thrown open, and out streamed the warriors to ambush Thorn and the children. As soon as Thorn heard the chilling command from above, he ordered the children to get up and run past him along the river. Without the slightest hesitation they did as Thorn demanded, running as fast as they could with Beatríz in tow behind Elli, who was leading the small pack. They were very fast, but the large warriors were faster and were quickly closing in on them. But unknown to Sutante's troops, they were also closing even faster on Thorn who was lying hidden in the grass across their path.

When the ferocious fighters had reached the place where Thorn was lying, Thorn raised his outstretched arms and legs and tripped the first five warriors who, in turn, caused the warriors behind them to trip. While they were falling over him and into one another, giving the children critical extra time to get away, Thorn slipped out from underneath the jumble of flailing limbs and ran through the cattails unseen. Like a deftly thrown spear, Thorn dove into the water, arms and legs clasped to his torso for minimal splash and maximum speed.

By the time the warriors had gotten to their feet, gathered themselves and looked toward the place where someone or something had entered the water, Thorn was already a third of the way into the broad river and considerably downstream. He was now swimming in the direction of the children with all but his eyes beneath the water. The warriors searched frantically along the shore for the source of the splash, and when they soon saw nothing, resumed their pursuit of the children, who by this time were getting tired and slowing down, even though they continued to run as fast as they could. Eventually, Jamie said he had to stop and that the others should keep going; but Elli halted everyone. They could hear the pounding of heavy warrior boots closing in on them. Elli looked all around, as did Jamie and Alex, but they saw no place to hide. Even the cattails had thinned, no longer able to provide sufficient cover. She knew they would not be able to outrun the warriors, yet that seemed the only option remaining.

"Run!" Elli shouted, and like a single organism the children started running again, bunched together to ensure that no one outran another.

Elli was looking and trying to think of something else they could do besides continuing to run a race they were surely—and shortly—to lose.

Suddenly, perhaps thirty yards ahead, Elli saw what seemed to be the same lights that had led them to Thorn now hovering just above the ground. "C'mon! Run toward the lights! They may be trying to help us—and we have nothing to lose finding out." The children ran straight for them but, as before in the woods, the Fire-eyes kept their distance while continuing to advance in the children's direction. Elli was wondering how long her friends and she would be able to keep running before being caught. Then, when it seemed as if she could no longer feel her legs moving beneath her, Elli saw the Fire-eyes stop and move toward the shore of the river. She had no idea what these Fire-eyes were intending for them, and whether it was for good or ill. But when she neared the spot where they were hovering in the cattails, Elli spotted—barely visible and extending from the near shore to the other side of the river high above, ending atop a sheer cliff—a rope footbridge. "Guys!" yelled Elli, between one gasp for air and the next. "Look! There's a bridge! Let's go—as fast as you can!"

The footbridge was narrow, and permitted them access in single file only. It had uneven log flooring and just one low rope on each side of the bridge to serve as meager railings. The night was even darker over the river, so they struggled simply to walk and not lose their balance in the veiling darkness. By the time they were about halfway across the bridge, the Fire-eyes were gone and the enemy had discovered them. With yelps and grisly snarls and screams, the warriors started across the bridge after the children. Here, too, the enemy could move faster than the children, and so the distance between them was—once again—collapsing. Looking back several times, and listening intently, Elli guessed that the fighters would be nearly upon them by the time they had all reached the other side. Alex, who was in the rear, also realized that it might be impossible to get away, even if they reached the top of the cliff before the enemy reached them. He yelled to Elli, the person foremost in his heart, "Ewi! You keep wunning with the othews! I wiw fight them with my knife!"

Elli remembered: they could use their knives as special tools. "Alex! When you are the last one to the cliff, take your knife and try to cut the ropes so the bridge falls!"

"But," replied Alex loudly, "thew ah so many wopes, and the knife is vewy smaw!"

"I think it will work, Alex—you and I! If we can cut quickly, we may have a chance! If not, we'll be right there to fight, and they can only cross one at a time!" Elli yelled back with feigned optimism to encourage Alex.

When the four children had stepped onto the cliff, and with the enemy within twenty-five feet of them, Elli and Alex swung fiercely at the dozen ropes holding the bridge in place. To their astonishment, they found that one swing at each rope was all that was needed to cut them, almost as if each rope was just waiting, wanting, to be cut. In mere seconds, the final rope was severed and all of the warriors, including one who was about to strike Alex, tumbled ninety feet below into the deep and rapid river, ejaculating screams of rage and terror the entire way. The children ran up another of the long and grassy slopes that lined the river and never looked back until they were up and over the crest of the hill. Only at that point did they stop and, crouching low, peer back over the top of the crest toward the place where the bridge had fallen into the river to learn if any of the warriors, by whatever means, were still pursuing them—or if there would be any sign of Thorn.

~SIX~

THORN LET THE RIVER current carry him swiftly downstream, his eyes fixed on the shoreline for any sound or sight of his friends. He dared not shout for them for fear of disclosing to the swift and relentless enemy either his whereabouts in the water or the children's presence on shore. The understandable—and wise—absence of communication between them led, however, to the exceedingly unfortunate circumstance of Thorn passing by the children while they had stopped to allow Jamie to catch his breath. And by the time Elli had seen the Fire-eyes, Thorn had been swept underneath and well beyond the bridge that, in the darkness, he had failed to notice. Thorn listened intently for the sound of the warriors' feet—or their voices—while he floated, but heard nothing. Then, as he swam as quietly as possible across the persistent current to the side of the river on which he had left the children some minutes earlier, he heard the loud, chilling shouts and screams of the warriors far upstream.

Thorn reached the shallows where cattails were growing. The blood-curdling noises coming from the enemy had abruptly stopped, as if directed by an order. All was quiet; Thorn heard only the light gurgling and lapping of the river among the cattails.

Thorn knelt in the cattails and considered the situation. He concluded quickly that if anything had happened to his friends it must be connected to the screaming of the warriors. Ever so gently Thorn rose and began walking slowly under partial cover of the cattails back upstream in search of his companions. He struggled with the current and the mud—and the water grasses that snagged and entangled his legs.

As Thorn cast his eyes separately about him, like the single eyes of two heads and minds, he noticed in the nearly complete darkness what appeared to be the vague outline of a corpse floating toward him. He shivered from the thought that it might be one of his friends—perhaps Alex, who was the largest of the four. But when he reached out to keep the body from floating past him, he could tell from the feel of the clothing and the size of the body, although substantially submerged, that it was one of the warriors. Thorn examined carefully the vast width of the river and noticed several more bodies of what he presumed to be warriors floating heavily downstream and past him.

Thorn inspected the body he had seized, and failing to find any obvious wounds, he decided that this warrior had drowned—and that likely the others floating past him had come to the same end. But, how did they drown, and how many were still alive? And, most important of all, where would he find the children and in what condition?

Thorn released the body to passing waters, then continued his own journey upstream. He concluded that if any of the children had been captured, they would have almost certainly been returned to the log cabin. That would be his first destination.

Before long, Thorn had the guard tower in sight. He crawled on all fours, taking advantage of the thicker growth for concealment. Soon Thorn could see the moving outline of a single guard in the tower ahead. When he was within about ten feet of the cabin, still hidden by the cattails and the darkness, he stopped to listen. The only sounds he heard were pacing boots and occasional whispering voices emanating from the huts. The doors to the building were still wide open, suggesting perhaps that none of the band of warriors had returned. When Thorn heard the sound of the boots diminishing from where he was crouching, he carefully stepped out of the water and moved quickly to the side of the building nearest to him. From there he inched his way along the outside of the structure until he was next to the door opening, careful to open his eyes only slightly, so as not to let their glow give him away.

Thorn heard nothing that would evidence the presence of anyone inside, so just inside the doorway he opened one eye slightly. Seeing and sensing no one, Thorn peered into the seeming vacuum, opening his eyes completely, which meant popping them from their sockets and casting two wide and dancing glows as he searched the room feverishly: it looked almost as if his eyes were lanterns being swung by two different searchers. The cavernous space was empty. The warriors, for whatever reasons, had not returned, and he therefore suspected that he would not find the children at the enemy outpost. And, if any of the children had been caught, dead or alive, he was certain that their captors would be returning to the modest fortress, and that there would be noises, likely soon, signaling their approach.

Thorn slipped silently back into the shallow water behind the cattails. He paused to gaze briefly at the shimmering beauty of the eternal heavens that belied his anxiety, and then began to crawl carefully downstream. A full moon was just beginning to rise above the great cliffs in the far distance. Thorn continued crawling until the guard tower was out of sight, at which point he resumed his journey upright.

He had walked for a short time when, in the moonlight, he saw a string of logs just ahead of him, lined up downstream, but apparently not moving with the current, as if they were—all of them—caught on something. When Thorn got closer, he saw that the logs were the remnants of a walking bridge that began near his feet and that must have spanned the river to the top of the tall cliff on the other side. It was evident that someone had sabotaged the bridge at its connection atop the cliff. Hope began to rise in Thorn's breast. Likely, he thought, his companions had crossed the bridge and then cut the connecting ropes while the warriors were in the process of crossing toward them, sending them to their deaths below. But how, he asked himself, was he to get to the top of the cliff? And even if he found a way to the top, would he be on course to find his friends? And how far would they have traveled by the time he reached the top of the cliff where they had no doubt been moving steadily inland from the river?

At the very least, he had to find cover before the daylight only a few hours away. The forest he called home was receding from the shoreline and growing on increasingly higher hills the further he went downstream. He could cross from there to the trees to spend the night, but he would be dangerously exposed during the crossing. Besides, traveling to and from the forest for the night would waste precious time he needed to find his friends—and perhaps even make finding them all but impossible. Thorn decided, for the time being, to press on downstream, skirting the barely concealing shoreline as the cattails and other plants continued to thin. While he walked, his eyes continually searched the cliffs for any possible way to the top. The glare from the moonlight above the cliffs made it difficult for him to discover potential opportunities, the cliffs being a virtually featureless silhouette against the sky.

Thorn had walked for nearly another hour and the moon was now overhead. The cattails appeared only sporadically, leaving him with nothing but young short reeds that barely covered his knees. He crouched to once again crawl along the shoreline. Then, as he resumed his journey on all fours, he noticed in the distance a set of tiny lights that he was quite certain were those of Fire-eyes. He didn't know if they had seen him. Perhaps they were searching for him. In his forest he called home they were always friends. Outside the forest there was no way to tell. The odds were against them being friendly, so he decided to lay himself slowly down in the water and wait to learn what the Fire-eyes would do next.

As soon as Thorn was lying flat along the shore, with only his two eyes protruding half-opened from the water, he saw the Fire-eyes move as a group toward him. They stopped within about thirty feet of Thorn and then one of them broke rank and came and hovered about an arm's length above his head. It remained in place for a few seconds and then returned slowly toward the waiting squadron, pausing every few feet and turning to look at Thorn, evidently signaling him to follow. There was really little choice, thought Thorn. If they were friendly, they would want to help him. And if they were aligned with Sutante Bliss, then the Fire-eyes would either lead him to the enemy or the enemy to him.

Thorn stood up resolutely, all eight feet of him, stepped onto the shore in full view of any sort of creature that might be present for a hundred yards around, and walked briskly in the direction of the Fire-eyes. They quickly began themselves to move downstream in the same direction and away from Thorn, careful to keep the same distance between them and their follower. After some time the shoreline began to wind and curl. The cliffs reached increasingly higher into the sky as he continued his way north, which both worried and discouraged Thorn as he contemplated the whereabouts of the children. Soon, a tree line of tall, gnarled oaks and large weeping willows began to appear along the river's edge and thicken in numbers as he traveled. Perhaps this was the cover he needed for the remainder of the night to which the Fire-eyes were directing him—or, at worst, an enemy encampment.

The Fire-eyes then stopped abruptly and flew slowly across the river, finally halting after several minutes to hover once again next to the most imposing of sheer cliffs that Thorn had yet seen on the other side. Puzzled, Thorn kept walking along the shore among the oaks and willows, constantly looking all about him, and then stopping when he was directly across the river from the Fire-eyes. He stood staring at the Fire-eyes and wondered why they would situate themselves across the water if they had wanted him either to take shelter where he was or to continue on. Although he could not make out any features on the cliffs that were encouraging, his vision was obscured by the darkness and the continuing glare from the moon, as well as by the moonlight's deceptive shadowing where he could see the face of the cliffs. The Fire-eyes finally moved toward him, stopped, and then returned to their original hovering position along the face of the cliff. That the Fire-eyes wanted Thorn to go to them was now certain, although their motive was not. And so Thorn dove into the river as he had done hours earlier and swam the one hundred yards or so to the other side where he found himself treading water beneath the Fire-eyes who were clustered about a dozen feet above him. When he looked up at them, he exclaimed softly, "But of course!"

~SEVEN~

THE FOUR CHILDREN SLIPPED quickly beneath the crest of the slope over which they had just run and sat, facing a star strewn sky to the east.

"Is everyone okay?" asked Elli, struggling for air. "I don't think we'll have to worry about them anymore—or, at least for the time being. But, we are still in the open, and I think we'd better head for that line of trees for the night," she added, referring to a stand of trees off to their left in the distance and growing over the next knoll, rising to the east.

"But, what about Thorn?" asked Jamie.

"I don't know how Thorn will be able to find us, and we can't just stay here and wait," replied Elli, apologetically. "Besides," she added, with a heavy heart, "we don't even know if he's still alive. We know he faced the warriors on his own to give us the chance to escape; he would be disappointed I think, if we stayed here just waiting and hoping."

"But, but . . . but . . . what if Thawn is huurt, Ewi?" asked Alex, in a distraught voice. "We can't just . . ."

"Alex," interrupted Beatríz, "now that the bridge is gone, we don't have any way of going back, even if we wanted to, and we don't know how Thorn would get to us without the bridge. Do you understand?"

"Yes," said Alex; he understood.

So off the four went, trotting straight toward the trees at the bottom of the valley a good half mile away. Within ten minutes they were under the cover of a long and wide grove of chestnut trees, the leaves of which, seen from a distance, shimmered softly and welcomingly in the starlight.

They built a small fire about a hundred yards into the grove for warmth and security. A barely visible column of thin smoke rose from the treetops, and the fire itself was well hidden from any eyes that might be peering in from outside the trees. They nestled under their skins and were facing the fire, watching a few moths dance above the flames and listening to the chirping of two or three crickets in the grass nearby. No one said anything for a while. Finally, Jamie asked Elli, within intended earshot of the others, "Elli, do you believe Thorn—and Hannah, and Mr. Peterwinkle?"

"What do you mean, Jamie?"

"I mean, who do you think was telling the truth about the Queen being dead or not?"

"Well, I believe both of them are telling the truth."

Jamie waited for Elli to continue her explanation. When she said no more, he persisted. "Do you mean you believe that both Hannah and Thorn were telling the truth because of the silver amulet saying they were both telling the truth?"

"I mean," Elli continued, "I believe that both of them were telling the truth because they have shown themselves to be truthful people."

"But, Elli, they can't *both* be telling the truth. How can we release from prison a Queen who is dead?"

"I don't know," replied Elli, almost matter-of-factly.

"Elli, I'm trying to understand!" insisted Jamie, a bit exasperated.

"So am I, Jamie."

"So because you believe Hannah is telling the truth, you believe our mission is—still—to help release the Queen from her imprisonment?"

"Yes, that is what I believe."

"And, because you believe that Thorn is telling the truth, you also believe that the Queen is dead?"

"Yes, I believe that, too," Elli said, without a hint of reservation or doubt in her voice.

"But, Elli, I'm still confused, and I don't know what to think or believe. I don't even know that our mission makes sense any more. How can you believe in releasing a dead Queen from prison and have that be the basis for this dangerous mission?"

"Jamie," she said quietly, but with an inexplicable certitude, and hoping that the others were also following the conversation, "I don't understand how we can possibly release a dead Queen Taralina from prison. And what I don't understand, I cannot possibly believe in—nor can I genuinely accept what I don't understand. Therefore, I don't accept and believe that we are going to be releasing a dead Queen from prison.

"On the other hand," she said, with a firm but quiet emphasis, "I believe that both Hannah and Thorn are telling the truth as truthful people, so I believe, dead or not, that my mission—*our* mission—remains: to attempt to release the Queen from prison. I can't believe in anything more about the mission at this point, because I don't understand anything else. And if I didn't believe in Hannah—if I *couldn't* believe in Hannah—then we'd have turned back days ago."

Jamie, and the other two who, indeed, also were listening intently, still did not quite understand, but they understood and believed in Elli as a truthful person who was telling the truth, and so that was good enough for them—at least for the night, and time being, anyway.

"Elli," Beatríz said, speaking for the first time, "one more thing."

"What's that, Beatríz?"

"Do you think—or, do you believe—that Thorn is still alive?"

"I can't believe either way," Elli said, with the same certitude and resolve that characterized her remarks to Jamie moments earlier. "But I have great hope that Thorn is not finished, either with us or with this business, regardless of what may have happened to him." Elli paused, and all remained silent for a few moments.

"Beatríz," Elli continued, "I'm not saying I'm optimistic about Thorn; the evidence would suggest the contrary. In fact, it all seems, and even at times feels, so defeating. But, I *am* saying that I still have great hope regarding Thorn. And all of our mission, regardless of anything, relies on this hope."

The four friends drifted off to sleep, trusting the low fire, the trees, and the night itself—and, in a way, Elli's hopefulness—to keep them safe until morning.

Because the long and steep rise from the valley floor was facing east, it was not until mid-morning that the sun's rays found the children through the trees and awakened them. They had slept soundly all night and felt remarkably refreshed. There had been nothing approaching a dangerous incident throughout the night, but just in case, Alex had slept with his knife held fast to his chest. For breakfast, three of them gathered fresh berries that were in conspicuous abundance in the late morning light in the bushes among the trees and water from a nearby spring. They had crossed the diminutive, gurgling stream just moments after entering the grove the night before. Beatríz had been gathering chestnuts that were scattered about the clearing and placing them in the newly fed fire. She knew they were fresh because she could hear the ever eager and always clever squirrels looking for them; besides, she had actually heard several drop from the trees during the night.

When they had finished breakfast, packed up their few items and doused the fire, they decided to head north as far as the trees would take them, following as much as possible the stream that meandered largely in that direction. But they quickly discovered that the forest was only about two miles wide, ending northward at the bottom of another grassy knoll which rose eastward. This hill, however, was much taller and broader than the one behind them from which they had entered the woods during the night. Accordingly, the small band of brothers and sisters traipsed back to the other side of the forest and followed its path up that smaller of these two hills, remaining hidden among the trees about thirty yards from the forest's edge. As it was already well into the afternoon by the time they began their ascent eastward, they made camp for the night at the crest of that first knoll, one of a series of like encampments yet to come.

For the next several days the foursome trudged up and down small knolls that soon became not insubstantial hills, wondering constantly how many there were and how high they would climb before the topography changed, allowing them, hopefully, to head north for an extended distance and with comparative ease. At the crest of each one they ascended they invariably, and rather discouragingly, saw hills on the northern side of the tree line that were much taller and wider than those over which they were climbing on the southern edge of the trees. They needed to head north, but if they did so now they would be in the open, perhaps for hours, before they found other tree cover. They never suspected that they were being followed, about two day's distance behind them, by Unpersons and Fire-eyes loyal to Sutante Bliss. The Fire-eyes could sail through the air only as fast as an ordinary person could run, but their advantage was that they never needed to sleep—not having bodies requiring rest.

Finally, by nightfall on the fifth day of climbing a seemingly endless succession of increasingly larger knolls that turned into foothills, they reached the beginning of what they desperately hoped would be their final foothill to climb. Once again, they camped deep inside the forest to prevent anyone from seeing their fire. The night was especially cold, so they huddled close to one another, overlapping their skins and sharing body heat to stay warm. Even as they felt the toasty glow of the fire on their faces, they could see their breaths, like so many tiny ghosts being expelled into the haunting night air.

"How many more of these hills are we going to climb, Elli, before we finally go north toward the mountains?" asked Jamie.

"I don't know, Jamie. I'm hoping we'll find a way north that will keep us from being in the open, but I'm not sure we can head east much longer;

at some point soon we *have* to go north, and the options may not get better than what they've been," Elli replied.

"Elli?" asked Jamie. Elli said nothing, waiting for Jamie to continue. "Elli, I want to go home," he said, in a voice that was choking back tears. Beatríz and Alex nestled closer to Elli.

"I know, Jamie," she whispered.

"Are you angry with me for wanting to go home?" he asked. "I'm so frightened; I feel like such a coward."

"No, Jamie, I'm not angry with you. I want to go home, too. We all do." She paused, reflecting deeply, and added, "But we won't be able to get home now—without leaving it behind."

"What do you mean?" asked Jamie.

"Home is inside of us now; and we'd be leaving it here if we tried to go back. And," she added, for everyone's benefit, "it's okay to be frightened and to not want to do something. I'm frightened too; all of us are, Jamie. What matters is what we do with the fear. But without being frightened there's no way to be courageous. That's how I see it."

In just a few minutes the eyes of each child were closed, even as the eyes of others were open—and peering at them from just beyond the reach of the firelight and its concealing glare. A number of the Fire-eyes aligned with Sutante Bliss had just caught up with the children whom they had been pursuing for some days. They hovered high in the trees for a brief time and then retreated to report their discovery to Sutante's forces that were only a half-day's journey behind them. Fire-eyes couldn't speak, of course, because they had no mouths, but there were those who could "read their eyes."

Just as there appeared in the still starlit sky that dim—almost dark— crawling light of dawn that was yet an hour or so away from breaking, Jamie rose and awakened Alex to help him with breakfast. By the time the morning sky had extinguished the last of the stars, Alex and Jamie had trout from a nearby stream frying in the fire. This new sound along with the sweet smell of broiling fresh fish awakened the others, and soon all had eaten their fill and were on their way. They began, again under cover of the forest, to trudge up this longest of the hills thus far climbed toward the sun that had not yet appeared above the hilltop. It was much steeper, and the ground less even, than the knolls they had struggled against to this point, and they learned as they climbed that smaller hills were folding themselves into larger ones, making the actual top of the hill elusive.

The children stopped frequently in the moist heat to drink water, but climbed on throughout the afternoon and early evening, their arms and legs growing fatigued from pushing back the limbs of trees and shrubs. The sun never did appear, as the sky spread out a thick veil of clouds extending to every horizon. By late evening the sky and earth seemed to melt together into a single darkness, so much so, that the weary climbers decided that it would now be safe, and certainly faster, to continue their ascent on the grassy edge of the forest. At one point, Alex said, "I think we should stop now and fi-finish owu cwime tomauwo."

"I doubt it's much past eight o'clock, Alex," Elli replied. "I think we should go another hour and see if we can't reach the top. Is that okay with the rest of you?"

Over the next half hour or so it seemed that the cloud cover was thinning as they climbed, and they could once again see a division between earth and sky. Finally, the veil of clouds was gone, giving way to a starry black sky and a light breeze. The dewy earth shimmered an iridescent blue, and the stars were so bright they created shadows in the rippling grasses and among the quiet rustling trees. At times the shadows appeared to be advancing like ghostly traveling companions.

At Elli's suggestion, the children were about to climb the rest of the hour in the trees, when the forest that had been their traveling companion for a number of days came to an abrupt end, and they were suddenly, and unexpectedly, standing atop this last of the mountains' foothills heading east—exhausted, but in awe at the sight before them. They stood in silence for a minute and then sank heavily to the ground, staring ahead and below them. None of them had ever seen so vast a sky before, and they felt they were experiencing what it must be like to sit on top of the world. For far beneath them, perhaps a thousand feet or more, lay a misty and sparkling cover of continuously billowing clouds extending all the way to the eastern and southern horizons, and extending north where, on that horizon, the pointed hats of snow-capped mountains were poking through.

What was beneath the vast blanket of rolling clouds they had no idea, but they decided to suspend further speculation and travel until morning. And so they returned to the trees just below the crest of the hill and made camp as usual deep within the forest cover. They dined on nuts and berries, and finished reluctantly what remained of the chestnuts they had roasted a few days earlier. Then they lay down for the night, the bright glare of the firelight blocking out the stars that were otherwise peeking through the treetops. Lying snugly around the fire, and on top of their skins because of the surprisingly warm and breezeless air, all of them drifted off to sleep, each with sad thoughts of Thorn.

In the middle of the night Alex awoke suddenly, as if awakened by noises he hadn't consciously heard or couldn't recall hearing. He shivered in unaccountable fear and moved himself next to Elli. Beatríz awoke at the same time, but she had actually heard something—in the distance. She lay quietly, listening intently for any further sounds. Alex put his hand on Elli's arm and stared mildly at his soundly sleeping friend. In the flickering light of the embers he could see Elli's neck and just a bit of the library key poking above her shirt, twisted on its chain. Ever so slowly, Alex took his hand that was on Elli's arm and reached for the key.

"Alex!" Elli whispered loudly and sternly while grabbing Alex's hand. "What are you doing?" It may have been the case she was awakened before Alex's hand had even touched the key. "Were you trying to take the key?" she asked, in angry disbelief. They lay, staring into each other's eyes, Alex replying tearfully,

"No Ewi! I wouldn't take the key! I wa was just touching it! That's aw!"

"But, why, Alex?" Elli asked, her anger receding quickly.

"Be becuz itz the onwy thing we have fwum home." Alex began to sob lightly under his breath. "I'm sawy, Ewi."

"It's okay, Alex." She put her hand on his shoulder, pulling her face closer to his. "I understand. It's okay. And if you ever want to touch it, just ask me, okay? But, I can't take it off; you understand that, don't you?" He nodded immediately in assent. "Let's try to get back to sleep, then, okay?"

"Okay." And Alex closed his eyes with a half-sad smile.

Jamie had awakened to the exchange between Alex and Elli. After the conversation had concluded, and while gazing up at the starry sky now visible with a low fire, Jamie's mind lingered tentatively on Alex's reference to home. Alex was homesick. Elli and Beatríz were homesick, too. And what about him, Jamie? He certainly wanted to go home—or, at the very least, to leave Bairnmoor. But it wasn't the same for him, he thought. He did find himself at that moment, beneath the soft, glowing blanket of stars that seemed so familiar, feeling homesick—for the first time ever, he thought. But he didn't really want to go home—to his house and parents and older brother. He never really wanted to go back there; never, for as long as he could remember. Jamie's mind lighted stealthily on images of his brother and parents, as if conjuring up pictures too boldly might bring them to life.

His brother, Tyler, never missed an opportunity to berate or belittle, or otherwise to humiliate, him, even to the point of creating opportunities. He recalled the time that his brother, pretending to be their father, called his second grade teacher to tell her how well Jamie was able to play the Star-Spangled Banner on his trumpet, and how great it would be if she asked Jamie to play for the class. Thinking, as Tyler intended, that Tyler's voice was really coming from Jamie, she insisted to Jamie that he play the Star-Spangled Banner for the class on the day before the fourth of July. However, when Jamie opened his case to get his trumpet, he realized to his horror that his music was missing. It didn't matter, she said; she had set aside the time for him, so he was going to play. And if he was really that accomplished, she said, he didn't need the music anyway. He remembered a series of notes erupting from the horn that didn't remotely resemble the patriotic tune, or any other tune for that matter, and the kids began to laugh and then to jeer, as if there were twenty-five Tylers taunting him. That was the longest half minute of his entire life.

But, it wasn't all that unusual. Such moments had occurred repeatedly in his life for as far back as he could remember: times that Tyler would pretend in front of others that he, Jamie, had farted, or would tell others that he peed in his bed at night, which he did. And he recalled, now vividly, but long suppressed in his memory, that his parents never intervened on his behalf, or that, if they did try to curtail Tyler's behavior, it was disingenuous—which Tyler construed as encouragement of his actions. Sometimes they even laughed along with Tyler, thinking him funny, even clever. He, of course, was their "genius" son, about whom they loved to broadcast his talents, virtues, and accomplishments. When Jamie complained to his parents about Tyler's behavior, they told him simply to "stop whining like a little girl" and to "grow up." After all, they'd say, it was all in good fun.

No, he was homesick; he knew that now, for certain. But what he was homesick for was not his parents and his brother, but for the mom and dad and brother he never had and so desperately wanted. He was still waiting for them. He believed they were there—somewhere—and that one day he'd 'go home' to them. And, like the lone tear that held fast to his lash, reflecting the starlight above and refusing to fall, he clung firmly within his soul to a tiny sparkle of irrepressible hope as he drifted back to sleep.

Beatríz remained awake for some time. She listened intently for the sound she had heard briefly earlier, like the sound of roaring men—many men—in the distance. As she lay listening, she heard no more of that sound, but did hear, in the distance, as if coming from the other side of the hill, what sounded like the sad murmuring of young children. The barely audible lamenting continued for a long time, until Beatríz finally joined the others in slumber.

No one rose before dawn, and it wasn't until late morning that the first of the friends, Jamie, awoke. He was hungry, and started to think about breakfast, but he wanted even more to see if the cloud cover on the other side of the knoll had lifted. He put on his boots and scrambled as quietly as possible through and out of the trees to the top of the ridge. He stood there staring and yelled back, "Guys! Guys! Come here! Look! The clouds are gone! It's amazing!" The other three awoke and scrambled from their beds to join Jamie. When they reached him, they gazed—once again, as they had the night before—in wonder. Far below them was a vast swamp and river that began at the foot of the knoll and stretched in width eastward for perhaps half a mile where, on the other side of the water, another forest began. This forest was taller than the one through which they had been traveling in recent days, and displayed a different variety of trees.

The river portion of the wetlands flowed oddly northward for a mile or so before bending westward and out of sight behind the still-larger hills that lay between the adventurers and the mountains in the north. The forest, like the cloud cover the night before, stretched to the horizons in the east and south and appeared to end north at the snowline of the mountain tops many miles away. The children returned to the campsite among the trees and sat down on the ground. The fire was all but out.

"Well," began Elli, "we have a decision to make. We either continue east across the swamp and river, only heaven knowing how we'll accomplish that, or head north now, which," she then concluded after a pause, "which may be our only option."

"But we'll be exposed on those hills," said Jamie. "And we can't tell for how long."

"Whichever way we're going at this point," offered Beatríz, "we'd better get going and eat later. I heard last night what seemed to be the sound of men shouting in the distance behind us. If it was the sound of Sutante's forces, then they can't be very far behind."

"Should we get out owuh knives, Ewi?" asked Alex.

"No . . . not yet, at least. Just make sure," she said firmly, making eye contact with each of her friends, "that you leave them accessible when you pack up."

The children took little time to gather their things, extinguish the fire and begin what seemed might be an endless and hazardous trudge north, initially through the line of trees and then, shortly, across the first of many steep foothills toward the mountains.

They had hardly begun their journey when, suddenly, not more than a hundred yards away, the clamoring sound of Sutante's forces could be heard. They stopped for a moment, and when they realized that the enemy was advancing from all sides except the east, they scrambled to the crest of the hill looking down on the swamp and descended as quickly as possible, Beatríz holding tightly to Jamie.

The moment they reached the bottom of the hill far below, they both heard and saw enemy forces pouring over the crest like so many ants from a disturbed hill.

"Now! Get out your knives! Beatríz, lie down behind us and keep your knife close, though it won't be great as a weapon now that you've used it on the Mortejos."

Jamie shouted, as if involuntarily, through the din of the enemy forces careering down the hill and the loud pounding of his own fear within, "I'll go to meet them first! Alex, you protect Elli and Beatríz!"

"No, Jamie! We stay together! We'll surround Beatríz! When we fall, we'll try to fall on top of her!"

"Alex! Alex! Where are you?" Elli screamed, startled to see that he was no longer with them.

"Ewi! Ewi! Guys! Thew ah stones in the watuh! Look! We can walk on them!" Alex shouted, while stepping from one to another, and then stopping to face Elli.

"Alex! No!" Elli shouted back. "Those aren't stones; they're giant snapping turtles, and the swamp is full of alligators! Look! All around you!"

"No! C'mon, guys!" yelled Alex, as he continued to step from one turtle back to another, as if to illustrate their means of escape.

It became clear to the others that the turtles were their only option. They signaled for Alex to keep going as they also stepped quickly onto the backs of large turtles that numbered in the dozens, their toothy mouths wide open as if awaiting an imminent feast. The turtles, being within only a couple of feet of each other, enabled the children, even while assisting Beatríz, to move quickly from one to the next until the assembly of turtles ended, perhaps thirty yards from shore. The warriors, ecstatic that their quarry had found only a temporary means of escape, jumped onto the backs of the same turtles. First there were four, and then eight, and then another four. And so the steady flow continued until it was evident that most of the turtles' backs would be covered with enemy forces and that dozens of fighters armed with knives and hatchets and swords would momentarily be setting upon them.

"Here, Beatríz, you take my knife!" insisted Jamie. "You need whatever magic it has more than I do," he added, while he grabbed Beatríz's knife and pressed his own into her hands. The enemy warriors bore down on the children.

"Kill them! Kill them!" screamed the Wolfmen and Unpersons and other warriors as the first of them drew near.

Elli rallied her friends, shouting, "Let's fight to the end for each other! I love you all!"

~EIGHT~

"But of course!" Thorn repeated quietly to himself. For there, immediately above him, were juniper limbs, two to three feet long, growing out of the rock, and nearly bare of needles. And he could see, however faintly, another set of limbs off to the right of the ones just above him. He could not tell whether there were others scattered about the face of the cliff that were within reach and sturdy enough to hold him—as well as in sufficient numbers to lift him all the way to the top. Whether to attempt to climb the limbs was not in question. The worst thing that could happen would be for one of the limbs to break, sending him plummeting to his death. But, as far as he could ascertain, this was the only chance he had of reaching the children.

Thorn, with his own long and strong limbs, stretched and grabbed hold of two branches just within reach and hoisted himself into the juniper clump. Once he was secured, he looked for other branches in the blackness with his lantern eyes, but saw none besides the ones to the right. At the same time, he was startled to see the Fire-eyes about thirteen feet above him. Thorn grabbed one of the limbs to his right while holding fast to where he was situated. That turned out to be a wise decision, because as soon as he applied the least amount of pressure on the limb it broke. The entire juniper bush was dead and of no use to him.

He strained his eyes to see other branches above him, but saw none. The Fire-eyes remained where they were. Perhaps they were hovering once again near a set of limbs not yet visible to him and signaling where he should reach next. Without further hesitation, Thorn stood up ever so cautiously, being certain to lean his body against the face of the cliff. He then reached about as high as he could—on his foot fingers—and found a single limb to grasp. With both hands he hoisted himself up, confirming that the Fire-eyes had indeed led him to another sturdy set of limbs. When he was secure in those, he saw the Fire-eyes move and hover at another spot about a dozen feet up and to the left. Thorn stretched to reach where the Fire-eyes were floating and, sure enough, discovered a new set of limbs on which he could rely.

Thorn continued in that fashion for some hours until, finally, he hoisted himself one more time to the top of the towering cliff. The faint orange curtain of dawn was also lifting itself over the other edge of the cliff many miles away. Thorn sat, hands clasped around his knees, and simply rested for a time. He looked about and saw stretching for miles in all directions a hard rock plateau, like an expansive tabletop, strewn with the crumbs of thousands of boulders of different sizes. There were also pockets of sand scattered all about him, as if a giant god had tried in haste with a single sweep of its hand to wipe the table clean, leaving behind not only many rocks but sand that had fled to the safety of hundreds of holes and crevices. Some of the pockets of sand were as small as several feet in diameter—others as large as a football field. As Thorn sat, gazing out across the barren flatland, he saw nothing on the horizon to the east and south except sky. To the north, well beyond the edge of the plateau, was an immensely tall chain of snow-capped mountains extending in a line east to west as far as the eye could see, both ends shrouded by clouds before they dipped below the horizon. Thorn, for all his centuries of age and travel, was now in entirely unfamiliar territory.

He pondered his companions' circumstances, and knew that while they needed at some point to head north they would likely travel east first, seeking a more charitable place in the topography to change direction. He surmised correctly that heading east from the river where the children had crossed the bridge they were encountering a series of knolls and hills, increasing in height as they journeyed. Thorn couldn't hazard an educated guess as to what was beyond the foothills far to the east, but perhaps he could gain some evidence by heading east himself to the edge of the plateau. From there he might more accurately speculate on the path that Elli and her friends had taken.

At this point, he didn't need water, having drunk his fill, both intentionally and involuntarily, while plying his way down and across the river, but knew that he would need moisture in another several days—and there appeared to be no place on the plateau where water would be found. He knew that if there were even the slightest amount of water available to him, there would also be at least some vegetation. But he could see nothing anywhere that seemed alive.

Fortunately, Dactyls can store water much more efficiently than humans. He only hoped that the children would encounter water frequently. The sun had bounced from the top of the plateau and was rapidly heating his surroundings. In the distance undulating heat waves made the land itself seem alive. He decided to find cover behind a large boulder and hide in its shadows, first on one side and then on the other until evening. Traveling in the cool of the night he would be able to more than make up time and distance lost during the brutally hot daylight hours.

He spotted a large rock a few hundred yards away and went there to rest for the remainder of the day. Sitting against the rock in the shade, Thorn rested with both eyes closed and without movement.

Many hours later and shortly after the sun had set, Thorn was suddenly aroused by the sound and feel of a brief but stiff wind passing close overhead. He opened his eyes—but dared not open them fully, knowing that any eye-glow that might enable him to see danger coming could also help any danger see him.

He remained very still, as if he were simply a set of sticks piled loosely together, listening and watching the sky. He would not leave the cover of the rock until it was fully dark, perhaps in another couple of hours. Thorn closed his eyes once again and resumed his rest. Another two hours passed and a nearly full moon was just beginning its own journey in the night above the plateau, casting a soft bluish glow across the landscape as it traveled. Thorn was startled to instant alertness by the sound and feel of large wings slapping the air all about him. He looked up and saw a huge black shape descending rapidly upon him, like a vast cloak being thrown over him by unseen hands. Before he knew what was happening or could muster any sort of effective defense, Thorn felt the claws of a gigantic bird closing themselves around his arms and legs—and his body being lifted swiftly into the air.

Up, up, and up Thorn was lifted, and at a speed faster than any he had ever encountered. The force of the bird soaring skyward threw back Thorn's head, but at that angle he saw that a supposedly extinct double-winged condor, the largest of all creatures in Bairnmoor, had captured him. High above the earth the condor carried Thorn before shooting abruptly north toward the mountains.

The condor, with all four wings plying the air with fierce rapidity, was flying as fast as an arrow, or so Thorn thought. It was certainly faster than any other creature in the world, bar none, and the dangling of Thorn beneath the bird seemed to provide little, if any, drag. Yet the force of the wind would have made it impossible for Thorn to hold on. In that regard, some ten thousand feet above the ground now, Thorn was grateful for the condor's strong grip on him—even if the bird's talons were digging painfully into his skin. And other than the loud slapping of the air, the condor made no other sound or movement, as if oblivious, or at least indifferent, to its gangly cargo.

Thorn was more than frightened; he was speechlessly in shock, and feeling weaker and less alert by the minute. He wondered if the altitude was causing him to lose consciousness and control. He shook his head back and forth as best he could, striving to remain alert. But, it was no use. As the condor was beginning a slight descent to its aerie just below the snowline on a large outcropping of rock, Thorn lost consciousness. Little did he know that his absence of awareness was not only because of the altitude or the wind relentlessly battering him, but also because of the loss of his blood from wounds inflicted by the condor's talons.

With the upper set of slightly smaller wings now beating the air in a direction opposite that of its large wings below, the condor deftly slowed and hovered for a moment above its nest. It then released its hold on Thorn and dropped him heavily into the nest some thirty feet beneath the bird. And there he lay, motionless, while the condor dove like a shooting star off the ledge and into the night sky, its feathers glistening brilliantly in the moonlight.

Thorn began to regain consciousness and, with it, an increasing awareness that he could move neither arms nor legs—and his head only slightly. He was caught in something, but with his initially blurred vision, he could not tell what it was. When he could see clearly once again, Thorn saw that the sunlight from above was dim and only indirectly apparent as it drifted and dripped among what he could now ascertain was a dense covering of heavy branches holding him motionless. With clarity in vision came also clarity of mind, and Thorn suddenly realized where he was— and why. He was part of the condor's nest, and how many hours or days the condor had taken to cover him with about six feet of branches, he couldn't know.

But he was glad for three things: that he was still alive, even if terribly hungry and thirsty; that the bird had mistaken him, as had the children, for a stack of sticks; and that the bird was not his natural predator. But stuck he was, and he began to wonder how he was going to work his way out of his predicament. What if the condor discovered him, he asked himself? Would the enormous bird immediately kill him, simply toss him from the cliff, actually try to eat him, or . . . just leave him where he was as an integral part of the nest's structure—to die a slow death?

The only member of his body that he could move at all, other than his fingers, which could grab nothing within their reach, was his head. His neck was uncannily strong and his teeth exceedingly tough, so he decided to bite a branch within reach of his mouth and attempt to move it. But just as he was able to clamp his teeth onto a thick branch, the nest shook violently and became entirely darkened from above. Only a few ineffectual dabs of light were visible through the thick sides of the nest. The nest vibrated again and again as the large bird, following its harsh landing, was attempting to settle itself into the cavity close to Thorn's head. Thorn was astounded that he wasn't crushed, and grateful that the structure of the nest imprisoning him was also protecting him.

There was nothing else to do. Thorn released his mouth from the limb and screamed. "Help! Help!" The startled condor moved about quickly in the nest, painfully pressing on Thorn's body parts while he was looking all around him for the source of the noise.

"Ow! Ooow!" Thorn yelled as the condor looked abruptly one way and then another, its eyes looking more puzzled than anxious or worried.

"Help! Help! Help me!" Thorn screamed again.

The bird dipped its head downward and beneath his suddenly raised breast, and then jumped from the nest and settled next to it, its four rapidly flapping wings creating turbulence not unlike a sudden squall at sea.

"Help! Heeeelp me!" repeated Thorn, more desperately.

The condor poked its head into the nest, noticed the talking branches, and began pecking away at the nest with a speed that was matched only by the ferocity of its screeching! Within a short time the condor had pulled away all the nesting material that was holding Thorn fast. When the final piece was lifted and cast aside, Thorn lay motionless, including his two large eyes now popped from their sockets and staring into a single large yellow eye that was also motionless, and staring directly at him.

~NINE~

THE BIRD COCKED ITS head from side to side, staring at Thorn first with one eye and then the other.

"Well, what do we have here?" the bird inquired, much to the shock of Thorn upon hearing the condor speak.

"Well, certainly not just a pile of sticks for your nest, I can assure you!" Thorn replied indignantly, and with a tone of authority not consistent with the moment's obvious imbalance of power.

Equally surprised when he heard Thorn speak, the Condor immediately asked, "Who and what are *you*?" asked the bird.

"My name, if you please, Mr. Bird," said Thorn, more deferentially, "my name is Thorn, and I am what's called a Dactyl. I have lived for hundreds of years in the Forest of Giant Trees more than seventy-five miles to the west."

"Then, what, might I ask, were you doing on Flat Top?" interrogated the condor.

"Flat Top? What's Flat Top?" asked Thorn.

"The plateau I plucked you from several days ago. And a nice bunch of sticks for my nest I thought you'd make—and may *still make*—depending on your answer." The bird leered at Thorn. "No friendly forces have passed through this country for many years, Mr. Sticks."

"Um, if you please, Mr. Condor, it is Thorn—no Mr., just Thorn— and I am not an enemy of yours, I can assure you."

"Well," replied the bird while sizing up Thorn below him, "one like you could hardly be an enemy to *me*, but the question is whether you *represent* the enemy."

"And who would the enemy be?" asked Thorn, careful to remain entirely still, although he was dying to stretch his limbs, and especially his right leg—which was bent above his head.

"That, Mr. Sticks, depends on your answer, now doesn't it?" replied the bird.

Thorn wasn't sure what to say, or not to say, not knowing the loyalty, or at least the sympathies, of the condor. He certainly was not going to correct the bird again regarding his name. But while he hurriedly considered his answer, the bird spoke again.

"No answer is an enemy answer as far as I'm concerned, and silence will only get you tossed from the ledge to your death below—and, I might add, to ultimate use in my nest that you have just now caused me so inconveniently to tear apart."

"I am loyal to the Queen—or, shall I say, I *was* loyal to the Queen," answered Thorn, hoping that telling the truth wasn't ill advised.

Between the two barely visible holes of Thorn's nose, the Condor now placed the tip of his beak, the fine fuzz encircling the bird's jaw making Thorn's face itch to the point of tears. The condor spoke again, but this time more emphatically. "And what were you doing so far from home?"

"I was looking for some friends of mine," Thorn said. "But," he continued quickly, "I will tell you nothing about them unless *I* know that *you* are not *my* enemy. Otherwise," he added, now sitting up and away from the bird's beak, with a note of self-confidence that belied his quaking fear, "you may as well go ahead and turn me into the pile of *sticks* you keep calling me, because I will say no more."

The condor raised his head out of the nest and sat beside it, still looking at Thorn. He breathed out a long breath from his nose, stirring the air about Thorn's face. "I believe I saw these friends of yours—four of them—several days ago. I saw them while in flight, trudging through a tree line many miles southwest of here. I assumed they were small Unpersons scouting for Sutante's forces. But I wanted nothing to do with them; far be it from me to become involved with Sutante's loyalists or his property. So, who are these friends of yours?" the bird asked, this time expecting an answer. Thorn was silent.

"Suppose I told you I'm acquainted with Hannah?" said the condor.

"Hannah?" replied Thorn, his eyes now involuntarily protruding from their sockets. "What do you know about Hannah?"

"Only that she's our last hope, and has been seeking the restoration of Bairnmoor. She's been watching for a mythical child to come one day and release the Queen and restore her reign. Everyone loyal to the Queen knows of Hannah—as does Sutante, who's been continually searching for her, to kill her, and so once and for all kill the myth that Hannah is responsible for keeping alive. Sutante knows that subjugated people with a little hope, even in small numbers, can be extremely dangerous to those who rule with the scepter of despair." The condor cocked his head at Thorn, signaling it was now his turn.

"What I *can* say to you," replied Thorn thoughtfully, "is that the story you tell is the truth, as I know it, and that my task in this business was first to lead my very human friends safely out of the Forest of Giant Trees. It has since become a task of accompaniment, since I believe that one of the girls is in fact the one of the myth. All four of my friends, as would be evident to you upon a closer examination, are children—the likes of which have not been seen in Bairnmoor, to the best of my knowledge, for hundreds of years."

"So," said the condor, with a most calm and resolute voice, "I can see I must help you find your friends, and the sooner the better, assuming Sutante's forces haven't already found them—*and* that we are able to find them *now* before they do."

"Mr. Condor, I am so relieved to hear you say this, and grateful for your assistance."

"Don't be too grateful; there is more self-interest at play in assisting you than you know," the condor replied, almost apologetically. "But you and I seem to share the same loathing of Sutante and the same affection for Hannah. I am alone now," the bird continued, more slowly and pensively, "and I'm seeking my mate. She disappeared a long time ago—when she didn't return home. I don't know if she's alive, but I'll continue looking until I die. There are no other condors remaining; of that fact, I am quite certain."

"I, too," said Thorn, in a similar voice and demeanor, "am all that remains of the Dactyls; but, I have no belief that my mate survives—anywhere. I stopped looking for her a long time ago."

"I don't expect my mate is alive, either, Mr. Sticks."

"But, I believe you just said you are still looking for her," replied Thorn, sounding confused, which he was.

"There's a huge difference, Mr. Sticks, between belief and hope. Of course, beliefs can lead to hopes, and some hopes can result in some beliefs. But I am merely *hoping* I will find her alive." He let out a soft, sad screech. "And I'm not optimistic. If I were, I would have stopped searching a long time ago. No, I'm simply hopeful."

And so it was that Thorn had a new, or at least a second, name. While Thorn was pondering the condor's words, and also wondering if *he* had a name, too, the bird took off in rapid flight down from the mountain ledge. It flew south and east, as if it were heading for a predetermined spot in the distance where he might find the children, assuming they were able to continue their journey unimpeded. When the condor was above the river, he descended suddenly and with lightning speed, folding tightly against his midnight blue body his four wings. And just when it seemed he was going to dive at a terrifying high rate of speed into the river, the condor just as suddenly unfolded his wings and turned at a ninety degree angle so that was he was gliding swiftly just above the surface of the water. Within no time at all he had dipped the tip of his beak into the water and scooped up a fish; he then rose like a Roman candle back into the sky and headed back to the nest.

Thorn was left to himself for about half an hour, after which the condor returned—with supper for Thorn. Thorn had never eaten uncooked fish before, but this first time was not as awful as he had anticipated, given that his hunger was far greater than his sense of the abominable. There was also some water remaining in the lower jaw of the condor's beak, which he gave to Thorn as if providing water to a baby bird. In all, the nourishment and libation were a bit distasteful and rather humiliatingly delivered, but Thorn was grateful beyond words for both the thoughtfulness and the refreshments.

When Thorn had eaten and drunk to his fill, he asked politely, "May I ask your name?"

The condor looked up, as if he were expecting to see his name written across the sky, and then said, "She called me Starnee. It means Night Star." He looked back at Thorn. "We have no time to lose. If we still have any chance of finding these friends of yours alive, we must leave without delay."

"What do you mean by *we*, Starnee? You from the air, and I from the ground, I suppose?" he asked nervously, since he'd never flown before—except in the condor's talons.

"That will never do. I'm not going to lose you, too!" replied Starnee. "You'll simply climb onto my back and grab the lower parts of the feathers behind my neck—and hang on tight."

"But it will be dark soon. How are we going to see anything at night?" Thorn asked, with puzzled lips.

"My sight is keenest after nightfall; I'll watch for movements in the trees and meadows. You, Mr. Sticks, will watch for the small light of a fire—or perhaps a column of smoke absorbing the moonlight."

Within a minute or so, Thorn had found an elevated spot on the rocky outpost from which to jump onto Starnee's back. "Are you ready, Sticks?" Starnee asked, cocking one eye back at Thorn who, wide-eyed and staring at Starnee, was now settled deep behind Starnee's neck and grasping the feathers as if he were already being tossed to and fro. And then, before Thorn could utter a sound, much less an answer, the condor launched himself and his cargo abruptly up and over the cliff, descending rapidly thousands of feet below where each would be able to see what he was looking for—assuming *it* still existed, and its existence and their search converged.

It was the deep blue and purple of that part of the night sky when the sun had long ago slipped from view and a kind of scant "sun dust" was left clinging to the eastern horizon. As quickly as Starnee had leveled off above the grass-tufted mountains, heading southwest, the "dust" had fallen away from the edge of the world, giving way to total liquid blackness behind the stars and a just-rising moon. They were soaring perhaps a thousand feet above the terrain, the horizon of which unfolded itself from smaller mountains to foothills, and then from the vast plateau to a seemingly endless chain of gigantic knolls that, also in the process of becoming gradually smaller, made it seem as if Starnee were merely climbing higher and higher. The air was freezing, but the wind seemed to circle over and around them, as if Thorn was encapsulated in a bubble of still, balmy air that accompanied them on their journey. He settled himself in the thick down beneath the feathers, gazing at the motionless sea of stars above while awaiting further instructions from his carrier. The various textures of the terrain passed swiftly beneath them, so fast was Starnee flying, and yet it seemed to Thorn that time was becoming slower. He had no idea how long they had been in flight or how far they had flown. And, like a passenger in a car at night, he became mesmerized watching Starnee's black wings wiping the sky clean of stars the way a windshield wiper wipes away the sparkling droplets of rain at night, only to have them suddenly reappear.

Starnee had passed a number of ascending strips of forest between knolls before he saw the one that he was looking for. "We're turning east now, above that narrow forest below where I believe I saw your companions. Watch carefully for light and smoke, Sticks; I'll watch for movement!" Starnee shouted into the wind.

Thorn hung his head over the right shoulder of the upper wing, intently surveying the earth below while gripping tightly the stems of

Starnee's feathers. It was amazing to Thorn how little the great bird had to flap his wings to maintain his speed as he began a long glide just above the forest canopy, which was bathed in moonlight.

They had flown for perhaps half an hour when Thorn thought he'd seen a tiny light blink through the foliage as they passed overhead. "Starn-ee! I think I just saw a small light." Thorn felt himself suddenly thrown to the right as Starnee banked sharply left and thereby sent all of Thorn's body, except for his hands, skyward as Starnee completed a one hundred eighty degree turn while descending sharply. They were flying so close to the treetops now that Thorn thought he could hear branches glancing off Starnee's body and lower wing tips. Starnee had slowed their speed to such an extent that he was now moving his wings continually in a series of slight undulations.

"There!" Thorn shouted, as a now much larger flickering light passed lazily beneath them.

"I saw it!" screeched Starnee when they were well past the point of discovery. "Unfortunately," Starnee added, with a firm sense of urgency, "there was a lot more light and a lot more movement than could be made by simply four children. Whether or not that large group includes your friends remains to be seen. I'll circle back and we'll spend the rest of the night in the trees a good mile south of their encampment. Then, in the morning, we'll have you get a close look at them."

"How am I going to get a close look at them, Starnee," asked Thorn, nervously, "without their getting a close look at me?"

"We'll talk about that at dawn, Sticks." Starnee completed his wide circle and then lighted ever so gently in a protrusion of treetops, barely rustling the leaves as he lowered himself into the branches with folding wings, not unlike the deft movements of a ballet dancer. And there, for the rest of the night, the bird and its "sticks" slept.

~TEN~

ALEX, THE FIRST OF the four companions who would engage the enemy, raised his knife. "C'mon! C'mon! I'm not afwaid of you!" he yelled, even though inside it seemed that his very heart had stopped from the terror that was coiling itself around him. In just a few seconds, the roaring, toothy giant would attempt to drive his hatchet into Alex's head. Along with Alex, the other three screamed as well, "Yeah! C'mon! We're not afraid of you!"

Then, just as Alex had set his blade in the air to repel the downward thrust of the creature's weapon, the distance between them began quickly, and then much more rapidly, to increase. Indeed, the distance between the four children and their pursuers grew as the turtles on which they were standing swam, as if purposely, toward open water in the direction of the opposite shore. Suddenly, the remaining turtles on which stood many of the astonished enemy warriors reared up and hurled their cargo into the swamp. Just as suddenly, and with razor-sharp jaws, the turtles snapped off the heads and limbs of the Wolfmen and other warriors as they struggled in the water to get to shore. Nearly half of the enemy forces were wiped out in less than a minute of tumult, leaving the remaining warriors on shore shocked and speechless.

Soon all became still, and every living thing seemed sealed in silence while Elli and her friends drifted noiselessly, and with scarcely a ripple, toward the distant forest. Every so often each turtle on which one of the children was riding would strain its head back and around, as if to ensure that all was well with its unharmed, but exhausted passenger. With no sense of urgency the large green shells continued a direct and lazy course toward the opposite shore.

By the time the turtles had beached themselves to allow their passengers to disembark, the sun was hanging large and reddish-orange in the west, just above the peaceful hill they had earlier descended in a panic. The enemy was nowhere to be seen across the water. The children watched as the turtles turned swiftly around and scrambled back into the water. Not thinking for a moment that the turtles would understand, the children—nevertheless—yelled "Thank you! Thank you!" and waved. All four turtles immediately stopped dead in the water and cast a look back for a long, lingering moment, as if to say they *did* understand and the children were *welcome*. And then, as if in military formation, they returned their heads to the forward position and in a single movement dove out of sight.

The four children, realizing their exposure on the shore, also dove out of sight, just inside the edge of the forest, where they sat and told Beatríz all that had just happened with their carrier turtles. Soon the conversation turned to what to do for the night that would soon envelop them in darkness. They walked further inland, finding the going easy, as the space between the trees was substantial and relatively free of shrubs and brush. During the roughly thirty minutes they traveled due east into the forest, they noticed that the trees were both much alike and much different, one from another. Many of them had numerous long and thin, rope-like branches that draped, some nearly to the ground, making them look more like giant jellyfishes than trees. All of the trees were large, some giant, varying in foliage.

As the darkness began to enfold them, none of the four children felt threatened by the forest—nor did they seem frightend by its possible inhabitants. But each one sensed sadness in the air. Perhaps it had less to do with the forest than with their recent experiences. It was time to make camp. Decades, if not centuries, of fallen leaves had created a ground that was as soft as the nicest mattress and as warm as a down comforter. They cleared a small area and built a low fire that offered some light and security, though hardly enough heat over which to prepare any sort of meal. They were ravished with hunger now, and yet there seemed to be nothing suitable in the forest for them to eat. However, grateful for the finish to the day, Elli, Jamie, and Alex fell asleep without effort upon settling themselves into the leaves—which smelled of golden autumn days back home. Beatríz did not have to struggle to fall asleep, but she forced herself to remain awake, feeling a curious and enveloping affection for the gentle woods. She reached up and found several branches hanging close overhead, and began to gently finger and stroke them. They felt like no branches she had ever felt before. The closest tree in resemblance she could think of was the weeping willow, but these branches seemed more alive—more like animals, or even persons, than like the branches of trees. The stroking relaxed her beyond her resolve to stay awake, and she soon joined her friends in a deep quiet slumber.

The children had been asleep for several hours, and along with the bright stars overhead came a light but steady breeze through the trees. Beatríz awoke lazily to the sound of what she had heard in the distance the night before—a light, thin moaning sound, as if from a hundred mourning women encircling their campsite from a great distance. It was a light, thin sound of sadness, in various voices and instruments, becoming gradually louder. The music of vocal grief and instrumental lament drew ever closer, as if seeking solace and comfort. Not the least bit frightened, Beatríz made no sound; she just lay still and listened. She reached up again for the branches she had been stroking earlier, only to discover they were not only swaying in the breeze, but also vibrating ever so slightly and producing the most pleasant of barely audible sounds. And then she realized that the larger sound surrounding her—like a song—was coming from the trees themselves, their branches and leaves quivering and rubbing against each other. And she discovered that it was, indeed, a song, with several harmonic parts and numerous voices and instruments blended in concert with one another. Beatríz suddenly felt the gentle brush of slow-rolling drops on her cheeks as she began softly crying, as if sharing with the forest whatever sorrow it seemed to be shouldering and wanting to reveal. She continued to stroke the branches and leaves, letting them slide through her half-closed hand.

"Elli! Alex! Jamie!" Beatríz whispered, loudly enough to gain their attention while still maintaining the atmosphere that had settled around her and that she did not wish to disturb. There was no answer.

"Ellie! Alex! Jamie!" she repeated.

"What, Beatríz?" asked Elli, opening her eyes. And then Elli also heard the wind in the trees. Alex and Jamie also awoke, and the three of them just lay still, listening.

"Beatríz," Elli said, in a hushed voice. "What is it?"

"Yeah, wa wa tis it?" asked Alex, mimicking Elli's tone.

"The trees!" replied Beatríz, joyfully. "It's like they're crying—or whimpering—and singing! If you stroke the branches, you can feel them vibrating in the wind, making music; and if you're really quiet, you can hear them ever so slightly singing or playing. I know they're making music because I can hear the melody and the harmony!" She added softly, but excitedly, "It's all so very beautiful, isn't it? And so very sad?"

All four of them remained quiet until, after some minutes, the wind died and the music stopped. It was the earliest hours of the morning and still completely dark. And all four of them, deep in wonder and thought, drifted back to sleep, the fire all but out.

The dawning sun, not yet visible through the trees, was settling a soft dim light on the thick haze that covered the circle of ground on which the children were sleeping. Jamie and Alex were snoring lightly and, from time to time, mumbling in their sleep. None of the four friends were yet awake to see a sheaf of tiny purple flowers lying close to the head of each. Beatríz could smell the fragrance of the flowers in her dreams. Then, startled, she became aware of something soft and fuzzy rubbing gently and intermittently against her exposed cheek as she lay on her side in the leafy hollow of her bed.

"Alex!" Beatríz whispered, smilingly, her eyes still closed. "Stop it!" The gentle brushing continued. "Alex! Stop it! Please!" But still the brushing continued against her cheek. "Alex!" Beatríz whispered sharply, with a giggle. And then she reached to push away whatever it was that Alex was using to tickle her cheek and awaken her, only to realize in an instant that it was something alive, but not Alex, which was nuzzling her cheek and making no sound. Beatríz put back her hand to her side ever so slowly and then said, haltingly, "Guys! Guys!" She paused. "Guys!" she now screamed. All three awoke at once. Elli sat up.

"What is it, Beatríz?" Elli asked, rubbing her eyes and trying to see her through the haze that had gathered about them during the night.

"Don't you see it, Elli?" Beatríz asked, incredulously.

"See what, Beatríz?" Elli asked, puzzled by Beatríz's cry. "I don't see anything. You must have been dreaming, Beatríz. Everything's fine, and it's not quite morning for us—the sun is up, I'm sure, but we can't see it, so it's still pretty dusky out."

"Elli," reaffirmed Beatríz, "something was touching me, just a minute ago, and if it wasn't one of you, then . . . then . . . what was it?"

It was then that Elli noticed the flowers not far from Beatríz's head, smelled the light sweet fragrance all about them, and observed that there was a loose bouquet of flowers next to each one's headrest. "You're right, Beatríz. Something *has* been here. And whatever it was has left us all flowers!"

The four friends were now sitting up, and the flowers were the only things of color visible under the barely bluing sky that was silhouetting the treetops.

"Butweece!" asked Alex, "what wuzzit?"

"I don't know," said Beatríz, sounding now more reflective than up-set. "But it was soft and fuzzy. And I tried to get everyone's attention by not speaking too loudly in calling for you. Then, when I finally yelled for you, it must have run away. But I didn't hear anything."

"I wonder," said Jamie, "if it has anything to do with the noises last night."

"You mean, *music*, Jamie. It wasn't just noises; it was music," she in-sisted, "and it was coming from the trees."

"Well," Elli said, "obviously these flowers didn't come from the trees."

Each of them was fingering the flowers in wonderment when into the clearing, through the swirling smoky haze blanketing the ground, stepped what at first appeared to be a tall white horse—the biggest horse that any of the children had ever seen, whether in real life or even in pictures. How-ever, it became almost immediately apparent to all but Beatríz what it was.

"Beatríz," said Jamie, softly, frozen in place—out of amazement. "It's a unicorn—a white unicorn—just like the ones you see in paintings and hear about in fairy tales!"

The unicorn stepped deliberately toward what had been the fire and, within several feet of the children, lay itself down on all fours, turning its head to look at them. "I'm not here to hurt or frighten you, I can assure you," said the unicorn, calmly. "And, it was I who had left the flowers for you. A sort of welcome gift, you might say."

"I, I didn't know that unicorns existed or could talk," said Jamie, without thinking before he spoke.

"Well, it's more the case in this part of the country that one would be surprised to know that humans existed," replied the unicorn.

Alex spoke, as if waiting for his opportunity to lay down the rules. "We ah not afwaid of you, unicone, and we ah not going to tew you anything."

The unicorn chuckled warmly and without any hint of condescen-sion. "You don't need to tell me anything. It is *I* who must tell *you* some-thing." The unicorn paused and shook out its dazzling white mane. "My name is Childheart," said the unicorn, as if to begin a monologue, which, in fact, it was to be. "And I don't know your names. But this much I *do* know about you.

"According to Hannah, you," Childheart began his statement, nod-ding to Elli, "may be the long-awaited fulfillment of the prophetic poem that predicted, centuries ago, that a child would come to us and release the Queen." The unicorn then repeated for them the story they had heard from Thorn, as well as from Hannah.

"Now, quite frankly, children," Childheart said, and cleared his throat, "I don't *know* for a fact that you"—again, nodding to Elli—"are this child who is to come, or if there is to be another—or any at all. In all events, I seriously doubt there will *be* another, authentic or otherwise. But, even if you *are* this chosen child, I have no idea how you are going to release a Queen from imprisonment who has been dead for more than three centuries." On hearing another—*from* Bairnmoor—verbalize his own doubts, Jamie gave special ear to what the unicorn was saying.

"What I *do know* is that this land is slowly dying, that this forest is slowly dying, and that I, too, am slowly dying. Indeed, I'm afraid that both this forest and I are nearly at our end, and that, without a return of the Queen in the near future our end will come sooner rather than later.

"I also know that you are beyond brave to come to us from wherever you came, and however you came, and that I will do all I can to assist you, including giving my life for you, if that is required."

Elli broke into the monologue: "My name is Elli, and these are my friends," she said, nodding to each in turn, "Beatríz, Alex, and Jamie. I must say to you, Childheart, that *they* are the ones beyond brave. They *chose* to travel with me, understanding as much as possible the dangers. I, on the other hand, did not exactly *choose* to come here."

"What do you mean, Elli?" asked Childheart.

"What I mean is," Elli said, and then pausing to consider carefully her next words. "What I mean is . . ."

"Ewi! You can *not* tew him anything, wemembuh?" Alex broke in.

"Don't worry, Alex, I won't say anything I'm not supposed to say," Elli said, reassuringly, but with a tone of slight reproach for the interruption. Turning again to Childheart, Elli continued her explanation. "I was told by someone I cannot name that I was *supposed* to come to Bairnmoor, and that I myself could choose not to come, but also that the future of your land somehow depended on my coming if it were to survive at all. I was also told I needed to come with three friends—these, who, amazingly, agreed to come with me. And, Childheart, I have no idea—that is, *we* have no idea—how the four of us are going to be of any help to you and your land. We have nothing—really, Childheart, nothing—to offer you. But, we will do what we can. We have been through a lot already, so we're willing to keep going as long as we are able. In any event, there is no going back."

"I suspect Hannah, or another, has told you to trust the source of all things, the Good, apart from whom your mission would be entirely without hope," said Childheart, "although I need to be frank with you and tell you that the Good, if it yet exists independent of the Queen, has provided no assistance to this forest—or even to me individually as the one charged by the Queen to be, as she decreed, 'the Belover' of this forest."

"Childheart," asked Beatríz, "what was it that seemed to be sad music coming from the trees last night?"

"You heard songs of lament, dear child. For many centuries this largest of all forests in Bairnmoor was known as Symphony Forest, or Forest of Joy, where daily the trees would make beautiful and joyful music. People and animals and creatures of all sorts would come from all parts of Bairnmoor to listen to the forest's music and be comforted and encouraged, gladdened and strengthened, even healed, by its balm." Childheart rested his head on his front legs and shifted his long tail next to his eyes, as if he were about to cover them. "Now," the unicorn said, with a fading voice and glazed, motionless eyes, "now, the trees play and sing music, but only at night, and only in the form of songs of sorrowful remembrance and grief—and only when they feel safe doing so."

"But, what happened, Childheart? Why are you and the forest dying?" Elli asked.

The unicorn started, as if suddenly being awakened from sleep by a loud noise, and jumped to his feet. "But, my, what a fine host I've been!" Childheart said, with self-chiding in his voice. "You must be terribly hungry. Wait here. I will return shortly with food and drink. And then, while you eat and get refreshed, I will tell you the story of what for centuries has made this place 'The Forest of Lament.'"

Within minutes, Childheart had galloped off with barely a sound beneath his swift and agile feet and returned carrying a basket of fruit and nuts, and plant milk, for his guests. Then, while the children ate politely, but greedily, Childheart told them this story.

"The Queen of Bairnmoor, Queen Taralina, ruled this land with only the force of the Good that was in her and the love that it radiated—like the sun—throughout all parts of her Kingdom. She ruled by the authority and power of the Good for many centuries before my time, though she remained forever a child. Even when she was reported to be nearly five hundred years old, she had the features and beauty of a young child in a woman's body, with the heart and qualities of a child. Indeed, all who lived in Bairnmoor were children of one sort or another, some with more 'childnessness' than others, but all imbued with the Spirit of Childnessness that seemed to fill all of Bairnmoor.

"She loved me very much, and in that love, in the name and the power of the Good, she charged me with the awesome, but joyful, vocation of loving the trees of this forest. I was known as Childheart, the Belover, and the trees were my Beloved. As long as the Queen's love filled me, I had limitless love for the trees of the forest, loving them as I would a family. And Symphony Forest thrived and brought joy and the benefits of love to untold millions of others over the centuries.

"Then, as incredible as it seemed to virtually everyone, we heard there was one closest to the Queen who was not satisfied with the Queen's love and rule, who was himself in love with power and who raised up arms against her. He promised the people of Bairnmoor, and especially the people of his own land in the far north of the country, greater material prosperity, with no end to the growth of abundance and self-determination. He alleged that the Queen was actually 'treating them like infant children' and preventing them from fulfilling their potential and establishing self-rule. In short, he leveled against her the charge that she was *enslaving* them and condemning them to a life of perpetual immaturity, when what they were meant for was adulthood and authority over their own destinies, filled with infinite possibilities and limitless choices, and capable of becoming the leading world of all worlds everywhere.

"This one, Sutante Bliss, demonstrated for people the invention and fabrication of things and machines that had never entered the minds of others—things that could make life far easier and more enjoyable, with the promises of less work and more leisure, greater happiness, and both self-empowerment and cosmic dominance. And, amazingly . . . " Childheart's voice trailed off into deep, private thoughts.

"'Amazingly' what?" asked Elli. She and the others simply stopped eating and waited for a while to see if Childheart was going to continue.

"Well, many of the people—an increasing number—joined their voices with Sutante's voice, challenging the Queen to respond to the allegations. They demanded that she countervail his charges with defenses and proposals of her own for providing the freedoms and possibilities that Sutante Bliss was advancing—and insisting on demonstrations of her ability to do so.

"Many of us pleaded with her to parry his evil thrusts, but . . . " Childheart gave a seemingly bottomless sigh. "She never answered Sutante—nor any of her people, including those of us closest to her. All she would say was, 'Nevertheless, I love you.' It was as if," he said, "she was simply letting them win.

"Since she ruled solely by the authority and power of the Good and its force of love, she had no military, and she asked for no defense. And even when thousands rallied to defend her, vowing to fight to the death, she begged them to lay down their arms—and thousands of her loyalists had already fallen in various parts of her Kingdom.

"Sutante Bliss quickly overran her castle, chased her to the vault beneath the castle and there killed her by his own sword—and entombed her. Sutante then ordered that a clay likeness of her dead body together with the killing sword be cast for permanent public display, and that the vault be sealed against anyone and anything going in—or out. As it happened, as soon as the massive door that had always been open was closed, it locked of its own accord, so that not even Sutante Bliss could enter. The whole of Bairnmoor quickly learned that this door of an unknown material was incapable of being opened by anyone except—except by a child with a diamond key, according to the prophetic poem inscribed on the front of the door, a poem never before seen by anyone until the door was closed.

"This is the poem that Hannah has kept through its ritual retelling every year on the anniversary of the Queen's death:

> *At close of time the door be shut*
> *Against the child within without;*
> *The lock a seal against the death*
> *Of nothingness about.*
>
> *Through space and time a child shall come*
> *To open this eternal door;*
> *The Queen, released from imprisonment,*
> *Will spread her life forevermore.*
>
> *The child shall come with forces fierce:*
> *Evil, legions of children to meet;*
> *And with the sword of right and good*
> *Adultish nothingness defeat.*
>
> *From some dimension far beyond*
> *The reach of our eternity;*
> *The child shall come and open wide*
> *This portal with a diamond key.*

"As soon as the Queen was dead, there was no longer childnessness irradiating those whom she loved and charged with loving in return. Without the unlimited love of childnessness that was hers alone to provide, those of us called to love have had less and less love to give. So those in need of love for their very existence are dying a slow and increasingly painful death."

"Then, *you* are dying, Childheart—and it hurts you more and more?" asked Beatríz, incapable of holding back tears.

"Not physically. In that way, feeling less and less is its own source of sorrow. But far greater than physical pain is the pain of losing those you love, a little more every day," replied Childheart, with tearful eyes.

"And with Sutante Bliss—what happened next?" asked Jamie.

"Nothing of what Sutante Bliss described was true," Childheart continued, "and none of his promises were kept, except, of course, in very distorted, manipulative and evil ways, and then only for those closest to him or otherwise pressed into service on his behalf, with rewards for service and penalties for refusals to serve him.

"All forces in the world are now marshaled and controlled by Sutante Bliss in his insatiable pursuit of power and wealth and the advancement of his kingdom—putting at risk, I believe, the whole of existence."

"Excuse me, Childheart," interrupted Elli, "but when you speak of the whole of existence, what do you include? I mean, you don't mean the world that we come from, surely?"

"I mean everything, Elli. I know nothing of your world, but I can assure you that if you were summoned here, it is not solely because of Bairnmoor. We learned long ago that the Good is at the heart of *all* existence, and that without its control, all things cease to exist—or die—be they animate or inanimate in nature. The question to ask yourselves, I suppose, is whether your world is dying. It is either growing or dying—there is no in between, even among things we consider inanimate."

Elli and her friends were now given some time to ruminate before Childheart made the closing remarks to his narrative.

"Sutante Bliss has now managed to subjugate virtually everyone, and with their forced labor he has built himself the most magnificent of castles, as well as a large fortress that encloses within it, like a museum piece, the once-beautiful and welcoming—and now by comparison diminutive—castle of the Queen. And around his own castle he has built a towering fortress that is guarded by heavily armed warriors, including Wolfmen, that number in the thousands. Even the impenetrable door to the Queen's vault, now inhabited by nothing threatening, is guarded by dozens of warriors."

"Why," asked Beatríz, with incredulity, "would Sutante need all these warriors within the fortress itself to guard the dead Queen's vault?"

"Simply because of the inscription on the door—discovered once it was closed."

"But," asked Elli, reentering the conversation, "does Sutante Bliss himself believe the prophecy will come true?"

"Sutante Bliss and Evil itself, Elli, believe nothing. They only fear and then react accordingly. And," Childheart added, "notwithstanding all appearances to the contrary, Sutante and his evil power can create nothing; they can only destroy—and only childness love can expose him for what he is and reveal the nothingness of the world he has fashioned."

"But, what does Sutante Bliss now fear, and for what reasons?" asked Jamie.

"He fears anything that could possibly threaten his power. He also fears childnessness, for it alone held sway before his revolt. And so immediately upon killing the Queen and assuming power over Bairnmoor, he killed many young children, enslaved the rest, and forbade the teaching and training of 'childnessness.' Only 'adultness' is permitted in Bairnmoor."

Beatríz, who loved words, quickly interjected her only seemingly unrelated question: "Why, Childheart, does there exist *childnessness*, but apparently not *adultnessness*—only *adultness*?"

"Because, Beatríz, childnessness is the essence of the quality of childness. But adultness has no essence," answered Childheart, acknowledging with obvious delight the critical relevance of her question.

"Wa . . . wat is 'adowtness?'" asked Alex.

"'Adultness' is the opposite of 'childness' and its love, and of what the Good creates and sustains," answered Childheart, but not so certain he had answered well enough for Alex—or any of them, for that matter—to understand.

Childheart stood (to stretch his legs)—as did the children, thinking the conversation was concluded—and then lay down again.

"Perhaps I can explain it in another way. Under the Queen's rule, if in fact it is *rule* we are talking about at all, all were called and encouraged—and so expected—to reflect childness; to possess, as it were, the essence of childnessness. The quality of childness consists of truthfulness, honesty, and trustfulness; of wonderment, belief, and obedience; of gratefulness and contentment; of hopefulness and courage; of joyfulness and love; and, perhaps most of all, of humility, without which none of these other qualities could exist. Childness also includes a sense of the community and of the whole being larger and more important than any single individual. Paradoxically, though, it is in community where we achieve truly and more effectively our individuality.

"We have always believed, and lived as if we believed, that our own individual identity and well-being are tied up inextricably with the identity and well-being of the community—and all of Bairnmoor. Indeed, with the full development of childnessness, there is an individual awareness of participating in a larger, collective consciousness—not erasing individual identity, but creating an infinitely greater sense of identity, in which the individual is knowingly and lovingly subordinate to the community."

By this time the children had drawn close to Childheart's head and were lying on their sides while they ate.

"Not surprisingly then, Sutante Bliss trained his loyalists and overseers to inculcate in his subjects the qualities of 'adultness': the qualities of suspicion, mistrust, and cynicism; of dishonesty and lying, as well as fear, selfishness, judgmentalism, and haughtiness. As people of all ages began to behave with greater adultness, the childlike features of their faces began to fade and reflect the increasing emptiness of their very being. And so, for example, the quality of truthfulness has a facial quality, as does the quality of trust. Suspicion has no face; neither does selfishness. Almost all people are now Sutante's 'adults' and Unpersons. Even the children who are born are not born any longer as children, but as Unpersons, and raised from the first moments of birth to cultivate 'adultness' as they grow. You will notice in no apparent—and I emphasize *apparent*—children you encounter, anything but guileful smiles and unwelcoming—even hateful—eyes, and skeptically scrunched noses and mouths. Even these features, starved of any authentic emotions, fade with time."

The children had finished their early morning breakfast and were struggling to comprehend all that Childheart had told them. By this time the sun had appeared through the trees, the ground fog had lifted and the sky was sapphirine. But the colors of sky and flowers, and the delight of their encounter with Childheart, belied what would be the darkening of the day, which was shortly to unfold before them.

~ELEVEN~

STARNEE GREETED WITH ALERT eyes the smooth crest of the orange sun just emerging from behind the low-slung hill in the east. The forest floor would yet be shrouded in darkness, so now would be the time to send Thorn on his mission.

"Sticks!" Thorn remained fast asleep. "Sticks!" Starnee yelled, while he ruffled his neck feathers and, at the same time, ruffled Thorn to consciousness with his beak. Thorn had slept as well as he had ever slept in recent months, and awoke feeling refreshed, strong, and alert.

"I'm awake, Starnee—and ready. What's next?"

"I'm going to take you in my talons and drop you just above the trees as we approach the camp. When I've hovered to within several feet of a good spot for the drop, I'll release you."

"And then?"

"You'll need to work your way—*noiselessly*—to a place above the camp another hundred yards east of the drop site. There you can descend and perhaps get a good look at what's there, including how many warriors, and of course noting—hoping for failure here—any evidence of your friends' presence. After your reconnaissance, make your way back to the drop-off point and wait for me."

Within a few minutes following their brief conversation, Thorn and Starnee were aloft. Very shortly thereafter, having hardly taken flight, Starnee dropped Thorn into the trees and turned back.

Thorn grabbed the first available branches—with only his feet—and so came quickly to rest upside down. In his younger days, when he did a lot of tree climbing simply for the sheer pleasure of it all, he could easily have bent at the waist nearly a hundred and eighty degrees and grabbed with his hands the branches onto which his feet were holding for dear life. But those more limber days were well behind him, and he had to spend several minutes moving his feet inch by inch along the branches until he was close enough to other branches he could grasp with his hands and thereby right himself.

Once righted, Thorn made his way limb by limb toward the encampment. Soon he was well concealed in the trees just above the western edge of the enemy camp. The sun had risen from behind the hill, and there was just enough light slanting onto the forest floor for Thorn to get a clear and detailed view of the situation. What he saw startled him. He could count only fifteen warriors, none of them Wolfmen, but he also noted, incongruously, dozens upon dozens of horses and mules, with each animal pulling a covered cart or carrying a concealed load. It appeared to Thorn that the cargo consisted both of weaponry of various sorts and of food, enough of each to supply a war party of hundreds of troops for many days. He also noticed that a number of mules were carrying large, but empty, cages. While taking note in his head of all he was seeing, a loud, but distant, cacophony of screeching voices filled the air, startling both Thorn and those just beneath him. The din of both fear and rage continued for five chilling minutes, then faded quickly and disappeared.

The sun was high overhead when Thorn had returned to the drop-off point. Thorn waited and watched for several hours, but there was neither sight nor sound of Starnee who, Thorn believed, was going to be at the spot by the time he had returned from his reconnaissance. Several more hours passed, and the shadows had now lengthened into a blanket of charcoal across the top of the forest.

The night sky was full of dozens of small drifting clouds, and the rising half moon shone dimly through the tufted phantoms floating leisurely by. For reasons that had to be serious, Starnee failed to show. And now that night had fallen completely, Thorn knew that, even if Starnee returned before dawn, he would not try to find him in the dark. Accordingly, Thorn settled down just beneath the tree tops where he could rest each of his limbs, albeit not altogether comfortably, and watched the clouds drift overhead, their edges backlighted brightly by the hidden moon; there he waited restlessly for what he desperately hoped would be a more promising morning.

As soon as a hint of pink wash appeared on the eastern horizon, Thorn poked his head through the canopy of leaves and searched the sky for his new friend. In this fashion, Thorn spent the first several hours of the morning, constantly turning this way and that for anything in the sky that might become Starnee. Nothing was stirring above or below him. An uninterrupted sheet of clouds covered the sky. Then, breaking the stillness of the skyscape, Thorn saw a vast and dark cloud of birds sailing north-ward on the far western edge of the horizon. It was impossible for Thorn to ascertain the number of birds in the flock, but what was more than evident was that many of them were carrying a single burden beneath them which, on closer inspection, even at this great distance, could be none other than the silhouette of a much, much larger bird the size of . . . Starnee. It had to be Starnee. There was no mistake. But what brought shivers down Thorn's otherwise insensitive back was the unmistakable lifelessness of Starnee's body against the dawning sky. He was held aloft and carried upside down by dozens of birds, each with its own spot of skin to grab hold of with talons or beak. The thought of all the piercing, of the awful fight that must have led to Starnee's capture, and of the likelihood of his being dead, made Thorn weep.

Thorn shed his first tears since the disappearance of his partner, Pop-lar, hundreds of years ago; he shed them now for Starnee, for his other companions, for his utter sense of helplessness, and for his near despair over Sutante Bliss.

But he had a decision to make—quickly and decisively, regardless of what had happened beyond his control and knowledge. He needed to keep looking for his friends, or he needed to look for Starnee. He knew that finding his friends who were so far ahead of him would be nearly impossi-ble, now that Starnee could no longer assist him. His singular focus to this point of helping the children was now going to shift to helping Starnee, if there was any Starnee left to help. And so, without further pause, and without allowing his emotions to dictate his actions, Thorn descended the trees and headed west, watching carefully for any signs of enemy life. Once night had fallen completely, Thorn planned to head northward in the open across the grassy hills. By that time, he hoped the earth would once again be shrouded with cloud cover, precluding the moon and stars from shad-owing his presence against illuminated grasses and fields. His further hope was that the birds would have to travel short distances with long breaks, so heavy was their spoil from battle.

It was as Thorn walked quickly just inside the tree line, using for bal-ance his staff that he (almost miraculously, he thought) did not lose in the midst of all the tumult of his journey thus far, recalled the screeching noise of the previous morning. He reasoned that what he heard was the sound of Starnee being ambushed by some sort of predator birds that were hunting, uncharacteristically, in a pack. They were likely of the falcon variety, no doubt trained by Sutante Bliss to marshal their forces as a single entity.

Only evil could do that, he thought. Only evil *would* do that, he thought. If falcons, they were among the fiercest of predators, unusually strong for their size, faster than any other bird of prey—besides the condor, fearless in pursuit, and relentless in battle. As a pack, they would be virtually invincible against any other creature—or gathering of creatures—in all the land. What he could do to assist Starnee, even if he found him alive, Thorn had no idea whatsoever. Only the Good could do anything now, if the Good still existed—if the Good *ever* existed, he thought—apart from the Queen, that is.

When it was dusk, and becoming extremely difficult for Thorn to see his way along the nearly black forest floor without the full use of his eyes— given their readily detectable glow—he had traveled about as far west as he guessed necessary before heading northward to follow the course taken by the falcons. Because it was yet light, Thorn rested inside the forest until night had fallen completely. When darkness advancing from the eastern sky had finally pushed the last strip of pale grey light below the western horizon, the cloud cover *also* followed the dusky sky over the edge and out of sight. Discouragingly for Thorn, the stars were as bright as ever, and even without the moon that had not yet risen they outlined the shape of Thorn sharply against the glistening, dew-gathering grass. Thorn's one positive thought was that at least he could move more quickly with the light of the stars illuminating the way before him.

Thorn traveled half the night without resting, climbing and descending two large knolls before he stopped just over the top of the third one. As he sat he became absorbed in thoughts of Starnee and of the Goodness of the Queen that could have prevented all of this from happening—all of the evil that had happened, and was continuing to happen, even before her death. "Why," he had asked himself so many times, "why did she not fight, fight for the Good and let the Good continue to reign in the land of Bairnmoor? What did she gain by letting—and that's what she did, she *let*—Sutante win; and she *had* to have seen it coming, hadn't she? Perhaps," he allowed himself to think, "she wasn't all that she claimed to be, or, more accurately, all that others said she was and that everyone else simply accepted without question. Maybe, in the final analysis, she was just a fantasy—or a charlatan! It had all seemed so real, so perfect, so *true*—for so long."

Thorn lay back on the warm wet grass and gazed up into the sky— as he had done that night on Starnee's back. Suddenly, similar to what happened when Starnee was flapping his wings while Thorn was reclined behind him, a large black "wing" of something flew overhead in the near distance, abruptly wiping away the stars from Thorn's vision, only to have them just as abruptly reappear. Thorn sat up quickly and looked for the black shape. He looked and looked, and then he saw it—heading directly toward him, as if it had seen him. Thorn scrambled back over to the other side of the knoll and crouched in as much of a ball as he could manage with pieces of arms and legs and a torso that were each three feet or more in length. He settled into a shape that would have appeared to almost anyone, especially high in the sky, as a pile of sticks. But, within minutes, the dark cloud of whatever it was had stopped to hover in the sky above him, obviously not believing he was a pile of sticks, or else, like Starnee, looking for just that sort of thing. Regardless, Thorn kept as still as a pile of sticks and waited, at this point without fear, but with the fervent hope against an encroaching despair that his mission would not be delayed or dismantled by this encounter.

The dark cloud hovered for some time, and Thorn peeked through his arms and legs with scant slits of eyes to learn whether the cloud would continue on its way or approach him. He hadn't long to wonder. The dark mass began slowly to descend toward him. At that moment Thorn knew he had been seen, and so he scrambled to his feet and began to run, back up and over and down the knoll. At least, he thought, he could fight more effectively on the run, as well as gain a small amount of additional distance in his quest to find Starnee—and perhaps he'd even find some sort of cover under which to hide, be it a crevice in a rock, a cave, or even a tree; none of which, he knew, was likely.

But it was no use. The cloud descended to within twenty feet of Thorn and followed him, making an almost deafening humming noise, like that of a thousand bumblebees approaching. And just as he was about to stop and turn and fight, he heard the most unusual voices shouting in succession over the hum.

"Stop!"

"Stop, Thorn!"

"We know who you are!"

"We are here to help you!"

"Please, stop!"

Thorn stopped (since he couldn't run anymore, anyway) and turned and looked up. His eyeballs began to pop out of his sockets involuntarily at the sight before him, and he had to push them back in with his fingers. He had lived in Bairnmoor for a very long time and thought he had seen everything. The uninvited visitors, who seemed, indeed, to know who Thorn was, were now hovering just above and around his head, with some even beginning to land on the ground beside him, as if dropping from fatigue.

"Who *are* you?" demanded Thorn.

"We, Sir Thorn, are, of course, a host of angels! Have you never *seen* or *heard* of a host of angels before?"

"Well, um . . . no, I haven't ever seen a host of angels . . . and I have to confess, the image I've always had of angels, to the extent that I thought they existed at all, was something else entirely. And how do I *know* you're angels?" Thorn insisted, trying to force his voice through the droning.

"Because we say so, and angels never lie!" a number of the "angels" replied, as if a choir, and as if they'd answered that question before.

Thorn paused briefly to consider the answer, which made no sense to him.

"May we land around you, Sir Thorn?" one of them bellowed. "We are getting rather tired of hovering."

"Ye . . . yes, by all means! Please do!" said Thorn, agreeably, still puzzling over their answer to his simple question.

When all of about two hundred and fifty of the "angels" had landed, not one of them daintily, revealing once again the brilliant starry sky above him, Thorn spoke, tentatively.

"So judging from what I see in this dim light, it would seem that I have been visited from the sky by dozens of, may I say, flying toads?" He then added quickly, as if he had forgotten himself, "And please correct me, if I am wrong."

One of the (rather large and plump) toads, the size of a muskmelon, hopped laboriously forward and spoke. "If you mean, by 'toads,' *Cannotoads*, then you are correct, Sir Thorn."

"What's a *Cannotoad*?" asked Thorn.

"I understand. Please forgive me," said the self-described Cannotoad. "I assume you have neither seen, nor heard of, us before. We are Cannotoad Angels. And a host of Cannotoad angels has been visited upon you, Sir Thorn—which means that the Good has smiled favorably upon you."

Thorn, despite his weariness and a sense of urgency, attempted to focus on what was happening to him at the moment. Two feet in front of him sat a fat, warty toad who had rather diminutive—and, one would think, entirely ineffective—feathery wings protruding from its back. "So you would have me believe that you are . . . *angels* who are *toads* who can *fly*, and that you are here for my benefit, is that correct?"

"That is correct, Sir Thorn," the Cannotoad said, with an exceedingly wide smile that made Thorn want to laugh—and for the first time in many years.

"And assuming you are angels, how do you know that the Good has smiled something upon me—what was it?"

"'Smiled *favorably* upon you," answered the Cannotoad, deferentially, but with a wide grin.

"Yes, *favorably* upon me. How do you *know* that the Good has smiled favorably upon me?"

"Because we were told to say so, and none of us ever lies, so it must be so."

"May I ask *who* told you?" asked Thorn, becoming restless.

"I really do think we should focus on the 'favorably' part of all this, Sir Thorn, since time is precious to you and I doubt that you are really going to get all your questions answered to your satisfaction. Please correct *me*, if I am mistaken."

"You are correct," said Thorn, who then—first looking around to avoid squishing one of his celestial visitors—sat down on the grass. "So how do you know who I am? And how do you propose to assist me, as you said, *favorably?*" asked Thorn.

"We are here to reunite you with the children you accompanied out of the Forest of Giant Trees."

"You mean, *Elli?*" asked Thorn, his eyes once again beginning to protrude.

"Yes, and the others," said the Cannotoad.

"How many others?" asked Thorn, quickly and apprehensively, desperately wanting—and not wanting—to know the answer.

The Cannotoad paused before answering, putting one foot to his mouth, his few fingers drumming against his lips, as if pondering. "Two—no, three—others. So, four, total."

Thorn broke out into such a wide smile that one might have thought he was mimicking the Cannotoad.

While the rest of the angels sat around them, Thorn and the Cannotoad spokesperson continued their conversation.

"Where *are* the children?" asked Thorn, excitedly. "And are they okay?" he added quickly. "And, oh, do you have a name?"

"They are many days' journey on foot from here," answered the Cannotoad. "They are in fine shape, notwithstanding all they have been through, or so we have been told—we have not actually met them yet, you see—and," said the avuncular-looking toad, extending a front leg, "I am Butterfly."

At the mention of the toad's name, Thorn burst out laughing—a genuine laugh, a belly laugh, the first genuine belly laugh he had experienced, like the wide smile, in many years. He was embarrassed that he did so, but was also unable to contain himself. While he continued to laugh, the toad continued to speak, as if entirely untroubled by Thorn's rude assessment of his name.

"As I said, I am Butterfly, the chief archangel, and these four other archangels"—whom Thorn saw hop forward into the circle in succession as each one's name was announced—"are Roogerd, Weeplop, Mannywart, and Bill. We are here to bring you back to the children as quickly as possible; they are in the Forest of Lament far to the east beyond Hill Swamp River."

Having heard tales from a few others who had been through them only once, and hundreds of years earlier, Thorn had only the vaguest notion of what the Forest of Lament and Hill Swamp River were, but he knew they were at least a couple of hundred miles away. "And how are *we* going to 'bring me back as quickly as possible' if we are, as you said, several days' away on foot?"

"We are going to *carry* you, Sir Thorn; it's a mode of transportation reserved for only the *most favored* ones," replied Butterfly, with another wide smile of what appeared to be chest-protruding pride—but couldn't have been, given, as Thorn would soon learn, that angels cannot be self-satisfied.

Thorn thought it a dubious proposition, and it must have showed on his face, for Butterfly immediately followed his remark with another. "We are not able to fly very fast, and, as you also noticed, our landings are not very pretty, but we have carried without incident precious cargo much larger and heavier than you before, and we will carry you in comfort, I can assure you. If we leave tonight, we can be back with the children within a dozen hours or so."

"So," Thorn said, collecting his thoughts, "that sounds actually all very wonderful, but I cannot go with you at present because I am trying to find a friend of mine who is hurt, if not dead. He is a giant condor, and his name is Starnee, and he was helping me find the children when a large pack of predator birds—falcons, I think—attacked him and carried him away. I only know this because yesterday I saw the birds from a distance carrying a limp body that I knew to be Starnee's." Thorn then explained, in an abbreviated form, so as not to waste time, what had happened to him since he lost track of the children at the river.

"Well," said Butterfly, "let me consult with my colleagues and determine how we should proceed." Thereupon Butterfly huddled with the other four Cannotoad archangels. When the short—as in three second—meeting had concluded, Butterfly turned and said to Thorn, "We will leave a unit of twenty-five angels with you while the remainder of us divide into groups and try to locate your friend. When we have found him, we will do what we can for him, if anything, and bring you to him. Those angels remaining behind will protect you from everything that can harm you, I can assure you."

Within a minute, hundreds of Cannotoad angels lifted from the ground like slow, laboring helicopters and flew northward in a number of small and imperfect formations. Thorn, who was worried about whether his new friends would find Starnee and, if they did, whether they would find him alive, was also wondering at the same time how his *de facto* guardian angels were going to protect him from much of anything, much less from everything. He struck up a conversation with Weeplop, the only archangel left behind. "Weeplop, may I ask you a few questions about yourselves?"

"Of course," replied Weeplop, delighted to be asked. Weeplop hopped next to Thorn.

Thorn lay back on the grass and sorted out the questions in his mind. All of the angel toads but Weeplop closed their eyes and began to snore—or ribbit—softly. His first question was, "Why is Butterfly called Butterfly; it seems rather incongruous to me, given—how shall I say it, and with no offense intended—given how *indelicately* he lands?"

"That one is easy," replied Weeplop, with an indulgent smile. "That is his nickname, which reflects the opposite of how one thinks about him. It was given to him by the chief angel when he put Butterfly in charge of the rest of us as a way to remind him of the posture he is always to take in his relations with others: that of humility. It would be rather hard to be otherwise with a name like that, or so the argument goes. And it's not that the rest of us land more elegantly, but then, we are not the leader of the group."

Thorn was becoming a bit anxious over the apparent slumbering of all his protectors, and was glancing around to see if anyone else besides

Weeplop and him was awake as he posed his second question. "So, tell me, Weeplop, if you would: why are you called Cannotoad angels?"

"That one is easy, too. We are called Cannotoads because we are toads who, as angels, cannot do other than good."

"You mean, you *can't* do bad, even if you wanted to?" replied Thorn, with confused doubtfulness.

"No. I mean we cannot do bad of any sort, including *wanting* to do bad; we know only how to be and say and think and do good, which makes us exceedingly reliable, wouldn't you say?"

"Yes, but," Thorn offered, while his mind was spinning, "I can't understand how anyone could only *want* to do good."

"Well, by the same token," answered Weeplop, in a matter-of-fact tone, "I don't understand how anyone could want to do other than good. And I certainly don't understand how some can want *only* to do bad, which is true for more creatures than you might imagine."

"I'd say you are pretty lucky, then, Weeplop," concluded Thorn.

"Actually, being fortunate is more with you," answered Weeplop.

"How could that possibly be, Weeplop?"

"Because you are *free to choose.* Free to choose to be and do bad, and free to choose to be and do good. We don't have such freedom. We are not even free to *love*," said Weeplop, having to feign a tone of sadness because he didn't really know what that sort of sadness was, except that he assumed he would be sad if he were free to choose and could *experience* the inability—or refusal—to love that other creatures possessed.

"How can you not be free to love?"

"Because love is a choice. We, who have no choice, are simply good— or, shall I say, simply doing what would be called good, if we were able to choose." Weeplop cocked his head to one side and blinked. "I mean, it's hard to say I am actually good or doing good when I can't choose to do otherwise; but, that's the best explanation I can come up with." He glanced at Thorn for a look or word of understanding.

"But don't you choose all the time whether to do this or do that, and how to behave?" asked Thorn, really wanting to understand.

"Yes, we choose, Sir Thorn, but it's all in the context of what is already good."

"Well, then, my last question for now, Weeplop, is: how can all of you protect me from anything, and especially when it appears that everyone but you is asleep?" asked Thorn, more anxiously, being aware of all the possible dangers and no longer distracted by his intellectual curiosity.

"Oh, no, Sir Thorn—they are not sleeping; just meditating—just *being* good. If there is any sign of possible danger, they will be ready immediately to defend you against harm, I can assure you." Thorn wondered if Weeplop said, "I can assure you," simply out of habit.

"But, if you'll pardon me one more time, how *will* they protect me?" Thorn asked, again with a tone of skepticism.

"Our saliva, of course! It can cripple or kill any who are doing, or who are intending at the time to do, evil. Our tongues are able to strike at very great distances and leave whatever we touch with a moisture that is most toxic," answered Weeplop, confidently.

"What happens if you happen to strike someone or some creature that is *not* doing evil?"

At that moment Weeplop, Thorn, and the rest of the Cannotoads heard the sound of squadrons of toad angels approaching from just beyond the next hill, but still out of sight. "Here they are," said Weeplop, hopping toward the crest of the hill below which Thorn and he had been resting. "They will have news about Starnee—I can assure you!"

~TWELVE~

CHILDHEART EXPLAINED TO THE children that they would need to travel northward from now on to reach The Mountains beyond which they would find the castle of Queen Taralina—and the fortress of Sutante Bliss. He also said, to the children's dismay, that he would not be accompanying them, as he had the continuing vocation of loving the trees as long as he was able. As the young people started to protest, he assured them that there would be no further danger while they journeyed through the Forest of Lament. They were free to travel by day or by night, but he encouraged them to use one part of the day to rest—and to watch intently for any spies in the sky during the remainder of the day. He also told them that as they neared the base of The Mountains, they would encounter a river called Sleeping Guard (the children wondered if it would be the same one they had crossed to get to the Forest of Lament) that would divide the Forest from The Mountains, and so mark the end of the land over which he could provide protection. Once they crossed the river, they would be in the land of The Mountains, and so subject to all the forces and dynamics contained therein, with nothing that he knew of to assist them, except the Good. He added that they would easily find places to cross the typically slow and shallow river that would mark the end of the Forest to the north.

Before saying goodbye, Childheart gave them more than enough food to last until they reached The Mountains, and Elli posed a couple of additional questions that were weighing heavily on her mind. She first asked, "Childheart, how are we going to cross the mountains? And what is their name?"

Childheart pawed gently on the ground, as if he were writing something, shook his head, and then said, "Elli, I don't know how you are going to cross The Mountains. I have never been in The Mountains, much less crossed them, and I have met no one who claims to have done so. As far as a name is concerned, there is none, and to the best of my knowledge there has never been a name given to The Mountains, except, "The Mountains." No one has ever needed, or even wanted, before the rise of Sutante Bliss, to enter The Mountains. We name things we come to know. Because no one has ever known The Mountains, they remain otherwise nameless."

"Ewi, w . . . why don't we give The Mountains a name?" Alex asked enthusiastically.

"Alex, that's a good idea; and I think we will, once we get to know them," she answered, before turning her attention once again to Child-heart. "Childheart, I have one final question, and that is . . . " Elli paused, perhaps wondering if it were a question to which she actually wanted to know the answer. "That is, why did you question, when you mentioned the Good, whether it still exists or even ever existed?"

Childheart lowered his head and pawed once again at the ground, as if embarrassed to tell the truth. "Elli, I have only sensed the presence of the Good in the Queen. I have witnessed no other manifestation of it, except as an extension of the Queen. I would like to say simply that the Good *will* go with you, but I'm afraid I can't. Nevertheless, I do *hope* that you will travel in the will of the Good, regardless of what transpires—I hope you will forgive me if I have now said or done anything to hamper your journey."

"Childheart," said Elli, sympathetically, sounding almost like a loving parent, "you have done nothing but assist us on our journey, and for that we are forever grateful. And as far as believing in the Good is concerned, I have come to think that it is more important that I live *as if* the Good is guiding me, and hope my belief will follow the experiencing of its good-ness. Already, in fact, I have come to think that the Good not only exists, but is also with us, because there is no other satisfactory explanation I can think of for why any of us is here!"

Childheart, not knowing whether Elli was referring to every creature, or just to the four—or five—of them when she said "any of us," decided to depart from Elli and her friends simply pondering the question.

"Fare thee well," said Childheart. "I do wish and hope you find the Good in all that unfolds ahead of you. I already long to see you again."

"And, oh yes," he added, just as he was beginning to turn away from them, "beware the Den of Liars. I know little about them, but I have learned over time they consist mostly of Unpersons and that they try to trick journeyers into taking the incorrect way through the first mountain beyond the river—a way which, invariably, leads to death. I am told they *never* tell the truth."

"Fare thee well, Childheart," answered Elli. "And we hope also to see you again." When the others had said their goodbyes, Childheart turned and headed west through the trees, pausing here and there to nudge a branch or nose a leaf. At the same time, the children, following Elli, headed north.

The four continued their journey northward without incident for several days until they came to Sleeping Guard River, marking the end of the Forest of Lament. The water was low and the river narrow. They could easily step across in a matter of a few minutes. The foothills began just to the other side of the river. As the four of them stood and stared at the tall rocky face of The Mountains looming before them in the near distance, each of them was feeling that peculiar fear of the unknown about which one ought to be frightened.

It was early morning, the sun had not yet risen above the forest, and the children decided to take breakfast of what remained of the food Childheart had provided them. They ate in silence, all of them gazing across and up and down the other side of the river, wondering what the coming days would bring. The river gurgled around the stones visible above the water, and they could hear a number of birds chirping from trees well inland across the river, though none of the children would have described them as cheerful.

As the sun was peering above the trees to the east, Elli and her companions decided to head for The Mountains. The crossing was a bit wet for Beatríz who stumbled on the rocks, but otherwise uneventful. When they reached the other side they walked inland, leaving the sight of the river behind them in the dense thicket of bushes, tall weeds, saplings, and mature trees through which they struggled. The ground was dry, hard, and extremely uneven, with boulders of all sizes impeding their journey, including some as big as a house. When Elli saw Beatríz getting scratches on her face and arms, she stopped and decided that two of them would lead Beatríz, one hand in hand beside her, pushing away as much as possible the trailing foliage that Elli in the lead left behind and was unable to control.

By the time the sun was directly overhead, they had climbed to a long, narrow, and rather smooth plateau of flat rock. It was bare of flora except for a few grasses and wildflowers growing out of the cracks and crevices. On the whole, it was a pleasant place to stop and rest, perhaps even to stay for the remainder of the day and night. The remaining hours of light would give them a chance to explore along both sides of the plateau that skirted out of sight in opposite directions behind the hill's rocky face that gloomed before them. Elli and Beatríz stayed back to build a fire and prepare a meager supper from what was left in their knapsacks. Jamie and Alex decided to explore in tandem some distance in one direction along the plateau, and then turn around and explore roughly the same amount of distance in the other direction, time permitting before it was too dark.

A couple of hours later Alex and Jamie returned to the campsite and reported nothing noteworthy going east. They then headed west, as if following the lead of the sun. Perhaps three hours later, and just as the sun was dipping out of sight behind the tall grassy knolls beyond the Forest of Lament in the distant west, Alex and Jamie stepped back into view and, when they saw the other two companions, shouted, "Elli! Beatríz! Guys!"

Quickly the scouting party of two stood before the girls huffing and puffing, able to say no more until each had caught his breath. "There are two caves that seem to be tunnels of some sort not far from here," reported still-huffing Jamie. "They remind us a little of the tunnels underneath the Forest of Giant Trees; smaller tunnels branch off in other directions once you are inside, but they are made entirely of rock and very spacious, at least at the beginning. We went into both a short way, but saw nothing to indicate an end close by in either of them."

"They ah scaawy caves," added Alex.

"Why do you say that, Alex?" asked Beatríz.

"Because something made them."

"He's right about that, guys," said Jamie. "Something, or more likely some*one,* has made them. We saw all kinds of marks that indicated blasting or metal blades striking the rock, and it seems that a lot of the rock that was removed was dumped below the plateau, though not recently, as far as we could tell."

They spent a warm night on the flat rock under the stars, with a low fire and a restless Elli intermittently dozing, watching over them. In the morning, Elli roused the others just as it was light enough to see. All agreed they would eat something later. They still had as much as four days of food remaining, including some chestnuts from their trek eastward up and down the knolls, and a bit still from Childheart. They gathered up all their things and followed Jamie to the site of the caves. The sun had risen just above the trees when they arrived. They sat and discussed the caves as an option for continuing northward inasmuch as climbing the mountain immediately before them didn't seem feasible. Their only other option was to continue walking, either east or west, in the hopes of finding a better way up and into The Mountains—a slight valley perhaps, or some sort of rocky mass that wasn't too steep to climb. It was uncertain where the caves would lead them, but at least for a while they would take them northward. The one major caveat was that they could easily become lost, perhaps irrecoverably, in the apparent maze of tunnels branching out just inside the opening of each cave.

They decided to create a rope by weaving together vines and saplings, and that two of them would travel with the rope first into one of the caves and then into the other, as far as it would stretch. By late morning, they had a durable rope in excess of a hundred yards in length. Once again, Alex and Jamie would do the exploring while Elli and Beatríz remained behind to grip the rope—and keep a lookout for enemies of any sort—or, better, for friends. For the first thirty yards into the cave to the left, Elli and Beatríz could hear the voices of the boys talking to each other and could even communicate with them from the mouth of the cave. Beyond that distance all became suddenly and eerily quiet. Elli yelled for them, but received no reply. The only evidence to Elli and Beatríz of life at the other end of the rope was the vibration they felt as the two boys continued to uncoil and gently stretch their line.

Perhaps an hour had passed when Beatríz heard the sound of feet padding the ground softly not far away. She whispered her discovery to Elli who couldn't hear them. It was the sound of only two feet, as far as Beatríz could tell. Elli reached for her knife and put it into the top front of her skirt and beneath her shirt. She put a finger to Beatríz's lips and both sat as still as garden statuary. The sound grew louder so that Elli too could hear the footfalls approaching. Suddenly, from the east, a figure appeared, as if out of nowhere, and stopped, staring straight at the two girls, and looking ghostlier than any person Elli had ever seen. Elli recognized up close what she had only seen from a distance and in the dark some days before. And Childheart had warned about them. There was no mistaking it. It was an Unperson, without clothes and of indeterminate age. Even in its nakedness, Elli could not tell if it was male or female, although the body type appeared to be that of an older boy. It had the characteristic featurelessness of an Unperson's face.

Elli stood and faced the Unperson, lifting Beatríz to her feet as she did so. Elli noticed the faint outlines of eyes and ears and nose and mouth on the creature, but they were so blended into the rest of the face and head that she was certain they would have been invisible, or at least indefinable, in dusky light. Elli said nothing; and she was not afraid. She waited for the

Unperson to say the first words or otherwise to make the first move. The two stared at each other without facial expression, gesture, or words on the part of either for nearly two minutes. Finally, the Unperson spoke to Elli. Its voice had the muffled sound of one speaking behind a mask.

"I do not know who you are, but you want to go through the mountain, yes?"

"Perhaps. Why do you ask?" answered Elli.

"Because I can help you, and there is only one way through the mountain, so you need to choose wisely," the voice said, sounding as if the words had been rehearsed and spoken from rote.

"Why would you want to help us?" asked Elli, in a tone more of curiosity than of skepticism.

"Because we want all people to go through the mountain safely."

"And why would our safety concern you?" pressed Elli.

"Because we are good and care about everyone."

Of course, Elli and Beatríz knew they were speaking with one of those from the Den of Liars. Elli did not want the visitor to have any idea there were two friends already inside one of the caves, so she dropped the end of the rope and then got to her feet, being sure to stand firmly on it. She then said to the Unperson:

"Would you please tell me then which way is the way through the mountain?"

The Unperson pointed to the cave to the left and said, "You must go that way to get through the mountain."

Knowing from her conversation with Childheart that nothing the Unperson from the Den of Liars said was true, Elli assumed the cave to the right was the only possible way through the mountain. However, just to make certain (since she genuinely *wanted* to know), she fingered the bracelet and asked the question under her breath, "The cave to the right is the correct way through the mountain, is it not?" The amulet failed to glow, indicating that it was *not* the way through the mountain—an answer that, of course, puzzled Elli. If all the members of the Den of Liars could only lie, then it must be the case, she thought, that the cave to the left would not lead them through the mountain and that the only cave remaining—to the right—would be the correct one. She fingered the bracelet and repeated her question in a different word order, but it reaffirmed its original verdict in the absence of a glow. Elli then asked the silver bracelet whether the Unperson was telling the truth, and again it failed to glow, signaling that he was not, exacerbating Elli's confusion.

Trying hard to remember what Hannah had told them, Elli said to herself, "So, if the Unperson is lying when it says that the cave to the left is the way through the mountain, and it is not true that the cave to the right is the way through the mountain, then neither must be the way through the mountain, and we must look for another way." At that point, Elli saw a luminescent mist gathering behind and to the side of the Unperson. As she stared at it, the spectral form of Hannah appeared and spoke to Elli.

"Elli, one may say something that is accurate and factual, but still be lying, if the intent is to deceive. Truthfulness is always a *relationship* between one person and another involving thought, speech, or action. Deception is at the heart of all lying; lying is at the heart of all guile; guile is at the heart of all 'adultness'; and 'adultness' is at the heart of all that is evil."

"Hannah, where did you come from and how did you get here?" asked Elli, in a low voice of astonishment and wonder.

"Elli," asked Beatríz, in a whisper, "who are you talking to? Is Hannah actually here?"

"I don't know, Beatríz, but I can see her and she's talking to me," answered Elli.

Hannah replied, "Does it matter where I came from or how I got here?"

"But, Hannah," replied Elli, disconcertedly, wanting desperately to understand the moment, "are you really here, or am I just imagining you?"

"Dear girl," answered Hannah, now smiling at Elli, "is there really a difference, if it's all true?"

Hannah then added, while she was fading from sight, "Remember, only truthful people can speak and act the truth, and only that which is true is real."

"But, Hannah," said Elli, pleadingly. And then Hannah was gone, and Elli looked back at the Unperson.

"Elli, what did Hannah say to you?" asked Beatríz.

"Just this, I think: this Unperson is not telling the truth, but I believe the cave to the left will lead us through the mountain."

"But how can that be?" asked Beatríz, troublingly puzzled.

"Because while the Unperson is *stating* what is true, it wants us to *believe* that what it is telling us is false, and therefore is being *untruthful* while telling, in some fashion, the *truth*." Elli then spoke to the Unperson. "I believe you are telling the truth, and we will indeed try the way through the cave to the left."

At that point the Unperson became visibly distressed, and a vague look of terror appeared on its face, along with its oversized hands, which then covered it. Suddenly, from behind the Unperson, another much larger Unperson appeared, dressed in ragged clothing. It ran at the Unperson who had spoken to Elli, grabbed it around the neck from behind and thrust a knife into its chest. The smaller Unperson fell, crumpled, to the ground, and the slayer ran back into hiding just as Elli had pulled her own knife and was ready to attack it. Instead, Elli ran to the downed Unperson who, upon looking into Elli's eyes and seeing her knife, looked even more terrified than before, though already mortally wounded. Elli returned the knife to her skirt and knelt by the Unperson. She gently pulled the Unperson close, cradled its head in her lap and stroked it. She looked at the wound and saw that the strike had been deadly. The Unperson stared at Elli as she held its head, and its vague features began to relax and soften. With a look of disbelieving gratitude, the Unperson nuzzled against Elli's lean stomach and closed its eyes.

"Elli!" screamed Beatríz.

"It's okay, Beatríz!" Elli yelled back. "Another Unperson stabbed this one and then ran. The wound is to the heart. He can't hurt us now. I'm simply holding him until he dies."

"But, Elli, he wanted you dead, and lied to you so it would happen!" Beatríz shouted, more in confusion than anger.

"Perhaps," said Elli. "But, then, what a pathetically sad existence he's known—and could he really have known any better, or done any differently?"

That seemed to settle it for Beatríz. "Is it a male, Elli?"

"I don't know," said Elli, "but the Unperson already seems to me to be more of a person than it seems not to be."

Beatríz, following the sounds, walked to Elli, sat down beside her and stroked her hair. The two sat together with the Unperson for about half an hour before Beatríz started. "Elli! The rope!"

~THIRTEEN~

WHEN VIRTUALLY ALL OF the angels on the expedition had landed in a single—and not altogether elegant—descent, Butterfly reported to Thorn they had found Starnee, that he was in awful shape and near death, and that fifty angels were left behind to tend to him as best they could. Butterfly would take Thorn to him presently.

Thorn soon found himself carried on the wind by dozens of Cannotoad angels, all of whom either lifted him from underneath or pulled on him from other parts of his body, angel positions for transport made possible by wings that could reverse themselves. Hundreds of suction-cupped feet adhered to Thorn's body, enabling Thorn to feel both securely held and as if he were flying under his own power. Within minutes they had reached the spot at the top of a long and high hill where Starnee was located.

When they landed Thorn upright to avoid crushing the kind toads underneath, in front of him a very battered and bloody Starnee was lying motionless on the grass. He had bald spots where feathers had been torn from his body by the talons and beaks of the falcons, and the feathers on his head were matted with blood. There appeared to be no place on Starnee's body that had escaped the onslaught, and Thorn wondered how it was that Starnee could possibly have survived—and whether he was alive now.

All about him, as if in a fairy ring, were fifty Cannotoads protruding their tongues out and onto a multitude of wounds on Starnee's body. Some were working on the large bald areas in pairs or in groups of three, while others individually worked their way through the feathers to locate injuries. Some of the tongues were barely visible, so close to Starnee's body were some of the toads working, but others had launched their tongues great distances to find and reach the wounds, including places on one side of Starnee or the other that were beyond the sight of the toads who owned the tongues. And the sound was something you might expect from a hundred cats lapping up milk.

Thorn stood staring at the large patient and the many healers hard at work. He wondered how their saliva would not be toxic to Thorn; perhaps, he thought, they were only closing the wounds and readying the body for burial.

Butterfly suddenly hopped next to Thorn. "I know it must be tough to see, but I can assure you we've dealt with worse, and that your friend will be fine. The toads know what they're doing and consider their work a labor of goodness—a difference, I might add, that seems lost on so many creatures who can choose to do good. The same work perhaps, but a different outcome, or a better outcome, because it *is* a labor of goodness or, as it could be in your case, a labor of love. Very powerful and effective."

"Why," Thorn now asked, "is the saliva of these Cannotoads not toxic to my friend? Or is it a different saliva?"

"We all have the same saliva; and none of it is toxic unless we are dealing with creatures who are doing, or who seek to be doing, evil. The toxin comes from rejection of the healing and revivifying properties of not just the saliva, but also of the Cannotoads' goodness and their work. If you are one who seeks light, and wholeness, and goodness and love, then we can offer significant therapeutic assistance. Otherwise, those we help experience our assistance as something toxic. But, you've already had a long night, as have many of us," said Butterfly, sounding weary, "and so we urge you to get some sleep. You'll be entirely safe here. We'll awaken you in the morning. By that time Starnee should be his old self, whatever that was, and then we'll execute a plan for the next day or so."

Thorn stepped through the circle of Cannotoad angels and put a gentle hand on Starnee's brow. He then walked slowly away from his friend and lay himself down in a lone spot of tall meadow grasses, clasped his hands behind his head, and began to count the stars. When he had reached fifteen he was fast asleep.

Thorn felt a familiar nudge—and then heard a familiar voice. "Hey, Sticks! C'mon, wake up! You're wasting our time; we're ready to go!" shouted Starnee as he shoved Thorn with his beak.

Thorn sat up, startled, but smiling. "Oh my . . . oh my . . . I am so glad to see you, Starnee!"

"Well, that makes one of us!" said Starnee, cocking his head to one side to signal a tease. "Just when I thought the journey had ended it's only getting longer—and, who knows, maybe more difficult yet. C'mon over and talk with Butterfly and his officers; we need to get going."

Butterfly explained that he had arranged with Childheart to meet him back at the Forest of Lament, with an initial stop along the river where Childheart would either be there waiting or would have left a signal for them. If a signal, then they would travel inland due east from the spot he had marked. It was settled that the Cannotoads would take the lead and have Starnee bring up the rear with his ever-watchful eye. Butterfly gave Thorn the choice of being carried by either Starnee or the angels. Thorn pondered his two options briefly and said, without waiting for Starnee to offer an opinion, he thought it might be a relief for Starnee to fly without him for a day or so and let his wounds heal some more; therefore, Thorn would allow the Cannotoads to carry him. Starnee said nothing, and, as planned, they took off to the northeast for the roughly two day journey to the Forest of Lament.

~FOURTEEN~

Elli looked all over the ground quickly and frantically for the rope. "Beatríz! It's gone! Here! You hold the Unperson! I'll run into the cave and see if I can find it!" Elli disappeared into the cave. Beatríz heard Elli yelling deep inside for the boys, and then, immediately thereafter, she heard Elli running back to her. "It's gone—probably far into the cave, Beatríz!" Elli plopped down on the ground. "Oh, no! This can't be happening!" Elli cried, beginning to shed tears. "This can't be happening!"

Beatríz reached to wipe away Elli's tears even as her own began to fall. She also fingered the Unperson's face to wipe away any of her own tears that must have fallen on it as she continued to stroke its head. Something seemed different about the Unperson, however. "Elli. Elli—look. Look at the Unperson. It feels to me as if its features have begun to change a bit. What do you see?"

Elli glanced over at the Unperson and was surprised by what she saw, setting aside for a moment her preoccupation with finding Alex and Jamie. "Beatríz!" Elli said, as she moved closer to Beatríz and touched the Unperson's face. "His eyes and nose and mouth are more defined—and, and, his wound, Beatríz! His wound has stopped bleeding and seems to be closing—and he seems to be breathing better! Keep stroking him, Beatríz! I'm going to get a skin to cover him with—and then I'm going to start making a new rope. I've got to go in after the boys. Even if this *is* the way through the mountain that doesn't mean they can't also get lost *on* the way through. They still haven't returned, and it's been an hour and a half, at least judging by the sun. And besides, who knows what else they've encountered. I'd like you to stay with the Unperson as long as he is still alive, and also tend to the rope that I'll tie around a stake, okay? And I'll leave you my knife and take yours."

"Okay," replied Beatríz, as if it all made perfect sense. But, of course, nothing was going to make perfect sense in Bairnmoor, not for the time being, anyway—and perhaps never. What made sense to Beatríz was trusting Elli. And besides, Beatríz was now focused on her patient.

It took Elli several hours of feverish work to complete a second—and even longer—rope. The sun had now dipped once again behind the large hills on the other side of Hill Swamp River far to the west, and dusk had fallen fast and deep. Elli coiled the rope, tied the short end to a stake just inside the mouth of the cave, and then had Beatríz and the Unperson position themselves in the permanent shadows next to the stake.

"I think that's it, Beatríz. I'll find my way back no matter what using the rope, with or without the boys."

"But Elli, why don't you wait until morning? It's late and it has to be getting pretty dark; I've felt the chill of the sun's absence for a while now," said Beatríz.

"It's not going to matter, Beatríz, in the cave; and besides, I'm not going to be able to sleep anyway. And you'll be safer by yourself in the dark. I'll be sure to be back before daybreak, even if I haven't found the boys by that time." Then she added, reluctantly, "And if I don't return, leave the Unperson in the cave with some food, go carefully down the hill, and re-cross the river back to the Forest of Lament. Wait there in the trees for Childheart." With a promise from Beatríz, Elli left.

Beatríz sat with the Unperson, his head in her lap, and listened to him breathe in his unconsciousness. She continued to stroke his face while she considered her circumstances. It was only days ago that all were together and feeling an incipient sense of providence, albeit unaccountably so. Now, she sat alone—with an enemy—all her companions and friends met along the way no longer present; not one of them. She doubted she'd see Thorn again. She doubted she'd see all of her companions again, hoping against hope that at least one of them would return. She decided she would have preferred to have herself gone missing, and even be dead, to having everyone else gone. But, as pessimistic as she felt, she hung onto a pearl of hope as if it were the only thing palpably left of all that she had been and done—and of her life with the others. Could the Good—if it, or he, or she, existed—work all this out for the good? For everyone's good? She wondered.

Beatríz dozed with her head against the rock wall and one hand resting on the rope at the stake while, the entire time she slept, she continued to caress the Unperson's face and body with the other hand. It was not clear how long she had been asleep, but was awakened to what she at first thought was the voice of Elli getting closer with as yet muffled and indecipherable words. Immediately upon being fully roused, she realized that the voice was coming from the Unperson, and that he was not lying next to her any longer.

"Why did you save me?" asked the Unperson, in words now clearer and sounding more sincere than before.

"Where are you?" asked Beatríz, nervously.

The Unperson reached for Beatríz's hand and held it. "But, why did you save me, and what is your name, and who are you?" the Unperson asked again.

"Please. Let me see your face, and then I'll answer you as best I am able." Beatríz scooted herself forward and reached her hand toward the Unperson's head, ever so carefully and tentatively. The Unperson took gentle hold of her hand and placed it on his face. What Beatríz "saw" with her fingers simply amazed her. It was as if all of his features were now as clearly located on his face as were her own, and she was even more amazed to realize she was "seeing" directly in front of her a very young—and a very handsome young—man, perhaps not much older than she.

She spoke again: "My name is Beatríz, and I come from another kingdom you know nothing about, just as I knew nothing about your kingdom until a few weeks ago, when my companions and I found ourselves very suddenly and inexplicably in your land. I did not know I was saving you; my friend, Elli, and I simply wanted to show you some kindness before you died. But I am so very happy you have lived. Are you still hurt?"

"No. Your love has healed me, inside and out, and, at least for the time being, I am no longer an Unperson. I'm not at all certain what I am, but an Unperson I am no longer, and I have only you and your friend to thank."

"And what is your name?" Beatríz asked, still feeling his face and finding herself unwilling to remove her hand, as if by removing it his face might disappear. She hesitated and then asked, "And why are you part of the Den of Liars?"

"I know they used to call me 'Kahner,'" he replied, "but I have not been called that for many, many years—really, not since before my actual memory of being a person." Kahner became quiet for a while. He then told Beatríz all he could remember, which wasn't a whole lot: that he had been brought by armed creatures while he was still very young to this place, to be brought up by the Den leaders, all of whom are Unpersons; that he must have had a family of some sort of whom he has no memory; that he has been trained to think and act like an Unperson for many, many decades, owing until this moment full allegiance to the "great and marvelous Sutante Bliss"; and that, accordingly, he had lost his independence of mind, his capacity to feel with his heart, his imagination, his sense of right and wrong, and therefore his personhood, together with all of the features that are associated with being a person, both inside and out. Only *now*, thanks to Beatríz, was he beginning to experience what it was like once again to be a person. That was all he could recall for Beatríz. So he asked, "So, why are you in Bairnmoor?"

"All I can say to you, Kahner, is what we have said to everyone else we have met who has asked, and that is: we are children from another world and have in some way been brought here to accomplish something—maybe an impossible something." Beatríz then recounted to him all that had happened to them to the very point of Kahner's encounter with Elli. When she had finished, Beatríz asked, "Why did that other Unperson try to kill you?"

"Because my lying did not work—you chose the tunnel that I did not want you to choose; if anyone's lies ever fail to be effective, that Unperson is eliminated by the executioner of the Den—who is always near." He then explained how he had tried to deceive them, confirming Elli's theory, and how, to his considerable regret, her friends may now be lost.

"But, I still don't understand, Kahner: if we chose the cave that contains the only way through, then why do you say that my friends may be lost?" asked Beatríz, now becoming petrified with fear.

"Because I deceived you twice. The only way through The Mountains is the known way, even though it is located only in the cave to the left. The double deception ensures that people who enter the caves will perish there, regardless of which one they choose. The chances of your friends finding the one way amidst the numerous tunnel options and without becoming a victim of the vast maze beneath the mountain—and perhaps Blackfire—are almost nonexistent," Kahner said, with reluctance in his voice.

"What is this maze you speak of, Kahner, and who or what is Blackfire?" asked Beatríz, who felt she was about to go crazy.

"It is an actual maze, built by the dragon, Blackfire, reportedly, and in the center of which, if it even has a center, Blackfire supposedly lies in wait for any 'lost ones' to kill—and maybe eat," Kahner added hesitantly. "I have never seen the dragon—no one has. There are, however, numerous stories of burned bodies being discovered in various parts of the cave, often with nothing left on their bones, and of a few who have escaped and lived to tell about losing their limbs and being horribly burned by fire from a source they could not see. These caves, and The Mountains containing them, may be the only place in the whole kingdom of Bairnmoor that Sutante Bliss does not rule."

"Why do you call the dragon Blackfire?" Beatríz asked quickly.

"Everyone has called it 'Blackfire' since before time, or so the legend goes; it is said its fire is so much hotter than any other that it burns its own light, which is black, and that it can burn anything into, well, into nothing at all—as if the thing never existed in the first place. It is also said that the dragon is as old—or, as eternal—as 'the Good,' and that there is great antagonism between them. Why any Good that might exist would allow such an evil creature to exist is incomprehensible—at least to me."

"Do you believe in the Good, then?" asked Beatríz, hopefully.

"I don't know that I do—or that I don't," said Kahner. "I don't know if I believed in the Good when I was young or not. It has been, like the story of Blackfire, only a legend, and certainly of no consequence to me or to my existence as an Unperson."

"You are so different, Kahner, and not at all like the Unperson we first encountered—I don't understand it," said Beatríz.

"It's because I *am* a different person, Beatríz. I was nobody, and now I am somebody. I did not exist before—no, I couldn't have. You see, it's as if you *loved me into being*."

He added, "I belong to you, now, Beatríz. Please, tell me what I can do for you in return for your goodness shown to me."

"Well, first, I want you to belong to yourself, not to me, and second, I want you to help me, if you possibly can, to find my three friends who are somewhere in this cave, including Elli, who took the other end of this rope that is tied to the stake."

"I see the stake, Beatríz, but I do not see the rope, except a remnant of one that is only about ten feet long; it seems to have been broken at that point," said Kahner.

"Oh no! Oh no, Kahner!" cried Beatríz, putting her hands to her face and covering her eyes.

"It doesn't matter, Beatríz—really, it doesn't. I know the way through this particular mountain, to the Valley of Plenty on the other side, and much of the maze as well. And I can see in the dark very well, so I will be able to follow their tracks. We'll find your friends, as long as Sutante's forces—or Blackfire—haven't found them before we do.

"But we should go now, Beatríz; we have a lot of ground to cover, and we will need to proceed rather slowly so we don't miss any signs of your friends trailing off from the only way through."

"Kahner," Beatríz said, almost interrupting him, "Elli told me in no uncertain terms that if she did not return by morning, which I believe it is now, I was to return to the Forest of Lament and wait for Childheart. I promised her I would do as she ordered. I know you know the way, and that Elli had no idea we'd be having this conversation, but I think we should do as Elli instructed me."

Kahner tensed and looked worriedly at Beatríz, and as if he were trying to formulate a reply that would persuade her to change her mind. But he smiled, and relaxed, and said simply, "Of course, as you wish."

In no time at all, Beatríz and Kahner were on their way back to Sleeping Guard River and, on the other side, the Forest of Lament. Kahner held Beatríz's hand with a firmness she had never known in any other hand before—not even her father's. And Kahner moved so much more easily and quickly around and over the rocks—and through the brushes and bushes and trees—than did she and her companions. Yet not once did a branch touch her face; not once did she stumble; not once did she grab something hurtful.

By the time the sun was directly overhead, Beatríz was ready for the coolness of the water, regardless of how deep they might find it. She was feeling unpleasantly hot and sweaty on the outside, but pleasantly cool and secure on the inside. Just as she had experienced other sensations and emotions for the first time during her time in Bairnmoor before encountering Kahner, so Beatríz was experiencing a whole new set of emotions and feelings for the first time ever since she met Kahner only a day earlier. All of them were in some measure to be treasured, each in its own way, even the hard and horrible and sad ones.

Just past noon, the sun still high and the two seemingly alone under the bright blue sky, Kahner and Beatríz reached the river. It had grown some since she was last there, and the water was now about knee deep and forty yards across. The bottom, as before, was strewn with smooth rocks of various sizes and shapes, many of them concealed below the water. When she mentioned she had acquired the bruises visible on her legs from stumbling in the earlier crossing, Kahner said he would solve that problem by simply carrying her across. With her arms about his neck, and her head resting against his lean shoulder, Kahner carried Beatríz across the river to the Forest of Lament. (The only lamentable aspect of the entire crossing, as far as Beatríz was concerned, was that it lasted such a short time.)

Since Beatríz had no idea where to locate Childheart, and it was just past noon in a bright sun, the two decided to rest, at least for the time being, under the canopy of a large tree, its cascading branches encircling them nearly to the ground. Indeed, shortly after settling down, Beatríz recommended they stay where they were and simply wait for Childheart— who had found her the first time, and at night. And so they slept from sheer exhaustion, Beatríz's head resting against Kahner's shoulder as if they had been friends for a very long time.

Several hours later, with the sun no longer visible through the trees, but not yet set, Kahner built a fire and went to the river to catch a couple of fish. Beatríz remained behind and stayed alert for the presence of Childheart. Once Beatríz and Kahner had eaten, they lay down next to each other and tried to get some more sleep. Kahner stretched out an arm so that Beatríz could lay her head on it. In a matter of minutes, Beatríz was deep asleep, and peacefully so. Kahner stayed awake simply to mull over in his still rusty brain all that he had just experienced that day, the plight of Beatríz's friends, the story of Beatríz's journey, where exactly he had come from, and what the future might hold. A light breeze, as if out of nowhere, but as if it were a live and knowing breeze, began to sway the branches and rustle the leaves. Kahner reached for one of the serpentine branches rocking gently just above him and began to stroke it; the leaves felt good in his hands, and he continued to caress them until, as had Beatríz and the others before him, he began to hear a light—almost symphonic—sound, not unlike that which might be produced by thousands of stringed instruments lightly bowing. He listened carefully, wondering if he hadn't heard this sound before, but he could recall nothing of the sort from his past. It was as much a wistful lullaby as anything else, and it was soothing, even though the tune was pensive and somewhat sorrowful. Kahner had never before heard anything so beautiful. He whispered to Beatríz: "Beatríz! Beatríz! Wake up!"

Beatríz stirred and opened her eyes, turning to look at Kahner who was staring down at her. She smiled. "What, Kahner?"

"Can you hear the beautiful music, Beatríz? What do you think it is?"

Beatríz replied quietly in a relaxed, contented voice. "It's the trees, Kahner." She explained to him eveything she learned about the Forest of Lament from Childheart. "The trees must feel comfortable with you; I think they are singing and playing for you, Kahner," Beatríz said with another smile while looking toward Kahner's eyes. They remained "looking at each other" for quite some time, although it seemed as if no time had passed whatsoever, when the porcelain stillness was broken by Childheart, who appeared suddenly and noisily next to the fire as if by magic. They turned to look at Childheart, and Beatríz exclaimed immediately upon hearing him approach,

"Oh, Childheart!" Beatríz began to sob uncontrollably.

"It's quite alright, Beatríz," Childheart replied soothingly. "I am glad to see you as well, dear girl. But, I do not know your new companion, and it troubles me to see none of the others with you. Is that why you are crying?"

Beatríz nodded, still weeping.

Childheart turned his head ever so slightly and looked at Kahner. "Well, then, would you please tell me who you are and, if you know, what has happened to the others?"

Kahner recounted to Childheart all he learned from Beatríz about what had occurred since the four children had left Childheart, including his confrontation with the two girls. Shortly after Kahner began to speak, Beatríz stopped crying and laid her head against his shoulder, occasionally sniffling and heaving a sigh. At times she would offer a word or two, or nod when she wanted to emphasize something that Kahner was saying. When Kahner had finished, Childheart said to both of them, "I am profoundly saddened by the news, but I am exceedingly happy that you are both here, and I remain hopeful that the others—all of the others, including Thorn—yet live and continue to have an important part to play in this strange business."

"What are we supposed to do, Childheart?" asked Beatríz, imploringly.

"I don't have the foggiest idea what you are *supposed* to do, Beatríz, but I can tell you what I think would be advisable, at least from my perspective," said Childheart. Beatríz's eyes encouraged Childheart to continue, please.

"First of all, dear children, I have already begun a search for your friend, Thorn, outside of the Forest. I approached some angels I know and requested their assistance."

"*Angels?*" exclaimed Beatríz. "There are angels in the Forest of Lament?"

"Well, no, not exactly. It just so happened that I saw them encamping near the river two days ago. And while we have not seen each other for many decades, I felt certain they would want to help once they heard your story. As I speak, they are searching for Thorn, and I have little doubt they will find him, regardless of his circumstances or condition. It may take some time, though, especially if Thorn is in some woods somewhere and not able—or willing, for some reason—to signal his presence to them."

"Childheart, thank you so much. If they find Thorn, what will they do with him?" Beatríz asked.

"They will bring him to me, at least initially," said Childheart. "After that, we'll have to see—how things are, and how he is."

"Childheart, will Thorn be able to see the angels—and would *we* be able to see them if they were here in front of us?" Beatríz asked, with that sort of curiosity that is often a respite from abiding sorrow.

"Oh my, yes, and you may have seen them already without realizing it," said Childheart.

"What do they look like, and how can we know who they are if we see them? Do they have wings, and are they rather small?" asked Beatríz. "And," she added, uncertainly, but suggesting to Childheart the expected answer, "are they beautiful?"

"They do have wings, Beatríz, and they are actually quite small. And I and others, and perhaps Thorn, should they have found him already, think them beautiful, but you will not know them as angels even if you see them, unless that is their purpose," he said. Childheart blew through his mouth and shook his long white mane. "But we must attend to what's next for the two of you now."

Childheart lay down on his stomach. The fire was dying out and the stars above shone as if it were their first night to appear, each one trying to outshine the other. Kahner got up and put a few more logs on the smoking, barely visible embers. Almost immediately, hidden flames rose from the ash, curled about the logs and licked them hungrily.

"I would like you to remain here for another day. If Thorn does not arrive by then, I will advise you one way; if he does, I will advise you another way. I must be about other business for the remainder of the night, but I will check back with you sometime during the day—and well before dark. Try to rest if you can; I'll bring with me fresh food and drink." Childheart was quiet for half a minute, and then he abruptly got to his feet, stared momentarily into the fire, and trotted off, disappearing quickly into the fluttering woodland shadows and in the direction of the river to the west, the river that the four companions had crossed several days earlier on the backs of turtles. Kahner and Beatríz settled back down for the remainder of the night and slept until daybreak, awakening to the sound of Childheart's sudden, rapid and loud reappearance.

"Beatríz! Kahner! I see they've found Thorn. They will be here short-ly!" Beatríz and Kahner could hear in the sky an approaching drone.

~FIFTEEN~

WITHIN SEVERAL MINUTES THE droning of the angels was directly over-head, and both Childheart and Kahner noticed it came in the shape of what Childheart knew to be Thorn. But it was a Thorn with something that looked, high above them, like moving flesh, with lots of small pieces of tissue fluttering nearby, as if tethered by threads to Thorn's body. As the cloud of angels descended slowly through the trees, Kahner described to Beatríz what they could scarcely believe was transpiring. The Cannotoad angels settled Thorn to the ground in an upright position, all three specta-tors greeting with unbridled delight Thorn's wide-open eyes and as wide a smile as he could possibly muster with his short, thin lips.

"Thorn!" Beatríz exulted, as she ran toward the arrivals, her arms opened wide. The Cannotoads pulled back and allowed the two of them, shedding free-flowing tears of joy, to embrace—which they did for a long time, saying to each other repeatedly only, "Oh, Thorn!" and "Oh, Beatríz!"

When Thorn and Beatríz had had their initial fill of mutual affection, Childheart had everyone sit about the low fire. He introduced Kahner and Beatríz to the Cannotoads, introduced Kahner and himself to Thorn, and then had Thorn tell his story of all that had happened since the night he became separated from all four children. Then Beatríz spoke. During this time Childheart distributed baskets of food and drink sufficient to satisfy everyone, although Beatríz thought that whatever it was the Can-notoads were eating was gross, mostly because she could tell their meal was moving.

Suddenly, there was a peace-shattering screech from above.

"Oh my! Oh my!" exclaimed Thorn. "Starnee! We forgot all about Starnee!" Following Thorn's lead, everyone looked up, and, sure enough, there was Starnee, situated comfortably in one of the tall trees nearby, un-able to reach the ground because there was not enough clearing for the condor to land.

Thorn, profusely apologetic, introduced Starnee to Beatríz, Kahner, and Childheart. Starnee was more amused than annoyed by their neglect of him, and seemed genuinely perturbed only by Thorn's decision to have the Cannotoads carry him to the Forest of Lament instead of riding on Starnee's back.

With Starnee now part of those assembled, Childheart spoke again, this time so Starnee did not have to strain to hear. His plan was that the three original companions, including Starnee, should not under any circumstances become separated. Accordingly, Childheart advised that Beatríz and Thorn ride on Starnee above The Mountains to the other side of the caves and from that vantage point attempt to find one or more of the three children who were last seen going into The Mountains. Starnee did not know if he could fly that high, but he would certainly try; if he failed, according to Childheart's instructions, he was to return to where the Cannotoads would encamp themselves near the caves.

"But," interjected Beatríz, her face flushed and sad and her voice full of perturbation. "But, what about Kahner, Childheart? We cannot leave him here—and *I* will not leave him here alone, regardless of anyone else. Kahner can come with Thorn and me."

Childheart reared up sharply, frightening everyone except Starnee. He shook his mane twice, and then he pawed the ground, as if he were writing thoughts to himself. "Beatríz," Childheart finally said, in a voice that was as relaxed as Beatríz's was not. "I have no intention of recommending that Kahner remain behind and alone. But that is quite another matter at the moment. What concerns me is your insistence not only on your own way, but for your own sake, and not out of a fundamental concern for the rest of the mission party, nor out of concern that you try to do what it is that the Good would want you to do—and therefore what is best." Kahner said nothing and was expressionless during the conversation between Childheart and Beatríz.

"But, Childheart," protested Beatríz, "it *is* out of concern for everyone—and I mean, *everyone*—that I will not leave Kahner behind alone, or, really, behind at all. It wouldn't be right."

"Beatríz," Childheart said again, followed by a moment of intended silence, "it would no doubt be good to take Kahner with you, or good for you to remain behind with him, but it may not be for the best. I dare say, Beatríz, that your standard for what is good here has more to do with you and Kahner than it does with anyone or anything else, including 'the Good.'" Beatríz's face began to redden. Childheart continued.

"I had a dream last night, Beatríz, and because of that dream I have decided that I will leave the Forest of Lament and help you find your friends. This is not what I want to do. I love these trees more than anything or anyone else, and I do not want to leave them. Indeed, once I leave the Forest I may not ever return. Yes, it would be good to stay, for the trees and for me, but it would not be for the best, and could even in the long run be the very worst thing for me to do. It was clear in the dream what *I wanted* to do; but, it was also clear in the dream what *I was being called* to do, and the two do not presently coincide. I am telling myself one thing; the Good, or what I will consider to be the Good, is telling me another. And so I believe for you, Beatríz."

"But," Beatríz added, as if there were another—more subtle—way to persuade Childheart of her position. "How do you know it was the Good speaking to you—I thought you didn't know if the Good still existed, or if it ever existed, apart from the Queen, who is now dead?"

"I don't *know*, dear child, whether the Good exists, but what I can tell you are three things that favor my recommendation: I know my own voice of what I want; and I also know of another voice that is telling me what I ought to do; I know that my voice puts me first, and that the other voice is putting not itself but consideration of everyone first; and, third, that that same voice in the dream showed me precisely how we are to divide up ourselves. I don't *know*, Beatríz," Childheart repeated, "that the Good exists and is the voice I heard, but to behave as if it were the Good speaking to me would be the most *faithful* thing for me to do. Concern for others is always good, no matter the consequences or errors. However, primary concern for oneself and one's own wants is *always* an error in judgment. But, Beatríz," Childheart said, and then after a lengthy pause concluded, "it is your decision to make." Childheart then waited patiently for Beatríz to speak—who was considering Childheart's surprising words.

"I apologize, Childheart. I'll do as you say, in part because Elli told me to go to you should she not return, and I agreed to do so. I also will do as you say, because apart from you and your recommendations, Childheart, I have no idea what I otherwise *ought* to do. If I must leave Kahner, I will be devastated, but I see now that there are worse things than that, and that I am not the one who should make this judgment. But," she continued hesitantly, "I don't understand why you will not be able to return to the Forest of Lament once you leave it, Childheart!"

"That explanation will have to wait for another time, Beatríz."

Childheart said Kahner and he would go into the caves together, with Kahner riding him and pointing out the way. To try to reach the others on foot at this juncture would be futile, he said. A small number of Cannotoads would do reconnaissance regarding the enemy's operations in the area, but most of them would wait along the river outside the caves, their presence stretching for some distance both east and west, and so preventing anyone else, whether friend or foe, from approaching the caves. The plan for all who were traveling, if possible, was to try to meet just outside the caves, wherever they exited on the other side of the first set of mountains. If, after a reasonable length of time waiting outside the caves, the two groups were not able to meet, Childheart said they should each continue their journey north alone over the remainder of The Mountains, with or without Elli and the two boys, hoping to find one another again.

The entire assembly then prepared to disperse. Childheart, Kahner, and the Cannotoads would head north for the caves, while Thorn and Beatríz would make their way west to the river where they would meet Starnee and mount him from the trees by the water's edge. All said their goodbyes and well-wishes. Beatríz hugged Childheart's neck; he kissed her cheek.

Lastly, while the rest of the traveling party waited patiently off to the side, Beatríz and Kahner embraced, whispering to each other private words of separation and dreams. Their tears of joy and sorrow, flowing freely, mingled as Beatríz caressed Kahner's cheeks with her own. And then they stepped back from each other, said nothing more, reached their fingers for a final touch, and departed.

~SIXTEEN~

"It's vewy, vewy dahk in hew," said Alex to Jamie when they had walked for about thirty yards into the mouth of the left cave, unraveling the vine rope as they went, each holding onto it and letting it fall behind them on the soft powder that layered the stone path. The idea was to keep walking until they had completely unraveled the coil and then carefully stretch it against Elli's grip outside the cave. Alex's fear was less for the dark than it was for the winding nature of the path, which almost immediately upon entering the cave began to branch off into several different directions, each alternative route continuing the branching, not unlike the spreading limbs of a tree. By the time they had advanced perhaps seventy-five yards into the cave they had entered more than a dozen different branches. Their initial expectation, quickly disabused, was that the main cavern run would be noticeably, if not markedly, larger than its tributaries, perhaps comparatively straight as well, but oddly, Jamie thought, all of the tunnels were serpentine and of roughly equal size. The one advantage, if it could really be such, was that all of the passageways were exceedingly wide and tall, as if built for an army and its armaments to pass through.

As they walked slowly and with careful steps, clinging to the side of the passageway, they didn't realize they were now not only carrying the vine coil, but slowly dragging the vine tail itself, Elli having let go of the rope when she stood to face the Unperson not long after the two had entered the cave. The silence was complete, like the darkness, and when they spoke there was never an echo, as if they were traveling round and round in an enclosed circular passage with thick wooden walls. For the first time since they entered the cave, Jamie felt as if the cavern were some sort of catacomb, but there was no evidence of this, and he certainly said nothing to Alex. Jamie felt the urge to hold his knife before him, but thought better of it when he realized that if he dropped the knife he might lose it forever.

Jamie suddenly stopped. "Well, Alex, that's the last of the coil. Let's start pulling on it gently and find the point of tension; we'll then know how much slack we still have to travel some more—although my guess is that, regardless, we are not going to find anything just up ahead that's remarkably different from what we've already discovered. Probably just more of the same." The two of them pulled on the vine and learned, to their amazement, that they were gathering in numerous feet of slack. Finally, after bringing in almost fifty feet of vine, the rope would give no more. "Well, Alex, we've got quite a bit of additional vine to work with, so we may as well use it." But, as Jamie had reasonably suspected, the additional feet of exploratory rope gave them only additional feet of the same passageway.

"I think we should go back now," said Alex, his voice thick with trepidation, when they had used the entire length of vine. "Thew is eviw in hew, Jamie."

Jamie shuddered. "Why do you say that, Alex?"

"Becuz the dahkness is eviw, vewy eviw, Jamie."

"Well, we need to head back anyway; that was the plan when we ran out of rope," Jamie answered, not wanting to explore Alex's thought any further since there was nothing they could do about it anyway. Alex lifted the rope while Jamie coiled it back up as the two of them headed back toward the mouth of the cave. They traveled in reverse much more swiftly and came quickly to a startling discovery: the rope, about halfway down its length, was caught on a jagged piece of cavern wall. Alex did not understand the significance of the discovery, but Jamie felt the chill of death down his spine. When he lifted the rope from what had snagged it, he learned what he had feared most—that the only tension on the rope had come from its being snagged; there was no tension beyond that from the hand of Elli. Jamie took the lead and continued to coil the rope as they retraced their steps. Just as he feared, he came to the end of the rope, the two of them still well into the cave. "Alex, this is the end of the rope, and we are far from the mouth of the cave where Elli and Beatríz are sitting. We're going to have to try to get back without using the rope."

"I don't undustand, Jamie. Whew is Ewi and Butweece?" asked Alex.

"For some reason, Alex, Elli let go of the end of the rope. Something must have happened to them, because Elli would never have willingly let go of it," replied Jamie. "So we'll have to be careful to make sure we retrace our steps and not get lost on the way back."

The immense challenge now, as Jamie knew well, was to keep to the side of the cave going back and be able to discern when they were still on the course they had taken going in, avoiding the same branching off they had avoided earlier and not mistakenly take a branch that was not part of the initial route. A single false move could possibly doom them, but he kept such knowledge, like his fear, to himself.

The two of them bypassed three separate branches on their way back that Jamie was certain they had avoided earlier. However, it wasn't long before the inevitable happened: a fourth branch—one that left Jamie in doubt. He could not recall whether they had turned here at the wall or not, and the more he struggled to remember his steps at this critical junction the more doubtful he became. Alex clung to Jamie's shirt with both hands, ensuring that he would not lose Jamie even if they together lost their way.

Suddenly, the boys heard a high pitched voice calling for them, seemingly far away, as if from another world. "Alex! Jamie! Alex! Jamie!"

"Ewi!" Alex yelled back. "Hwew ah you?"

"Elli! We're over here! Can you hear us?" shouted Jamie.

"Jamie! I hear you! But barely! Where are you? Are you okay?" Elli, answered, feeling the most hopeful and happy she had felt in days.

"We're fine, Elli, but I can't tell you where we are! Stay there! I think I know where your voice is coming from, so we'll try to come to you! Just keep calling for us!" yelled back Jamie, against silence and darkness that felt to Jamie like conspirators determined to hold them.

"Alex! Jamie! Alex! Jamie! Alex! Jamie!" Elli repeated rhythmically, as if she were a small sharp bell tolling endlessly on a rolling merchant ship buffeted by constant wind. "Alex! Jamie! Alex! Jamie!" After a minute or so, Elli yelled, "Jamie! Where are you now? Are you getting closer?" But she received no reply. "Aaaaaalex! Jaaaaamie!" she yelled, frantically. The silence was palpable, like a stone rolled across the mouth of a tomb, shutting everything in and everything out. Elli struggled to maintain her mental stability. She could return to Beatríz and the Unperson as she had planned to do, with or without Alex and Jamie. But she was too close to finding them now to leave off the search.

"Beatríz! Can you hear me? I've found the boys!" Elli yelled. She waited. But there was nothing from Beatríz either. Elli recalled that she had instructed Beatríz to go back to the Forest of Lament were she not to return by morning, but Elli had lost track of time entirely. She did not know if she had been in the cave for two hours or ten. Elli began to walk once again in the direction of her companions' voices, continuing to call for them without answer while still uncoiling what little remained of her rope. Soon, Elli had uncoiled the rope completely. She continued on, gripping tightly to her end of the rope, dragging it as she went, and expecting any moment tension from the stake. Elli knew something awful had happened to her friends in the cave not far away, and so she drew her knife, ready to strike.

And then what had no doubt happened to Alex and Jamie, and without warning, Elli slipped on the powdery floor of the passageway that dipped sharply downward, and she began to slide, swiftly and uncontrollably. She yelled for the boys as she slid, and tried futilely to stop herself by attempting to dig her heels into the hard, smooth floor that carried her deeper and deeper—or, was it, somehow, higher and higher—into the depths of The Mountains.

As Elli flew down or up in the dark tunnel at a tremendous speed, she felt no longer that there was anything at all on which she was sliding. As if speeding air were escorting her, she felt no rush of wind. And then, whether Elli was becoming accustomed to the light, or the light was becoming accustomed to her, the darkness began to recede. Like the invisible powder on which she had been walking on the passageways, there was now what seemed like a visible powder that was parting like the Red Sea in front of her as she flew into it. The billowing dust flashed into view just before reaching her hurtling body and roiling around her, shimmering like the ground that glimmered in the starlight on that night when she became separated from Thorn. Soon, when the iridescent powder was flying past her, it created thin, overlapping sheets of continuous soft light, so fast was she—or the dust, or both of them—traveling. Elli felt weightless and without any sense of direction, but saw all around her what looked like the brightest stars she had ever seen whizzing past. Finally, the dust completely encircled her as she traveled through this strange space of darkness and light, with nothing illuminated by the light except her own body.

Elli had no idea how long she had been traveling, but all of a sudden she was beginning to fly directly into the powder that like a benign soft wind slowed her down, cushioning her fall to the very end. She hit the ground as if—well, as if—there weren't any; she simply stopped moving and found herself sitting in what she might best describe as stardust. It completely covered her, but she had no difficulty seeing and breathing and moving in the dust. She stood up. She surfaced above the dust, and stood in the midst of something that she knew she was unable to describe to anyone else. The closest she could come to putting it into words was by thinking of being inside a giant black gemstone that radiated light, which shimmered and pulsed and varied in intensity, as if it were something alive and ever-gloaming. The inner surface of both floor and walls was smoother than any material she had ever seen or touched, and she was standing in the middle of a vast tubular tunnel that extended itself in both directions, with no ends in sight.

Then Elli heard a roar that the blackness itself seemed to generate, at the same time terrible and awesome, and so loud that she was certain her eardrums would shatter. She was trying to determine where the roaring was coming from when it abruptly stopped. Elli waited silently, looking and listening. When she neither heard nor saw anything further, she yelled, trembling from both fear and wonder, "Hello! Who's there? I'm not afraid of you!" Then, with a combination of both fear and hope suddenly stirring within her, Elli heard Alex and Jamie yelling.

"Elli! Elli! We're right here! We're trapped!"

"Ewi! We ah hew!"

"Where is 'right here?' Jamie?" Elli cried out, desperately, looking this way and that.

"I don't know, Elli—I don't know!" Jamie yelled back. "All I know is that we're floating in some sort of dust that shines; we aren't hurt, but we can't touch bottom—and we can't move!"

Elli looked immediately behind her at the pool of stardust. "I think I know where you are! I'll try to reach for you!" Ellie got down on her hands and knees and was about to penetrate the powder when she saw her shadow in sharp outline against the dust from a bright light that had come up behind her. She stood and turned around.

"That will never do!" bellowed a voice from the dazzling light in the distance that was streaming at her. The white light was so big and bright that Elli was unable to see its source.

"Step away from the stardust and approach me!" the voice commanded.

"But I don't know what I'm walking toward—I can't see!" Elli yelled back.

"Come forward!" ordered the voice. Elli began walking toward the blinding light that, surprisingly, did not hurt her eyes. As she walked, the light began to dim and to continue to do so until she saw in front of her, perhaps twenty yards away, a dragon. It was a dragon that was as tall as the biggest building in Millerton, its tail perhaps thirty yards long. It had a head that resembled that of a horse, but with two inordinately large eyes that occupied the entire width of the top of its forehead. But perhaps most startling of all, the dragon was emanating light from every spot on its body, including the crown of spikes along its back that stretched to its tail, the talons on its four feet, and its scales, which covered everything but its eyes. Elli could not yet determine the dragon's color, but its stunning beauty already enthralled her, despite her terror. Indeed, it was a terrifying beauty, she thought.

Elli had stopped within ten yards of the beast when it instructed her, calmly and soberly, "Far enough." Elli faced perhaps the most beautiful creature she had ever seen or even imagined. She saw now that the dragon was entirely white, except for its eyes, which were sapphire blue. And she was beginning to hope in the friendliness of the gorgeous creature when she spied not far behind the dragon, in glimmering shadows, a mammoth pile of skulls and bones, all of them burnt—or eaten—clean of any flesh. There may have been others deeper into the shadows, but Elli knew, at the very least, that she was looking at thousands upon thousands of humanoid remains, and she felt, upon noticing them, a sudden and aching chill from head to toe. A vision of Hannah and her words played upon her mind like an epiphany: "Remember, all that is ugly is not bad, and all that is beautiful is not good." But how would it apply here, she wondered?

"Who are you?" asked the dragon, sounding sinisterly playful.

"My name is Elli, and I'm a child," answered Elli, with the concision of a captured soldier.

"And what were you doing in my caves?" the dragon asked, with eyes that penetrated hers painfully, making her desperate to look away, although she refused to acquiesce to such intimidation—or, was she rendered incapable of looking away, she wondered?

Elli had been through this questioning before. So far, the endings had been favorable. She had the strong sense that this ending would be otherwise. "I can't tell you anything else, except that I was in your caves attempting to find my two friends—whom you, apparently, have found. May we go now, please?"

"A polite piece of prey—how about that?" said the dragon under his breath, as if speaking to himself alone. "No, the three of you may *not* go!" the dragon thundered. Then, in an almost lilting voice, he added, "One of you must stay as a sacrifice, and I don't care much who it is; but one of you will most definitely stay. It is the price for being here." The dragon smiled a most gentle, but yet wicked-looking, smile at Elli. "Well?" the dragon asked, and in such a friendly tone, that Elli felt another chill up and down her spine. "Otherwise, I will simply choose myself." And, again, there was the same smile, this time wide enough to reveal innumerable razor-sharp teeth that reminded Elli of those she had seen on a *Tyrannosaurus rex*.

"Then it will be me," Elli immediately said. She had nothing to think about. She was not about to place the decision in the hands of either of her friends.

"No!" shouted Jamie. "No, Elli! It *can't* be you!"

"Ewiiiii!" shouted Alex, in great agony. "Ewi!!! Wet me die instead!"

"Take me, dragon!" screamed Jamie.

"Enough!" roared the dragon, releasing as he yelled the hottest of fires, except that its flames were black! "The 'Elli' it shall be," he ordered.

The other two began yelling again for the dragon to choose one of them. But the dragon shouted, "Silence!" Alex and Jamie became still. "I don't *have* to stop at one."

With heightened awareness that comes from being extraordinarily frightened, Elli now wondered quickly if there was another option. Perhaps if she got to know the dragon, she thought.

"Mr. Dragon, before you kill me, would you please tell me where I am—and who you are?"

The dragon wagged his head from side to side a couple of times, not taking his flashing eyes off of Elli. "Most impressive. Most impressive," he said. "Very well: I do not myself have a name, but I am known in the world as 'Blackfire.' And you are *here*—that's where you are."

"And what is here called, and where is here located?" Elli continued in a conversational and not at all petitioning voice, almost forgetting the horrible event that she was almost certain was going to unfold—and sooner rather than later, no matter her "chat" with the dragon.

The dragon smiled a smile of genuine enjoyment, and allowed the dialogue to continue for yet a little while. "You are in a White Hole, and," he added following a pause for emphasis, "it is located everywhere, and nowhere. It is infinitely distant from everything else, but it is also infinitely close to all things. All light comes from, and finally returns to, the White Hole."

"Blackfire, you are about to do another evil thing—another, I would say, *cowardly* thing—by killing me, or any of us, and I want to know *why* you would commit this evil?" Elli demanded, for she knew she had nothing to lose.

Blackfire laughed—a loud belly laugh. "Yes, I suppose it *does* look to be rather evil doesn't it? Of course, it all depends on one's perspective, wouldn't you agree? Does a lion commit an evil deed when it kills a gazelle? Or any animal that hunts for its meal? Do you commit evil when you kill another in self-defense? It depends on perspective, little girl, and my perspective is entirely different from yours, and you are in my world now! And now I will take you. And, frankly," Blackfire added, as if to toss Elli a favor, "you won't feel a thing, it will happen so fast."

At that moment Alex and Jamie appeared—involuntarily, as if lifted by invisible large hands—above the stardust, shouting "Nooooo!! Nooooo!!" But there was to be no more delay. The dragon pointed its mouth at Elli and blew the hottest and blackest fire one could imagine and, in an instant, it was over. Elli's body and bones were burned into a small pile of black ash, with a tip of something tiny and black poking from the ashes that was apparently not consumed by the fire, but which no one seemed to notice, including Blackfire. Alex and Jamie collapsed to the glassy surface, wailing in abject self-abandonment and anger, pounding their fists and pleading to be taken, too.

Then, without another word, Blackfire blew a breath at Alex and Jamie with such ferocity that it lifted and hurled them in swirling, speeding clouds of stardust back down the black-diamond-like tunnel. And before they realized what was happening to them, the two boys lay lifeless on a green grassy slope outside the mountain, opposite the side they had entered. Their inert bodies were resting at the upper edge of a shallow valley at the mountain's foot. A rushing stream of fresh spring water could be heard gurgling from the bottom of the valley some distance away. A black key was lying by itself out of sight of the two boys who were not close together, and a small cloud of buzzards circled eagerly overhead.

~SEVENTEEN~

NEITHER KAHNER NOR CHILDHEART said a word as they drove at a fierce gallop through the Forest of Lament toward Sleeping Guard River and the caves on the other side. What words could weigh anything against the burden that each one carried in his heart and mind? Before long, and while it was still very light, Kahner and Childheart saw the river, which at Childheart's speed was coming swiftly upon them. It was rather narrow, but extremely deep at that point, and Kahner wondered how Childheart would choose to cross it. When Childheart did not slow down, but reached the shore of the river at a full gallop, Kahner fell down against Childheart's neck in fear, anticipating a catastrophic crash into the water. But with the river flying suddenly beneath him, Childheart, as if with wings, leapt across fifty feet of water, landed mildly on the other side, and trotted to a stop.

"Straight up the slope, Childheart, on that flat piece of ground way above us, just beyond the trees," said Kahner, the only one of the two who was breathless. Childheart began climbing the slope, as if effortlessly, and reached the long plateau within a matter of minutes. There in front of them were the mouths of the two caves, the blackness looking all the more foreboding in the bright sunlight that set them off from the glistening grey rock out of which the caves had been cut and bored—and seemingly blasted with an intense and disintegrating heat.

Kahner dismounted and the two of them rested a while, taking nourishment and water from a supply satchel that Childheart had provided Kahner to carry. When they had refreshed themselves briefly, given their sense of urgency, Kahner, with a nod from Childheart, remounted and led Childheart into the cave. The two of them proceeded slowly so Kahner could examine with his night vision, developed over years of practice, the prints in the deep dust. When Kahner had determined at one point well into the cavern that there were still three sets of footprints altogether, he advised Childheart to gallop straight ahead for about a mile. Childheart wondered how Kahner could see the prints at such a pace; it concerned Childheart, but he said nothing to Kahner.

Kahner told Childheart to stop. Kahner looked down and saw only two sets of prints. "We have the two boys, Childheart, but Elli took a different route before this point. We'll walk ahead and see if they took the next tunnel veering off to the left." Once there, and noting that Alex and Jamie had, indeed, taken the left fork, Kahner told Childheart that if they went another half mile and took a passageway off to the right they would end up on a path on which all three sets of prints would inescapably find themselves. He then explained that their turn to the right would take them actually to the left and beneath the main route on which they were currently traveling.

"Are you certain of this, without a doubt?" asked Childheart, probingly.

Kahner hesitated a moment, and then said, "No. I can't say that I am that certain, but I think I am as certain as I can be."

"Fair enough," answered Childheart, leaving Kahner to believe that his answer satisfied and pleased Childheart. And so they galloped another half mile and there entered the passageway to their right, descending sharply downward and to their left beneath the way above. The two now trotted along at a rapid pace. After some minutes Kahner yelled again for Childheart to stop, which he summarily did, as if taking orders as a subordinate. But Childheart was merely being obedient to that which was summoning him on a journey not his own. Kahner then asked Childheart to make his way one slow step at a time until he told him once again to halt. They traveled in the pitch-black darkness another twenty yards or so when Kahner, as if sounding an alarm, yelled, "Stop!" Kahner dismounted Childheart and walked into the darkness some ten feet in front of the stationary unicorn.

"As I suspected, Childheart: I stand at the end of both sets of footprints—I mean, the prints made by all three of them. I knew that unless any of them returned to the main route by way of their path of departure, all of them would end up in the same place from opposite directions, as I feared would be the case."

"Go on; tell me everything," encouraged Childheart firmly.

"When you step forward to where I'm now standing you will be able to reach out a front leg, Childheart, and find the sharp drop-off that your three friends had stepped into," Kahner said, adding after a brief pause, "no doubt to their deaths, I'm sorry to say." Kahner was quiet again, momentarily. "No one knows what's at the bottom, or even if there is one, because no one has ever returned from entering the drop-off, not ever, Childheart. It's our legend that a dragon named Blackfire lives at the bottom of the shaft where he lies in wait for live food, and over the centuries there has been plenty. Some have even offered the opinion that there is some connection between the dragon and the Den of Liars inasmuch as the Liars control Blackfire's access to food. Certainly no one has ever reported evidence of Blackfire's presence outside the caves."

"Let's not allow this tragedy to alter our commitment. Let's get back to the main route and exit the caves as soon as possible where, I can only hope, the others on our expedition are waiting for us already," said Childheart, heavy with sorrow and dropping tears, but still driven by resolve and an overarching sense of purpose—regardless of what might unfold in the coming days. Kahner grabbed Childheart's long thick mane and pulled himself back onto the unicorn's back. As soon as he had fastened himself to Childheart's neck, Childheart took off in a gallop, trusting only Kahner's eyes and verbal instructions of "right" or "left" or "steady" or "stop." They had to slow when they came to the sharp rise that took them underneath and around the main route to the point at which they had departed from the main tunnel, whereupon they headed north once again in a bolt of determination.

None of those traveling on the mission north, whether through or above the mountain, had any notion of how wide it was, including Kahner who had been through any number of times while an Unperson, but Childheart figured that Kahner and he had ridden from the south about a dozen miles already, with no end in sight. They quickly logged another couple of miles when the two of them heard a loud roaring sound in the near distance and felt vibrations beneath them that signaled, perhaps, the advancing presence of the dragon. Childheart stopped immediately to provide Kahner a brief opportunity to determine if possible the precise nature of the sound. Almost immediately, however, Kahner knew the cacophony of voices and the hard tramping of perhaps two hundred feet to be those of approaching warriors, including Wolfmen and others, traveling swiftly south—and so coming towards them.

It would be less than a minute before the warriors would discover them, so Kahner told Childheart to go back as quickly as possible about twenty yards and take the first tunnel to the right. The two had just gotten far enough into the side passageway to avoid being seen by the warriors as they were passing the opening. Childheart and his rider were fortunate to find the other side of a shallow bend in the passage that hid them from view. When these forces belonging certainly to Sutante had traveled well beyond the opening to their hiding place, Childheart and Kahner began walking slowly and silently back toward the main route. Their mutual concern was whether any of the enemy would notice the recently made hoof prints heading north through the cave and decide to turn around and give chase.

Once they had returned to the main route, the two companions continued walking stealthily until the din from the enemy warriors had dissipated into a faraway murmur. At that point Childheart, without any prompting from Kahner, catapulted forward. They galloped for another several miles before Kahner prompted Childheart to slow down enough to take a sharp left hook, which sent them deep down and back to the south for what seemed to a now-impatient Childheart an interminable length of time. Over the course of two hours they galloped and walked and trotted through one passageway after another, the only indicator of correctness coming from Kahner's sharp directives. Fortunately, all the passageways were tall and wide—and certainly large enough for the easy movements of a mythical dragon, as well as enemy troops.

Just as Childheart thought they should stop and rest for a short while, Kahner told Childheart he thought they were near the end. So they made their way for another several minutes as swiftly as the twists and turns would allow until Childheart smelled the sweet perfume of lush green grasses indicating that they were approaching an entrance—or, in their case, a most welcome exit. Indeed, another wide turn to the left found them rushing toward a small circle of bright daylight in the distance, Childheart galloping so fast toward the opening that Kahner hardly believed the unicorn's feet were, even apart from a leap, touching the ground. Childheart slowed abruptly and, like a train braking hard and then crawling tentatively through a station, began to walk ever so slowly from the cave opening into the daylight.

Childheart was filled with mixed and contradictory emotions as he led Kahner into the light that initially blinded both of them. Enveloped by sunlight immediately upon leaving the cave, Childheart lived momentarily only an emotional existence, unable to see or know anything except that which was inside him. In that moment he was deeply grateful for their safe passage through the caves with its many hostilities, devastatingly saddened to have left three dear friends behind in its cruel depths, sorrowful over his permanent departure from the Forest of Lament, desperately eager to see Beatríz and her friends, anxious about what the ensuing hours would unfold and hopeful that an obedience to the elusive, inscrutable Good would result in some as yet unimaginable restoration of Bairnmoor—or, if not, the annihilation of all existence. It occurred to Childheart that it was only in that moment and because of the presence of these children that he was able to feel and begin to understand the full evil force of all that had transpired in Bairnmoor since the deposing of the Queen so far in the distant past.

Childheart's spirits began to lift as he became acclimated to the light and he saw stretching out before him a beauty that mountainous grandeur alone can produce. As he stood motionless before the soft grasses that were waving like a vast mountain lake in the firm but gentle wind, Kahner astride him, Childheart was held unresistingly captive to the enthralling combination of dry cool air, sapphirine blue skies, the tallest of majestic and snowy mountain peaks, an expansive valley of grasses, trees, and wildflowers, and a blazing yellow sun that outsized everything, as if painted by a small child with a large brush.

Kahner, noticing buzzards, shouted, "Childheart! Look—down and to the left, maybe a hundred yards! I think it's a body!"

Childheart sprang into a gallop and quickly scattered the carrion birds that were flying low over a body lying sprawled face down in a patch of yellow flowers. Kahner jumped from Childheart's back and gently turned over the body. Childheart started and shook his head. "It's Jamie! Is he dead, Kahner?"

Kahner put his face in front of Jamie's. "I don't feel any breath, Childheart." He felt around Jamie's neck. "And I can't find a pulse—but he's still very warm!"

"We need the angels, Kahner. If anyone is going to be able to save him, it will be the Cannotoads," said Childheart, anxiously scanning the horizon for signs of the rest of their search party that just might include some of the healers.

"Let me do to him what Elli and Beatríz did to me, Childheart—at least while we're waiting," said Kahner, with an almost fevered anxiety. "They just stroked my head and my face and my arms!" As he finished speaking, Kahner had already cradled Jamie's head in his lap and was stroking his hair, brushing his cheeks with the backs of his hands and speaking softly to Jamie.

"Do whatever you think you can, Kahner. I'll search for the others. Yell for me if you see anyone!" shouted Childheart as he darted away and out of sight, following the ridge of the valley around and behind a large protrusion of ancient rock.

Kahner continued to stroke Jamie, but it only seemed that Jamie's body was getting cooler by the minute. Perhaps, thought Kahner, it had more to do with being in the long mountain shadows that were now rapidly fanning themselves out across the valley than with what was happening to Jamie's body by itself. "C'mon, Jamie! You don't know me, but this is for Beatríz and Elli and Thorn and your other friends! C'mon! You can make it! I know you can! You have to! Please! They need you! We all do!" cried Kahner, in a forceful whisper. As he rubbed and caressed and talked, Kahner wondered for the first time if he *could* love someone into health, if he was able to love at all, or if he could even know what it was. But, he thought, can I love with Beatríz's love somehow? Or with Elli's love? Does it have to be mine, and mine only, or mine at all? "Oh, Jamie—you were so special to Beatríz, and I never even got to meet you!" Kahner said, as his hands slowed in discouragement.

Kahner lifted Jamie's head and held it fast against his own bare chest made thick and sinewy by decades of long and heavy labor in mines and fields and orchards. As he did so, he caught a glimpse of the southwestern sky and noticed a single dark spot extremely high up, no doubt having just cleared the lowest portion of the top of the mountain through which Childheart and he had just passed. His heart was conflicted with both fear and hope, not knowing yet what the looming spot would portend.

Kahner continued to cradle Jamie's head and caress his body while keeping his eyes fixed on the spot that was drifting toward him in a wide downward spiral. Soon he noticed two gargantuan wings that, to his relief and delight, must be Starnee. Kahner set Jamie down gently and stood to signal his presence to the bird and its two passengers. "Starnee! Thorn! Beatríz!" But there was no need to shout his location; Starnee's trajectory indicated that they must have seen Kahner since first clearing the peak. Kahner sat down again and lifted Jamie's head into his lap and began once more to massage him lightly.

As soon as Starnee landed, Thorn and Beatríz jumped from Starnee's back and ran hand-in-hand toward Kahner.

"Kahner! Kahner!" Beatríz shouted, her entire face an ecstatic smile. Her joyfulness shone in delighted, tearful eyes. It was as if Beatríz could now see Kahner and no longer needed her tight hand around Thorn's fingers for guidance.

As Childheart cantered back into their midst, Beatríz was kneeling next to Kahner, hugging him in her distress and tears over Jamie while telling him how worried she had been. Kahner hugged her once and then continued stroking Jamie. All of the others kneeled, too, and examined—or simply touched affectionately—Jamie's body. As far as they knew, or could see, which was very far indeed, there was no enemy within miles of them, so Childheart asked everyone to gather in a tight circle, including Kahner and Beatriz and their patient, and report their respective experiences.

Childheart told Beatríz and Thorn and Starnee about Kahner's and his eventful journey through the mountain and of the large gathering of warriors, including Wolfmen, marching south. The others, including Kahner, were fixed on Childheart's words. When he reached the point at which they had thought all three of the other children had been lost, Childheart, upon mentioning Jamie and glancing at him, noticed that one of Jamie's toes was moving. Immediately, Beatríz, who was seated next to Kahner and also stroking Jamie's arm, began to whisper into his ear words of affection and encouragement. All became silent and watched.

Several minutes later everyone noticed Jamie give a heaving breath and open his eyes ever so slightly! "Yay!" everyone yelled, together with, "Jamie!" and "You're alive!" Thorn ran to get fresh water from the spring-fed stream located at the bottom of this side of the valley they had noticed from the air, and Beatríz grabbed some food from Kahner's satchel. Just as Thorn was beginning to return from the spring with the water, Jamie was sitting up, his back leaning against Kahner's chest. Then he spoke.

"Alex! You're alright, then!" Jamie said, with sudden energy and excitement, as he twisted to look up at Alex, only to discover to his immediate consternation that it wasn't Alex at all. "Who are *you*?" Jamie asked, "And where is Alex?" Jamie looked quickly at each of them for the answer. It was Childheart who walked over to Jamie and provided it.

"Jamie, we found only you, lying unconscious with no one else in sight. We know about the three of you stumbling into the deep shaft, or whatever that hole is, but we never expected that you—any of you—would live to see the light of day. There is no sign anywhere nearby that either Alex or Elli survived along with you, unless you know something different." It was at that point that Jamie had collected himself enough to be able to tell his part of the story, including in detail their experiences at the bottom of the shaft with Elli, Alex, and Blackfire. All listened in silence—tears flowing freely.

When Jamie had finished speaking and had learned who Kahner was, Kahner said, "We should have seen Alex's body inside the cave on our way out, but we didn't. That means that his body might be here somewhere." And then, as if cued by Kahner, Thorn yelled up the hillside,

"I've found Alex! He was hidden by a rock so we couldn't see him from the air! I'm afraid he may be dead! I'll carry him up!" And, with that, Thorn hoisted Alex's body onto his shoulder as if Alex were as light as a large bag of straw, and began walking back to the group—when his eye caught something in the grass that looked familiar. "Just a minute! I see something!" Thorn then gently laid Alex's body on the ground and picked up the object. "It's Elli's key!" shouted Thorn. He put the key in one of his hidden pockets, hoisted Alex back onto his shoulder and climbed the shallow rise back to the group.

With some confidence and cautious optimism, Beatríz and Kahner began to do for Alex what they had done for Jamie. Jamie, like the others, sat anxiously nearby watching and discussing all that had happened after they separated, including Starnee's story. Within a matter of two or three hours, and by the time a hazy dusk had fallen over all the valley and the dark blue sky was unveiling a few of its brightest stars, Alex began to stir and yelled for Jamie—who appeared immediately in front of his face. When Alex saw Jamie, he yelled, "You ah ugly, Jamie!" And then Alex gave out a big smile, laughed and immediately reached for his friend. "I'm s-s-soo gwad you ah okay, J-J-Jamie!" He paused and looked around, visibly happy to see everyone, and then suddenly frowned. "But hwew is Ewi?" Alex asked, apparently not recalling her death. Alex was able to recover his memory of most of what had happened during their time with Elli in the presence of Blackfire, but he could not remember—nor was he willing to believe—that Elli had been killed.

All of them helped build a campfire just inside the mouth of the cave, with Starnee participating by fetching the bulk of the wood from just below the tree line several thousand feet up the mountain. While the supper of fish and edible roots cooked in the fire, Childheart called for a group meeting. They had to decide what to do the next morning, and determine who was going to carry—and so safeguard—Elli's key. The first decision was the easier of the two and handled quickly, since the options were limited. They would cross the valley—and so the river—going north and try to get part way up the mountain that was much wider and higher than the one through and over which they had just come. No one knew, of course, what their traveling party would discover on the other side of the mountain, should they even be able to cross it. How many other mountains would there be? How high would they reach? And how far would they extend?

Clearly the warriors they had already encountered had been able to make it from Sutante's fortress, unless, of course, they had never been to the fortress and simply originated in and remained among the visible mountains as a first line of defense—or offense, as the case might be. But at least there had to be messengers who traveled from the fortress to where they were now located; there had to be a way for individuals to get through or over or around what lay between them and the place from which Sutante Bliss now ruled. But it didn't mean they would be able to find that way, even if it existed, or whether, if they found it, they would be able to take advantage of it. It was difficult for them to imagine that such a way would not be heavily guarded. Regardless, they would break camp in the dark and head out at first light, well before the sun would find them around mid-morning.

But who should carry the key was the next and much larger question. As soon as Childheart raised the issue, Alex spoke. "Hwew is Ewi? I want to know *hwew* she is! The key bewongs to Ewi!" Alex insisted, as if the others were keeping a secret from him.

"Alex," Jamie said, kindly, but very firmly, as if there should be no further conversation about it after he had spoken, "Elli was killed by Blackfire, deep in the ground, don't you remember?" Jamie paused while Alex buried his head in his hands and rubbed his scalp, trying to remember. Jamie spoke again, this time reluctantly. "Alex, she was bur . . . she was killed by Blackfire, right before our eyes, and then he blew us outside the mountain—do you remember now?"

Alex *did* remember now, and he began to weep quietly to himself. With tears in his own eyes, both over Elli's death and over Alex's grief, Jamie went over and put his arm around Alex. "I'm sorry, Alex."

"But I want to know hwew she is *now!*" Alex replied, as if he hadn't heard a word Jamie had said.

"Alex, I just told you she *died*! You need to stop wondering where she is and believe me. I wouldn't lie to you."

"Not so fast, Jamie," Childheart said, shaking his head, as if to command attention to his words, both said and soon to be voiced. "When one stops wondering, one stops living in the real world; and we wonder because we hope. And, even if we have lost our hope, we can still hope that we will hope again—at the very least, we must always hope for hope." All about the fire were so quiet that they could hear the water of the many springs along the hillside rushing to join the river at the bottom of the valley like young children dropping their play and running home for supper in the late summer evening. Some were trying to understand what Childheart had just said. Others simply pondered his words. "But," Childheart finally continued, interrupting what felt like a sacred stillness, "we must decide, at least for the time being, who among the three children will carry the key."

"I want to cawwy Ewi's key," said Alex, seeking comfort.

"I'll carry it," Jamie volunteered.

"I don't want to carry Elli's key," said Beatríz.

Childheart considered their responses. "Well, I'm not certain we actually have a choice in the matter. The prophecy speaks of a young girl with a key who would release the queen, and that must be you, now, Beatríz."

"But, but," Beatríz stammered, "that is a diamond key, as you said before, Childheart, and this is only an old library key."

"That may be, dear child, but Elli was told to never take it off, so there has to be some connection between this black key and the diamond key, whatever that is, or at least between the key and this mission. There is no doubt a connection between a key and a young girl. You must, therefore, carry the key, now, Beatríz."

"But I don't *want* to, Childheart. I can't be Elli. I'm not as capable—or as brave—as she is!"

"Well, Beatríz, I accept your explanation, which is, at least in part, why you must carry the key." He paused and gently pawed the earth with a front hoof. "Beatríz, it's not about whether you want to do this or not; what it means to live truly is never fundamentally about what we want. It's about that which calls us, that which summons us, to speak and to act, regardless of our desires. And yet," Childheart said, smiling at Beatríz, "it is the case that only as we know what we truly want that we can then know—*against* that—what we otherwise truly ought to do and say. In a word, I suppose, it is learning inwardly the inescapable contrast between our own voice of *desire* and the always-present and different voice of *ought*. Without accepting the truth that there are always two distinct voices speaking to us, we will simply assume, erroneously, that what we want to do is what we ought to do.

"This mission, Beatríz, isn't about Elli any more than it is about you; that much I already know without knowing anything else about it. No, Beatríz, as I suspect you well know, you are being summoned—by something or someone—and hopefully by the Good—to carry the key. You can, of course, refuse to do so, and no one will say anything more about it. But it seems clear that it *is* what you ought to do."

All were quiet again, waiting for, well . . . just waiting for they knew not what would—or should—come next, but recognizing that it was truly a sobering, even a sacred, moment. After half a minute or so, Beatríz held out one hand, and then, after a slight hesitation, the other one. "As you think best, Childheart," she said.

Everything decided, and with the key about Beatríz's neck, they turned in for the night in and around the mouth of the cave. The low but continuously maintained fire remained a steady companion throughout the night, thanks to the efforts of Thorn who alone needed no sleep. Under a full moon he and Starnee kept guard as the first line of defense outside the mouth of the cave, with Thorn sitting next to the opening and Starnee crouching low behind a large protrusion of rock some distance downhill from the encampment. It was unique to the Bairnmoor condors that they could *half sleep* by simply closing one eye, which is precisely what Starnee did. Everyone else slept, although Beatríz, who was resting against Childheart's massive chest just inside the cover of the cave, gazed up into the sky at the moon that was rising with seemingly magical speed above the mountainous horizon. She wondered if the moon's full phase, which Childheart mentioned earlier in the evening, would be an omen of good things for the day soon to follow; and then she, too, slept.

~EIGHTEEN~

WHEN ELLI SAW THE bolt of light shooting toward her and felt the searing heat of the black flames about to devour her, she closed her eyes and braced herself for what she hoped would be an instantaneous death. But in that same moment—in that same infinitely brief moment before her death—she felt herself, with eyes still closed, lying on cool grass, a dappling of warmth and light dancing all about her as a multitude of clouds wheeled rapidly across the sunlit sky. The feathery breeze carried the aroma of wild flowers in August—of Queen Anne's lace and chicory, of clover and black-eyed Susans. As she lay there, utterly content, she assumed that she was experiencing the soothing qualities of the "peaceful death" that everyone always spoke of, but of course knew nothing about. She wasn't sure if she was going to—ever, perhaps—open her eyes, so unutterably relieved and contented was she, when a soft croaking nearby made up her mind for her.

Opening her eyes, Elli was overwhelmed by what she saw. Lying on her side, she was looking out at a beautiful lake that was perhaps three blocks in diameter and nestled in a canyon with steep, sheer cliffs around three-fourths of the lake's circumference. Elli was looking down and toward that smaller, open part of the lake that had a white sandy beach and, immediately beyond that, the thick soft grass on which she was lying. Beyond the grass behind her and also encircling the cliffs was a wide ring of meadow grasses and wild flowers. Beyond the meadow stood a dense wood, mostly of broad oaks and tall poplars. The oak branches, swaying gently in the high, stiff wind, were squeaking delightfully, and the poplar leaves were rustling and tapping against one another, all like a lunchroom full of young girls squealing and chattering excitedly. The mourning doves were cooing. She now saw the widely scattered clouds in the deep blue sky moving swiftly past the bright sun. Elli could hardly imagine a more beautiful place on earth—especially since this was the place where she chose to spend most of her time in the late spring and early autumn when she could enjoy it all by herself.

The place was, in fact, Quarry Lake Park, about three miles from her house on Lake Ridge Boulevard. It never ceased to tickle her funny bone when she thought about the name of her street. There was, after all, no ridge, no lake, and no boulevard anywhere near her street! She was amused by how often developers would name streets after topographical features that bore no resemblance whatsoever to the streets themselves. She knew that in the country it was different. If there was an Oak Lane, it was because there really was a lane and it was really running through or alongside a lineup of oak trees. Or, in the case of a road she was familiar with, there really was a Night Ghost Circle, because there really was a road in the shape of a circle, and wisps of marsh gas that appeared like ghosts, drifting across the road at night from the nearby swamp. It was as if, she thought, people had to make up a name to create an identity that reflected a more pleasant reality than what actually existed, rather than naming something for what it was. Instead, the name itself became more important than the thing it was supposed to be referring to.

She wondered about her own name in that regard. What did it mean for her to be named *Elli*? When she asked her parents how they named her, they said, rather sheepishly, that they were on the way to pick her up from the adoption agency when they realized they were supposed to have picked out a name by that time. Being only two blocks from the agency, and already late for the appointment, her father saw a billboard with many of its neon letters missing. All that remained of the two words were the letters E, L, L, and I, which put together spelled—and so he exclaimed to her mom—"Elli! That will be her name! Elli!" She never did ask, though, what the actual words on the billboard were. Someday she needed to ask.

Elli now lay there completely confused. "What just happened to me?" she asked herself. "And to the others? Or, did anything at all happen? Did I really go to the library with my friends and speak to a man named Peterwinkle? Or am I waking from a dream and don't remember going to the park and falling asleep here? Or, am I truly dead and just beginning a new existence, or whatever it is one calls the state of being after death?"

She heard the croaking once again, repeatedly so, as if it were hailing her. Elli sat up and turned around. And there, sitting on the ground not three feet away, was a very large toad. Indeed, the toad was the size of a muskmelon, and it had—yes, it really did have, she could see—little translucent wings on its back, looking as if a child had been playing dress-up with it by taping the wings from a tiny stuffed angel to its back. Elli began to giggle. "My, you're a funny-looking thing!" she squealed.

And then she started, gasping loudly, when the toad replied, "Well, if that's the case, then I suspect I could say the same is true about you. But, then, I'm not in the business of saying unkind things to you, or to anyone else, for that matter. But I am in the business of helping, and I am here to help *you*. And my name is Butterfly."

Elli began to giggle again, feeling embarrassed about it but not being able to stop. "But, Mr. Butterfly, excuse me for giggling again, and it's not because you don't look nice, but I have to say you don't resemble a real butterfly at all!" The toad made no further sound or any movement but simply waited for however long it took for Elli to become tired of laughing. When Elli had finished, Butterfly continued.

"I, young lady, am a Cannotoad—a Cannotoad angel—and I come from Bairnmoor, and this is the Lake of Imagination, or, as it is sometimes called, for descriptive purposes, the Lake of Probable Impossibilities, that I, together with other Cannotoads, manage and—now, mostly—safeguard."

"Excuse me for interrupting, Mr. Butterfly, but I know this place as Quarry Lake Park, on the Earth, just a few miles from where I live. Are you saying that I am not at Quarry Lake Park, but someplace else?" Elli furrowed her eyebrows and bent slightly toward the toad. "And, if so, am I dead? And why am I here at all, if I'm anywhere? It's all so confusing to me, Mr. Butterfly. Why, I don't even know if I'm really talking to you, or if I am still asleep and only dreaming you. How do I even know you—or any of this—is not a dream I'm having?"

"Well," Butterfly offered, screwing up his mouth first on one side and then on the other. "Well, . . . how do you know that I'm not asleep and dreaming *you*?"

"Because I am who I am," said Elli, and she added, "so I am not the product of anyone else's dreams or imagination!"

"Really?" asked Butterfly, cocking his head to one side as well as he could, which wasn't very far. "Well, I am who I am, and I could say that I'm not the product of your dreams or anyone else's imagination, except that, well, it's not quite that simple, you see, for either one of us."

"Can I touch you, Mr. Butterfly, to see if you are real and I'm not dreaming you?"

"I dare say, young lady, that is a slippery slope of proof without end. If you can dream me, then, of course, you can dream you are touching me as well, no?"

"Yes, I suppose so," said Elli, looking momentarily baffled.

"Besides, perhaps it doesn't matter whether it's a dream or not, or whose dream it is," Butterfly added, raising the pitch of his voice at the end the way young girls do to emphasize an assertion by seeming to ask a question.

"But," Elli quickly added, as if she had been suddenly awakened from sleep, "do you know who I am and anything about me and about my journey—if there was one—in Bairnmoor? And what happened to me when Blackfire tried to kill me? And am I, in fact, dead?"

"That's partly why I'm here, Elli!" announced Butterfly. "And let me say first that, from my perspective, you are most certainly not dead—although it could appear that way to everyone else you've left behind—and you are still in Bairnmoor, although, I understand, you are also in your park not far from your house back in your world." Butterfly looked up at Elli, waiting for her to nod, which she did. Butterfly then went on to explain to Elli that she had likely traveled through a White Hole made mostly of light and that she was now existing perpendicular to perpendicular time, which meant that she was now living in a third realm of time, quite apart from the time of the other two realms, which however was much closer to the first realm of time in which she was accustomed to living.

Elli's mind spun, striving to comprehend all the toad had just told her. "But, where am I, then?" pressed Elli, but respectfully so.

"As I said just moments ago, the most accurate answer to your question of where you are is the Lake of Imagination."

"And, where is that, if it's not back where I'm really—or originally—from?"

"It's in your imagination, of course, dear girl, as the name itself indicates. And," he added, with a slight change of tone signaling an altogether different issue, "as far as 'where you are really—or originally—from,' I wouldn't be so quick to answer that question; what, after all, *seems most real* to you may, in fact, turn out to be what is *least real*."

Elli, impatient with trying to figure out conundrums that strained all credulity, demanded, "What do you mean by 'the Lake of Imagination' is *in* my imagination? If it's in my imagination, then it is *not* real, correct?" she asked, as if she had grabbed control of the conversation.

"Elli, you as much as anyone should see it differently. Indeed, you have *seen* it differently. It's just that you are treating your doubts as if *they* were real, when they only *point* to what's real."

"I'm not understanding you at all, Butterfly, not at all, and," she added in a tone of desperation, "I need to make sense of what's happened to me, and what's now happening to me, and what is *going* to happen to me! I feel so entirely lost!" Elli bowed her head and was about to begin to weep.

"Dear Elli," Butterfly said, softly and slowly, as if his words were molasses dripping from his thin lips, and then he walked, albeit awkwardly, next to Elli and sat down beside her so that both of them were looking out over the lake. They sat silently together for a few minutes, before Butterfly cut gently into the palpable silence.

"All that is true, and so all that is real, to the extent that anything is true and real, besides the Good," said Butterfly, deep in thought, "is what is ironic and metaphorical. It is the casting away of the literal (as finite and incomplete, and derivative) and then journeying on the basis of simile that is the way to truth. What is true," he said, before pausing for emphasis, "is never what it seems to be, and always infinitely more than it is—like a poem, Elli." Butterfly now turned his head as far as he was able so that both of his eyes were looking up and into Elli's, and he smiled at her—or so Elli thought, when she turned her eyes to meet his.

"What do you know about a poem I am supposed to write?" Elli asked, looking down at Butterfly with a furrowed brow.

"Nothing more than that, Elli, nothing more than that. But Bairnmoor understands from its mythology that you are to write one, and that is why you are here."

Elli, her brain aching from numerous hard thoughts tumbling about and over and into each other, looked back up toward the lake. As if trying to put a jigsaw puzzle together one piece at a time, not knowing what the final picture is supposed to look like, but simply searching for pieces that fit together, Elli asked, "What exactly is the Lake of Imagination, Butterfly?"

"As I said earlier, it is in the Lake of Probable Impossibilities where those with baptized imaginations may envision, and act in accordance with that vision. And only the imagination of an appointed child may be baptized in these waters. You are here, Elli. Therefore, you have been called to have your imagination baptized."

"What does that mean, Butterfly, and how does it happen?" Elli asked, yielding now to the Cannotoad's train of thought.

"It means that when you are baptized in these waters, you may imagine anything about Bairnmoor's future that you believe you are *supposed* to imagine—what you *want to have to imagine*—and it will, in its own way and time, come to pass. How it happens," Butterfly said, as if stating the obvious, "is that you dive deep into the lake until you no longer feel the urge to breathe. It is then that you will begin to imagine the Bairnmoor you have been summoned to imagine; and, when you have done so sufficiently, you will find yourself surfacing from the water and, at that point, gasping for air and marshalling all your internal forces to advance the vision you have been given," said Butterfly, not pausing before continuing.

"On the other hand . . . " Butterfly began again.

"But," interrupted Elli, "what if I do not *want* to have my imagination baptized and I do not *want* to imagine the future of Bairnmoor, but simply . . . simply want to be left alone?" she asked anxiously, yearning for at least the possibility of choosing otherwise—including, perhaps, going home to Lake Ridge Boulevard.

"As I was about to say, Elli: on the other hand, if you choose *not* to have your imagination baptized, then you may simply walk back to your earthly dwelling where life will be just as it was for you and your friends before you ever started your journey toward Bairnmoor and, shall we say, your journey *away* from your land of *improbable possibilities.* No one will think that anything at all has happened to you, and only you and your friends will share this event, as if having shared the same dream."

"I can just . . . right now, I mean . . . just walk right home?" she asked, almost giddy in her excitement and relief.

"Well, I don't know about walking *home,"* answered Butterfly, reflectively, "since I'm not at all certain where home for you is, Elli, just as I suspect *you* do not know where home is for you. But, yes, you may walk back to your house, and to your school, and to your friends, and to your parents—indeed, to the way everything was before you left. No one will know you were missing, and no one in Bairnmoor will pass judgment on your decision."

"I'm not sure . . . I don't know what you mean by even *me* not knowing where my home is," Elli said, thinking perhaps she had finally caught Butterfly stumbling in his own thinking.

"All I mean, Elli, is that a house is not itself a home—nor is your town, or your country, or any other place by itself, at all a home. Only that place where you know once and for all who you really are, and live on the basis of that knowledge, can be home. And, as well," Butterfly added parenthetically, "you are known for who you truly are in that place that is really home for you."

"But how can things go back the way they were? So much time has already passed by," Elli asked, trying to fit this piece of the puzzle into other pieces of an apparently whole new and yet to be disclosed picture of reality.

"Oh, bumbles, Elli! No time whatsoever has passed by. As soon as you began to step toward Bairnmoor you stepped out of your time altogether and into no time at all. Indeed, according to the world of the Good, time is merely a dependent subset of that which is timeless."

"Before I decide, Butterfly, may I ask a couple more questions?" Elli asked, with a mild note of entitlement in her voice.

"By all means, fire away, and I'll do my best to answer them."

"First, Butterfly, how did I get here—at the Lake of Imagination, I mean?"

"Well, it's indubitable that you arrived by virtue of the White Hole, as I mentioned before. And you will undoubtedly want to know what that is," said Butterfly, turning his gaze over the lake now to the face of Elli who was nodding, "yes."

"Well," Butterfly said, and then he paused to scratch under his chin. "As I understand it, Elli, all light comes from and returns to the White Hole, and in the White Hole it is said that one is both infinitely distant from, and infinitely close to, everything else, including, of course, what you call your world and the world of Bairnmoor." Elli was startled to hear from the toad what Blackfire had said to her, and she didn't know what to think or say. Butterfly continued right on, however: "It is also recounted in our mythology that all *goodness* comes from the White Hole and returns there. It is a place, if it can be called a *place* at all, where all that is imagined is real and all that is real is imagined. Of course, that means there can be no evil there, since evil can neither imagine nor be imagined."

A lengthy, almost comfortable, silence ensued. Butterfly then broke the silence, as if he had forgotten something. "It can scheme, of course—evil, I mean; but it cannot imagine."

Butterfly, who during the entirety of his long answer to Elli's short question had been looking up at the sky, lowered his head to once again eye Elli, wondering if she was following his train of thought.

"Blackfire, Butterfly. Who or what is Blackfire? And did Blackfire send me here?" Elli asked, more relaxed than at any time up to this point in her conversation with Butterfly.

"I don't know anything about Blackfire, Elli, and I don't care to know. All I know is that no one has ever seen Blackfire—or seen Blackfire and lived to tell about it, although some have returned from nearing his presence severely burned, or so I've been informed. Apparently he kills all who actually enter the sphere of his presence. Certainly no one has ever returned to indicate otherwise."

Elli wasn't clear whether Butterfly was including her in the all-inclusive class of 'no one ever having seen Blackfire living to tell about it,' but at least for the time being she kept it to herself. "He's a very evil creature, isn't he, Butterfly?"

"Well, I couldn't really say. The mere fact that he intentionally kills does not make him necessarily evil, although it would ordinarily be pretty strong evidence. But, of course, it is *whom* you kill and *why* you kill, as well as *how* you kill, that largely determines, according to universal standards of right and wrong, whether your behavior is good or evil, regardless of what others may think. On the other hand, is Blackfire even subject to universal standards of right and wrong—or, as some have suggested—" Butterfly then began to add, but decided to let what he was thinking remain unspoken.

"And Queen Taralina, Butterfly. If she was the Good, or came from the Good, why was she not immortal? I mean, everlasting?"

"Well, of course, dear girl, if you think carefully about it, something can be everlasting without being immortal, as long as it depends on something immortal for its continued existence. I don't know that I, or anyone else, ever thought of Queen Taralina as being immortal. But there was always a sense that her reign would never end—and our mythology affirms that."

At this point, both girl and angel seemed rather ensconced in private reveries until, breaking the mood, Butterfly announced, not looking at her, "I think it's time, Elli, for you to decide."

During the silence, Elli thought about her life from the earlist events she could remember to the time she decided to talk with the others about going to Bairnmoor, and then to the time that they and she had spent in Bairnmoor already. And she thought about what it would mean for her—as well as for her friends—to go home to Millerton. Butterfly was right, of course; she could feel it, even if she could not quite understand it: her home with her parents and brother never quite felt like home—at least, not the sort of home she longed for where, as Butterfly so truly stated it, she knew who she was and lived on that basis—and others knew who she was. She knew that her three friends felt very much the same way, although she didn't know whether they would articulate it in the same way. And that there was no place she knew of—aside from Bairnmoor—where she thought she and the others *could* feel at home.

But, it was true, and she knew that Butterfly was suggesting so: namely, that she *did* feel *at home* in Bairnmoor—even, amazingly—when she was fleeing for her life from the warriors chasing her across the rope bridge. It was as if, even then, she was running just as much to get home as she was running to escape from something, and getting home had nothing to do with Millerton. But she also knew that once she decided to be baptized in the Lake of Imagination, there would be no going back—she would become a servant to her imagined vision, and going home to Lake Ridge Boulevard would not be a part of it—ever. And then, when she thought about dying old in Millerton, perhaps never having known who she really was, or dying young in Bairnmoor, and already in the process of discovering who she was, the choice was clear. Nevertheless, she added, as if involuntarily and from some lingering doubt, "I wish, though, that I could wait until I really felt I was *ready* to decide, Butterfly."

"But, that's just it, Elli," he returned, blinking his eyes like one who was just awakened from an afternoon nap. "Those who act truly, and so according to the Good, are *never ready*—and never feel they are. If you wait to act until you are ready, dear girl, you will never act."

"I just wish I could believe in this thing, or someone, called the Good, Butterfly. It would all be so much easier."

"I don't know about it being easier—I'm an angel, after all. But I do know faith is about action more than belief—and that if we act truly, true belief, where it's necessary, will follow. You will certainly never be ready by waiting for enough belief. That much I do know, Elli."

Nevertheless, it would be, ironically, those very hoped-for words that would initiate the baptism of Elli's imagination. With the simple statement, "I'm ready," the dozen Cannotoad angels holding Elli aloft well above both the lake and its steep stony sides released her to dive head first into the clear blue waters and begin her long descent.

Like an arrow shot fast and straight and true, Elli slipped into the water almost noiselessly, as if the lake was whispering its welcome to her. Elli did not open her eyes to the deep and dusky water sliding rapidly past her body like a fine satin sheet, until her velocity stopped and she found herself floating gently downward. When she opened them, she saw all about her the clearest water she could possibly imagine. It was nearly dark, but the water seemed to take the meager sunlight that was able to cut through the depths and reflect it on itself and so multiply it, like trillions of atomic mirrors that catch one tiny flame from a single candle in a vast sea of darkness and multiply its light exponentially through reflection and refraction.

Elli, as instructed, began to pull her body through the water toward the bottom. Very quickly, however, she became aware of an increasing desire to breathe. The desire became quickly a desperate one, and the muscles encasing her lungs constricted painfully like knives stabbing at her chest in their effort to prevent the lungs from expanding and filling with water. In her struggle to keep from panicking, Elli stopped, and was about to launch her body with abandon back to the surface when she realized in that same instant that she would never make it. So she pulled again toward the bottom, with all the strength that was in her, and discovered that, as she continued to dive deeper into the now pitch-blackness, her desire to breathe was lessening and her chest was beginning to relax. Before long, Elli's desire for air dissipated entirely, and Elli began involuntarily to wonder whether this wasn't the way fishes felt in the water. She stopped swimming and spun upright, looking all about her. The blackness seemed so dense that she wondered if any light at all could penetrate it. And, then, the blackness thinned and became a darkness that was less like dusk than like dawn, and within a few moments she was viewing a panorama all about her as clear as crystal of what she knew to be Bairnmoor, although none of what she saw had she ever seen before.

There were tall, majestic mountains in the distance, and in the foreground stood a mighty and expansive fortress of stone enclosing another fortress, which in turn enclosed what Elli knew immediately to be the castle of Queen Taralina. She saw that a fierce battle was underway outside the fortress, where many human-like beings and other creatures were being killed. Some of her companions in the midst of the battle were running toward the castle with the enemy about to fall on them, and various friends were injured—perhaps even dead. And she saw the door to the mausoleum and somone's hand reaching for the keyhole, and a key dropping from the hand. But where was she, she wondered? The scene blurred, and Elli blinked in the water, hoping it would clear, but it didn't. She saw someone fall hard against the mausoleum door, but she couldn't see who it was. Then everything went dark, as if the darkness was itself part of the scene—as if she herself had suddenly become entombed inside the panorama.

Suddenly the darkness fled, along with the entire vision, and in that same moment Elli found herself surfacing from the water, gasping for air and standing before Blackfire—and the black fire that was hurtling toward her and about to incinerate her body, which it did, leaving behind the only evidence of her having ever existed in Bairnmoor: a small pile of smoking ash, and a black key.

~NINETEEN~

THE NIGHT PASSED UNEVENTFULLY, and as daylight was just beginning to
melt the night sky above the imposing mountains, Beatríz woke Childheart
with a start.

"What is it, Beatríz? It's not yet dawn. You can sleep some more;
you're going to need it for today's journey."

"But I hear some rumbling in the distance, inside the mountain."

When Childheart, too, felt the vibrations and heard the sound of
rapidly tramping warriors, he rallied everyone from sleep and said they
would be moving out before breakfast, it being evident the enemy in the
caves had learned they were on this side of the mountain and were racing toward them. While it would be some time before the warriors would
reach them, Childheart wanted to cross the wide valley before dark and
establish camp on high ground, if not get back into The Mountains themselves, and do so before the pursuing enemy discovered them.

With amazing dispatch, the seven sojourners broke camp and gathered all their belongings, including firewood to be carried by Starnee, to
begin their march before dawn. They traveled two by two: Childheart and
Beatríz in front, Alex and Jamie behind them, and Kahner and Thorn
bringing up the rear. Starnee flew ahead by himself to scout the mountain
for any sort of promising opening as well as the presence of any enemy.
Because of the unevenness of the ground and the depth of the grasses hiding it, the party found that hiking down into the valley and across it was
more difficult than they would find the going back up to be. It was early afternoon before they reached the end of the valley floor and the beginning
of the long low rise to the base of the next group of steep mountains. They
stopped, ate, and refreshed themselves for half an hour before continuing on. While they were eating and drinking, Starnee flew into view high
above and then descended to land next to Childheart and Thorn, who had
been whispering together.

Starnee reported both good news and bad. The bad news was that he could find no opening into the mountain. The good news was that there was a narrow, barely visible path that wound its way like one S stacked upon another all the way to the snow line and, presumably, either beyond, around, or through the mountain. The path, he added, looked unused for a long time. Starnee was not able to fly to the snow line on these mountains, so much higher were they than the initial part of the range that had last engaged them. Indeed, it was not at all clear how Starnee could be helpful from that point onward. The one thing he would be able to do was to deposit the wood at that place on the mountain path where they would camp for the night. In the meantime, he would scout for enemy forces, including both those that might already be in the vicinity and the ones soon to emerge from the mountain behind them—the one on the other side of the valley, against which they had just made camp.

This northern half of the valley was in fact much less steep than the half they had descended, which made progress easier than expected. On the other hand, the shallow incline of the valley obscured the fact that this side was also much longer than the opposite side, so that it was taking them longer to get to the base of The Mountains before them. At one point, midway between the edge of the valley floor and The Mountains—which seemed to them to be forever in the distance—there was a slight rise and then a long level area of ground to travel across that hid from view the tunnel opening on the other side of the valley—a tunnel through which the enemy would soon be marching. That meant that only Starnee would be aware of the enemies' exit from the mountain; and there was no doubt that Sutante's forces would be well on their way along the valley floor by the time Childheart could lead his party to a place where the enemy would be visible once again. They could only hope to find encampment on high ground from which to defend themselves, if need be.

By late morning the six of them had reached the base of The Mountains and the beginning of the narrow path that snaked its way efficiently upward and quickly out of sight. They rested for only twenty minutes, refreshing themselves with crackers and water, and then began the climb in single file. They were heading to a place halfway up the mountain that Starnee told them widened into an area big enough for them to spend the night. It would also be, to everyone's dismay, that point in their ascent beyond which Starnee would not be able to land and travel with them.

It wasn't long before they were high enough to see the enemy advancing rapidly up the long shallow slope from the valley floor in the distance below. Childheart's train of travelers, moving like a determined caterpillar along the path, was making good time, and it would still be light when they finally stopped for the night. Fortunately, they were able to do all their climbing in the daytime, since negotiating the quickly changing path all along the precipitous drop-off at night would have been harrowing and risky. On the other hand, Sutante's forces would be able to watch them climb the entire way to the place where they intended to camp for the night. Already, Beatríz could hear the rumbling and screaming drifting up the side of the mountain from the various creatures that, still far away, were clearly pursuing them. Soon the rest of her climbing party would be able to hear them as well. At last they stumbled one by one onto the plateau—at the same time beginning to hear their pursuers.

Childheart considered the likely defense of their position during the night, relieved that only one member of the enemy at a time could advance to the small plateau where they would be resting—and trying to sleep. But he guessed the enemy forces numbered about one hundred and twenty-five, which meant their leaders could rush and sacrifice one soldier at a time until very soon the defenders would be overwhelmed and killed, injured, or taken captive. After a brief discussion involving everyone sitting around a low fire, it was decided that for the night Thorn and Childheart would settle themselves next to the continuation of the path beyond the resting place and watch for any signs of trouble from above. Starnee would lie at the entrance to the path going back down and watch for anyone, or anything, coming up. That left Kahner and the three children to sleep close to each other between the two watch stations.

As a deep and dusty twilight drifted down over the vast valley, the group could hear and see the enemy forces approaching to within five hundred yards of the mountain face and the beginning of the path. The moon would not rise above The Mountains across the valley until late into the night, so for a long time there would be no moving shadows to help them spot the enemy forces climbing toward them. Although it was impossible to see the faces of those they were chasing, simply spotting their aggregate presence high above was sufficient to turn the dozens of troops into a heightened level of raging hostility and screaming anger. With the remainder of the party standing close behind, Starnee and Childheart surveyed the situation below, wondering how many of the enemy would begin the climb—and when. They also wondered whether the enemy was aware of the risks of trying to follow the nearly invisible path during the night.

Once darkness had settled, the adversaries could no longer see each other, and Sutante's forces became eerily quiet. Childheart and Starnee eyed one another, each wondering if the other had figured out what was happening below, but said nothing. Finally, when the hour was near midnight, those who were watching suggested the others sleep. Childheart announced they would head out as soon as the path became visible again in the early morning—or whenever they could hear or see the enemy climbing the path, whichever happened first.

The three children and Kahner then lay themselves down for the night near the fire, Beatríz and Kahner snuggling close. Sad about Elli and wondering what she was supposed to do with the key, Beatríz lay awake. "After all, it's a *diamond* key that is supposed to release the queen," she thought, "and this one is just an old skeleton key to get us back inside the library." She was so glad she had met Kahner, though, and thought how, but for him, she would have fallen completely apart over Elli's death. Now, she needed to use the strength of her bond with Kahner to help her do whatever was required of her, no matter how frightened she was. And, she had to admit, as much as she did not want to carry Elli's key, the presence of its chain about her neck enabled her to feel closer to Elli, almost as if Elli were there with them in some way. It was in these final thoughts that Beatríz found peace, and then sleep.

On occasion throughout the night the three watchmen would hear something that made all of them start, but in each case they determined it was merely a loose stone or perhaps a small nocturnal creature looking for prey.

A chilly light wind rose with the first of the hidden sun's rays diffused like a wash of thin watercolor across the eastern rim of the overcast sky. The wind, rolling over and down the mountain's long face from the north, awakened Childheart who had been sleeping the final hours of the night. Thorn, who had been awake and alert the entire night and noticed Childheart's blinking eyes, greeted him.

"Well, it's morning. I've heard nothing of note all night, and it's not yet light enough to see the enemy below. My assumption is if they were moving already we'd at least be able to hear them."

"Let's awaken everyone, grab what we can to eat from our individual stores while packing up, and continue up the path. By the time we head out, we should be able to see Sutante's forces—and the path—with some clarity," said Childheart.

While all who had them stuffed their skins back into their packs and the others doused the remains of the fire, they munched on whatever they could find among their belongings, two or three quickly bartering with one another. One person wanted berries and another roasted chestnuts. Still another traded for some of the dry bread from Hannah that remained and continued to be tasty. When it was time to part with Starnee, Thorn stepped out from the small gathering and stated that he thought it wise for him to accompany the condor. No one should travel alone any longer, he advised, and Starnee had a long and difficult assignment ahead of him. Starnee was going to try to find a lower elevation at the crest and fly over The Mountains as far as they would take him until he reached the end and, supposedly, the beginning of Sutante Bliss's fortressed location, stopping along the way wherever there was a place to land and rest.

Despite Starnee's strong misgivings, especially given the distinct possibility of failure deep into the unnavigable mountain range, everyone else agreed that the two of them traveling together was wise. All said their goodbyes to Starnee and Thorn. Just as Starnee and Thorn were preparing to take off, Childheart, who had said his goodbyes and had walked to the edge of the plateau to check on the status of the enemy forces, shouted back to everyone, "They're gone! They're all gone! And I have no idea where they could have gone to, since they're not visible in the valley going south and are obviously not climbing the mountain—at least not from that location."

Starnee said that he and Thorn would look for the whereabouts of the enemy warriors—and so for another, perhaps far easier, way either into or over The Mountains—and try to let their companions know about anything discovered before they had either ascended above that point beyond which Starnee could not fly or otherwise disappeared inland. The plan was to meet on the northern side of the mountain range, Thorn and Starnee heading east beyond The Mountains until they located Childheart's party. Either party, upon reaching the end of The Mountains, would search or wait for the others no longer than four days, and then do whatever they could to locate the southeastern corner of the fortress enclosing the Queen's castle. There they were to hide and wait for another guiding word—and for "the girl with the diamond key" if she were not already present. Whose word that would be was not clear to anyone, but without more word there was no more mission. There had been that necessary word from someone at all times past on their journey, first from Peterwinkle, then from Hannah, Thorn, and finally Childheart. It was now another's vocation to bring the word, and they could only hope—at least *in* hope—that the messenger would find them when they needed him, if there was any messenger, and anyone left to find.

Childheart harbored privately the growing belief that death and annihilation of the whole of Bairnmoor was preferable to the eternal reign of evil. Perhaps this vast mountainous region, having the verisimilitude of an infinite something, would be the staging ground for the beginning of something's end, preempting, as the Good's last resort, the advent of the eternal rule of nothingness. Without the existence of something, there would no longer be nothing either. As beautiful as the apparently lifeless mountains were by themselves, without someone to appreciate them as such, they would cease to be. What if in these mountains there was to be found their true mission: all of them to die as the beginning of the end of all things—to die in order to begin the annihilation of the world, and so the annihilation as well, of the nothingness of evil, enabling the Good to begin something again? Childheart did not know what to believe, although he knew how to act, regardless of what was true. But of these thoughts he said nothing to anyone.

As soon as Starnee and Thorn took off toward the west, where it looked as though the mountain tops were less elevated, Childheart, with Beatríz as rider, led the remainder of the travelers on the steep and narrow path upwards, with nothing but a sheer, deadly drop at its outer edge—and so with no room for error. Each step would be either a step into life or a step into death, and no one knew how long it would continue to be that way.

Up and up they trudged in the dark, the snaking path taking them farther horizontally than vertically. The air was now crystalline clear, the sun just beginning to suggest its concealed existence beneath the tall eastern horizon, and it was cold and getting colder with each step they climbed. Every so often the entire party would stop and sit on the path to rest and take nourishment, but at the cost of getting colder without gaining ground.

Soon they began to enter the tall and cloudy snow covered cap of the crest. Beatríz knew because the moisture was frosting her face and making her shiver. Light flurries blew in an icy, stiff wind as they labored up the mountainside, finding it as difficult to see the path immediately in front of them as it was in the dead of a moonless night. They toiled for hours with few breaks in the raw, thin air, seldom knowing if they were stepping on stone or snow or ice, their legs becoming weary and weak, and their ankles sore. The sunlight provided little help, and yet they were racing it to reach some sort of suitable campsite before darkness fell, the temperatures dropped precipitously, and they were no longer able to see anything. All were praying against the waning light for a way at least *into,* if not a path *through,* the mountain well before that.

Time moved far too quickly as the five travelers moved at a snail's pace, feeling what was in front with nearly frozen toes before committing to another step—though their feet would soon be too numb to feel anything. Already, there were slight squeals and voices of surprise that pierced the wind, indicating someone had slipped. Childheart had thought earlier, prior to the climb, about the possibility of tying everyone together, but rejected the idea when he realized that a fall by any one of them would almost certainly mean a fall by another one—or all.

On they labored, and cold piled on cold until the temperature had dropped to near zero. With clothes from Hannah and skins from Thorn, Alex, Jamie, and Beatríz were thus far able to stay warm, as was Kahner, who had fashioned his own clothing early on that was suitable for the climb, and was accustomed to being naked in the elements as a member of the Den of Liars. But a couple of them wondered aloud what it was going to be like when the elevation went much higher and they were no longer moving to help keep warm.

Finally, darkness fell fast and hard. Childheart was not happy about having to stop on the narrow path for the night and hoped they would encounter a widened area soon, not unlike the rocky shelf on which they had spent the previous night. Fortunately, he came very quickly to an opening in the face of the rock to his left, obscured by a protrusion. He had not seen it in the waning light and shadows, and would have passed it by but for the fact that he was continually brushing against the mountainside to avoid the edge. The cleft in the rock was low and rather narrow. Childheart suggested that Jamie and Alex travel on all fours to see how far and just where the side passageway would take them. Unfortunately, regardless of any promising quality that lay ahead on this alternate route, Childheart knew what likely no one else had yet thought about, namely, that given the size of the opening, he would not be able to travel with them any longer.

What the two boys soon discovered was that the opening led to a narrow path of rock that wound between two granite walls, soon enabling them to walk. What was not clear was whether this secondary path was passing through a crevice in a single mountaintop or between two different mountaintops. Childheart encouraged the boys to travel further to see if there was any reason for at least some of them to take this alternate route—or at least use it for shelter for the night.

Alex and Jamie continued walking carefully in the darkness that was nearly complete. After about five minutes Jamie shouted back, "There are no more walls! Just air—and really high winds and a drop-off—on both sides! And it's very narrow! I'll crawl on it for a while and see where it goes!" Within another ten minutes, Jamie shouted back, "It's like a bridge to another mountain, and on this other side where I now am there is an area, maybe forty feet in diameter, where we could actually rest if we can all get through. I'm heading back now!"

"No! Stay there, Jamie!" Childheart ordered loudly against the muffling rock. "I'm sending Kahner and Beatríz through to you! Alex, wait for Kahner!" Childheart shouted.

"I know you can't fit, Childheart! I knew it right away!" Jamie yelled back. "I'm coming back and we're all staying together!"

"No!" shouted Childheart, with an almost personal anger in his voice. "All of you are taking the alternate route, and I will continue on until I can find a way inland and hope, then, to meet up with you again!"

"Childheart," Kahner said quietly, but firmly, "it was agreed by all, including Thorn and Starnee, that no one would travel alone. Beatríz needs to be with the others. I will accompany you, if you will let me."

"I'll come, too!" Beatríz said, imploringly. "I don't want to be separated from Kahner again!"

"Beatríz," said Kahner, "you need to . . ."

"Be the one to go with Childheart, then," she said emphatically, interrupting him. "I have been with him since we left the first mountains."

"And I was with him the entire time going *through* those mountains!" answered Kahner.

"Children, enough! You're acting childish. This is not about what *anyone* wants. This is about what is right and best for the mission before us." Childheart then pronounced, in a tone that reminded Beatríz of her school principal, "Beatríz, you must remain with Alex and Jamie. Your options for travel through these mountains, as demonstrated just now, will be better and more numerous with the others. We need to get you, Beatríz, to the Queen's castle. But I *will* take Kahner; he is correct about the group decision. Besides, Beatríz, you are already shivering with cold, and all of you can rest now for the remainder of the day and night and get warm. I think there is even enough wood among you to have at least one more fire."

Immediately, as if just this moment had been anticipated for a long time, Beatríz whispered something into Kahner's ear and hugged him— then quickly walked through the opening. Without any more delay, Childheart and Kahner decided to chance a further climb. It was now getting so cold, and the wind was swirling so harshly, that Childheart knew that if they stayed where they were for the night it would be where they stayed forever.

~TWENTY~

THE TOP OF THE sun was barely visible from behind the rough edges of
granite and snow and ice in the far eastern sky when Starnee and Thorn
finally saw mountaintops low enough for Starnee to fly over to the north.
The trick would be to continue to find elevations no higher than these
until they had crossed the entire mountainous divide between what now
seemed a distant past and their immediate future.

Having already flown for nearly three hours due west in the early
hours of the morning in search of a promising elevation, Starnee needed
rest before turning north. He settled himself and his large shadow racing
before him on the ground below onto a slightly elevated piece of flat rock
just above the foot of the mountain range. Since Starnee was only minutes
from the valley, he left Thorn and went fishing. Soon he returned with fish
and water, which Thorn had prepared his palate, as before, to unnaturally
accept. Twenty minutes later, as the sun was effortlessly lifting from the
eastern rim of the jagged horizon, Starnee, with Thorn securely aboard,
leapt heavily from the rocky shelf, dipped precipitously, and then, like a
speedy swimmer, scooped the air beneath him with all four wings and
climbed rapidly to the point of intended entry over The Mountains. The
air was crisp and cool, apple fresh, and Starnee felt the warmth of the sun's
rays through the thin blue air while Thorn took comfort in a small nest of
feathers and down just behind Starnee's neck.

They flew uneventfully for about an hour over and around and between the steel-gray peaks that seemed to lunge at them suddenly from all
directions. The poultices of ice and snow plastered randomly over fissures,
cuts and crevices were the only variations in an otherwise stark grey texture stretching in all directions. Starnee yelled back at Thorn through the
roaring wind that they should begin to look for a place to land. For this
purpose, simply because the higher he flew the less three dimensional the
earth appeared, Starnee descended to a point where he could better see a

landing spot—and where Thorn feared they would fatally clip one of the rocky peaks and ridges that were racing past them on all sides. Starnee flew for another half hour without spotting a suitable place to land. There were no—even precarious—small valleys to settle into as a last resort, since the landscape of mountaintops was like a sea of tall and wide stalagmites that were joined at their bases, with no level spaces visible between them. The few horizontal strips of snow or ice they saw that were otherwise suitable for landing were impossible to fly into between the rocky walls that all but enclosed them.

Starnee realized to his private dismay that unless he found someplace to land within the next hour, he would have to land involuntarily wherever he happened to be once he no longer had the energy to remain aloft. There was no turning back now; it was an hour and a half back to the valley, and, besides, there was nothing suitable for landing they had flown across to this point. Finally, he communicated the predicament to Thorn who, despite the freezing wind that felt like needles impaling themselves into his tight skin, cast both eyes toward the ground in search of a landing zone.

The sun was now so high and bright that the nuance of shadowing that might disclose a promising spot was entirely absent. As they neared the end of another half hour of flight, Thorn could hear Starnee breathing. It wasn't laborious, Thorn thought, but what was worrisome was that this was the first time he had ever heard Starnee breathe at all. Thorn was now looking so hard at the ground that his eyes began uncharacteristically to water, diminishing his ability to see. Starnee was just staring straight ahead, focusing all his energy on remaining aloft and hoping that Thorn would spy something soon.

"Thorn . . ." Starnee rasped. "Anything?"

Thorn knew now that they were in dire straights: Starnee had never called him Thorn before.

"Nothing, Starnee—simply nothing at all—and I don't think we are going to find anything," replied Thorn, resignedly. "Do you?"

"I can go perhaps another ten minutes, and then we'll have to abandon the sky. I'll do the best I can, Sticks, but you'd better prepare yourself for quite a rough landing. Hold tight with both hands, but keep a look out. If I say 'jump!' do so immediately, and without asking questions, got it?"

"But, Starnee, I'm not . . ." Thorn interjected.

"No 'but,' Sticks; just jump when I tell you to!"

Starnee was now breathing as if every breath hurt his lungs, and Thorn could feel the heaviness Starnee was feeling as their speed diminished and a slow and inescapable descent was underway. Starnee was banking unstably one way and then another when, just as they rounded a sharp peak, Starnee noticed on the upper side of another peak dead ahead a narrow shelf of rock that was both devoid of snow and just wide enough to accommodate Thorn. At one of its short ends it became a tiny bridge between that peak and a second one. Starnee flew directly toward it and yelled for Thorn to be ready to jump. Then, just as Starnee appeared to be heading directly into the side of the mountaintop, he pulled up sharply and hung for a brief moment in the air, fluttering just above the shelf and yelling huskily, "Jump! Now!"

Thorn sprang awkwardly from Starnee's back and landed with a loud thud about fifteen feet beneath the bird—then watched in horror as his flailing friend dropped from the sky like a heavy stone. Starnee's body hit hard against the rocky face of the mountain, bounced sharply away, and then hit the opposite mountainside at a fierce rate of descent before crashing out of sight thousands of feet below into a tiny crevice of deep snow.

"Starnee! Starnee!" yelled Thorn, peering over the edge on all fours. But he knew, this time, there would be no Cannotoad angels to save him. The only reply to his call was a barely audible echo of his own plea bouncing back to him, as if mockingly, from the indifferent world that now engulfed him. Thorn lay on his stomach for a long time, peering over the edge of the outcropping at the barely visible dark hole made by Starnee's body plummeting to the unforgiving ground. The sun was almost directly overhead, and the peak at Thorn's back was blocking the stiff northeast wind, enabling Thorn to feel sufficiently warm in his exhaustion and sorrow to fall asleep involuntarily.

Thorn awoke rather suddenly to swirling snow striking his body in the dusky light of early evening, the only evidence of the sun being an orange-to-red glow above the peaks in the western sky that was barely visible through the turbulent storm. There was no more hope in Thorn. If there was any to be found, it needed to be with those who would hope on his behalf. Thorn's mind was racing inside his inert body. Should he just go back to sleep and die right there, not far from his friend? Should he try to save himself, as impossible as that was, knowing that he at least died *trying* to live? Or should he deliberately join Starnee, and lie *alongside* him, their mutual resting place providing perhaps the only place of preserved meaning among these otherwise eternally meaningless mountains?

Thorn rose, having decided to hope against hope—and so bet against despair—even if it meant taking only one step from that forsaken and forsaking place on which he had been lying for several hours. He would move forward from that place, one step at a time, whether a step into life or a step into death. Each step taken would be taken in the face of doubt and in the absence of belief, as an act of true faith. He would be one who insisted on living eternally regardless of what was otherwise true or false, otherwise enduring or ephemeral. In that way also he would pay eternal homage to Starnee and to their friendship, and to all his friends who together were attempting the impossible for something larger than they themselves.

Thorn crawled away from the sheltering rock and along the narrow, short stone bridge that connected the peak where he had been to the one toward which he was heading, hoping to find better surfaces from which to climb down. Once across, he began his slow, tentative descent with the intention of first trying to locate Starnee's body upon reaching the base of the peak, as impossible a task as that seemed. His one comfort, aside from at least trying to live, was the knowledge that in the event of his likely fall and certain death, he would fall in or near where Starnee disappeared. Whether he continued to live or to die, Thorn was determined to move for the sake of the Good, come what may, and, in that way, choose his own destiny.

The wind swirled tightly and rapidly around the wide cold peak to which Thorn was clinging, forcing him to grip as best he could with all four sets of fingers to keep from falling. The snow was thickening the air to near whiteout conditions now and gathering across his eyeballs, sticking to his lenses like freezing sleet against a windshield. Thorn blinked continually to clear his vision, but felt the sharp, resistant crystals of snow and ice already clinging to his eyeballs tearing at his lids with every blink. He descended perhaps two feet in the course of ten minutes and then paused for a moment, laying his forehead against the rock in utter exhaustion. As if hallucinating, he saw the four children standing along the rock with him and urging him on:

"One more step, Thorn; just one more step—you can always do one more step." As the voices and apparitions faded, he knew he could not allow himself to think about the ludicrously impossible distance he would have to travel to get across The Mountains and back to a part of the world that could sustain him. Nor could he calculate and dwell on the impossible length of time that any chance of success would have to take him. He could think only about taking one step at a time, and doing so for those with whom he had made a covenant.

He knew he needed to reach that point far down the peak that ended in the fingerling of snow encasing Starnee, and that he had to keep going regardless of the frigid darkness and driving snow obscuring his vision and stiffening his limbs. Stopping meant death. Life required movement. And so, one thin, frozen limb at a time, Thorn reached for a place he felt he could grab hold of before releasing another limb to grasp.

For better than three hours Thorn descended at a snail's pace through the fiercely darkening and snow-swirling skies that increasingly prevented him from seeing anything except the features to which he was clinging near his head. Thorn was now having difficulty feeling the rocky wall with his numb fingers, including those on his feet. He knew that he would have to find a place to stop, if not for the remainder of the night, then at least until he could warm his fingers and rest his arms and legs.

One step at a time he descended, feeling heavier as the moments passed, in part because of his tiring limbs, but also because the whipping snow was clinging to his body and accumulating, like ice on a plane's wings while in flight through a storm. Finally, Thorn could no longer tell if his next step was a secure one, so frozen were the fingers on both his feet. But then suddenly, Thorn spotted just eight or ten feet beneath him a black spot that indicated a small cave into the mountainside big enough for Thorn to stop and rest. It was there, he was certain of it. If he could just keep descending for another ten minutes he would reach it!

Within the vortex of swirling snow and an icy wind that slapped his head against the sharp stone wall, Thorn scraped about the face of the mountain with the one free foot, trying to feel something on which he could partially settle some weight, but the swinging motion caused him quite suddenly to lose all the other grips, and he fell, plummeting into the unkind darkness—enshrouded in screaming wind and his own silence.

~TWENTY-ONE~

"Well, climb aboard, Kahner. Let's see what we can find—or what can find us, perhaps. At least we have a path—for now. It may not lead us anywhere favorable, Kahner, but sometimes just having a path is enough."

And so Childheart, with his mount aboard, pawed and padded insecurely into the darkness and labored up the path, their heads bent toward the ground against the sharp icy wind and slapping flakes of snow hurling themselves at horse and rider. They continued in this fashion for nearly four hours without speaking except for the "Okay!" that Kahner repeatedly shouted, as if to himself, before Childheart would take another step. It seemed as if they had traveled nowhere during that entire time with each barely visible step on the path looking to Kahner like the one taken before. And yet, after another hour, Childheart called out that he thought they had journeyed around the peak and were now heading due north, because the wind was no longer pouring over the mountaintop. The accumulation of the snow on both the path and their bodies was slowing them considerably, and each of the travelers was beginning to think that stopping and staying on the path for the night would soon no longer be even a bad choice, but an inevitable one. They knew that what remained of this now short night might for them become an eternal one. Both Kahner and Childheart became lost in thoughts that warmed them on the inside while the increasingly numbing forces of bitter wind and snow were "warming" them to their harm on the outside: Together, as if in a conspiracy, warm memories and bitter cold were lulling the two sojourners towards a painless entrance into an endless night's sleep.

Kahner was lost in remembrance of Beatríz's caresses on his face that gave him love and saved his life, and Childheart was replaying in his own mind the most joyful of all the beautiful music that the Forest of Joy had gifted Bairnmoor over the centuries. But Childheart also heard something else breaking increasingly into the music he was hearing; it was the sorrowful songs of the Forest of Lament, reminding him that any death of his would certainly mean the death of the Forest and so the silencing of all of its music for all time. The unicorn slowed to an involuntary stop, reflecting on what a relief it would be to end it all right there.

As if intended for his own ears, Childheart yelled, "No, Kahner! We can't stop! We can't stop! We can always take one more step—one more step! We must *not stop, no matter what*! Let nothing but the Good stop us now! Nothing but the Good!" Childheart thought he might hear—if only brief—words of confirmation from Kahner, but there was nothing, and Childheart shuddered when he no longer felt any movement on his back of the companion who had been riding with him and barking out the command for each successive step.

"Kahner!" Childheart shouted. "Are you awake? Kahner!"

Just when Childheart was certain he was carrying an unconscious, if not dead, rider and friend, Kahner yelled out, "Childheart! There's something up ahead! It's a light! It's a light!"

Childheart strained to raise his sore and tired eyes to see what it was that Kahner was seeing, but saw nothing in that lightless world—not even the snow flying sharply into his face. Childheart concluded it was just a winter mirage of Kahner's hallucinating mind on the brink of shutting down. Childheart nevertheless yelled back words of encouragement, "Kahner, let's head for it! Stay sharp! Let me know what else you see!"

Kahner, as if newly roused by whatever he thought he saw, and by both the sound of his own voice and the words from Childheart, screamed back to Childheart despairingly, "They're gone! They're gone, Childheart! Where did they go?"

Childheart yelled back immediately to keep Kahner hopeful and alert. "It's okay, Kahner! It must still be there! Just keep looking! We'll find it!" He heard nothing in reply from Kahner, but Childheart could tell from a slight movement of the rider that Kahner was still with him, toward what end it made no sense to think about. Death had become a grasping, palpable presence.

Then Childheart heard Kahner yell once more, as if in a voice that hadn't spoken in a very long time, "I see it again, Childheart! The light! It's up ahead!" And he added, quickly and desperately, "But it's going away, Childheart! Hurry!" With that directive Childheart labored against the elements with what would most certainly be a final surge of energy and strength and speed, expending all to keep the two of them alive a moment longer. In utter abandonment, Childheart no longer looked toward the ground for the solid footing that Kahner would bring into view with each successive step, but, instead, focused straight ahead into the frontal assault, determined even in failure to make a noble end.

This was now the swiftest that Childheart had traveled on the path since he first set foot on it thousands of feet below. As he anticipated a fatal misstep that would send unicorn and rider into oblivion, Childheart suddenly saw the light himself, and there was no mistaking it for a mirage, since both he and Kahner noted the appearance simultaneously, shouting in unison, "The light!"

The soft beacon halted lazily some thirty yards ahead, and Childheart slowed his pace to a determined walk. As they drew closer to their quarry—or predator—both Childheart and Kahner could see that what had appeared to be a single floating light was actually many smaller lights, facilely cutting through this darkest of nights like a tight school of phosphorescent sea nymphs in quiet ocean depths. They knew they were almost certainly being beckoned, but for whose sake?

Approaching to within ten feet of the Fire-eyes, Childheart and Kahner saw them suddenly disappear off to the left. However, perhaps another thirty yards in the distance, they noticed what they assumed was a second set of barely visible Fire-eyes. These moved suddenly closer to Childheart and his rider, but abruptly stopped and backed away, as if also beckoning the two of them to follow. Carefully once again, Childheart pawed at the ground at the sound of an extremely weak "okay" drifting down from above. And then after a few more steps there appeared abruptly—in the rough, frozen mountainside next to them—a cavern that led deep into the mountain, reflecting soft light, and perhaps promised warmth, in the distance.

Childheart paused at the opening, gazing momentarily at the Fire-eyes hovering in the distance, and then turned into the shelter of the cave. They walked slowly down the tunnel of polished and multi-faceted rock, both sides of which played with the dim illumination that was emanating from the far back of the cavern, as if tossing balls of twinkling light back and forth. The sharp and measured clopping of each of Childheart's hoofs on the smooth cavern floor reverberated so loudly that it echoed like a dozen galloping horses in fierce pursuit of conquest were producing the cacophony.

Childheart and Kahner walked for nearly half an hour without appearing to be any closer to the source of the light, and the Fire-eyes that appeared to have gone in ahead of them were nowhere to be seen.

Perhaps those they last saw outside and beyond the cavern opening were the same Fire-eyes they had just earlier lost from view. It was less frigid inside the cave, and they continued toward the light that was now beginning to brighten as they reached a widely curving tunnel, the angle of which was becoming increasingly more acute. Childheart noticed that the echoes from his footfalls had lessened and were now almost entirely behind them. They rounded a sharp corner and halted. They could feel a light, warm and fragrant wind from an opening fifty yards ahead. Neither said a word as they basked in the gentle breeze and let their eyes adjust to the soft light shining through the opening. Childheart resumed the journey, and soon they found themselves at the other end of the tunnel. There before them, spreading for many miles in all directions, and entirely surrounded by the tallest and sheerest of mountain walls and sharp, snow-pocked peaks, was a valley of woods and springs and creeks, with wide swaths of meadow grasses and wildflowers, fruit orchards and wheat fields. Everything reflected in an effulgent shimmer the canopy of a stunningly brilliant, star-washed sky.

Kahner dismounted and stood next to Childheart, both of them gazing across an isolated, idyllic world that suggested a Bairnmoor in better days and centuries earlier. Most amazing of all was that this bucolic expanse was thriving at nearly fifteen thousand feet above sea level in the midst of the harshest and most frigid and lifeless of places in all of Bairnmoor. Indeed, on the other side of the tunnel through which they had just traveled existed an eternal winter of blinding snowstorms, cutting wind, and a cold so cold that nothing in its clutches could exist meaningfully.

There was no continuation of a path outside the cavern, except an ancient-looking and overgrown one, that suggested anything had either come from or gone into the tunnel for a very long time. Except for one small sliver of rogue space through which they could see the landscape below, the entirety of the hillside around the opening consisted of an uninterrupted thicket of tall and wild junipers that extended steeply to the valley floor. If anyone knew of the existence of the tunnel it wasn't because it was visible, and excursions up the hillside through the thicket would have been tortuous—perhaps even impossible.

Grateful for the salvific warmth of the summer night, Kahner and Childheart rested for about an hour, then turned their attention to finding a way to the valley floor, eager to learn something about this new world—and, finally, where they were—and why.

"Where do you think we are, Childheart?" asked Kahner, staring bewilderedly at the vista before him.

"I've no idea, Kahner. By the laws of nature, it shouldn't be here; so something strange is afoot. Stay alert. Let's find a way down, hopefully without being seen."

"Childheart!" Kahner whispered guardedly. "There's room to move up and to the right. Maybe it can lead us around the thicket. Besides, I don't see any other way."

"Okay, let's go. Climb aboard, but stay low."

~TWENTY-TWO~

LIKELY HALLUCINATING, STARNEE SAW a cameo of his mate, Mythena, lovely and glowing against the blackness roaring past him as he plummeted through the stormy night sky. Invisible darts of ice stormed his eyes, their lids no longer able to close and protect him from the wintry assault. His wings, surrendering to death, folded close, and his speed accelerated toward the base of the peak on which moments earlier he had deposited Thorn. Starnee could only hope that providence would somehow preserve his friend against his own fate, the lone consolation of which was that death would come with a collision he would never feel—or recall had ever happened.

What both amazed and frightened Starnee was that he *did sense* his hurtling into an ancient drift of snow at the speed of a comet, that he *did experience* it, and that he *knew,* and *continued to know,* it had occurred. He felt no pain, only a warm blanket of darkness enveloping and caressing his body, as if trying to rescue and protect him. But he saw and heard nothing. Was this but an initiation into death? Starnee wondered. Was death, then, a friend you immediately became intimate with, even before you knew what—or who—it was? Or, was he yet to be smashed—and obliterated—leaving no discernible remnant of his ever having existed?

Suddenly Starnee was in a sky awash in stars as big as Christmas ornaments, and Starnee was rising swiftly to meet them. He was no longer cold, and he could now close his eyes. But Starnee kept them open, for the warm and soft wind was soothing them, and his vision was fixed on the enchantment of the celestial lights. Instinctively, he spread his wings, slowed his ascent, and glided effortlessly on the balmy currents that were drifting upward to catch and cradle him aloft. It was then that Starnee looked groundward—and was just as delightfully enchanted by the vista beneath him.

Stretching for miles and miles lay a valley of deep forests and wide meadows shimmering under a glaze of stardust and surrounded by tall, jagged mountain peaks that sparkled so brilliantly in the starlight that Starnee could scarcely tell where ground ended and sky began. Soaring effortlesslessly on caressing drafts billowing up to carry him, Starnee was as contented as an infant in its mother's arms.

Starnee's reverie was momentary, however, for he quickly remembered Thorn, and the frozen peak on which Starnee had both saved and abandoned him. He had been hoping against all odds that Thorn would be able to survive the mountain peaks and reach the northern side of the broad range still hundreds of miles away. Now, Starnee was fervently hoping for Thorn to fall—right where Starnee had left him—and actually expecting it, perhaps at any moment. Starnee continued his effortless gliding for a number of hours, gaining strength from it and using it to scan the heavens for any movement against the sparkling lights above that would signal Thorn's soaring presence.

And, then, like watching a black comet shooting skyward from behind the tooth-edged horizon, Starnee saw a rapid succession of interruptions in the canopy of lights, as if they were turning off and on, one right after the other, and in a perfectly bowed line streaking straight up. Starnee knew without a doubt it was the body of Thorn that was shooting toward the stars. Knowing that Thorn's swift ascent would brake and reverse itself quickly, sending him once again groundward, Starnee took off, as if catapulted, toward the tiny mass that was streaking overhead.

Thorn, who, like Starnee before him, was gaping wide-eyed at the celestial display toward which he was soaring, and feeling the embrace of a soft warmth rushing to comfort and reassure him, was startled by his sudden flop into the deep feathers and down at the back of Starnee's neck. Thorn shouted a welcoming "Starneeeeee!"—and Starnee barked back . . . "Grab tight!"

Thorn yelled through the muffling feathers, "I have never been so happy to see anyone in my entire life!" He caught his breath. "You're alive! I'm alive! And we're clear of The Mountains!"

"Yeah, it's all pretty good stuff, Sticks, but not so fast with your elation. We're not clear of The Mountains yet. We're just between them. But, take a look below. I don't have any idea what it is or where we are, but that's where we're headed. Hold on!"

And, with that, Starnee banked sharply to his left, bringing the ground into view for Thorn to see for the first time—his two bulbous eyeballs protruding through the feathers toward the world below. There was so much that he wanted to talk with Starnee about, but right then the glory all around him left him speechless.

~TWENTY-THREE~

ELLI BECAME AWARE, FIRST, of the delicate breeze that was cooling her flushed face. Next, she felt herself lying in a pool of water that felt like flowing silk soothing the rest of her feverish body. Then, Elli detected some barely audible whispers echoing from a number of directions, as if they were coming from a distance in a vast hall, and felt something delicate stroking her head and pulling tenderly at her hair. "Am I *actually* dead now?" Elli wondered. "Or, had I died the first time I left Blackfire, and this is just a continuation of that same event? Or, am I simply still in the process of dying, and whatever is happening to me now is simply another step or stage on the way to death? Or," Elli asked herself in the luxury of this moment before opening her eyes, "am I waking slowly from a dream and will soon find myself in my soft bed, cooled by morning breezes wafting through my open bedroom window?"

Better yet, she thought, would she find herself on the verdant grass of Oak Ridge Park where she had only *believed* she had found herself before, just to learn now that *that* was a dream, and this time an awakening for real? And then she wondered, "What *is* best and happiest in life, after all? Are they necessarily the same? And is one dependent on the other? Or are they perhaps incompatible with each other?"

Setting those thoughts aside, Elli wondered whether opening her eyes to an awakening in Millerton would be what she really most wanted—if she had a choice, and *did* have a choice, about where to be, and whether to be happy or not.

Her mind drifted back to the events, whether real or not, of her visit to the Lake of Imagination. It was as if her mind was now floating atop currents without any volition on her part to make thoughts drift in one direction or another. It was almost as if she was being *given* these movements of her mind—in the same way, it seemed, she was given this protracted time specifically for wondering—and, perhaps, even gifted so much more in everything leading up to this moment.

Elli felt no urgency to open her eyes and reveal to her conscious mind whoever it was who was attending to her. She was apparently in a place of no immediate danger—where the intent was to soothe her body, make her comfortable, and patiently wait for her to awaken. What *did* she hope to discover?

She understood now what she wanted. She wanted to be in the Queen's castle and on her way to the burial vault. But it was one thing to be in the castle and quite another to be going to the vault—especially since, she suddenly realized, no longer feeling its presence about her neck, she had no key! And the only one she had had was almost certainly not the key she needed, at least according to the prophecy.

Elli opened her eyes only slightly to get the barest glimpse of her immediate surroundings without being noticed—like opening her bedroom door just a tiny crack late at night to learn if her parents' door was closed before slipping unnoticed down the stairs.

But, she *was* noticed, and so Elli opened her eyes the entire way—to look into another set of eyes that were watching hers attentively, as they likely had been doing for a very long time. The sky blue eyes that greeted Elli's were glistening with warmth. They were the eyes of a young woman seated next to Elli.

Elli was lying in a large rectangular pool of water, soft as olive oil, and female attendants beside her in the water kept her floating still and close to the mosaic tile edge where the "watching woman" was seated. Leaning over Elli, the woman looked directly into her eyes. The woman's long wheat-blonde hair nearly grazed Elli's face. She wore a sleeveless, multilayered dress of sheer metallic chiffon that draped like liquid silver over the curves of her body. The hem was draped on the brilliantly colored marble floor. She sat motionless on a settee. Elli focused her eyes about and above and around the girl, who was perhaps no more than seventeen or eighteen years of age, and observed that the two of them were in a large hall with high ceilings supported by flying buttresses of carved stone.

Elli sat up on the satin cushions provided by the attendants and only then realized she was naked. She was surprised that she was not the least bit embarrassed, giving no thought to covering her pubescent breasts or any other part of her body. Elli felt strangely safe, and that surprised Elli as well, for she had no idea where, or in whose presence, she was. Her first thought was that she was in the palace of Queen Taralina. Everything looked like the palace interiors she had pictured in her mind since she first heard fairy tales about kings and queens as a small child. She noticed the open terrace well behind the seated woman that revealed in the far distance a meadow and trees in the grip of a sunless, late autumn grimness.

Elli looked back into the eyes of her watch keeper. "Where am I?" asked Elli, in a tone that was almost matter-of-fact, "and how did I get here, and who are you?"

"In the order in which you asked the questions," replied the young woman, and just as matter-of-factly, as if all was now settled between them, "you are in the castle of the Princess of Bairnmoor. We found you unconscious outside the furthest gate to the castle grounds—and naked and feverish, I might add. My name is Santanya and this is my home. They call me 'Tanya.'" Her voice was warm and welcoming.

"How long have I been here?" asked Elli.

"We found you and brought you here nearly thirty days ago. I have been watching you almost constantly since your arrival."

"But," Elli said, with a long and considered pause, "are you a friend or an enemy of Queen Taralina?"

"That depends on your perspective, of course," replied Santanya. "I mean, I have always both adored and admired the Queen, and that remains true even now, when it comes to her legacy. I do not view her in the way my father views her. Upon her death, my father assumed the mantle of 'Eternal Ruler of Bairnmoor.' My only brother died in battle defending my father, and my father is determined to seal his rule against all enemies, real or potential—or even imagined." Tanya was by this time lost in thought and speaking as if she were no longer aware of Elli's presence. Elli, for her part, was still looking into Tanya's eyes, staring at the realization that she was face-to-face with the daughter of Sutante Bliss!

"What do you know about me?" asked Elli. Tanya motioned delicately for the attendants to once again lay Elli back into the water.

"Well, first of all, what I don't know is your name."

Elli understood the danger if she lied, and Tanya knew it. "My name is Elli."

"Is that for Eleanor or Elizabeth, then?" asked Tanya.

"It's just Elli. Nothing significant about it except it was all my parents could think of before they arrived to pick me up at the adoption agency."

Tanya continued smiling at Elli. "Well, Elli, I can tell you everything I know about you rather quickly, because I don't know very much. But, I do know what I know is important." Tanya shifted on the settee. "I know you are one of a small number of children not from Bairnmoor—four in total, I believe. I know you are on a journey and one of you has a key that some believe . . ." And here Tanya paused, and then said again, "That some believe could alter the course of the history of Bairnmoor were it to reach inside castle walls once belonging to the Queen.

"I know you have others from Bairnmoor assisting you in your quest, and that my father wants desperately to find the key and destroy it before the prophecy of a poem can be fulfilled." Tanya paused and then continued. "Elli, my father says it is only that: a poem—and so without truth. But I know he worries privately, and that he is obsessed with finding the key—and the girl who owns it."

Elli glanced furtively at the attendants.

"They cannot hear, Elli; nor can they read lips. Now, I happen to believe that there *is* something to the poem's truthfulness—and even hope fervently that is the case. But the only way to find out is to get the girl with the key safely to the Queen's vault. And," she said, with emphasis, "without my help it cannot be accomplished." Tanya nodded toward Elli. "I see that you do not have the key; so I will assume there is another girl with whom you have been traveling who does, and that *your* mission is to help her fulfill *her* mission, and so fulfill the prophecy and return Bairnmoor to Queen Taralina." Santanya sighed benignly. "Am I correct?"

Elli sat up again, the attendants immediately assisting her. "I cannot tell you what our purpose is for being in Bairnmoor, regardless of whether you believe you know what that purpose is or not, Tanya. In fact, I'm not even sure I exactly know our purpose. Also," she added, "I do not have the key, and I don't know whether any of my friends now possess it or not.

"And since I no longer see how I can assist them," Elli said, with moist eyes, "I don't know how *you* can be of assistance to *us*."

Tanya's smile lifted from her face. "I have a plan. My father will trust me, and *that* will be my key to getting *your* key." A smile settled once more on Santanya's gentle face.

"How am I to know I can trust you, Tanya?"

"You can't, Elli. But, then, I think trusting me is the best you can do; is this not true?" Tanya did not wait for a reply, and Elli seemed unwilling to give one. Instead, Tanya motioned to the attendants and rose. She began walking away and said simply, "I will see you at dinner; we'll talk more then. There will be a fresh dress on your bed to wear—and in the closet all the lovely clothes you could possibly want while you are here. As I said, my attendants found you with nothing." She stopped and said over her shoulder, "Well, nothing except a knife lying next to you; it's in your room."

~TWENTY-FOUR~

"C'MON, BUTWEECE! YOU CAN do it! I know you can!" yelled Alex from the rocky ledge, as soon as he glimpsed the shadowed outline of Beatríz pushing on all fours against the darkness and the snow-hurling wind. Beatríz made no answer, focusing all her attention on ensuring she was setting her now numb palms on stone and keeping her balance. She never imagined that cold could really be this cold—or she could possibly *feel* this cold. She was thinking that it had to be a dream from which she would almost certainly awaken. But, when? When? Perhaps falling wouldn't be the worst thing in the world, Beatríz thought. They say you always wake from your dream before you hit the ground. And, if not . . .

Not once raising her head toward Alex and Jamie, Beatríz padded her palms and knees gingerly along, like one trying to avoid random spots of fire, except that her hands could feel nothing—nothing, that is, except the aching inside them from the weight they bore with each hand-step forward. How absolutely crazy this was if it was *not* a dream, Beatríz reflected. Who was she, anyway, of *all people—of all people*—to be doing this, to be on this mission? She, the *least* of unqualified candidates! How is it that with infinitely less demanding jobs they always want "qualified candidates only" to apply, but not with this one? She half chuckled at the irony. Almost *anyone* was more qualified than she to be on this mission! Indeed, almost *everyone*.

And yet, as Beatríz inched cautiously forward, she wondered if anyone could be qualified for this mission! The mission was so far beyond everyone's qualifications that it really didn't matter what fool was willing to "be chosen." Still, why she? Was it just random? And if random, then how could that be called "chosen"? That would make her selection more like a lottery. Or, was she simply one of the three (or truly four) most gullible people alive?

But, she *was* chosen! And she wasn't even the girl of the poem, although, she remembered, she *was* the girl with the key—or, the only key they had.

Beatríz—alarmed—shuddered and fell suddenly forward. But she smiled ecstatically when she felt the sturdy arms of Alex pulling her into his lap and out of the wind and snow. All three exchanged greetings and words of relief while Beatríz nestled urgently into Alex's embrace. They then moved just inside the mouth of the small cave at the back of the desolate overhang and built a small fire. Sitting behind the fire, their heads close to the ceiling and their bodies close together, they could feel just barely the heat from the few flames that flickered lamely in front of them.

They ate from their satchels while the fire died out and then moved further into the tunnel and slept, wrapped in each other's arms. Alex kept vigil in his light sleep, with the hand of his arm encircling Beatríz gripping tightly the hilt of his drawn knife. The wind outside whistled a harsh lullaby.

It was not yet dawn when they were startled from sleep. They sat up and tensed, wondering. What they noted first was a draft of warmer air, and then a faint rumbling and a dim light issuing quietly from the bowels of the mountain, as if from a distant lava.

Led by Alex on all fours, followed by Beatríz and Jamie, they traveled about a hundred yards, when the tunnel widened considerably, enabling them to stand and walk abreast. They noticed that the surface arching over them as well as the floor itself were becoming increasingly smooth until they were as smooth as the surface of a blown crystal goblet. As the tunnel turned ever so slightly, Jamie and Alex noticed the light at the suspected end of the tunnel was growing larger, brighter, and seemingly closer.

Suddenly, tiny bits of light no larger than a grain of sand were appearing in growing numbers as they walked, each speck bouncing from one surface of the tunnel to the next. The light ahead of them continued to brighten, and the bits of light were becoming rapidly, maybe even exponentially, more numerous. Within a few minutes the travelers were surrounded by the light. Jamie and Alex were amazed they could keep their eyes open; never had they seen so bright a light before. Was it now a single light—or was it actually gazillions of tiny lights that simply appeared to be a single light, every bit alive, but stationary?

They walked hand in tight hand for another several minutes until they came to the end of the tunnel. Here they would have walked directly into a solid, sheer perpendicular wall reflecting the gathered light had they not stepped together, still hand in hand, onto a steep and slippery slope that pulled them speeding beneath the wall and into the depths of the mountain. Not one of the children said a word or made any sort of noise. It was as if there were no words or sounds that could express what they were encountering, much less what they were feeling. It was as if they had no thoughts or feelings, but existed purely as an integral part of what was happening—not just *to* them, but *by* them somehow, feeling as if they were both actor and acted upon. Even Beatríz was able to see the light, although she didn't know she was seeing, or what it was she saw.

They were soaring in light—a tube of light—a ball of light—a womb of light. Later, but how much later—was it an hour, or a minute, or only a second, or even no time at all? The light with which they were seemingly one began to dissipate. Suddenly, it cleared into a heaven awash in stars that appeared to outsize the sky. In that very same moment they found themselves lying still, one next to the other, still hand in hand, on a wide blanket of warm grass sprinkled generously with stardust.

The children sat up and looked about them. An entire world of grasses and trees and brooks and meadows and cultivated fields, as well as hillocks, lay around them, stretching everywhere to distant mountains that enclosed the lush world. Scattered widely were a small number of tiny houses made of adobe and thatch. Dim lights were dripping from the windows. The air was summer warm, and there were soft, lazy breezes. And the night was snuggly quiet—too quiet, it seemed to them. They rose to their feet and decided quickly and quietly to explore their surroundings while trying to remain undiscovered. Alex said he would lead.

Noticing a narrow path lined neatly on both sides by wide oaks and tall poplars as well as a number of scattered maple trees growing thick and close together, the three children determined it best to survey from within the cover of the path this strange new world into which they had been flung. Besides, the constant chatter of the wind-rustled leaves overhead would muffle the sound of any footfalls they made on the hard ground. So they crawled to the path through the tall meadow grasses and stood to walk, treading gently on the well-worn track before them and stopping often to peer between the trunks.

They walked in this manner for several hours, seeing much that amazed them. What appeared to be stardust covered all that was ex- posed to the elements—to the extent that trees and flowers, and other living things, including a large owl that swooped down and just above their heads, seemed to have no corporeal form except that provided by the stardust. Even the trees they peered between were covered with dust that, when brushed away, revealed nothing they could see—or even touch. Perhaps most amazing of all, however, was that in the course of four hours of travel through several square miles, they detected no evidence of humanlike creatures, or even of animal life, apart from the owl. They were increasingly eager to peer into the lighted windows of the few cottages they passed at a distance. Tired from the walking and the weariness accumulated over several days' travel, the three companions decided at last to sleep next to the trees until morning. Each of them nestled into some tall grass that hid them from any who might be traveling the path during the remainder of the night, and slept. Beatríz lay with her arms about Alex. Jamie found a spot on the other side of the path outside the row of trees.

When Jamie awoke, he was certain they had slept more than enough hours to get them well into the light of morning. But the night sky seemed to be no closer to dawn than it was when they had first retired for the night. Jamie sat up, looked all around him furtively for signs of unfamiliar life, and whispered sharply to the others, "Beatríz! Alex!!" There was no answer, so Jamie tried again, just a bit more forcefully, but not so loudly that anyone in a nearby cottage would be able to hear. "Beatríz! Alex! Wake up!" Still no answer, Jamie rose and ran to check on his friends. He rifled through the undergrowth where he had left them lying (who knew how many) hours earlier. Finding nothing, he sprang from one side of the path to the other, scanning the landscape through the trees for any signs of Beatríz and Alex, frequently barking their names in a sharp whisper. Jamie decided finally to climb one of the oak trees. He was a nimble and experienced climber, having often scaled trees to elude his brother or hide from his parents. However, more than once he slipped and nearly fell to the ground when he attempted to place a hand or a foot on places where he (or something else before him) had inadvertently brushed away stardust from the branches. Once, he grasped a branch so hard that it lost all its stardust and sent the upper half of the branch crashing down on him, narrowly missing his head.

Nevertheless, within minutes, Jamie reached a spot near the top of the tree and settled himself where he could get a clear view of all that lay around him and up the path. There was no sighting of either of his companions; but, just as he was about to climb down, Jamie noticed a tracing through the field. The tracing could only have been caused by the brushing of stardust from some of the grasses by persons or other large creatures filing through the meadow. Jamie noticed that the trace extended from where Beatríz and Alex had been sleeping to the top of a low rise in the distance where it quickly disappeared from view.

Jamie climbed down from the tree, careful to not scrape away too much of the stardust with his hands and feet. As soon as he reached the ground, however, he pushed his way with abandon through the dense hedge of trees and grasses and into the meadow. He then followed swiftly the trail less visible at ground level that was left by a substantial number of travelers—hopefully including his friends.

As Jamie ran he scanned the horizon all around him for the first signs of dawn that would provide the compass he wanted, but the still dark sky was unhelpful—and he did not recognize the stars. Jamie had no difficulty following the trail, however, and when he reached the top of the rise he could see clearly where it continued far ahead of him, fading well into the distance of the shimmering darkness spread out before him.

Jamie shifted his backpack, secured it tightly and checked for his knife before he set out running. He ran unimpeded for quite some time until he came to a swift river where the trail abruptly ended. Flecks of dust from the stars rushed past in the racing and turbulent waters, flashing brightly for a moment before the current bore them briskly away.

The river at that point was about thirty yards wide. Jamie could not determine how those traveling before him had crossed it, and yet somehow they had managed, for he saw the trail continuing on the opposite bank. Swimming was out of the question, and there was nothing apparent to convey him across. Accordingly, Jamie would attempt the only thing that seemed possible, as hazardous as it was. He would wade across and hope both that the river was shallow enough for him to plant his feet on the bottom and that the racing water wouldn't carry him downstream against large stones scattered throughout the river—or pull him under its surface.

With searching feet Jamie stepped from the river's edge and into the water, finding that even there it was already waist deep. He could only hope the river wouldn't become much deeper. As it was, he would have to struggle mightily to keep his balance. Jamie leaned hard against the current, digging his boots into the sandy floor as he planted one foot after another. Halfway across he was heartened to discover that the riverbed remained only waist deep. But, just as Jamie's spirits began to lift, he planted his foot against what he thought was a heavy boulder—that suddenly slipped away. The stone released itself to the torque of the current, abandoning Jamie to the aggressions of the river that swept him headlong downstream.

Jamie struggled with an unnatural strength against the force of the undertow to remain on top of the water, but he could manage to surface only for brief moments to gasp for a small amount of air before being pulled under once again. His Herculean effort was nearly spent, and he was not going to survive without immediate assistance. Jamie yelled for help—or, at least attempted to. But there wasn't enough air left in his lungs to produce more than a single "Help!" which was audible only to him. As Jamie lost consciousness and went limp, the invisible arms of the deep current coiling about him pulled his acquiescent body beneath the surface of the churning water.

~TWENTY-FIVE~

STARNEE MAINTAINED A SHARP left bank and descended gradually on the cushions of warm air billowing up to meet him while he searched for a suitable place to rest. Seeing a river, he decided to follow its course, intending to land where Thorn and he could have easy access to food and water. Starnee circled a host of times in a wide spiral downward, surveying with Thorn's assistance the surprising landscape. Starnee then leveled off just above the rushing river and continued to follow the course of its turbulence in an easy glide.

Starnee had noticed a wide depression near the river in which to settle when he suddenly saw something—or someone—struggling in the water just ahead. He dropped quickly toward the creature and, as he came upon it, saw it slip beneath the surface of the churning water. In that same instant, Starnee launched his folded legs like torpedoes into the river and grabbed whatever it was in his talons just before it slipped out of reach. Within seconds, Starnee had landed, together with Thorn and his salvage, in the soft grasses of the depression. Oblivious to what had just occurred, Thorn heard Starnee yell upon touching down, "Sticks! I just pulled something from the river! What did I rescue?"

Thorn hopped down from Starnee's back like a youngster and quickly stooped over what was obviously a person who was lying face down and lifeless. Thorn turned him over and shouted, with astonished incredulity, "Starnee! It's Jamie!" Thorn immediately checked Jamie for any sign of life and then began to pump his chest with his hands. "I don't know if he's dead yet, but we have to get the water out of his lungs or he soon will be!"

Starnee sat, calm but concerned, and watched Thorn work on Jamie, wondering how Jamie had gotten there and where the other two children were. Of course, he also wondered where Thorn and he were, and what had happened to Childheart and Kahner! What had become of the elaborately woven fabric of their mission that now seemed to have unraveled?

Starnee heard sounds of fatigue erupting from Thorn. Jamie remained unresponsive.

"Sticks! Let me try." Whereupon Starnee flipped Jamie onto his stomach with the slightest nudge of a talon and pressed hard on Jamie's back with one of his feet. One hard push was all it took to eject the water from Jamie's lungs, inducing a sputtering cough and wide open eyes.

"Wha . . . what happened?" Jamie rasped, taking some moments to regain fuller consciousness.

"That's what *we'd* like to know!" exclaimed Starnee, joyfully.

"Starnee!" Jamie exulted. "Thorn! I'm so glad to see you! What are you doing here? And how did you get here? And how did you find me—and what happened? And where am I?"

"Jamie, Starnee just pulled you from the river!" said Thorn.

"Well, truth be told, Sticks and I *both* were involved in the marine salvage operation, Jamie." Then, turning to Thorn, Starnee said, "Let's see if we can't build a fire and get him warm before he freezes to death. He's shivering faster than a pair of bees' wings!"

Thorn told Starnee it might take too long to build a fire effective enough and suggested that Jamie might dry out more quickly if he simply nestled in Starnee's feathers. Starnee acknowledged Thorn's wisdom and lowered himself for Jamie to climb aboard.

Jamie quickly peeled off his soaked clothing and laid it across some tall grasses. With some assistance from Thorn, he then scrambled onto Starnee's back and burrowed hungrily into the soft thick down growing close to Starnee's warm skin. Once Jamie *finally* got settled, as if he were a small child tossing in his blankets for just the right position to be comfortable, Starnee and Thorn told first what had happened to them since the breakup of the entire group. When it was his turn, Jamie, now warmed and fully alert, recounted what had happened to him—and to Beatríz and Alex. When all had concluded their stories, including a slew of questions shooting rapidly back and forth, the three became quietly immersed in their own individual thoughts.

"It would seem," offered Starnee, "that we are in a place where the sun neither rises nor sets. And yet, oddly, one can't quite say that it's always night—not with all the light from all these stars . . . these millions of tiny suns! So," he added, confidently, "there is no point in waiting for some sort of daylight before continuing our search for Beatríz and Alex."

Thorn and Starnee decided it would be best for Jamie to remain in the feathers until his clothes had fully dried. Thorn would continue by foot on the trace as far as it would take him, while Starnee would conduct a broader search from the sky. They agreed that Thorn would stop and wait for Starnee and Jamie if he discovered anything notable.

With Starnee in flight and visible only by the swift and successive blackout of stars by his soaring mass, Thorn put stick to ground and began to trod and scan intently the glistening terrain. His eyes, bulging from their sockets and dancing separately all about, looked like a pair of circus glasses floating by themselves in the darkness up the path. For several hours the search by land and air continued. Every half hour or so Starnee would double back and check on Thorn's progress, at one point returning to the spot of rescue for Jamie's clothes. Finally, Starnee saw from the sky that Thorn had stopped, his eyes fully protruded and searching the skies as if to signal to Starnee that something noteworthy had occurred.

Thorn pointed out to Starnee and a now dried and dressed Jamie that the trace had disappeared at the edge of a thick woods, concealing where the path led next. Nevertheless, the progress of those they were trailing must have continued into the forest; so, into the forest Thorn and Jamie decided to go. Starnee, not able to accompany them, decided to learn from the sky where the vast forest ended, and so where, perhaps, the path continued beyond the trees. If he did find the path continuing beyond the woods, Starnee would simply locate Jamie and Thorn through the forest canopy and carry them to where the course resumed—unless, of course, it was evident that the earlier party that entered the forest at one end had not exited it at the other. Part of Thorn's job was to search the sky frequently with his eyes fully protruded so Starnee would be able to locate them through the treetops on his return flight from the forest's edge.

Thorn and Jamie paused before the edge of the forest, staring at the wall of tangled undergrowth that soared as much as eight to ten feet high. They glanced at one another and then began to push and pull against the defensive—resistant—foliage. They fought for better than half an hour to get little more than thirty yards into the trees, struggling at the same time to stay in sight of each another, relying on the light from Thorn's eyes. Thorn really needed to pop out his eyes for maximum glow, as well as to be able to signal Thorn, but he was constantly afraid of getting them scratched or tangled in the twisted thicket of bushes, saplings, and coiling vines. It was so dark below, and the forest canopy was so high and thick above, that no stars were visible to assist them. For all Jamie and Thorn knew, they had spent half an hour simply going in a circle.

"Thorn! I can't go any further! It's just too dense!" Jamie whispered sharply. "But there's a small opening in the undergrowth that may be big enough for us to crawl through on our hands and knees. What do you think?"

"I can't get any further either," replied Thorn. "Let's try it."

And so, on all fours and crouched uncomfortably low to the moist and musky ground, Thorn and Jamie crawled one after the other into the low opening.

Even after an hour of flight, Starnee was unable to locate a continuation of any sort of path at the opposite side of the forest besides one that began halfway up The Mountains more than ten miles away—and which appeared to have been unused for years. Concluding it unrealistic that the party including Beatríz and Alex could have gotten that far in the time they had been separated from Jamie, Starnee headed back to the spot where he had left his companions entering the forest and began to look for the light from Thorn's eyes; but Starnee saw nothing. He spent several more hours flitting from treetop to treetop and poking his head through the leafy canopy in an effort to find his friends. Again, however, he was unsuccessful. He even dared finally to make sounds that Thorn would be able to identify, but received no response. At last Starnee called loudly for them, but there was only silence.

Starnee decided to look more carefully along the edge of the forest that ended at the base of The Mountains, hoping he would find much closer than the one ten miles away the trail on which he could reasonably assume Thorn and Jamie would ultimately emerge. There he would wait for a while. Meanwhile, Starnee would continue to search frequently for Thorn and Jamie from any number of brief perches in the treetops on his way toward the forest's edge.

After what must have been in Starnee's mind several days of shuttling between reconnaissance along the forest's edge near The Mountains and searching for his friends from the forest canopy, Starnee discovered the vestige of a trail deeply hidden in a wide stand of mostly large junipers, winding its way down the mountainside to the valley floor almost directly across from where Jamie and Thorn had entered the forest. As far as he could tell, the ancient-looking trail—which evidently had not been used for many years—extended from a location halfway up the mountainside to a place well below where, again, because of the density of the overgrowth, he was not able to see whether it reached all the way to the forest's edge. Nevertheless, after considering all options, Starnee established a provisisonal home base and point of lookout on a mountainside outcropping high above the trail.

Disconsolate and weary, Starnee focused his eyes vigilantly for a number of days on the path below. He saw nothing come or go. And he likely would have failed to see the movement on the path even immediately below him on the mountainside had he not also heard whispering. Starnee cocked his ear and gazed intently for their source. At first he saw nothing, but heard what seemed to be light, familiar footfalls on the stone and grit and more than one hushed voice. He strained his neck over the edge of the outcropping. Suddenly, Starnee saw who it was. With unrestrained delight he screeched, "Childheart! Kahner!"

The unicorn and its rider, who had just left the cover of the well-concealed tunnel lip to travel up the path in order eventually to go down, came to an abrupt and startled stop, and looked up.

"Starnee!" they cried gleefully.

Starnee directed them to a clearing wide enough for him to land on, where they gathered for the quick shedding of tears and sharing of stories. Soon what to do next also occupied a good deal of their time and thought. Starnee was not happy about being left out of the action, but he recognized there was nothing he could do in a ground level search through the forest. Childheart decided Kahner and he would follow the mountain path down as far as it went and then enter the forest at that point, regardless of whether there was any further path going into the forest. From there they would travel about a hundred yards inside the forest. Starnee would continue general reconnaissance from the sky, but would remain in frequent contact with Childheart and Kahner. Any further separation among the group they considered to be intolerable.

Childheart and Kahner discovered after a small struggle of some hours that the path down the mountain had at one point in the distant past indeed entered the forest. Extensive and undisturbed overgrowth indicated, however, that no one had either left or entered the forest by that trail for many decades. Regardless, the two of them decided without delay or hesitation to enter the forest at that point where path and forest had at one time joined. The going was not unlike that which Thorn and Jamie had experienced, including the discovery of an old tunnel made of vines and other material lying along the ground—and far too small for Childheart to use. But Childheart was no stranger to forests and the impediments they presented, so his going was more expeditious than Thorn and Jamie's foray into the woods. Indeed, Kahner was amazed at the extent to which Childheart was able to handle the dense undergrowth and interminable hanging lattice work of coiled vines, sharply angled branches, and the thick, sticky moss covering nearly all of it. What Childheart could not trample summarily to the ground he could either push quite easily through with his horn or jump over with his massive legs. Kahner spent most of his time on the unicorn's back scouting and providing verbal direction and encouragement—as well as ducking branches springing back at him! The noise that Childheart and he created made it easy for Starnee—or anything else, for that matter—to locate them.

After a while, foliage gave way to mossy grass, and the trees began to grow broader and further apart, and without the presence of rogue bushes and saplings, so there was no longer any need to struggle. Only Childheart's light footfalls on the soft turf broke the otherwise complete silence. Off to the left there was a large clearing that Childheart and Kahner paused to consider. Kahner felt a cold wind brush past his leg, and Childheart remarked immediately thereafter, "Did you feel that?"

"Yes," Kahner replied. "I did."

"Something's afoot. Stay alert!"

Childheart wondered to himself whether they might be walking into something, not unlike an ambush, but suggested nevertheless, "Let's have a look around the clearing, Kahner; not that I have an especially good feeling about it."

Childheart stepped into the broad circle of open space that, fully cleared and meticulously maintained around the edge, appeared to be some sort of frequented gathering ground. The temporary flattening of the groomed grass suggested that a gathering had taken place recently, perhaps only hours earlier, involving as many as several hundred creatures. Childheart walked slowly toward the center of the clearing and then stopped. A cold chill began to encircle them, and they heard rustling all about them in the forest. They saw the foliage at the edge of the clearing yielding suddenly to invisible forces that were spreading and trampling it, and heard the sound of dozens of feet or paws running toward them from every direction. Unseen hands pulled Kahner from the back of Childheart and placed a cloth bag over his head. At the same time that Kahner was pulled aside from the unicorn and utterly immobilized, his body as limp as that of a dead eel, Childheart felt webbing drop from the sky and envelop him. The semi-opaque net restrained him so quickly and tightly that he fell off his feet, finding he was immediately suspended in air and promptly dropped harshly onto a cart or movable platform. Invisible hands pulled the net still tighter around Childheart while other hands rapidly bound his legs together. Nothing was said by any of the captors.

"Kahner!" Childheart yelled. "Kahner! Are you all right?" Childheart heard nothing in reply. He yelled again. When he concluded that Kahner could not reply, Childheart turned to his captors.

"Who are you, and why are you doing this?" The captors were silent. "Whom do you represent then, since you obviously do not represent yourselves? On whose authority are you doing this?"

As soon as both Kahner and Childheart were fastened securely to carts, those who had prevented the pair from proceeding on their own now proceeded with them, pulling and pushing the carts with ease and remarkable speed along a trail that was hidden beneath the ground foliage, yet familiar to those taking it. Stardust scattered itself from the plants alongside the carts like billowing swarms of suddenly disturbed insects, leaving the foliage, in the absence of its stardust, looking like large bites had been taken out of it.

The phantoms pulled and pushed the carts roughly through the yielding forest for what Childheart estimated to be several hours, although there was nothing against which to measure time. The carts stopped. Once again unseen hands lifted Childheart and Kahner and dumped them roughly into another cart being pulled by what sounded like horses, which immediately, and in company with many others, pulled them swiftly away.

After some time, the horses slowed to a canter on a flat stone surface and continued the journey for several more minutes. The cart then stopped, and the hands of many lifted Childheart and Kahner and carried them into an echoing chamber, depositing them on the floor. Other hands removed the nets, untied them, and pulled off their head sacks. Childheart saw they were in some sort of jail or stockade, and that Kahner remained unresponsive. He rose stiffly and went to Kahner. It was drafty, and Childheart concluded that a number of unseen hands—and whatever they were attached to, if anything at all—remained in the area of confinement with them. Once again Childheart queried his handlers concerning their capture, and, again, received no response.

While speaking, Childheart nudged Kahner gently with his nose, and Kahner stirred in a deep sleep. There were no windows, but the small stone space with a vaulted, outsize ceiling had one barred door that opened onto a dark stone hallway. Tiny torches high on the cell walls provided just enough light for Childheart to be able to recognize that the only other visible occupant of the room was Kahner. Childheart continued to nudge Kahner until finally, with labored efforts, he awakened.

"Where . . . where are we, Childheart? What happened? I remember the noises and the bag, and something wiped on my nose, and then . . . nothing else."

Childheart, too, recalled the substance that someone spread across his nose upon his capture, but evidently, he now reflected, Kahner did not share his own powers against which the potion had no efficacy. Childheart told Kahner what little he knew, and that he had yet to make any sense of it. Finally, the silence was broken by a voice nowhere visible speaking from the other side of the door, just outside the cell.

"You will be taken into the presence of Ashani—who will answer and decide all things. It would be foolish, as well as futile, for you to attempt either to fight or to flee."

"But who are *you*? And who is this one, 'Ashani'?" Childheart immediately replied, hoping to create a dialogue—about anything.

"I am a follower of Ashani, and Ashani is our custodian—our everything."

"But, who *is* Ashani?"

"I have just told you; I will say no more. But heed."

"Heed what?" Childheart said, pressing the conversation. But the follower of Ashani said no more and walked away, his feet slapping at the stone pavement.

Childheart and Kahner probed in their discourse with each other for understanding and wisdom, fully aware that all they said was being heard and noted. Accordingly, they made no mention of their companions or of the mission. But of the Good they spoke volubly, establishing their cosmic alignment and hoping thereby to learn as soon as possible Ashani's allegiance.

At about the same time the torches in the cell were appearing to go out on their own, other torches were coming down the hallway toward them. The door opened and a single voice among many mouths making various noises said simply, "Come with us."

Childheart was tempted to ask, "And to what does 'us' refer?" But he thought better of it and restrained himself. Kahner and Childheart walked side by side, neither one saying a word, Kahner holding tightly to the unicorn's mane. They walked, flanked on all sides by invisible guards, down a number of long halls and up numerous sets of stairs, until they arrived before two tall and wide bronze doors that, upon their arrival, began slowly to open. Into a broad and deep anteroom stepped the prisoners and their handlers.

Beyond the softly lit anteroom, not unlike a large narthex inside a huge cathedral, was a long open colonnade leading to a vast hall, in the middle of which was a sizeable circular theater built as a cone below floor level. Above the theater, which had concentric rings of seating drawing down to a circular staging area and a deep rectangular pit, was a presiding platform that, like the rest of the space beyond the bronze doors, was constructed entirely of marble. Even the chairs in the presider's space, as well as the large table set over the pit below, were of marble. Furthermore, it seemed that every edge of every floor, wall, and ceiling had in relief various borders sealed beneath gold leaf, and everywhere stood vessels and urns and candle sticks, as well as other accoutrements, of similar composition, including pure solid gold.

As they walked into a hall the size of a small river canyon, Kahner noticed, and noted for Childheart, the words that were carved high upon the walls and that extended in a single line around the entire hall, beginning and ending at the doors through which they had entered. Childheart looked up and was stunned to find the poem that, so far as he knew, was located nowhere but on Queen Taralina's chamber door. Indeed, the prophetic poem, other than orally recited and transmitted, was understood by everyone with allegiance to Queen Taralina to be physically—and inextricably—intertwined with the sacredness of the vault itself. Yet, inscrutably, here it was; and likely it had been here for a very long time.

The footfalls ahead of them ordered the way for Childheart and Kahner and led them around the upper lip of the theater to the presiding platform and a semicircle of chairs, with a large presider's chair located equidistant from the chairs on either side. A voice and hand together indicated that Kahner should seat himself immediately to the left of the large chair, while another voice and tug advised Childheart to remain standing immediately to its right. Those to whom the footfalls belonged then retreated from the space.

Applause erupted from the theater below. The torches dimmed, as if in obedience to the thundering hands, and the two guests noticed instantly the thin and slightly luminous outlines of heads and faces and clapping hands belonging to perhaps a thousand individuals who had filled the theater seats. The clapping came to an abrupt end, and music rose from a visible set of instruments to the far left that were just entering the hall. Childheart and Kahner could see two harps and several lyres, a flute, a recorder, a drum, some stringed instruments of various sizes, a couple of cymbals, and several other instruments they could not identify. At first it appeared the instruments were supporting and playing themselves, but as they drew closer it was evident there were faint outlines of bodies escorting and playing them.

Finally, behind the procession of instruments, a small man was advancing toward the elevated platform on an elaborately decorated litter constructed of gilded wood and silk curtains (drawn back), and which was carried by six attendants. The mass of his body, too, was nearly transparent, but the outline of its edge and features were much sharper and more effulgent, setting him apart from all others gathered in the hall. When his litter had reached the platform, assistants ushered him to the central chair; not once did he look at either Childheart or Kahner. He sat down, and immediately the music stopped.

"Ashani the Wise!" a lone echoing voice cried out, from no identifiable place. Those in the theater took their seats. Everything became quiet; the silence was hard, as if something forged. Then, the one called Ashani rose and addressed the assembly.

"Sons and daughters of Queen Taralina, we are once again at that time in our life together where we are called upon to offer thanks and praise to the Good for the gift of life past, and to beseech from the Good, by its continued love and mercy, the gift of life future, asking once more that dust from the stars that has renewed us and provided us sustenance will soon fall again and save us." Ashani raised his arms and intoned:

"Lord Good, you have been faithful to us since before time." Then the people, who had risen with the raising of Ashani's arms, responded:

"Accept our thanks and praise, O Good!"

And so the antiphon continued, with Ashani intoning petitions and those gathered in the theater responding immediately to each, accordingly.

"You provided us life in you and a way of life that is true to you through the life and example of Queen Taralina, your most humble servant."

"Accept our thanks and praise, O Good!"

"Your servant, Queen Taralina, loved us and cared for us sufficiently and steadfastly, but we wanted more, seeking to become lords of our own lives, and so turned against her."

"Accept our confession, and forgive us, O Good!"

"But even in our unfaithfulness to you, you remained faithful to us, and provided us a way of escape and protection from our enemies," Ashani prayed.

"Accept our thanks and praise, O Good!" responded the assembly, more loudly.

"You provided for us and protected us in flight, Lord Good, and brought us through the wilderness of darkness and death in The Mountains of Bairnmoor to this valley of light and life."

"Accept our thanks and praise, O Good!"

"You caused a quaking of the ground and a crumbling of The Mountains, and in your love The Mountains fell on our pursuers in the tunnel of our escape, sealing them in the death of their own devising," Ashani continued.

"Accept our thanks and praise, O Good!" replied the people, louder still.

"In providing for their *death beneath* The Mountains you provided for our *life beyond* The Mountains, both individually and in our life together: in this valley, where nothing comes in or goes out except by your will, and where you give to us in due course, according to your wisdom and love, the restorative and sustaining gift of your light that falls from the stars, where you reside in all your perfect Goodness," cried out Ashani, as if in a trance.

"Accept our thanks and praise, O Good!" said the people, more loudly.

"We have lived in your light, Lord Good, and by your light alone are we able to live; and so we beseech you in this hour of need, as our bodies and our lives are drawing their last from your hand and facing the end of their days, to shower down upon us once more the dust of your stars."

"Accept our sacrifice of praise and thanksgiving!" cried out the people, sharing the trance-like state with Ashani.

Kahner, listening to the words with increasing encouragement and thinking that at last they had many more on their side after all, looked keenly at Childheart for confirmation. But Childheart would not meet his eyes, and the reason became readily apparent when, upon the conclusion of Ashani's invocation, a portion of the floor at the bottom of the arena dropped away. Moments later the floor resurfaced, but with an individual who, hooded and gagged, was lashed to a gurney. Unseen hands then placed the gurney swiftly, but ceremonially, on the table straddling a now glowing and smoking fire pit.

Ashani raised a golden scepter and, immediately, nearly invisible hands removed the prisoner's hood while other phantom hands below the floor stoked the fire.

"Wait!" yelled Childheart, recognizing instantly that the individual about to be the liturgical sacrifice was Jamie. "Wait!" he yelled again.

Ashani lowered the scepter and, immediately, water was thrown on the fire. Ashani, continuing to look only at the person on the gurney, remarked to Childheart, "So, you know this person?"

"You know that I do," replied Childheart. "And if you are a disciple of Taralina, and owe allegiance to the Good, then why are you threatening to kill him?"

"I never make threats," replied Ashani. "We must sacrifice someone to obtain the Good's favor and ensure the continued salvation of my people. Tell me, why should it not be the gift to us of this one? Or of any of you?" Ashani then moved quickly to an interrogational voice, turning to look at Childheart. "Who are you? Where do you come from? Why did you come? And how did you get here?"

"How many of us do you hold?" asked Childheart, without the slightest waiver in his voice.

"We have captured two others like the one below and another creature from the forests beyond The Mountains. And," he added calmly, while nodding toward Childheart, "the two of you."

Ashani then rang a small bell in response to which a thick stone wall surfaced from the floor and completely encircled the chairs, stopping at a height of ten feet. A steel door in the wall opened and in walked two attendants, their bodies barely visible, who promptly lit the torch sconces. As soon as they had left Ashani looked at Childheart in a way that indicated it was now Childheart's turn to speak. Childheart began with his recollection of the day he first encountered the four children in the Forest of Lament. He said the children had come from a different world, and that they were on a mission about which they could not speak; that he was soon assisting them, feeling certain, at least at the time, that Elli was the child of the poem and that she would possess the key by which she would release the Queen from captivity.

When Childheart had finished, Ashani said, "This girl called Elli cannot be the child to release the Queen. That child would be grown and mature as a child, filled with childness and equipped with supernatural capacities and abilities beyond those of mere mortals. No ordinary child could possibly go into battle with the powerful forces belonging to Sutante Bliss, restore the Queen's life and resurrect her kingdom. How even a supernatural child is to accomplish that sort of mission is beyond imagination—infinitely more to imagine an ordinary child doing so. Besides," added Ashani, "you don't know whether this girl is alive and, if alive, where she might be in all of Bairnmoor. And then," Ashani concluded with a long pause, "the matter of the key: apparently she no longer possesses it?"

"And then you tell me that you arrived separately from the others, in three different ways, and that you, Childheart, and your young companion arrived here from the tops of The Mountains beyond this valley!

"My people have been here for hundreds of years. We arrived here after traveling for many days south through The Mountains, with Sutante's forces continuing to gain on us. The passage through The Mountains leading to this valley was long, and when the enemy was finally within earshot, we had no more food and water, and had to struggle forward without any more light. So close was the enemy at times that we could see the glow of their torches.

"It was only a matter of minutes before the enemy forces would fall upon us when, suddenly and inexplicably, the earth quaked and the ground shook and broke apart, and we found ourselves thrown through the mountain and spilled into this starlit valley—now fully exposed to the enemy, I might add. At that moment it seemed our chances of at least some of us surviving would have been better taken inside the passageway—where we were at least covered in darkness and had opportunities to hide.

"It was then the Good provided miraculously and mercifully for us. We had no sooner tumbled down the mountain and into the warm, starlit grasses outside the tunnel, with Sutante's forces about to spill forth from the tunnel and annihilate us, when the mountain quaked and this side of it dissolved, crushing Sutante's forces outside the tunnel and in the passageway—sealing them in, while sealing us out. There was now no way either into or out of the valley. And, until your impossible arrival, no one had ever discovered us. And no one has ever left here, except through death.

"Your unwillingness to tell the truth and so your inability to explain your most inauspicious presence, Master Childheart, leads me to the only reasonable conclusion: that you and your companions are scouts and spies for Sutante Bliss, and that his black arts alone can account for your presence here.

"We cannot allow you to ever leave this place. Nor can we provide any opportunity for Sutante's magic to be practiced on us. And any further delay in our sacrifice to the Good cannot be permitted."

Childheart scraped at the stone pavement, as if trying to extract something from it, sharply breaking the silence all about them. Then he spoke. "I see that you require the stardust for your continued existence? Am I correct?"

"With the stardust, our corporeal lives are revivified," began Ashani, now relaxed in his chair, as if the urgency of the sacrifice could safely cede momentary priority to some gracious explanation, if not simply decency. "The dust from the stars outlines our bodies and their features, as it does for all living things in this land. While the stardust remains, our bodies and very souls remain. We can touch, and be touched. And we can continue to live life as it was meant to be lived, faithfully and joyfully. When the stardust dissipates over time (as it is absorbed by our bodies—and our souls, we believe—to give them life), our bodies—and our souls—also dissipate. What remains is the *form* of a body that, though nearly spent, can yet do all the things that we could always do when our bodies had been fully revivified, but we cannot finally be seen, and we cannot be touched or felt or grasped. And, with the dissipation of our bodies, once complete, also comes the inescapable dissipation of our very selves. We are even now well on our way to fading entirely from existence. We can *feel* it. We can feel less faith, less hope, less love, less desire and less passion for the Good, less concern and care for one another, less interest in existence itself, until, we simply cease to exist altogether.

"And," he said, rather indifferently, Childheart thought, "it's not as if we any longer deserve to exist."

"Why do you say that you do not deserve to exist?" asked Childheart, suddenly absorbed in Ashani's story and quite unaware of Jamie struggling just outside the marble enclosure.

"We *did* (and therefore *do*) not deserve to exist because we did not defend the Queen. Some of us even joined in challenging her rule—challenging her intentions and the basis of her authority. Even, for a time, some of us participated in the actual effort to remove her from power—turning against her and aligning ourselves with Sutante Bliss."

So absorbed in the depths of his story that he seemed unaware of Childheart, Ashani continued after a short pause.

"When Sutante Bliss killed the Queen without her resisting in the least, many of us who had been most loyal to the Queen, even closest to her, found her passivity to be disgusting. There we were: risking our own lives to defend her while she was unwilling to offer even the least bit of defense of herself. When she died—when she simply, insipidly (we thought at the time), let her enemies win, we became ashamed of her and reluctant to admit any sort of allegiance, quite apart from any fear associated with such an allegiance.

"And then, when it was all over, and Sutante had actually won—when *all* of us opposed to her had actually won—everything suddenly changed for many of us, and for all of us who are now here."

"What do you mean, Ashani, when you say that 'everything suddenly changed'? You mean, you finally saw Sutante for who he was in reality?" asked Childheart.

"Quite to the contrary. We saw *ourselves* for who *we* are in all of our own reality—having nothing to do with Sutante Blilss. What was once shameful to us was now shaming us, and in refusing any longer to align ourselves with Sutante Bliss we were forced to flee for our very lives. But, of course," he added, in a tone of self-accusation, "from whom were we most fleeing: from Sutante or from ourselves?

"At the very least, we deserved nothing from the Good against whom we had been working, and when we found ourselves miraculously saved by the Good at just the crucial moment, we knew we had to offer thanks and do the most we could possibly do to show gratitude. And so, we determined that the greatest expression of penitence for our wrongdoing, and the greatest manifestation of our thankfulness, was to offer up our lives.

"We established a lottery to include all but the truly old and the infirm or disabled, as well as the young. We then summarily sacrificed the one chosen, whereupon no sooner had we made our sacrifice than the heavens showered down stardust upon us; and we became, with all living things beneath these skies, wonderfully alive and refreshed and aware of our presence before the Good—and its Goodness to us.

"But, over time, as we began to absorb the stardust, we discovered that our bodies began to dissipate. As the stardust diminished, so did we—so did all things living, although *far more rapidly for us.* Finally, when so many of our bodies were beginning to fade from existence, we determined to make another sacrifice. Within a matter of a few days the stardust fell gently upon us once again, restoring everyone's body and the corporeal presence of all living things beneath its dust.

"And so, yes, it is by this stardust alone that we are able to live and breathe and continue to have our being." Ashani paused and peered at Childheart.

"So it has come to pass that we have made many sacrifices over the years when our very existence was in the balance. We need once more to make a sacrifice, since so many of my people are dying—I along with them. Hence:" Ashani paused again before continuing. "Your one called Jamie."

"But I do not understand any of this, Ashani," Childheart said with mounting exasperation, "and Jamie is not even from among your people!"

"He, like the others in your party, is a gift to us from the Good—to give back to the Good, and so provide a reprieve for his people. Indeed," Ashani said as he stood and faced Childheart, "but for the supernatural gift of your presence, we would have to begin sacrificing the youngest among us who, until now, had been excluded from the lottery. Nevertheless, as I said, Childheart, we cannot allow any of you to run free, regardless of whether you soldier for Sutante Bliss or not."

"But, suppose you sacrifice this one we call Jamie and still the stardust does not fall?" Childheart retorted.

Ashani parried Childheart's retort. "Then we will continue our sacrifices until the Good is satisfied, even if it means sacrificing another one of our own in addition to all of you." He then stopped talking and displayed a demeanor that suggested that there was nothing more to be said. Ashani was about to resume the sacrifice, but Childheart again pawed at the pavement.

"Suppose, Ashani," bellowed Childheart abruptly, "I could have the Good bestow stardust upon you without making any sacrifice whatsoever? Would you then release the one on the pyre and all in our party?"

Ashani was caught entirely off guard, as if Childheart had redrawn his sword following the conclusion of a campaign and a laying down of weapons. "I do not understand, Childheart. Do you mean to say that *you* can bring the Goodness of the stardust to us without the sacrifice?" Ashani said, with almost scornful skepticism.

"Precisely," said Childheart sharply. It was not apparent whether his confidence was real or feigned. "In fact, Ashani, I will allow myself to be sacrificed along with Jamie, should I fail."

Kahner, sitting rigidly, his mind spinning, wondered what, if anything, Childheart knew that would account for this sudden turn of both conversation and events. Was Childheart more than what he, Kahner, thought he was? Did he have a special relationship with the Good? Did he have supernatural powers? Did he know when the stardust would fall—or was he simply hoping against hope that it must be time, given the condition of Ashani's people, and the urgent need for stardust—and swift intervention on behalf of Jamie?

Childheart lifted his head toward the heavens that were shimmering regally on the stone and marble surfaces from the wide-open ceiling above. He then looked at Ashani. "In two hours, when the stars have wheeled ten degrees in their course, stardust will have fallen, or I will set fire to the pyre on which the two of us will be lying. However, if the dust shall fall before the sacrifice is made, you shall free us and help us to leave the valley under your protection."

Ashani countered. "What makes you believe that we know a way out of this land, Childheart?"

"Because of your concern we *might leave*—and disclose the existence of this valley and your whereabouts to those outside the valley," replied Childheart.

Ashani looked hard at Childheart, and then glanced at the silent, unreadable skies. Ashani mouthed some soft words to no one in particular, and within seconds a barely visible assistant came with an hourglass. Ashani turned it over, and immediately the sand began to stream through the neck, as if in a race against time—or something else.

"So be it, Childheart," replied Ashani, "and may you succeed for the sake of all."

Childheart said nothing for the longest time as the ceiling of stars ran its course that would consume the distance at issue within less than two hours. Kahner, his eyes locked onto Childheart, sat restlessly in silence with the whole of the hushed assembly.

~TWENTY-SIX~

WHEN THE SAND WAS nearly finished, and Kahner was now looking alternately between the glass and Childheart, Childheart raised his head towards the skies and recited the final verse of the poem that was etched into the stone above before concluding, saying to the open sky above, "Our story is nothing apart from yours; and you have chosen in your story to include ours."

A few minutes later, with the conspicuous exception of several grains adhering to the glass tube as if trying stubbornly to hold bits of time in abeyance, all the sand had passed through. The walls surrounding Ashani and his two guests sank noiselessly back into the floor, and a number of unseen guards with visible instruments of death escorted Childheart to the base of the sanctuary. Ashani remained behind at the lip of the theater. Someone from below offered Childheart a flaming torch, which Childheart placed between his teeth. Childheart looked on Jamie, who was looking back at him in abject horror, and then straddled the prostrate boy so that his nose met Jamie's.

"You will feel nothing from the flame, Jamie," Childheart whispered tenderly between his teeth to the bound and gagged boy looking hysterically at Childheart. Childheart then rubbed Jamie's nose with his own, and the child instantly calmed and fell into a deep, deep sleep. Childheart, seeing that Jamie was asleep, turned and looked up at an expressionless Ashani returning his gaze. He then bent low to light the wood beneath the pyre.

Just as Childheart was about to set fire to the still-smoldering fuel, an object large enough to overshadow the bulk of the open ceiling above the theater soared overhead; it blocked out the stars and left the sanctuary so devoid of their light that it was as if for one brief moment the entire sky had been eclipsed. Everyone looked up at the suddenly shadowed sky, including Childheart and Ashani, but saw only the stars.

After the puzzling—and for Ashani, a troubling—moment had quickly passed, Childheart bent his head once again to drop the torch.

Suddenly, to the amazement of all, scattered particles of stardust began to drift gently down from the sky, wafting and sparkling, as if joyfully at play. All those in the sanctuary stood and raised their hands to the stars and began to praise and thank the Good while the thickening snow of starlight began to sharply outline—and then completely cover—everyone's body. Soon, the gathering stardust provided keen and distinguishable features to their faces and hands and feet. With the renewal of their bodies, all in the conical sanctuary began to dance in place before the Good and shout for joy. Childheart, who alone among the beings assembled gathered no dust and remained unchanged, observed the jubilation for a short while without moving or speaking. He then abruptly stepped away from the bier, dropped the torch onto the marble floor, and crushed the fire with one sharp strike of a hoof that generated a torrent of wind and sparks. The entire hall became suddenly quiet, and all in attendance knelt before the unicorn.

Ashani, from above, rose from knees which he also had bent, raised his sceptered hand, and shouted, "Hail to the Good! Let all the people say, 'Hail to the Good!'"

Whereupon all those gathered in that reverenced space stood and erupted in unison, "Hail to the Good! Hail to the Good! Hail to the Good!"

"Silence!" bellowed Ashani, and the noise subsided. When all was once again still, Ashani descended the steps and stood before Childheart. He bowed low and said, "Childheart, no one but the Good itself could do what you have just done, and I stand ready, along with my people, to honor you and obey you."

Ashani, rising, offered his scepter to the unicorn, but Childheart turned abruptly from Ashani, shaking his thick mane violently, and projected a firm voice out into the silenced assembly hall: "Ashani! And the people of this valley! Hear me! I am no more the Good than any of you, and I am, further, no more either its manifestation or its representative than any of you!"

"But, Childheart," replied Ashani, looking perplexed, "you did what you said you would do, and what no one else could have done. How, then, did you know the stardust would fall in response to your petition?"

"I didn't, Ashani. But I knew the time for its fall, given the recitation of your history, was imminent. I was hoping against hope it was now. More to the point, I did what I believe the Good would have wanted me to do, and so did so with only a meager hope, with no expectation—and, I might add, little optimism." He paused to emphasize his next remarks. "You need make no further sacrifices, Ashani, which serve only the purposes of Sutante Bliss, for the Good has shed its Goodness upon you, and not as a reward for thanksgiving and penance, but simply because the Good is Good and chooses to be so to you." He added, "And, is *this* not the Grace for which you lift voices of praise and thanksgiving—a Grace that, by virtue of being Grace, you have neither earned nor deserved?"

Childheart walked with the gentlest of echoing steps the short distance to the sleeping Jamie, bit easily through the ropes that had bound him, tore away his gag, and nuzzled Jamie's hair. Jamie opened his eyes and immediately asked, "Childheart, what happened?"

"Be still, my child," replied Childheart. "All is good. You may rise and climb aboard," whereupon Jamie, as if rushing home, scrambled off the bier, grabbed Childheart's mane, and pulled himself up onto the unicorn who had bent low for his climb.

"Ashani, I ask now, and without delay, that the others be brought to me and that you show us the way through the mountain. Further, on behalf of the Queen, Taralina, I ask your assistance in our quest to restore her kingdom. Come with us—you and your people—and help us battle Sutante Bliss and proclaim the truth of the poem's prophecy. There are only a few of us, and even with your help we are vastly outnumbered and woefully less equipped; so there is, I confess, little chance of our success. But, by our trust and rising certitude in the Good, we proclaim the poetic truth and attempt most humbly to advance its fulfillment. We, and the Good, need your help. Will you come with us?"

Ashani motioned for his people to be seated. Then, turning back to Childheart, he asked, "Do you believe that the girl who is with you is the one who is to release the Queen, according to the poem of promise?"

"She is, Ashani, the only girl we have; and, furthermore, she alone has a key."

"But, she is blind, Childheart, and far too young and unformed, and otherwise entirely incapable, to lead such a quest; and, besides, I have noticed that hers is not a diamond key. And yet you will advance the cause of the poem on this basis alone?"

"We advance the cause of the poem because we trust it is the poem of the Good; it is the Good, therefore, that must provide its fulfillment. Perhaps it is yet to be revealed who is the girl with the key."

"You seem to me to be a wise one, Childheart. Your evidence is lame, however, and any error would be disastrous. By any measure, it would be foolishness to attempt what you are designing to do."

"I cannot dispute what you aver, Ashani, but sometimes foolishness and wisdom must walk together on the same path."

Ashani paced with his hands behind his back for some time and then stopped to face Childheart, through the drifting smoke, from the other side of the pyre, its moist fuel still smoldering. "The other guests!" he ordered, while gesturing with his head to one of his court assistants. He motioned for Kahner to be led down the steps.

Within minutes Alex and Beatríz appeared, Thorn leading the way. At the sight of Childheart, the two children and Thorn hurried down the stairs and ran to the unicorn and their other companions, Kahner and Jamie. Joyful tears and long, affectionate hugs exploded. Then Thorn, Beatríz, and Alex all spoke at the same time:

"How did you get here?"

"Where have you been all this time?"

"How did you find us?"

"Do you know where Starnee is?"

"Do you know where we are?"

"What's happening to us?"

Childheart shook his mane, struck the pavement with a single hoof, and then said firmly, "Enough! Enough, all of you! There will be time later to indulge such questions—and answers, if possible. Now, we must be gone. Ashani will show us where he entered this valley and so, perhaps also, the way out—unless there is another more promising path to follow. Hopefully, once out of this valley and through the next set of mountains, we will be done with The Mountains altogether."

Outside the halls of Ashani, the trees and land, freshly dusted by the stars, appeared magically delicate and crisp, resembling a landscape of blown glass. All the people in the hall were now distinctly visible, and virtually all of them were smiling—but, less, it seemed to Childheart, out of joy than out of relief, Childheart knowing that real joy cannot exist between the poles of anxiety and relief, nor manifest itself beneath fear. "No," he thought, "if this were a people shaped by joy, instead of by fear and anxiety, they would be eager not only to point the way beyond the valley, but be the first to march through it." And yet he wondered whether this people, in being finally on their (albeit tortured) way to learning grace, might not also be on the way toward joy.

⌐⌐

Starnee spent what must have been, he thought, the better part of an entire day alternately soaring high and swooping low over the vast and thick canopy of forest leaves in search of his friends. Surprisingly, it was his neck and not his wings that tired most quickly and forced him to rest more times than he would have wanted to. He would have continued flying through the pain, regardless of how intense it became, but the sudden, frequent flicking of his head from right to left and back again over a lengthy course of flight caused his neck to stiffen, becoming immobile.

Finally, having surveyed half the length of the forest, Starnee decided to settle on a high cliff overlooking one end of the forest and reconsider his search strategy. He lighted gently on a lone branch protruding boldly into the star-speckled sky, folded his wings, and there simply thought, all the while continuing to survey as best he could the ubiquitous carpet of glimmering leaves. He had not yet covered the other half of the forest, but it was in the direction of Starnee's search up to this point that Kahner and Childheart had been traveling. "Could they have ended up inadvertently reversing their course?" he wondered. Was Starnee at that moment, then, further away from his friends than at any other time in his hunt for them?

At no time since Starnee entered the valley had he seen a single cloud, which is why he happened to notice what seemed to be a column of something resembling a cloud rising above the mountaintops in the distance. Indeed, but for the slightest cleft in one of the peaks, he would never have seen the column beyond the peaks that surrounded the valley. The cleft was but a fissure, and not even wide enough for Starnee to walk through, much less fly into. But the crack in the rock was more than sufficiently wide for Starnee to see the column and conclude it was some vast gathering of grey smoke that was almost, it seemed, propelled toward the black sky. It rose with such ferocity that it seemed to have burst through some barrier intended to contain its force.

Starnee realized further that beyond the valley there seemed to be no stars or other heavenly bodies of any sort whatsoever, and that a vague light was seeping just barely into the black skies from beneath the rim of the visible world and attaching itself to the jagged horizon.

Starnee decided he would start a new search over the other half of the valley forest and waste no more time getting there. On the way, however, he was determined to fly at his lowest altitude yet. He would not be able to re-survey nearly as much of the territory already covered, but at least he could better find openings through which he could see activity on the forest floor.

Starnee dove from the cliff, unfolded his wings, and leveled off just above the treetops. He was flying as slow as safe flight would permit at that altitude, so it would be nearly half an hour before he reached the beginning of the second half of the forest. When he had flown about twenty minutes, Starnee noticed a dim light poking briefly through the treetops. It came and went so quickly, however, Starnee wasn't clear about its location. He accelerated and lifted skyward, then doubled back in a wide turn well above the trees. He hoped the higher elevation would disclose the presence of the light more readily, if it was still there.

Starnee had just completed his turn when he saw a small spot of pale light off to his left. He circled high overhead and saw that the light was coming from the forest floor. It appeared to be some sort of large, ceilingless hall. He spiraled downward and made a slow pass over the opening just above the treetops, hoping to get a clarifying look.

Starnee had no idea what he had just seen, except for the appearance of numerous faint figures and (could it have been?) what he thought was a quick, but distinct, sighting of Childheart at the very center of the space. He circled back, looking for a place to light in the trees from which he could get a clear and sustained look at what was happening below, but without being seen. He was ready to act on behalf of Childheart immediately, if need be, but he also knew that readiness is not the same as preparedness, and that the latter is generally the more valuable of the two. The sudden appearance of what looked like glistening sifted flour drifting down lightly over the whole of the valley captured Starnee's attention. Starnee knew, of course, from the already frosted landscape, that it was dust falling from the stars. Starnee circled unseen several times around the opening, listening to what sounded like celebratory exclamations and chatter being raised to greet him. Had they seen him? Did they know anything about him? At last, he spotted a thicket of sturdy looking branches next to the clamorous opening and settled onto it as quietly as possible. Starnee then poked one eye furtively through the branches to assess the situation below.

He confirmed immediately that it was, indeed, Childheart, who was standing rather ceremoniously at the bottom of a vast inverted cone in the floor, with Jamie aboard and holding onto his neck, as if for dear life, not raising his head from within the security of Childheart's massive mane. Starnee listened and looked for anything that might require him to drop to the defense or rescue of his friends, knowing full well that once down, there would be no way back up; there was room to drop and flap his wings to halt his descent, but there was no room to take off. Should Childheart's party require his assistance, the act would become his own endgame—in a game he did not fully understand and never really wanted to be a part of.

Starnee listened with intense focus to the conversation that ensued between Childheart and an elderly man who appeared to be in charge of the gathering. He noticed the pyrrhic quality of the central table and the smoke that was ebbing lazily away beneath it. When he heard both the apparent leader and all those assembled in the concave circle hailing Childheart as "the Good," Starnee struggled to stifle a sudden urge to laugh.

Shortly thereafter, when the other members of Childheart's party appeared, and Starnee learned their apparent captors were going to free them, he yelled out, "Hey, down there! Hey!"

All looked skyward as if obeying an orchestra conductor and gasped when they caught sight of the head of a large bird stretched into the opening above.

"Starnee! Starnee!" a number of familiar voices screamed in delight, immediately settling the initial fears of everyone else.

"Starnee! Starnee!" his friends continued to shout.

"Enough of the slobbery! Just tell me what's going on here—and whether I can be spared the rather inconvenient trouble of having to sacrifice my beautiful self on your behalf!" Starnee bellowed from above.

"Starnee!" yelled Childheart, as if he was the only one not surprised to see him. "We're just getting ready to leave this place—and this valley— under the auspices of the people who occupy this land. Already, a party of our valley friends is assembling to accompany us to a hidden passage— perhaps requiring some excavation—that we hope will take us out of here. I'll learn shortly the direction we are going to be taking, and you can meet us at the edge of the forest where we'll emerge."

"Exactly where will this hidden passage take us, and," Starnee added, rather skeptically, "are they going with us, or must we do this alone?" Starnee paused and ruffled his feathers against the branches that were annoying him, adding, "And how do we know this isn't some sort of trap?"

"If it were going to be a trap, Starnee," replied Childheart, impatiently, "then it would be far less an opportunity to entrap us than has existed for the past however many hours or days we have been here. And, no, they will not accompany us through. They claim there are no stars outside the valley and, even if there are, no requisite stardust to sustain them. I suggested the Good will provide for them as it has thus far, and that, in any event, sometimes risking death is far better than ensuring life. But," Child-heart added, with a deep sigh of resignation, "they remain unconvinced."

Childheart promptly gathered his companions around Ashani and a couple of Ashani's assistants who arrived swiftly from the theater seating. Within a few minutes all was settled, including a direction to be followed, and Starnee took flight to meet his friends outside the forest.

~TWENTY-SEVEN~

WELL PROVISIONED, CHILDHEART AND his friends, accompanied by a small party led by Ashani himself, met an impatient Starnee outside the forest. From there they traveled many hours in the shimmering darkness, working their way along the valley floor on well-trodden paths, through newly glazed meadows and across small gurgling streams, until they arrived half a mile from the base of a mountain. It was this one, according to Ashani, that Childheart and his party would have to climb to reach the point of departure from the valley. Starnee flew a brief reconnaissance and reported that the base and initial side of the mountain were covered with an impenetrable thicket of tall juniper trees extending in both directions for miles. Childheart at that point whispered something to Kahner and then asked Starnee to carry the boy for his own look at the terrain.

"I don't know what *he's* going to see with his two *small* eyes that *I* haven't seen already with my two *large* ones," replied Starnee, with good humor, but also an edge of irritation, "but, as you wish; be back in a jiffy."

When Starnee returned, the boy jumped from his back and ran to Childheart. "It is, Childheart! It is!" Kahner whispered forcefully. Childheart then approached Ashani and asked him to point to the spot behind the junipers through which they were supposed to enter the mountain. Ashani pointed with certainty to the location.

"But that's the spot, Ashani, from which we only recently *emerged* from the mountain! Through that passageway one enters the most impassable mountainous terrain imaginable, with temperatures that will quickly freeze us and winds that, in any case, would shortly blow us off the mountain and into the oblivion from which we were miraculously saved only days ago! To return to *that* place and to try to continue on through The Mountains, perhaps for another two hundred miles or more, is beyond ludicrous. No," Childheart said firmly, "there is no way out through that opening." Childheart stared piercingly at Ashani. "What sort of inscrutable and unkind ploy is this? And why?"

"Childheart—and friends—there is no toying with you, I can assure you, and I cannot relate to what you have just described!" No one said anything further for quite some time, it being evident that Ashani was sorting things out. Then Ashani looked Childheart in the eye and said, "I myself have seen what is on the other side of this mountain through the very passage to which I'm taking you, and it is not as you describe it—I can assure you! I do not say you are not telling the truth, Childheart, or that you are even mistaken, but neither is my account any less the truth because it would seem to contradict your version of it. I will go with you—to the very place—and show you."

"Perhaps you are mistaken, Ashani. How many years has it been since you have passed through the opening?"

"Childheart," interrupted Jamie, "they say they had exited—and never entered—through that passage. You and Kahner, on the other hand, have entered through the passageway into the valley, but have never exited through it. Perhaps," Jamie said, diffidently, but, he thought, logically, "to exit through the opening is not the same as to enter through it, but more like looking at the back of something you have never seen the front of."

Childheart scratched the ground with a hoof, as if he was making some calculations in the dust in response to Jamie's rather stunning observation and hypothesis.

"Could it really be any less plausible than other things we have experienced so far in this world?" asked Jamie.

Childheart was already well into contemplating what Jamie was suggesting, and was struck, he had to admit to himself, that even their return through the valley to this very spot was just as unrecognizable as if it were an entirely different route, even though they had certainly traversed much of the same ground and used many of the same trails upon entering the valley. They had, in many places, witnessed both the front and the back of the valley—and they, indeed, were not the same. Sufficiently persuaded by Jamie's logic, Childheart relented regarding his suspicions, apologized to Ashani so that all could hear, and ordered a continuation of the journey.

Both Childheart and Kahner recalled with remarkable precision the path largely created by Childheart's horn and heavy hooves to push through the tall thicket to get to the valley floor. Their thought was, now that the trail had been recently blazed, that returning would be easier. Ironically, however, the trudging would prove to be far more difficult;

the overgrowth of trees and shrubs that Childheart had simply bent to the ground before them as they descended the mountain would soon assault them, having sprung back part way so that their long and sharp tops would now be pointing straight at the returning interlopers like so many arrows and spears.

Kahner had resumed his place aboard Childheart while Beatríz rode atop Ashani's mount. No one complained, but neither did anyone say very much, so arduous was the trek. After many hours and many rests the joint parties of seeming allies reached the small plateau in front of the black opening. Starnee was already waiting for them, of course. When Childheart saw him, he was about to greet the glistening bird with great enthusiasm, but stifled the impulse when he noticed Starnee's moist eyes.

"Starnee, what's wrong?" asked Childheart as he and Kahner reached the level rock.

Starnee blinked and then turned his head away to hide the tears that were just then spilling from his lower lids. He cleared his throat and threw his head back toward Childheart. "I'm not going with you, Childheart."

Childheart stared hard at Starnee. "What nonsense has gripped your mind, Starnee?" And then, as soon as Childheart finished speaking, he understood.

"The nonsense of perfect logic, Childheart. Look at the height of the opening. I can't fit into it, much less walk through it. But," he said, "you go on—I'll find another way, *over* The Mountains."

"But, Starnee," Thorn said, with alarm, having overheard the exchange, "we both know these mountains are far too high for you!"

"Sticks! Enough! I'll find a way over them!" Starnee retorted.

But Starnee knew, as did all the others, that the air even well below the peaks at every turn was much too thin to hold Starnee aloft, even assuming he could get enough oxygen to remain conscious during the flight. Any serious attempt would mean a certain stall—and then an irrecoverable drop, not unlike his fall after dropping Thorn onto the ledge during the storm.

"But, Stahnee, you haf to come with us! You haf to!" Alex blurted out.

"Starnee!" added Beatríz, "we need you—we can't do this without you!"

"There has to be a way, Starnee!" said Jamie.

All fell into a sad silence. Then Thorn spoke again. "Starnee, can't we somehow fall back into the hole we each fell out of?"

"Believe me, Sticks, I've thought about everything," Starnee replied. "Besides, would you really want to go back *there*?"

"Master Starnee," said Ashani, "you are welcome to remain here with us, and we'd be honored to have you as a part of our community of faith."

"I wouldn't be much good to you, Mr. Ashani. I have a hard time with faith even when I'm acting on it." Starnee paused and then turned his voice back to Childheart and his companions. "Look. I'll do everything I can to follow you—if the Good can provide stardust at just the right time, it can certainly find me a way out of something I've gotten myself into. Goodness knows I can't stay here. I'll find a way out; I promise. But you've got to get going—there is no more time to waste."

Childheart, in a quick discussion with Ashani, decided that Ashani's accompaniment was unnecessary. "Regardless of what we find, Ashani, we'll have to make do with that. And since you do not intend to join us on the other side of the mountain, there is really no point in your making the journey with us through it."

Childheart organized his traveling party and, with Childheart leading, they began their uncertain entrance into the familiar exit. Beatríz, who instead of Kahner was now aboard Childheart, glanced back, as if looking to catch a glimpse of someone just one last time.

Ashani was about to continue his conversation with Starnee, but the bird took flight as soon as Childheart and his friends had disappeared into the darkness. He caught the first current of warm air on which to glide and would determine his next course of action with the dispatch of someone who quickly reflected about everything and stewed over nothing. In seeking the lowest point over which to attempt a flight over The Mountains that encircled the entire valley, Starnee knew it would be no less suicidal than heading straight for the highest peak. But at least he would be *attempting* the least impossible of options.

To remain in what Ashani's people called Riven Valley was attempting nothing, and in its own way just as suicidal—choosing to die, at the last, in a place that offered him no options for real life. This place was no place for him. Starnee circled for half an hour on a broad updraft and calculated that the most modest of the lofty peaks were not far from the cavern through which his friends were now traveling. He set his eyes on a granite fissure that looked wide enough to accommodate his wingspan—and shot skyward.

Starnee stroked the air as if on a sortie to engage a powerful enemy—or to flee from it. He stroked and stroked and stroked with Olympian effort. He could feel the lift diminishing with increasing rapidity, and it almost seemed that the target was drifting further away from him the closer he got to it. Soon, however, he felt no air at all against his wings, and his speed decreased precipitously to a stall far sooner than he had anticipated. On the other hand, as he stalled and began his fall, time was slowing down for Starnee, and he thought of many things. He was genuinely surprised he had come as close to clearing the mountain as he had, and was actually disappointed in himself for not reaching it. He was falling fast, however, and held his wings (with their robust braking power) close to his body to increase his speed and accelerate what he was certain this time would be the end of his life's story. Once again, as he plunged toward the ground, a vision of his partner, Mythena, appeared behind his tightly closed lids, bidding him welcome—or was she waving goodbye? Then his free fall ended.

~TWENTY-EIGHT~

Beatríz wrapped her arms around Childheart's neck, as if to begin this leg of the journey asleep. But quickly she whispered, "Childheart?"

"Hm?" the unicorn replied.

"I don't know why the Good—I mean, if there *is* a Good—would allow so much badness. I mean, I don't know how I can believe in this one called, 'the Good,' when there is all this evil in the world."

"Hm," the unicorn replied again.

He scooped at the thick darkness, noting upon entering the tunnel the absence of the thousands of tiny bouncing lights that populated the place in their journey on the way out. He glanced back to see if they were there behind them, in the direction they had originally traveled, but everything around them was dark and eventless.

"Well, Beatríz, do you think there is, then, only bad in the world? Or, do you think it is mostly bad, with some moments of goodness?"

"Well," she said, "it seems there is good *and* bad in the world."

"And do you think the bad can create the Good—or create the Good without it still being bad, and only appearing good?"

"I guess I don't know how the bad can create anything good—else it, too, would have to be bad."

"But you think there is good in the world?" Childheart asked, prodding Beatríz into a keener thoughtfulness.

"Well . . . now I don't know." She shifted her weight toward the other of Childheart's ears.

"That's honest and fine. But, now, do you think I am good, Beatríz? Or, that I do genuinely good things?"

"Well, of course, Childheart! That's a silly question!"

"Well, I'd hardly agree that it's silly, given the consistency with which appearances deceive. But, if I *am* good or if I *do* good things, where did my goodness come from? Or, was it just an accident that I am good or do good things?"

"No. I don't see that your goodness is an accident, or . . . it really wouldn't be goodness, would it?" Childheart took several more steps into the vague light cast by a torch held by someone behind him.

"It seems to me there are only two options: either my goodness is fundamentally an accident or my goodness comes from something fundamentally good. You have to decide which is the more persuasive. But, if, as you say, my goodness is not an accident, then where do you think my goodness originates from?"

"I suppose some good person or being who created you?"

"So," said Childheart, threading the conversation through the facile fabric of Beatríz's curiosity, "you have to acknowledge, then, that something good *made* me good, while allowing me—as well as other good persons—to do bad things, some of which I know I have done, as I suspect of you as well."

Beatríz thought for a moment while shifting her weight to Childheart's other ear. "Still, Childheart, I don't see why the Good would allow the badness along with the goodness. Why couldn't—or *wouldn't*—the Good allow only goodness?"

"Perhaps because the Good, to allow for goodness, *must* allow for the badness—or, at least the possibility, if not the inevitability, of the badness. Else," said Childheart, who then sneezed, "else how could we *choose* to do good—how could we even really know what it is? And how can we behave in a goodly way if we cannot choose to do so? And if we have to be able to choose to do good, then, logically, we have to be able to choose to do bad. Otherwise," Childheart added, "what would it mean to be able *only* to choose and do good?"

"You mean, kind of like the Cannotoad angels—and their not being altogether happy—like we are, I mean," as she learned from Thorn, "about being able to choose only the Good?"

"Precisely, Beatríz. And when it comes to, say, the love of Kahner toward you: What would you prefer—finally, I mean? A love he had no choice but to have for you, or a love he could choose to have for you, even if you knew it meant he could choose not to have it—even if you knew he might *never* love you? Or, perhaps worst of all, love you and then stop loving you?"

"It would have to be his choice, Childheart, no matter what, or . . . or it wouldn't mean anything to me." Childheart said nothing more for a while, leaving Beatríz thinking, uneasily, that the conversation had concluded. But Childheart continued.

"Taking it a bit further, Beatríz, what would you prefer, if you had the choice, that is: that there be no hate as well as no love—or that there be some hate, and even perhaps very much hate, and maybe even mostly hate—and still have some love?"

"I would think the second of the two; yes, the second of the two, for sure," replied Beatríz.

"And so the same choice, only substituting badness and goodness for hate and love?" asked Childheart. "What would you prefer, finally? Mostly badness and some goodness—or no badness and no goodness at all?"

"The same, I would think," answered Beatríz, somewhat hesitantly. "Mostly badness and at least some goodness. But," she demanded, as if to bring the conversation logically, she thought, back to her original question, "*where is* the Good, then, Childheart?"

"Yes, now that's the question, Beatríz, you were really asking from the first—only you were not yet clear about it." Childheart's voice trailed off at the end, and then he paused—in his speech and on the path. "I can't exactly say, Beatríz, except might not the answer, and perhaps the answer to everything, begin with precisely that question: not '*whether* there is the Good,' but '*where* is the Good?'" Childheart then abruptly commanded everyone behind him to stop and keep quiet.

"Childheart," Beatríz whispered softly.

"Do you hear something, Beatríz?" Childheart whispered back.

"Yes. But, I don't know what I'm hearing, except that it's a low droning sound, and seems to be coming from below us."

"I can't hear anything," replied Childheart, "but I feel vibrations in my feet." He suddenly whispered more loudly, "Look sharp, everyone!" He then began again to lead them further into the tunnel.

The longer they traveled, the louder grew the sound so that others were beginning to hear it, too. The rising drone became an uninterrupted set of numerous and separate sounds, as if a very bad orchestra had each of its instruments playing tunes or notes at the same time that had nothing in common with each other, with most of the instruments percussive in nature.

After another two hours, the cacophony rose to a level that was painful to the ears, and then it diminished rather rapidly to the point where, once again, only Beatríz could still hear it. It was at that point, however, that a new—and ominously familiar—sound presented itself. In the far distance, but growing gradually louder—and so closer—all could hear the sound of on-rushing warriors, including Wolfmen and no doubt others, in apparent pursuit of their traveling party. It was difficult to determine from which direction the sound was coming; it seemed to be assailing them from every direction, including both above and below. Fortunately, however, the one direction from which the enemy did not seem to be approaching was the very direction in which they were traveling.

Without hesitation, Childheart ordered all the torches to be lit and the party to proceed with all dispatch down the tunnel, not worrying at that point about what else could see or hear them. At first, the sounds of their own flight covered the noises of their pursuers. Eventually, however, and alarmingly, they could hear more distinctly the hostile forces approaching than they could hear themselves in stride, and increasingly so. Abruptly, however, the noises of the enemy diminished almost entirely, as if someone had suddenly turned down a volume knob.

Childheart then yelled "Halting!" as he slowed abruptly and stopped before a T intersection. The torches revealed a masonry wall and two paved paths leading in opposite directions, as if the companions had reached the subterranean foundation of a large fortress. Huge blocks of quarried and shaped stones constituted both the wall and the two paths, neither of which seemed either different from each other or recently traveled. A soft layer of undisturbed fine dust had gathered along both stretches of path works.

What was different, however, was the startling appearance of two large eyes off to the left, accompanied by loud hissing noises and the all too familiar sounds of lazily stepping legs sounding woody against the pavement. Judging by their number and the lack of synchronism among them, Childheart determined, notwithstanding only one set of eyes, that there were at least two Mortejoses moving in the darkness not far down the passageway.

Childheart, motionless as an ice sculpture, ordered everyone in a careful but projected whisper, "Don't move or say anything; when I give the word, run as fast as you can down the other path. I—and Beatríz—will have to deal with the Mortejoses. Hold tight, Beatríz." Upon hearing the voice of Childheart, the Mortejoses became still, and the cavern had the feel of a silent crypt.

Childheart began to step in a slow, steady rhythm toward the eyes that he judged were about sixty yards away. "Now!" Childheart barked softly, with his first step, and the others led by Thorn sprinted away. Even apart from the appearance of the Death Eyes, there was no time for pausing or slowing in their flight, for the greater enemy was bearing down on them quickly. Childheart continued to walk toward the Mortejoses with the echoing sound of fearless footfalls as the creatures also began to step once again in the direction of the unicorn and its rider.

The creatures increased the volume of their hissing, and Childheart and Beatríz could hear the noise of saliva shooting between teeth. Suddenly, two other sets of eyes appeared in the darkness ahead, one set alongside the initial pair and another set more dimly just behind and above them.

"Beatríz," Childheart said calmly while continuing to walk toward the three Mortejoses, but with deliberate enunciation so she would be certain to understand him the first time, "I was hoping to do this by myself, but that may not be possible. I need you to slide off my back from behind, pull your knife, and then walk right next to me. When I stop, you stop. Then raise your knife to strike, and freeze. I'll shout 'Now!' when and if you need to help me. I can quite manage one at a time, but if two come at once, that will be a much more difficult challenge. Do you know what to do?"

"Yes, Childheart," answered Beatríz, in as brave a voice as she could muster—worrying now less about her own well-being than her ability to assist her friend.

"Okay, then. You may now get off—hold onto my tail and slide down," said Childheart.

Although keenly attentive to her duty at hand—or, perhaps because of it—Beatríz was momentarily surprised by her own calm in the midst of the dangers swirling about her, as if she were in the eye of a hurricane. The memory of her knife having already been used as a weapon "with extraordinary powers" was only fleeting. Side by side, Beatríz walking close to Childheart's breathing, the two soldiers of the Good approached the two pairs of menacing eyes up front. Then Childheart stopped, as did Beatríz—and, as did all the Death Eyes. The only sound now was a renewed faint one of Sutante's forces in the distance.

But the eerie, almost musical sound of woody legs suddenly began again, as the Mortejoses assumed their victims were paralyzed and made their characteristic unhurried approach. Beatríz felt herself wilting inside and her limbs becoming weak, and she struggled to remain perfectly still. The three Death Eyes and their hundreds of menacing feet were drawing close now, and Beatríz thought Childheart would initiate the order to strike with each successive wave of the advancing legs. She could feel the vibrations of their many feet keenly, just as she could feel the disturbance of warm air from the enemy heads that were now within only several feet of her own head. She wondered, "Will Childheart shout the order in time?"

Then, just as Beatríz could hold her arms clutching the blade aloft no longer, and thinking it was already too late for action, Childheart barked, "Now!" As she pulled sharply downward, Beatríz felt something both gelatinous and sinewy grip and then quickly release her knife, even as she heard one of Childheart's hoofs strike a different Mortejos—and so destroy that instrument of death in one fell swoop. Noting quickly, however, that she had failed at first to implant the knife into her own Mortejos's head, Beatríz quickly struck again, and this time found the skull. She clenched her body in anticipation of the Mortejos slamming its powerful body, if not its jaws, into her and launching her backwards. And backwards she went, bouncing hard off the pavement.

~TWENTY-NINE~

WITH THE ABILITY TO illuminate the path before him, Thorn was taking strides so long that it was difficult for the others to keep pace. Hearing the enemy continuing to close in around them, he wondered about the wisdom of Childheart's directive, and slowed for reconsideration. It was then that he, too, noticed an impending confrontation with a Death Eyes in the far distance that was swiftly bridging the gap between them. Alex and Jamie pulled up alongside Thorn, all of them realizing there was little time to decide what to do next. And Alex took no more time to decide. He pulled his knife and, his head bent toward the floor and screaming like he was either crazy or possessed by a demon, charged at the Mortejos full tilt. Thorn instantly took off after him, shouting "No, Alex! No! Stop! Come back!" But Alex behaved as if he was oblivious to anything besides his mission, and the glow from Thorn's eyes enabled Alex to better aim the blazing missile he had become.

Thorn ran his fastest, but realized he was not going to catch up to Alex in time. And yet, in virtually the moment Thorn realized he was not going to catch Alex, something happened that Thorn had never witnessed or even heard reported before. For just as Alex, with knife raised and head bent, was about to engage the Death Eyes in battle, an ear-piercing screech erupted from the vile beast as it summarily turned and fled. Alex continued to pursue the Death Eyes until he grasped that it was actually fleeing from him—or from whatever the Mortejos thought Alex was. Alex pulled up and Thorn joined him, the two of them simply standing and looking at each other, breathing laboredly and wondering what had just occurred.

"Alex," asked Thorn, between heaving breaths, "I don't know what you were thinking, but whatever you did worked! I don't think the Mortejos had ever had another creature initiate the attack; I think you utterly confused and terrified it."

"I was just so angwy! I went cwazy!" exclaimed Alex.

Thorn was going to ask Alex what exactly it *was* he was thinking, but paused before speaking, and decided that Alex's answer more than sufficed. Jamie and Kahner appeared suddenly alongside them, and Thorn simply responded to Alex, with a bit of preliminary laughter: "Yes. Crazy. I think that's what did it. Nothing had ever attacked the Mortejos before, and it had never before met a crazy creature." All of them laughed together, each slapping Alex on the back while he beamed—not because he was proud of himself, or they of him, but simply because he had pleased them.

⌒

Meanwhile, Beatríz lay stunned but conscious—and aware of a second crushing blow to one of the Death Eyes from Childheart; and, then, all became quiet, except for Childheart's—and her own—rapid breathing, and the mild but relentless din of Sutante's forces in the distance trying to encircle them.

"Beatríz, are you all right?" asked Childheart, bending his nose toward hers.

"Yes, I . . . I think so," she replied.

"Marvelously done, young lady—and brave warrior!" said Childheart.

"Yes, but I missed the first time, Childheart. I was lucky to get a second chance," Beatríz said, as she sat up and felt her head for any significant injury.

"I don't know about being lucky, Beatríz, but the fact of the matter is you didn't miss at all. You caught the upper lip of the first Mortejos, disabling him for a moment, and then you struck the head of the third Mortejos who was on the heels of the first one and ready to make a meal of you. After I killed the second Death Eyes, you gave me just enough time by your injury to the first one to finish him off." Childheart took a deep breath, sighed and added, "Interestingly, Beatríz, if you had driven your knife into the skull of the first one, as you intended, the second Mortejos would have gotten to you, for certain."

The eyes of all three Mortejoses were still alive with a slow revolving light from each that reflected dimly off the tunnel surfaces. "Quickly, if you can, Beatríz, climb aboard; we need to be heading back, hopefully finding our friends well before the enemy finds them or us first," said Childheart, as he kneeled for his rider.

As Beatríz mounted, she asked, "So, was that the Good helping us—I mean, helping me?"

"That's a question only you can answer, Beatríz. And the answer depends on how the moment shapes how you then live, if it does at all."

Beatríz *thought* she understood, but there was no opportunity for clarification. Childheart sprang back toward the T intersection, galloping with ferocious abandon; Beatríz had her arms about the unicorn's neck and her head buried deep in his flowing mane, utterly exhausted.

Past the intersection Childheart flew, not even stopping to allow Beatríz to grab a dropped torch, from which the ambient light emanated a considerable distance in front of them. So fast was Childheart racing that it seemed to Beatríz his hooves were barely touching the pavement. Within a few minutes Childheart and rider reached their three friends; they were standing together, as if waiting for them; and indeed they were.

"Thank goodness you made it back, Childheart," said Kahner casually, looking only at the firelight that was dancing in Beatríz's eyes—eyes that were turned only toward his.

"If it's true, as you blithely suggest, Kahner, there will need to be a lot more gratitude of that sort proffered to the Good before this business is finished," replied Childheart. It even occurred to Childheart that there was something in the tone of Kahner's voice that seemed not genuine; but he doubted Kahner was aware of it, and besides, there was no time to wonder about that just now.

"While you were fighting *your* Mortejos, Childheart, we—or, should I say, Alex—was fighting one of our own. I hope yours are dead?" Jamie asked.

"Thanks to Beatríz, yes, all three of them are dead. And yours?" returned Childheart.

"Ours simply ran away when Alex ran toward it head-on like a mad man!" Thorn replied quickly. "And then we heard you coming."

"Excellent. Well, let's be on our way," urged Childheart. "The enemy has, I believe, virtually surrounded us, and obviously has spent much time inside this mountain. How they have not already fallen upon us, I have no idea. I recognize we're heading closer to the enemy by continuing down this path toward the fleeing Mortejos, but it's tactically better than waiting to be caught between two different sets of forces, which is precisely what would happen if we simply remained where we now are. And," he added, "the forces coming toward us from the other direction are bearing down on us far more rapidly than those we'll be approaching. Assuming we encounter the enemy, and they want to fight, let Thorn and me do what we can to disable as many of them as possible for the rest of you to kill.

No better strategy occurs to me—unless it is something provided by the Good itself. Everyone must stay close together, and be ready—with your weapons drawn," Childheart ordered.

Childheart started to ask them to put out all the torches, but then changed his mind. He was worried about the enemy seeing them prematurely, but realized, more importantly, that they must not miss any opportunity, slim though it was, for escape before they were forced to engage in a fight. It continued to puzzle him though, that the enemy had not yet fallen on them; it was as if, Childheart thought, they were on paths that would never connect with their own.

The six of them set out at a swift pace, Thorn running far out ahead as a scout, since he could run the fastest without making much of a sound and had, of course, that natural ability to constantly light the way before him.

They followed the stone path that soon, and for quite some time, led the travelers on a wide—barely discernible—curve to the left and slightly uphill. Childheart and Beatríz reckoned that some of the enemy forces were perhaps only ten minutes away, and wondered if Thorn had already spotted their movement. They were soon to learn what now appeared to be the likely answer: They saw the eyes of Thorn bouncing in the distance like two fishing bobbers in disturbed water as he was running back toward them.

"Listen, everyone, quickly, please!" said Thorn, as he was slowing with labored breathing to rejoin the group. "We have no time to lose. There is a passageway up ahead that goes off to the left into the wall. It's very narrow, so we will have to enter it in single file." Catching his breath, Thorn paused briefly. "But, here's the thing. We will never reach the passageway before we encounter the enemy—unless, that is, there is a way of slowing them down. However," he offered quickly, "I have an idea: Childheart, you and I, I believe, can impede their progress sufficiently to allow the others time to get into the break in the wall. Once we have given the children enough time, Childheart, you and I will retreat to join them."

"But, Thorn!" objected Jamie, "we know the odds of your being able to join us this way . . ."

"Jamie!" Thorn snapped, interrupting him. "There is no other way to ensure that at least some of us, and especially you children, survive. This is no time for debate. Childheart, I think I know what to do."

"Then lift Beatríz off and climb aboard!" Childheart yelled to Thorn.

"No! Childheart! I'm staying with you, regardless of what happens!" Beatríz yelled, as Thorn removed her tenderly, but as rapidly as possible from the unicorn's back.

"Beatríz!" responded Childheart, in a firm whisper. "Now, all four of you—run like a hurricane! Jamie, you lead and take a torch. Be off now!" Childheart added, in a bellow that echoed down both directions of the tunnel as he and Thorn were already on their way toward engagement with the enemy forces, passing and leaving the children far behind in a white flourish. As ordered, the children already were racing at full speed, like leaves in a gusting wind.

Thorn leaned forward and directly into the wind that was coursing past Childheart's ear and told him his plan, which Childheart approved. Thorn would lie across the pavement once the two of them were well past the opening in the left wall. The on-rushing enemy forces would assume Thorn to be a small pile of sticks and logs they could easily hurdle without having to slow themselves down. As soon as the first of the forces attempted to jump Thorn, he would, as he did with the enemy many weeks earlier, raise his arms and legs and torso and trip them. They would fly head over heels, along with those who would be running close behind them. Accordingly, in front of Childheart, who would be waiting to spring from the dark, there would be forces reeling and piling on the pavement one on top of another.

Chidheart would then be able to attack several at once in their immobility and confusion, buying precious seconds for the children to get into the passageway. Once Childheart had given sufficient time to the children to press themselves into the crevice, he would, if he could, he insisted to Thorn, turn around and run in the opposite direction, leading any remaining forces on a chase past the children's escape route. At that point, Thorn, whom the enemy would not suspect to be other than the inanimate obstruction he had appeared to be, would race unseen behind the enemy to catch up with their four companions who had disappeared into the wall. Childheart would hope to escape from both enemy and tunnel by another way.

Thorn and Childheart quickly passed the exit through which they hoped the children would be able to pass unseen, and Thorn was on the ground and in position just as Sutante's forces with their torches were emerging from the darkness like so many lights being turned on in quick succession. The enemy never saw Thorn laying himself down on the path, and, fortunately, caught a glimpse of Childheart who, in the dim light from Thorn's eyes, had not yet disappeared into the shadows. Upon seeing Childheart, Sutante's warriors and beasts screeched and roared with greater ferocity. Childheart turned abruptly to face the enemy.

With delight at seeing their quarry now so close to capture or kill, those loyal to Sutante Bliss (if loyalty it was) pushed forward with abandon. Within seconds, the first of the warriors, four Wolfmen, were just beginning to make a shallow leap over the several branches in their way when Thorn raised all of his limbs just enough to trip them and send them flying hard onto the stone pavement. The second and third ranks of the enemy forces—trailing close behind and consisting of both Wolfmen and Unpersons—met the same fate, causing the remaining forces to stumble and fly into the pileup.

Immediately, Childheart launched his legs into the snarl of bodies attempting frantically to disentangle themselves to engage Childheart, screaming in their confusion and anger. There were perhaps twenty enemy forces in all, half of which Childheart was instantly able to either kill or severely disable with his hooves and horn. So horrifically efficient was Childheart in disposing of the enemy troops that within fifteen seconds or so of Childheart's initial assault, what little remained of the troops scrambled back across Thorn's inert body and retreated hastily into the darkness from which only half a minute earlier they had stridently emerged. Once Sutante's "men" were out of sight, Thorn rose and jumped aboard Childheart, stepping over the dead and injured as if they were a dozen land mines, a couple of which attempted lamely to ignite.

Childheart bolted away from the small killing field and almost immediately, upon reaching full speed, pulled up and halted abruptly, as if Thorn had just pulled hard on some invisible reins. There, in front of the fissure in the wall, Childheart ordered, "Here is where we part, my friend and potent warrior. Give the children a report that will lift their spirits." But Thorn did not move.

"I'm not leaving you all alone, Childheart!

"Thorn, the children . . . " But Thorn interrupted him.

"Yes, Childheart—a good report, indeed!" Thorn replied as he dismounted quickly and scrambled into the narrow space, glancing back to say, "Fare thee well, Childheart." Then, without further delay, he sprang on into the darkness that seemed to reach out to him like someone beckoning, but whose allegiance was unknown. At the same time, Childheart dove boldly ahead into the as yet undisclosed secrets of the mountain's black interior, shouting back, "And fare *thee* well, dear friend!"

~THIRTY~

JAMIE HELD ALOFT THE torch's flame, its pulsating light dancing on the jagged stone walls and playing games with the pathway ahead that seemed to press itself forward and change shape, as if it were a live serpent. With his other hand Jamie held tightly to Beatríz's hand. She, in turn, took the hand of Alex who was gripping hands with Kahner. Only occasionally did they have to duck or squeeze to get through, but even when the walls were not restricting, they had to move with caution because of the sharp jagged surfaces. They proceeded in this fashion for several minutes, pausing only briefly at one point along the way to listen to what was occurring back in the main tunnel: Thorn and Childheart battling Sutante's forces. Although wanting to stop and listen, and to wait for the awful sounds of destruction, injury, and death to cease—and then to stay and wait for Thorn—Jamie urged them forward.

When the sounds of intense battle rose and suddenly diminished and ceased, everyone knew that one side or the other had swiftly achieved total victory. Who was alive now? Only Thorn? Only Childheart? The two of them—or neither of them? Encouraged by the complete absence of further clamor from Sutante's troops, they hoped for a Thorn still alive and now making his way toward them. They prayed for a Childheart still alive and now making his way to an escape, separated—like Starnee—from everyone else.

After several more minutes of travel, Jamie stopped and whispered to the others excitedly, "I see a light up ahead! Keep as quiet as possible now." The light he saw, so far as he could tell, was something similar to daylight glowing vaguely into the passageway far ahead. He stopped again. "I think the end of the passageway is just ahead." It seemed to Jamie they must have walked half the distance to the light since first seeing it when, suddenly, the light disappeared. He stopped once more and mouthed back toward the others, with barely a sound, "The light is gone, and that means something is going on; stay quiet—be alert."

Finally, the four of them were close enough to see what appeared to be the end of the passageway not far ahead. There was still no further light signaling the end of the path, but Jamie could see the terminus in the light cast by the torch. Ever so gingerly the four companions stepped toward the back end of the stone corridor, only thirty feet remaining until their arrival. "And now what?" Jamie asked himself, for he could see nothing in the way of a continuation of the trail—nor any sort of exit.

Jamie motioned for the others to remain where they were while he stealthily investigated. When he reached the back wall it was as he initially thought: no apparent exit. It seemed their only option was to turn back, hopefully meeting up with Thorn, and then taking their chances in the broad main tunnel. But Jamie had definitely seen light that was not a reflection of his own. Where had it come from, he wondered. Jamie glanced carefully about the surface of the stony end. He noticed that the rocky face of the passageway's end had a texture that was at once very similar to, but also different from, that of the rest of the corridor. He also noticed that the back end of the passageway seemed to have been fitted *into* the wall, as if he were seeing a large stone that someone or something had recently pushed against and into an opening to the outside world—an opening he was certain had been there only moments earlier.

"Guys!" Jamie barked, but still in a whisper. "It looks like there's a stone blocking what is likely an exit—the one we must have seen the light coming from. I'm going to try to listen through the rock and see if I can hear any sounds of life on the other side. If I don't, I suggest we try to figure out how to move it out of the way. But," he added, with certainty that had been such a rare achievement on this journey, "clearly someone—or something—has just put it there."

Jamie pressed his ear against the end wall and cupped his hands around it. Listening intently, he realized they had not heard for quite some time now the sounds of enemy forces rushing from several directions deep inside the mountain, and he could not remember when he had last heard them. He was also surprised by the texture of the stone against which he was pressing his ear. Hearing nothing for just about a full minute, Jamie pulled back from the stone and pushed on it hard to no avail, then out of frustration punched it.

It was then he knew what was blocking their path was not a boulder at all, but the skin of some sort of creature which, at that moment of recognition and contact from Jamie, abruptly pulled away from the opening and turned like a whirlwind to face him. On noticing the blockage give way, Jamie yelled, "Look out!"—and then in a flash backed up, slamming into the body and arms of Beatríz, who then fell into the body and arms of Alex—who managed to stand his ground, catching Beatríz with both arms.

Apparently there was a large bulbous area below the head of the creature, but what protruded into the opening was a long pointed snout, not unlike that of a sawfish, that poked and thrashed at Jamie, barely missing his feet, which Jamie rapidly withdrew under himself. It was one of the creatures the children had all heard about—and actually heard—many weeks earlier, but had never seen: a Thrasher. And it was guarding the hole that led out of the mountain and into the light of day, or so Jamie and Alex thought from the tiny shafts of light that had flashed at them briefly when the creature turned to face them.

It screeched from a large mouth that was located at the base of its razor-sharp beak baring several rows of innumerable pointed teeth that were just as hideous-looking with its mouth closed as when it was open and salivating profusely. The children could feel large drops of saliva splattering against them when the animal assailed them with its saw-tooth beak whipping about and its lips hurling hideous sounds of rage and evil intent.

"Ahg!" screamed Alex, as fingers from behind gripped his shoulder.

"Children!" yelled Thorn. "There are enemy forces right behind me—we must keep going, and without delay of any sort, until we find a way out!"

"We can't, Thawn!" Alex yelled back. It was then Thorn noticed what was transpiring in front of him.

"Oh my . . . oh my!" Thorn said, and then, squeezing his way briskly past the children, he yelled, "Let me at him!"

"No, Thorn!" shouted Beatríz. "You can't, Thorn! He'll cut you into little sticks!"

"Well," replied Thorn, with fervent resolve, "so be it. That's apparently all I am anyway, at least according to our flying friend!" And as Thorn flew with his staff at the head of the creature to drive it into one of its eyes, Jamie grabbed hold of Thorn's legs in a bold and determined effort to tackle Thorn and pull him back toward the group before the Thrasher could cut into him. Thorn, indeed, fell hard to the ground, losing his grip on the staff. Thorn grasped wildly for his weapon while Jamie was pulling frantically on Thorn's legs. But Jamie could not draw Thorn back, for just as Thorn was reaching for his staff, the Thrasher caught Thorn's arm in its saw teeth and began to drag him toward its gaping mouth.

"No! Thorn!" yelled Jamie. "Beatríz, grab me and pull as hard as you can! The rest of you do the same!" Jamie gripped the jagged floor of the tunnel with his boots and pulled, straining every muscle and sinew. But the children were no match for the Thrasher—and were dragged along with Thorn toward the mouth of the vile creature.

"Let go, Jamie! All of you run through as soon as he pulls me free of the opening!" ordered Thorn.

"No! We're not letting you go, Thorn!" replied Jamie, through his clenched teeth.

Suddenly, the Thrasher lurched backwards with such ferocity that all the children, still holding onto each other and onto Thorn, found themselves being pulled rapidly out of the mouth of the cavern. All of them, except Kahner, whom no one noticed was missing, tumbled harshly in front of the Thrasher as its still-gaping mouth—without Thorn in it—was rising swiftly above them. And, then, like another recent battle, it was quickly over.

~THIRTY-ONE~

STARNEE WAITED CALMLY FOR the end that—this time—he was certain he would never actually experience. All of a sudden, however, as he was hurtling toward the ground, he felt himself being grabbed by dozens of tiny hooks that drove themselves mercilessly into his wings and body and that slowed him so rapidly he could feel his skin beginning to pull away from his carcass. He opened his eyes, but saw nothing—nothing, that is, except the ground slowing up to meet him, as if it were going to pause for a moment to welcome him into the earth.

He turned his head and strained his neck, but could not see what had apprehended him, and wondered if the falcons had ambushed him again. He wasn't ready for them, though he knew he should have been. Now all he could do was think how he might be able to face them and stand half a chance this time. But he knew he could do nothing until he was on the ground. Small vice grips were clutching and immobilizing him. He curled his head, awaiting the familiar assault.

"Starnee! It's okay. It's Butterfly, and all your other little angels!" His tone then shifted, as if Butterfly were interrogating a hostage. "But what in tarnation were you trying to do just now—kill yourself?"

Starnee said nothing as he grimaced in pain and allowed his rough but kind interceptors to land him.

"Just stay there now, and don't move a single muscle, Starnee!" Butterfly ordered, as he released the grip he had on the bird's scalp and rather sputtered the short distance to the ground. Starnee felt the hooks disengage from his skin and the tongues of the angel toads go to work immediately on his wounds, making their memorable milk-lapping sounds.

Butterfly hopped toward one of Starnee's eyes so aggressively that the condor thought the Cannotoad was going to crash right into it. As if teasing Starnee, Butterfly stopped abruptly just inches from Starnee's pupil.

"So," Butterfly began, almost scoldingly, "you mind telling me what this is all about?"

"Ah . . . " Starnee said, and then sighed. "It's a long—long—story, Butterfly, but just now I was trying, or, um, sort of trying, to fly over The Mountains to join some of my companions on the other side who are traveling *through* The Mountains to get there."

"You mean by, 'sort of,' I suspect, that you knew you couldn't possibly make it over."

"I thought it was for the best under the circumstances—unless you can think of something that would have been better," replied Starnee, not wanting, expecting, or anticipating an answer.

"Well, if you'd have waited another five minutes, you could have *found* a way over The Mountains, and *we* wouldn't have had to save you! How about *that something*?" Butterfly said, with a cock of his head punctuating the question and evident irritation in his voice. But he quickly altered his tone. "Never mind; it doesn't matter. What matters is we got here in time." Butterfly smiled that funny sort of way, and Starnee nodded ever so slightly to reciprocate.

"But wha . . . what do you mean, I could have found a way over The Mountains if I'd waited a few minutes? Where? How?" asked Starnee.

"Starnee: we can *carry you* over The Mountains!"

"I never thought you could fly as high as I can, much less fly a lot higher," replied Starnee, with sudden curiosity, raising his head off the ground for the first time since the hard landing.

"Oh, we can fly as high as we want," said Butterfly, matter-of-factly.

"But it doesn't make sense, Butterfly. I mean . . . ow!" he cried, reacting to one of the healers' efforts. "I mean, well, no offense little guy, but with a big body compared to, say, your insufficiently proportioned wings, it's a wonder you can fly at all!"

"My dear feathered friend," replied Butterfly, heartened by Starnee's emerging sense of humor, "we don't need our wings to fly. We're angels. But we do need them for balance and control, as well as direction."

When the Cannotoads had completed their healing labors, and Starnee had finished at about the same time recounting for Butterfly all that had transpired since they parted many days earlier, all of them assembled on the ground in a ring around the condor and their Chief.

"Do you know how long it will take the others to get through The Mountains—I mean, assuming they're not obstructed?" asked Starnee, hopefully.

"I've no idea; never been that way," replied Butterfly. "But I do know we've got a long way to go before we're clear of The Mountains," he added, as he twisted his head repeatedly one way and then the other, while gazing intently at the mountaintops.

"But," Starnee replied quickly, "how much *time* will it take us—can I get there in time to meet them?"

"Oh, that's not a worry—in no time at all; really. We'll just fly through the seam between The Mountains—and what lies beyond them," said Butterfly, with reticence.

"You're worried about something, though, Butterfly," said Starnee, now eager to be aloft and on their way.

"Angels never worry—it wastes time—and angels can't waste time. But, there *is* a consideration to be made," Butterfly said, and then paused to swallow, loudly, before continuing in a lower and slower voice. "The Corridor of Death . . . the seam, it includes the Corridor of Death."

"What's that, Butterfly?"

"It's that place where what you fear most and worry most about will tempt you to stop and pay heed. But, if you stop, you will . . ."

"But I won't stop, Butterfly," interrupted Starnee. "Don't worry about me."

"Remember, we don't worry; but I can assure you that you will *want* to stop, and that you will *beg* us to stop. And if you *will* yourself to stop, beyond merely *wanting* to do so, you will in fact stop, will be outside of our ability to assist you—and you will die. You will die in your worries and fears and be beyond the help of all others, including angels, and—and, perhaps, even the Good. Who can say?"

Starnee stared hard at Butterfly. "I understand; and even if I don't, I'm ready to go."

The plan was for Starnee to start alone and fly at the highest altitude he could achieve. At that point, the Cannotoads, flying alongside him, would grab him from both above and below and carry him the remainder of the way up and over the towering summits of rock. Once they had cleared the initial ring of peaks, they would enter the seam.

When Starnee had reached the loftiest elevation he had ever achieved in his long life, he was still more than 3,000 feet below the lowest of the mountain peaks. He relaxed his shoulders and spread his wings to soar. It was then that the angels clamped down on him, like so many little jaws snapping shut, and began to lift. They carried Starnee higher and higher, with blazing acceleration. Within mere moments, the entire set of mountains encircling Riven Valley was in the far distance below. "Why aren't they crossing The Mountains?" Starnee asked himself. Indeed, the Cannotoads and their precious cargo were at least as high above the tallest peaks as the valley floor was below them.

"Butterfly!" yelled Starnee.

"Yes, Starnee?" shouted Butterfly through the howling wind rushing past them.

"Why are you still climbing?"

"To get to the seam of course!"

"But . . . " Starnee stopped talking, deciding nothing that Butterfly would say would make any sense to him, at least not until after the fact, if even then. They were flying so fast, Starnee felt like a meteorite against the starry night sky.

And then, all of a sudden, Starnee felt the trajectory changing. Even more suddenly, the Cannotoads and he began to soar at a still higher speed across the diamond sprinkled sky until, with nary a jolt, Starnee saw they were now rocketing toward the ground. So fast were they racing toward The Mountains below that Starnee thought he saw at least a few of the stars whizzing past them. Stopping before hitting the ground seemed beyond impossible to him.

All went instantly dark, and Starnee felt himself floating, as if in outer space, but without the presence of the stars or other celestial bodies. Someone or something had turned off their lights, and he no longer felt the clutches of Butterfly and the other angels; he was utterly alone. But he knew he was still moving, or that something was moving, because he saw a single dim light in the far distance fast approaching. He then found himself entering a corridor, and he could see figures up ahead—moving, and making as yet indecipherable noises.

Now he no longer seemed to be moving at all; rather, on entering the corridor, it seemed that both the corridor and the figures were moving toward and round him. And the corridor was black—as black as lightless space—but with something of a sheen delineating its presence, as if it was part of some ghostly existence, part of darkness haunting darkness.

As the figures came closer, the distant voices became a din that got louder by the moment, even though he still could not identify what or who the figures were, or what they were saying. Suddenly there was a maelstrom of figures surrounding him and clutching at him, and screaming for him to help them. Starnee shut his eyes and tried to move his wings, but they were ineffectual, as he knew they would be.

He dared not look at the creatures that were screaming at him. But then, he heard amidst the rest of the innumerable voices, one that he recognized—the voice of Thorn, yelling for him: "Starnee! Help me!"

Starnee opened his eyes involuntarily and saw Thorn, bound and lying on a pyre, and about to be burned by wood that was hungrily awaiting only the small fire from a nearby torch to transform it into a raging furnace. Now Starnee could see that Jamie was on top, and bound like Thorn, and that he also was yelling for Starnee to save them. And then Starnee noticed Alex standing next to the pyre holding the torch, and an unseen and hideous voice ordering him to light the wood.

"Starnee! Starnee!" yelled the three friends, staring in abject horror at Starnee while they were grasping for him, beating the air wildly, and wailing and gnashing their teeth. Starnee yelled back at them:

"I can't! I can't!"

"Don't leave us, Starnee! Don't abandon us again! Don't fly away!"

Starnee yelled into the darkness holding him close to itself, "Butterfly! Butterfly, I want to go to them! I want to help them! I must go to them! I have to! Please, please, let me go!"

Then Starnee heard Butterfly's instant reply, much louder now that he was hearing Butterfly only in his memory: "If you *will* to go, then you will go."

Starnee clenched beak and teeth together so hard he thought his jaws would shatter, like a crystal goblet exploding. Gushing tears, Starnee yelled to himself, "No! No! I want to! I must! But I *will not!*"

The figures were now moving much faster and further away, the din diminished, and Starnee could no longer see his friends or hear their distinct voices. But just when he knew he had prevailed, Starnee heard the din once again increase and another distinct and familiar voice pleading to him. It was Beatríz! She was alone and wandering unaware toward enemy forces—vile creatures about to spring on her from behind a cavern wall.

"Starnee! Starnee!" begged Beatríz. "Where are you? Why have you abandoned me? Help me! Please, Starnee, save me!"

Starnee could see that concealed enemy swords were about to flash and lay open Beatríz's body, and that a rabid creature was readying its jaws to gnaw at her. She reached out to him, and he knew if he acted without further delay he could grab her and pull her to safety. He immediately stretched a leg, and he was only *inches* from her wildly grasping fingers, but his leg was not long enough. "Butterfly! Butterfly! Help me reach Beatríz! Just a little bit closer! Quickly!"

Starnee stretched his leg until it seemed to be tearing away from his abdomen, and he shouted, "I must this time! Butterfly, I must!" His resistance was weakening while his regret was growing. And then Starnee screamed, as if in the worst pain possible, "No! No! I will not, Beatríz!"

Beatríz let out a long and indicting wail, and then, in another instant, she was far away from Starnee, her pleas no longer reaching his ears, and all was quiet.

Just when Starnee thought the ordeal had come to an end, he heard the din increase a third time and a familiar voice distinguishing itself above the rest.

"Starnee! Starnee! My love!" cried out Mythena. "Why did you leave me? Why didn't you protect me? Why did you let them take me? But you can save me now, Starnee!"

Starnee looked around frantically, searching for the source of the cry from among a jumble of figures, all of whom were writhing in pain and calling out for help. And then he saw her, his Mythena, his beloved, above his head, struggling to pull a cart full of stones in her servitude to Sutante Bliss, and falling from the sky and being struck by many whips. Her claws were bound to render her harmless, and her back and wings and head were missing feathers and oozing blood, and wetting the ground red.

Suddenly, Mythena's voice became fragile and soft. She spoke in barely a whisper and looked lovingly into Starnee's eyes, and, despite the deafening cacophony all around him, Starnee could hear her distinctly, as if he was thinking her thoughts, and she his.

"I forgive you, Starnee! And I love you! Forever!"

This was the worst of all. "I must! I must!" Starnee screamed. "I must go to Mythena, Butterfly! I would rather rot in damnation for trying to save her and fail than live without trying! Butterfly! Do you hear me? I must! I must!—*Now!*" But he made no movement toward Mythena.

Starnee looked into Mythena's eyes, which were an alloy of pain and love, life ebbing rapidly from her body and her ember of being almost cold. And then, it was over.

Mythena, and all the other figures, and all the sounds, and even the corridor, were gone. Evening clouds appeared below him that stretched all the way to the horizon; and a dim light was glowing through the clouds and gilding their edges.

Starnee realized he was now soaring among and between and through the clouds on his own power—the Cannotoads nowhere to be seen. The sun's musty-colored rays were streaming skyward from below the horizon and refracting into a steel blue, twilight canopy of sky. The light was insufficient to give Starnee any sense of what lay beneath the clouds, so Starnee executed a wide descending bank down and through them. Immediately he caught sight of an old castle in the distance on a slight rise, and then noticed the ground welling up swiftly to meet him as he completed his turn. He barely avoided contact with a turret on a more imposing castle that suddenly swept into view right below him. He curled his wings and scooped the air to head vertically, just grazing the dark granite with the tips of his feathers. Once well above the castle and circling in reconnaissance, Starnee saw that the mammoth structure was built out of a sheer wall of mountain from which, no doubt, the stone had been quarried; indeed, it looked as if the castle had simply sprouted from the mountain's base.

Other than the side protruding from the mountain wall, the castle was anchored into, and surrounded by, a broad grassy mound that lifted it a hundred feet into the air. Encircling the mound was a wide and raging river that flowed from beneath the mountain, and then around the castle as a moat, before returning to hug the base of the mountain on its journey urgently southward. A tall steel gate in the mound wall signaled a drawbridge securely stowed.

Starnee continued to circle, surveying the terrain. He noticed the grass was brown, and that what few leaves still clinging to the otherwise barren trees, though flickering in the wind, were dead. Wherever he looked there appeared to be only the scarce plants and desperate flowers of late autumn. There were no trees or shrubs one would ordinarily find in winter, such as evergreens, and he noted, with a sudden tingling of his spine, that all the parcels of the once-cultivated land had been abandoned, perhaps for many, many years.

It occurred to Starnee that for as long as he had been flying the sky had not changed. The sun floating just beneath the horizon in the west had not moved whatsoever, and only a frozen sunset, Starnee determined, could account for what he was witnessing. There was little sign of life on the land, and the possibilities for living things would have to be severely limited, he thought. Certainly, he calculated, to the extent the land stretching away from him for miles and miles could provide little in the way of sustenance, the presence of resident creatures much larger than a shrew was highly unlikely, if not impossible. Wherever he looked, there was no evidence at all of persons or creatures of any sort—including a shrew.

The land was not devoid of beauty, but it was the beauty found in that which is nevertheless somber and sad. It was, Starnee thought, rather like a treeless Forest of Lament. A history of joy was evident; but the legacy of recent history was sorrow.

"Rowerowerowerowerow!" A startled Starnee looked sharply all around for the source of the sudden and ominous creature noise. He banked and looked back toward the mountain. All he could see far below was the back end of a large creature, the front of which was struggling inside an opening in the face of the mountain near the river egress. Starnee sailed cautiously toward the creature, maintaining a safe elevation. And then, all of a sudden, the Thrasher pulled itself free of the opening, its tooth-encrusted snout holding fast to the ground the top half of what Starnee instantly knew to be Thorn.

Starnee dove at the beast and seized its rear end, his talons digging deep into the creature's muscles. The Thrasher securely clutched, Starnee flew fiercely away from the hole, causing the creature to pull out the remaining half of Thorn with a harsh jolt, together with the three children who were locked like a chain to Thorn's legs. The beast wailed the most horrible of screams and in its agony released Thorn. The children tumbled over Thorn and sat up slowly. They were dazed, but alert enough to recognize Starnee and see him pull the Thrasher high into the air and hurl him against the face of the mountain.

The creature's deafening ejaculation of anguish and wrath was quickly silenced by the loud smack of contact with the stone, leaving the creature to make no further noise other than a single thud as it struck the ground. The children shouted for joy at the sight of Starnee and their rescue, even as they were scrambling over to Thorn to see how badly he was hurt.

One of Thorn's arms was severely gouged by the saw teeth, and it appeared as well that there was a hairline fracture on one of his legs extending from the ankle to the knee. But, aside from the pain, though considerable, Thorn's body seemed to work as capably as ever.

The children were wondering aloud what had been happening with Starnee during the separation and how he had managed to get across The Mountains, even as they were approaching Thorn, but were interrupted by shouting coming from a familiar person they thought they'd never hear from again.

~THIRTY-TWO~

ONE OF THE ATTENDANTS in the bathing hall escorted Elli to her room located at the top of a tall and rotund parapet: "I'll summon you for dinner in about fifteen minutes," the woman said, curtly.

When the woman had closed the door behind Elli, who was already busy examining the large, stately room, Elli thought she heard it being locked. She turned, and was tempted to try the door, but noticed that the escort had posted herself next to the latch, as evidenced by the shuffling of feet whose shadowed movements were visible beneath the door.

Elli looked toward the bed and saw a many-layered, diaphanous silk and chiffon gown lying in wait for her across the bed. She slid off the robe, put on the cream-colored gown that fell well beneath her knees, careful to stow in her new wide belt and sheath her knife that was lying next to the gown, and went to the large bay window facing east. Elli sat on the window seat and rested her chin on folded hands. She gazed across what she thought at one time must have been a stunningly beautiful land of woods and rolling meadows—now looking as if pensive in their late autumn browns and bare black limbs beneath a sunset sky full of brooding clouds.

Elli unlatched the leaded glass window and pushed it heavily out and into the warm and moist breeze. She was startled by a noise from behind; it was the curtains across the room fluttering, as if annoyingly disturbed by the suddenly freshening air. Then, just as suddenly, Elli was startled by another—much harsher—noise coming from outside the same shut and curtained window, as if something other than the breeze was disturbing the fabric. She sprang to that window and, again, with considerable effort, opened it. Far down below and out of her range of sight at the foot of the moat, Elli heard a screaming screech, a couple of monstrous thuds, and then familiar voices shouting, "Starnee!"

"Beatríz! Alex! Jamie!" Elli yelled. "Are you okay? I'm up here! In the castle!"

"Ewi! Ewi!" yelled Alex.

"Where are you?" shouted Jamie.

"I'm looking down from the parapet! I can't see you—step back from the wall!" Elli shouted back.

Alex, Jamie, and Beatríz dashed out into the broad swath of grass ringing the moat to look up at Elli while Starnee took flight. As soon as Elli caught sight of her companions, welling tears distorted her vision.

"Look, Elli!" erupted Beatríz. "The key! I have it!"

Elli blinked fiercely, saw the black key that Beatríz had lifted in both hands on the chain about her neck, and then, like old times, shouted decisive orders to her friends. "I can't explain now, but go back and hide by the moat wall! I'll be right there! And," she added quickly, with unrestrained excitement, "I'm bringing someone with me who can help us get to Queen Taralina's castle! We're so close now!"

Elli turned quickly from the window and ran to the door. It was locked. "Open the door! Please! Open the door!"

"I am not authorized to unlock what has been locked," said the voice behind the door, but not without a note of sympathy. "But I'll send for Santanya."

"Please! Hurry!"

Within seconds Elli heard the sound of scurrying feet. "Open the door, you fool!" shouted Santanya to the sentinel woman. The door burst open, revealing Santanya on its threshold and a dozen or so troops standing close behind her.

"Oh, Santanya! We've no time to lose! My friends are outside, and Beatríz has the key!" implored Elli, breathlessly, as she rushed toward the door with a sense of optimism, if not elation, she had never before experienced on the journey.

Santanya held up her hand, signaling Elli to halt her advance.

"*I* will help her, Elli. But you must stay here—where you'll be safe," answered Santanya.

"No! I don't care if I'm safe or not! I need to help my friends, Santanya!" shouted Elli, while staring fiercely into Santanya's fiery eyes.

"Well," retorted Santanya, taking umbrage, "*I* care if you're safe!" Santanya yelled, "Guards! Take this child to my chambers and go get the others who are outside the gate. Above all, apprehend the girl with the key and bring her directly to me—here! The other children can join this one."

Before Santanya had finished speaking, Elli sprang toward the door, startling Santanya, who stepped involuntarily back into the hallway. Elli then slammed the door shut and bolted it.

"Guards! Open the door! Break it down if you have to!" ordered Santanya, stridently.

Elli ran to the window and stepped onto the stone sill. "Guys! Run! Run! I've been deceived! I'll join you as soon as I can! Now run!" She heard their immediate cry from below.

"Starnee! Starnee!"

But Starnee had already anticipated the need. He swooped down to Elli who, quickly and heedless of the risk, had stepped outside the window and onto a narrow ledge where she was shifting her feet, inch by rapid inch, away from the opening. Just as Starnee had stopped mid-air, plucking Elli from the precipice, guards appeared at the window and flung their hatchets and spears at the bird that was scooping air ferociously with all four wings to remain stationary in flight. But the moment the weapons flew from enemy hands Starnee dropped like a rock, Elli firmly in his grasp, and then swept abruptly upwards—just before striking the ground. An enemy hatchet had found its mark on Starnee's forehead, but only the blood that was running into his eyes was of any consequence to him. Starnee shook off the rivulets of blood as he sped toward his companions who were now running through the tall meadow grasses beyond the moat's sward in the direction of Queen Taralina's castle.

To run faster, and to ensure he would not lose her, Thorn carried Beatríz on his back. They had covered about a third of the distance to the Queen's castle grounds when the enemy forces from Santanya's castle were crossing the lowered drawbridge in swift pursuit. Thorn yelled for everyone to stop. He then gave matches to Alex and Jamie and directed them to ignite the grasses behind them. Thorn hoped enough smoke would be sent on the steady wind into the face of Santanya's warriors to force them to circle round and attack from the windward side of the flames, giving the arsonists additional time to recoup some lost separation between the enemy and themselves.

Starnee had by this time dropped Elli to the ground next to Thorn before flying off again to divert the attention of the pursuers who had lost sight of their quarry behind the rising smoke. Suddenly, Thorn and the children stopped with alarm. They were being surrounded as enemy forces were now charging at them from the very direction in which they were fleeing. Everyone pulled a blade to defend Beatríz. Thorn and Elli stood

together to challenge the enemy approaching rapidly from Queen Taralina's castle to the front—Alex and Jamie stood their ground to defend the
mission party from the roiling forces again approaching from Santanya's
castle at the rear.

And then, when the two sets of attackers were within striking distance of the four children and Thorn, they let fly their knives, hatchets,
and spears, all of which sailed over the heads of the four companions,
as if miraculously sparing them. Thorn and the children cowered low in
the grass while peeking back and forth to see where the projectiles were
heading, and discovered that the two phalanxes of warriors were attack-
ing not them but one another! As soon as the battle lines for the moment
were clarified, Starnee swooped down and harassed the attackers to the
front while his companions began once again to run with abandon toward
Taralina's castle. A few warriors from both enemy camps ran swiftly to
overtake them, but invariably neutralized each other as they first fought
over who would catch the prize of their mutual pursuit.

A few of the attackers made it all the way to one or more of the children, but each of the children was able to fight them off—including Beatríz, who managed to strike a swift-footed warrior whom she heard closing
in on her just as he was about to snatch her from the back of Thorn. In
the act of striking forcefully at the creature, however, whose distance from
her she measured by the sound of his breathing, Beatríz caused Thorn to
lose his balance, sending him hard to the ground. The leg that was already
slightly fractured now suddenly exploded at the knee, rendering Thorn
useless as both carrier and fighter. Elli rushed to Beatríz's side and grabbed
her arm to lift her from the ground.

"C'mon, Beatríz! Run with me! Pick up your feet!" Elli shouted while
locking Beatríz's hand into hers.

As Elli and Beatríz ran, more of the enemy forces were closing in on
them from both sides, as well as from a reassembled rear flank. Starnee
had been effective in killing or injuring many, but Elli noticed additional
warriors pouring from Taralina's compound and rushing headlong in their
direction. Elli pulled at Beatríz's hand sharply to redirect their course.

"We have to go . . . this way. . . Beatríz! More are coming—in front
of us again!" shouted Elli, breathlessly. The two friends, joined now at
hand and heart as if nothing would—or could—ever separate one from
the other, were so tired they could no longer feel their legs, and knew they
were about to fall and be apprehended.

"Starnee! Starnee!" Elli, unable to see the condor, beseeched the sky. "Take Beatríz!" she screamed.

Starnee, who was embroiled close to the ground in a ferocious battle with a Wolfman and two Unpersons, heard Elli's plea and spun in the air to locate her. Quitting the immediate fight, Starnee shot toward the two girls, intent on doing as Elli had pleaded him to do, but without the slightest notion of how he was going to help Beatríz beyond that. Then he heard a voice that startled him, providing hope.

"Starnee! Keep fighting! I'll grab the girls!" yelled Childheart in a thunderous voice while he raced past Starnee in a flash of white across the battlefield.

Elli saw Childheart streaking toward her. "Childheart!" yelled Elli. "He's coming, Beatríz! He's coming for you!" she shouted as the two girls stumbled.

In a burst of dust that encircled all three of them, Childheart pulled up sharply next to the girls who had collapsed to the ground. Childheart kneeled. "Jump on! Both of you!"

In no time at all Beatríz and Elli were aboard Childheart and speeding against the impossible to get around both sets of enemy forces that were now joining and closing ranks from both ahead and behind to prevent the unicorn's further advance toward the castle. Kahner was still nowhere to be seen, as if he had existed only in their collective imagination. Starnee had dispatched summarily with a goodly number of "inconveniences" and was now flying just above Childheart and the two girls.

"Starnee!" yelled Elli, against the wind, "somehow we need to get into the castle! We have to get Beatríz and the key to Taralina's vault!"

Starnee acknowledged the child's reasoning without question or pause, snatched the two girls from Childheart's back, abruptly wheeled, and darted toward the castle. The forces from Taralina's compound continued to pour out like an open spigot, racing to encircle the perimeter to cut off and capture the unicorn and those they believed were still riding it. The other forces from Taralina's compound who had been battling the warriors from Santanya's castle well behind the new battle front suddenly adjourned their campaign, worked to disengage themselves from the fray, and scrambled back toward Taralina's castle. They split into two storming clusters of fighters, one pursuing Childheart and the other rushing to join in the compound's defense. Starnee circled tight and low over the castle, encouraging forces yet within the compound, both visible and hidden, to let fly lethal spears, hatchets, and other weapons, none of which, Starnee knew, would be able to reach him or the children he clutched close to his breast.

The castle was expansive, with lovely, but simple, parapets located at various places inside the low wall that softly girdled the towering castle and its grounds. There were also half a dozen higher parapets positioned at seemingly random places within the castle proper, one of which soared well above all the others. Nothing was conspicuously defensive about the structure of the castle, which fronted a long open staircase that advanced upward from the foundation of the castle wall toward the large bronze entrance doors. But the stairway and parapets were well guarded, as were three other doors in the castle wall providing access and egress—to and from someplace. Then Starnee noticed through the incessant hail of weaponry the enemy was flinging at him a small set of unremarkable stairs that led darkly down and beneath the castle—and which the largest number of tightly gathered warriors were protecting, as if expecting an attempt at penetration any moment. He was hopeful this was the way to the Queen's vault, but he noticed, in addition to its robust protection, there was no way either Childheart or he would be able to accompany Elli and Beatríz on this particular entry into the castle. Besides, it was impossible to ascertain whether the stairs descending steeply into darkness was the way to the Queen's vault or simply the way to ambush and capture—and maybe torture and death.

Childheart was continuing fiercely his course around the castle compound, hoping for a breach of some sort in the wall and, just as importantly, an absence of warriors blocking his approach. Starnee broke suddenly from his reconnaissance above the castle and descended sharply toward Childheart. The two of them were now racing side by side toward the looming compound, the two girls wrapped in Starnee's talons not noticing the ground as it flew by a few feet beneath them.

"No breach in the wall anywhere I could see!" Starnee yelled to Childheart, whose voluminous mane roiled against Starnee's feathers. "And there are forces now encircling the compound wall, as well as a large number inside guarding the gates and lying in wait." He paused to catch his breath. "There *is* an entrance going down from the bottom of the castle wall into the foundation of the castle that stands the best chance of being the opening we're looking for, but it's the most heavily guarded, and," he said, pausing again, less for breath than for emphasis, "there is no room for either of us to accompany the girls."

"Well," shouted Childheart, "I'll find a way of getting them over the outer wall if you'll take care of the guards!" Childheart did not wait for a reply. "Lead the way!"

Starnee barked orders to the girls to drop onto Childheart's back once more and then launched himself up and to the right, Childheart galloping close behind.

Starnee reached the castle grounds first and dove sharply toward the heads of the troops who were ringing ever more tightly the diminutive staircase. On his first pass he was able to grab the weapons of two Unpersons and fling them outside the wall, sending the two weaponless warriors scurrying for cover down the stairs. On his second pass Starnee was able to snatch the weapons of three more enemy forces, but not without a hatchet burying itself into one of his legs. As he spun up and away with the small cache of two knives and a spear, Starnee stretched his neck to extract the hatchet. Blood spurted into the wind and vaporized behind him. Starnee realized that Childheart might arrive quickly, depending on how entangled he had become in battle with those protecting the wall, so Starnee grasped the spear in one set of talons while he wielded a knife in the other and then circled back for what he hoped would be—perhaps would have to be—a final assault.

Just as Starnee was diving hard at the first of his remaining assailants, Childheart was racing toward a three-deep line of forces protecting the outer wall of the compound. Spears, knives, swords, and hatchets were ready for the onslaught and slaughter of the unicorn. Just as the warriors unleashed a dense volley of projectiles, storming with deadly aim toward the onrushing unicorn and its two riders, Childheart leaped over the phalanx of enemy troops and, with a brief touch on the ground behind them, bounded over the wall and into the courtyard already in tumult.

With Elli still clinging to Childheart and Beatríz to Elli, the terrible and beautiful unicorn, glowing in the dusky air as if it were drawing all light to itself, gored with its horn, and flattened with its front hoofs, and kicked with its rear legs, while Elli and Beatríz, with their blades, swiped at enemy forces closing in around them. The battle in the courtyard concluded with a sudden silence, save only the sound of rapid breathing emanating from the four friends and the clamor of steel and leather, boot and anger, encroaching fast from beyond the courtyard wall.

Childheart and Starnee stood, unmoving, next to each other, coated in dust and dripping blood. The children, without word or prompting from their two companions, jumped from Childheart's back, bolted down the short flight of visible steps and disappeared instantly into the black mouth of the tiny archway. Within an enveloping darkness Elli and Beatríz stood just beyond any view of the opening to the outside and listened to the clamorous din of hundreds of warriors as they descended from all directions on Childheart and Starnee. Neither condor nor unicorn intended to do other than fight to the last, if only to give the girls as much opportunity as possible to reach Taralina's vault. The two weary defenders of the mission stood, listing, in front of the stairs down which Elli and Beatríz had dashed moments earlier, waiting for the next—and presumably final—battle. As creatures and warriors by the dozens oozed from unseen places to the right and left, as well as over the wall in front of them, Childheart and Starnee each searched momentarily the other's eyes and then turned to face their attackers, talons and hooves tensed and ready.

~THIRTY-THREE~

ELLI CONTINUED THEIR DESCENT on the steep stone stairs with quiet abandon, Beatríz—stumbling, but remaining—in tow.

Having descended in complete darkness some eighty feet or so, they discovered a low alcove and passageway off to their left and stepped just inside to catch their breath and consider their next move. The two girls listened intently to one another's breathing, as if each was struggling to be certain of the other's existence, and said nothing. The original din above them had diminished markedly as they plunged into the thick bosom of damp stone and dank air. They felt as if they were carrion about to be swallowed.

Both of the wordless companions wanted to stay where they were until the fighting had concluded, but Elli and Beatríz knew it would be better to move on as quickly as possible using what remained of the noise above to cover their movement. Elli tugged gently on Beatríz, who complied immediately, as if waiting for Elli's signal. The girls continued their descent much less quickly, but just as urgently, and soon discovered a large wooden door blocking their path. Elli put her ear against it and listened; she whispered to Beatríz to do the same.

"Do you hear anything?"

"No. Nothing."

Elli tried the doorknob ever so slightly and, as she expected, found it locked. Elli felt around the doorframe for a key, but found only a hook on which it likely had hung. Then, something happened that made them gasp simultaneously, a noise with sufficient volume that they heard it echo behind them. Something on the other side of the door quietly unlatched it. Elli grabbed the hilt of her knife and drew it from its sheath. She gently pushed Beatríz behind her.

"Who's there?" Elli whispered. "Who's there?"

"Elli," offered Beatríz, softly, "I think I heard something running on the stairs."

"Above us?" Elli asked with a doubling of her alarm.

"No. On the other side of the door." She paused. "But it's gone now—the sound that is," said Beatríz.

"Okay. Let's go," Elli said, as she found again and tugged on Beatríz's hand. She turned the knob and pulled open the door that complained and resisted as if awakened after a very long sleep. Elli gripped her knife for whatever might seek to impede their progress and then slipped with Beatríz behind the door, the two of them allowing it to shut quietly against their backs.

The girls stood stiffly, Elli looking down a wide circular staircase illuminated by a flickering fire concealed well below the stairs.

"There's a little bit of firelight somewhere down the stairs that's allowing me to see again, Beatríz. Let's go."

They descended this new set of stairs for several minutes.

"Elli!" Beatríz said in a sharp whisper.

"What?"

"These stairs smell and feel like the very first stairs we went down, in the library."

"They look very much like them, too, Beatríz," replied Elli who, along with Beatríz, felt a chill of recognition.

As the girls continued down the stairs, a series of torches on the walls revealed at least one source of the light drifting up the staircase. But another soon disclosed itself when Elli and Beatríz reached the bottom of the stairs. Once there, around a tight corner, Elli and Beatríz stepped carefully into a vast hall made of polished granite floors and glistening marble walls, lit by torches stationed high in the vaulted ceiling of flying buttresses.

The space was perhaps seventy-five feet wide in front of them, with a ceiling soaring well above a hundred feet, and a length of hall going off to their left that could not be seen beyond a hundred feet, where it bent into complete darkness. Off to their immediate right was the other end of the hall containing what appeared to be recessed well within it—and to the astonishment of Elli—an apparent entombment chamber with a large metal door, barely visible behind several stone pillars. Beatríz was about to say something, but Elli squeezed her hand. "This must be it, Beatríz—the tomb, off to our right."

Elli couldn't see the keyhole because of the columns and shadows, but she was certain it had to be there; and she saw engraved writing on the door, although she couldn't read it. Elli continued simply to stand where she was, her arms interlocked with Beatríz's, perplexed by her inaction. "Why am I not rushing to the door?" she asked herself, and was about to take action, when they heard the sound of warrior feet and Elli saw forces emerge swiftly from the darkness to the left. She gripped Beatríz's hand fiercely and began to run to the vault. But Elli and Beatríz had not taken a single stride when they were stopped abruptly by Wolfmen and Unpersons who stepped rapidly from the recessed shadows surrounding the vault. It wasn't so much the enemy forces now completely encircling the two girls, however, that caught Elli up short, as it was the sudden appearance of an individual to her left who had just stepped from among the ranks of warriors and creatures and stood in the circle, facing the two girls.

"Kahner!" shouted Elli. Upon his sudden appearance all noise and movement promptly ceased, as if all within the hall were as startled by the vision as was Elli. Beatríz squeezed Elli's hand.

"Kahner?" asked Beatríz, thinly, breaking the silence in a voice that reflected both euphoria and puzzlement.

"Elli! Beatríz!" a beaming Kahner exclaimed, arms spread wide. "You have finally arrived! And you are safe now. I didn't know it was you—and didn't imagine it could ever be you!"

Kahner strode swiftly to Elli and hugged her; she stood unmoved, entirely bewildered, not sure whether their mission was about to be accomplished—or just had come to an unsuccessful end! Kahner then paused before Beatríz, laid his arms affectionately about her shoulders and drew her close.

"Oh, Kahner! I thought I'd lost you forever! Forever!"

Kahner released his arms and took Beatríz delicately by the hand while looking at Elli. "Come, sit down with me." Then, turning to a few of the forces close by, he ordered them sharply, but in a subdued voice, as if it would have a rippling effect on all of them, "As you were." Immediately the dozens of troops, mostly Wolfmen and Unpersons, lowered their weapons and retreated without delay to the far walls.

"Kahner," Elli said, emphatically, "what's happening? We need to get Beatríz to the vault—you know that."

"Elli, Beatríz," Kahner said, soothingly, "it's okay; I'm in charge now. I'll explain later. But what's more important is that *I* have the key—the *diamond* key!"

Kahner then pulled from inside his shirt a large key embedded with hundreds of diamonds. "Here, Beatríz—feel it!"

Blackfire

Beatríz reached out her hands and Kahner enfolded them around the key. "Is it really the diamond key, Kahner?" she asked him while she held the key in one hand and reached out with the other to touch his face. It was the face of Kahner—her Kahner, whom she loved beyond any love she had ever known for anyone else in the world.

Kahner smiled and said, "Yes. It's the diamond key, Beatríz. And it's yours. But," he added gently, "you need to put it around your neck now." And with those words he placed the chain from the diamond key in the hand that was caressing his face with its trembling fingertips.

"Here. Sit, and I'll put it on you." All three sat down, and then Kahner, as if remembering the library key for the first time, said, "Oh, but, of course, you'll need to take off the old black one, Beatríz. You won't need that any longer now that you have the real key." Kahner smiled again at Elli as he tenderly reached behind Beatríz's hair toward the chain holding the black key.

"No! Beatríz, no! You cannot remove the black key! You know that!" Then, turning to look hard at Kahner, she said, "Kahner, you know that, too! No one is to remove the key!" Kahner settled his hands lightly on Beatríz's shoulders.

"Elli," said Beatríz, with an almost motherly emphasis, "it's okay. It was only *you* that Peterwinkle told to not remove the key under any circumstances—and you did!

"Besides, Elli," she said with thick reassurance in her voice, "it's Kahner! It's Kahner! And he's giving us the key we need!"

Kahner withdrew his hands from Beatríz slowly, concedingly, and sat quietly, waiting with studied patience. He then spoke with almost exaggerated emphasis: "Actually, Beatríz, *you* now have the diamond key!"

Beatríz, without pause or hesitation, handed the diamond key to Elli, freeing her hands to reach back to gather her long hair and grasp the chain about her neck, which Childheart had placed there so formally many weeks earlier.

"Beatríz! No!" urged Elli, imploringly.

For the first time Beatríz thought, albeit fleetingly, that Elli was jealous—jealous that the key was actually supposed to go to *her*, that *she* was the girl of the poem—and jealous that *she* had Kahner, too.

Beatríz lifted the chain off her neck and reached out the key toward Kahner.

At that moment, Elli grabbed the black key while jumping to her feet and raced toward the vault. Kahner sprang from his knees to tackle Elli, but he was too late. Reaching the vault door before Kahner could give an order to stop her, Elli reached out to put the black key into the keyhole when Kahner grabbed Beatríz and yelled to Elli, "Stop!—I'll kill her! Stop! Or I'll kill Beatríz!"

Elli halted all movement with the key only inches from insertion, tossed the chain about her neck, the key still in her hand, and then turned around to face Kahner, who had a knife poised against Beatríz's throat.

"Kahner!" screamed Beatríz, with dismayed incredulity. "What are you doing? You're Kahner—*my* Kahner! *Our* Kahner!"

"You lied to her, Kahner. This is the key you need, isn't it?" said Elli.

"Just give me the key, Elli, or I will kill her—and still get the key from you," Kahner replied with cold arrogance.

"How do I know you won't kill her—and me—anyway?" retorted Elli.

"You don't. But you *will* be responsible for her death, and will watch her die—if you don't give me the key. Give it to me now, Elli!"

Disillusioned, heartbroken Beatríz cried out thickly through her sobs, "Don't give it to him, Elli! He's going to kill us both anyway!"

"Elli. I'm going to ask you just one more time," said Kahner, now with that coolness of voice and quietude of demeanor of one who has already won the war, and merely has to tie up the loose ends.

By this time, dozens of warriors were facing Elli with weapons raised and tensed for release. Elli knew now that as soon as she turned to reach the key into the keyhole she would be immediately killed, and most likely Beatríz as well. Could she move fast enough, though, she wondered quickly. And was she willing to try at the expense of Beatríz?

Elli began to lift from her neck the chain on which the black key hung. "Okay, Kahner," Elli said calmly. "Okay."

"No, Elli!" sobbed Beatríz.

Elli then stooped down ever so deliberately without taking her eyes off Kahner and slid the key and chain with one swift motion across the floor to Kahner's feet. Kahner gestured to one of the Unpersons to pick it up. As soon as the key was in Kahner's hand he released Beatríz—who fled toward Elli's voice and waiting arms, her one hand still clutching the diamond key.

Elli grabbed Beatríz before she ran into the door and drew her close, both arms encircling Beatríz's neck. With the black key delivered, Kahner turned to walk officiously back into the dark end of the hall. Only the barest ember of hope flickered in Elli's breast.

Kahner had taken no more than two strides with his back to Elli and Beatríz before he ordered, quietly, "Kill them both."

As the soft echo in the hall reaffirmed the order, Elli grabbed Beatríz hard at the shoulders and spun both of them around so that only Elli's back was facing the two executioners who had in that same moment launched their spears. One clanged stridently against the door where Beatríz had stood a moment earlier. The second blade, however, found its target on Elli's back, launching her forward into Beatríz—and, then, with Elli's fierce momentum, slamming the two of them into the door.

"Elli!" shrieked Beatríz.

The only subsequent sound before stillness gripped the whole of Bairnmoor was alarm voiced by enemy warriors who witnessed the vault door yielding to the impact of the girls—and the report of the door swinging shut as soon as Elli and Beatríz were hurled into the tomb.

End of Volume I